Taken by Storm

THE NOBLE LORDS: BOOK 2

DANELLE HARMON

OLIVERHEBERBOOKS

As children we all have our heroes, and when I was a little girl, mine were horses. This version of Taken By Storm is dedicated, with affection and long-standing admiration, to my own personal childhood favorite—the beautiful, indomitable, curious and charismatic 1930 American Triple Crown winner, Gallant Fox, on whom Shareb-er-rehh was based.

More in This Series

THE NOBLE LORDS

Prologue

The fire started as a spark set to hay, a twisting viper of black smoke before a draft from the stable's open door blew it into life.

With a savage, whooshing roar, the hay burst into flame.

Satisfied, the man tossed the lantern into the loose straw and stepped back as the fire's hot breath hit him. He stood watching the hay blacken, crackle, and disintegrate, mesmerized by the flames, feeling their heat pressing against his face and sucking the moisture out of his pores, drying out his eyes, searing the inside of his nose, and crawling into his lungs with deadly malice.

Take this, you bastard. Teach you to go breaking agreements. If I can't have the Weybourne fortune—and the horses—no one can.

Acrid smoke blackened the air, banked down from the rafters. Coughing, he whipped out his handkerchief, covered his mouth, and stepped back, toward the safety of the door and the coolness of the night beyond. Already, the fire was out of control, a frenzied demon swallowing up stacks of hay, leaping up the partitions that separated the empty stalls, and charging toward that one, single box at the end that was not empty at all.

A shrill whinny pierced the night, and then, hooves ringing desperately against wood.

The stallion was the most valuable horse in England, if not the world, but the man made no effort to save it. He heard its whinny become a terrified scream, felt the fire growing hotter, louder, angrier, pressing hot clothing against his skin, beginning to scorch, blister, and suffocate him. Smoke began to choke him, and he tasted burning wood and hay, turpentine, leather and dirt. Eyes watering, his lungs constricting in the searing heat, he retreated from the stable, the fire raging at his back.

From behind him came the stallion's frightened scream, piercing the hellish clamor of fire and heat. It was a horrible, ghastly sound of pure terror and he pictured the flames reaching for the proud animal, engulfing it, burning it.

Such a waste.

It could've been otherwise, Weybourne. You old fool.

Outside, the night air engulfed him like a cool blanket, and he sucked huge gulps of it into his lungs to rid them of smoke and heat. At his back the inferno roared, and he heard the great timbers of the stable caving in upon themselves, a last distant battering of shod hooves meeting wood ...

And then, a crescendo of thunder rising behind him.

He whirled and saw the stallion.

Wild-eyed with fury and terror, its tail streaming smoke and fire, the horse came charging out of the flames like a winged specter of death. It made straight for him; he saw the fire reflected in its savage black eyes, against its burnished coat, in its wide, flaring nostrils that burned an unholy red—

He threw himself out of the way just in time.

The great beast galloped madly off into the night, its mighty hooves making the earth tremble beneath him.

Shaken, his trousers smudged with dirt, the man pulled himself to his feet. Sweat poured down his hot face and sheets of fire snapped and popped and reached for him. Flames danced within the collapsed building like legions of angry devils. And now, faintly, he heard hoarse cries, and turned to see Weybourne himself running from the house, trailed by servants who were trying in vain to catch up to him.

"Shareb!" the old man cried. "Shareb-er-rehh!"

Silhouetted in the conflagration's bright light, the fire-starter moved backwards, and behind a stately elm whose leaves were already curling in agony against the intense heat. Smiling, he watched as the earl came rushing toward the stable, arms waving, old legs pumping, his night cap trailing from his head.

"Shareb!" the old man cried, and then his voice rose in a desperate scream of bleak agony: "*Shareb-er-rehh!*"

"Stop him!" shouted one of the servants, running as fast as he could. "My lord, no!"

Another section of the stable roof imploded, spouting a fountain of sparks and churning black smoke toward the stars above.

"*Shareb!*"

"No, milord! Don't go in there, *it's no use!*"

"Shareb-er-*rehhhhhhh*—"

The old earl ran blindly through the sheets of flame and into the burning stable; the servants charged toward the back of the building in the hope of gaining a safer entrance; then, there was only Weybourne's horrible screams as the fire caught him. His clothing ablaze, he came staggering out, gaining fifteen, maybe twenty feet, before he fell, clutching his chest.

The arsonist moved out from behind the elm and stood staring coldly down at the dying man.

"You ..." the old earl gasped, the flames glowing orange against his face as he dragged open his eyes and saw who stood over him. "Knew it was you ... did it for revenge, didn't you ... should have trusted my instincts about you ..."

The fire crackled and sighed. Pungent billows of black smoke enclosed them, cut them off from the shouts and screams and calls that pierced the darkness.

The arsonist knelt down to the old man's level. "Pity, pity, Weybourne. I suppose young Tristan told you all about me, did he not? Is that why you wanted to break the agreement?" He arched a brow, a faint smile touching his mouth as the earl stretched a wizened hand toward him, fingers clawing the glowing earth in a spasm of agony. "Well, *I'm* in debt, too ... and I'll be damned if I let you break your promise to me. Good-night, Weybourne. May you rot in hell."

He stood, still looking at that pitiful old hand reaching toward his boot. Above the fire's roar, he heard Weybourne's wheezing gasps, watched the feeble hand jerk and stiffen, saw, in the unholy glow from the burning stable, the skin going ashy and gray.

And heard, off in the distance, the thunder of hoofbeats.

Hard, fast, and furious.

The stallion was returning.

This time, the man slithered off into the night, while behind him the stable burned ...

And burned.

Chapter One

WANTED: Any information leading to the whereabouts of Lady Ariadne St. Aubyn, daughter of the late Earl of Weybourne, who disappeared on Sunday last following the stable fire at Weybourne House in which Lord Weybourne perished. Her Ladyship, who is nineteen years of age, is described as having a very small frame, a most remarkable shade of red hair, and has in her possession a bay stallion. A REWARD of ten thousand pounds has been offered by her brother, the new Lord Weybourne, for the return of said horse, of which he is the new and rightful owner. Enquiries may be made to Weybourne House, Brompton Road, London.

"That ought to do it."

Seated at the carved mahogany desk that was now his, the new Lord Weybourne scanned his words a final time, put his seal on the document, and briskly handed it into the care of his waiting butler. "Make sure a copy of this gets posted at every inn and public house from here to Kings Lynn, and get it into the *Times* as soon as possible." He picked up his gloves, took his hat from his valet, and slapped it atop his dark russet hair. "For all the good it will bloody well do. My sister is probably half-way to Norfolk with that horse by now."

The door opened and a groom stood there. "Your mare is saddled and ready, my lord."

"It's about time," Tristan said darkly, and slammed from the room.

Outside, the servants were already lined up on the lawn to see their young lord off. As he strode swiftly down the steps of Weybourne House, they quailed at the look in his eye, the grim set to his mouth.

"May God be with our dear Lady Ariadne, wherever she is," a maid whispered to the footman who stood rigidly beside her. She wrung her hands. "Oh, William, I only hope she reaches Norfolk before *he* does!"

"She has a good head-start," the footman said, out of the corner of his mouth. He kept his face fixed and attentive. "*And* Shareb-er-rehh. He'll not catch her."

Tight-lipped and silent, the servants watched as their new master checked his horse's girth, scowling at the animal as though damning it for not being one of the fast Norfolk Thoroughbreds. Tension crackled in the air, and tense sideways glances passed up and down their waiting ranks. Lady Ariadne had lost so much in the last two months alone. First the strange epidemic at the country house in Burnham Thorpe that had killed all but one of the Norfolk Thoroughbreds; then the London stable fire that had claimed her father, and nearly Shareb-er-rehh as well—and finally, the opening and reading of his will. It had been the final blow. Surely, old Lord Weybourne had meant well ... but to think he had been blind enough to bequeath Shareb-er-rehh, the last, and only remaining, stallion, to his derelict rakehell of a son. Who could blame Lady Ariadne for stealing the horse and fleeing London?

It was a good thing young Tristan was ignorant of their thoughts—and, where their sympathies lay. His handsome face exhibited no sign of grief as he passed the gutted stable on its black and ugly patch of charred ground, his eyes belied no emotion as the damp London wind skated over the rubble and brought with it the acrid stench of ashes and dead dreams. There was nothing in his countenance but fury—and grim resolve.

Sensing it, the mare rolled her eyes in fear as he pulled on his gloves, took the reins, and snapped out final instructions to his grave-faced butler. "If anyone comes looking for the reward money, put them off until my return. God knows I don't have the funds—*yet*—to pay it out. But I will, as soon as I catch up to my sister and get my hands on that stallion. *So help me God I will.*"

Then the young master of Weybourne swung himself up in the saddle, wheeled his horse, and in a clatter of hoofbeats, was gone.

"THERE SIR! IN THE STREET!"

Colin Nicholas Lord took one look at the dog and knew it was dying.

Gripping his bag, he sprinted as best he could toward the animal even as a woman broke from the confused group that milled around it. She hurried to meet him, her skirts flying, her face flushed and anxious. "Oh sir, they said you're an animal doctor! Please, do something to save our precious Homer—you've got to save him, sir, oh, *please* you've got to save him, he's my son Tommy's only companion and if he dies—"

The crowd parted, ushering him through. The big black mastiff was lying on its side, lips pulled back in a grimace of agony, body stiff, eyes glassy and staring into nothingness. A little boy, six or seven years old by the look of him, was huddled on the street next to the dog, his skinny arms wrapped around its massive neck, his bright blond head buried in its fur. He looked up, his eyes huge and blue, his cheeks streaked with tears.

"H-Homer... ." he choked out, "My doggie—"

"Let me get in here and take a look at him," Colin said gently. "May I?"

The boy's lower lip quivered, and a huge tear rolled from his eye. Wordlessly, he turned and fled into his mother's arms.

Colin knelt down on the cobblestones beside the dog. "Easy there, big fellow," he murmured, setting his bag down and running a calming hand over the animal. Beneath the heavy warmth of its hind leg, he found the femoral pulse beating too rapidly, too faintly; he lifted the slack lip, saw that the mucus membranes were nearly as white as the teeth they enclosed. But it was the dog's abdomen, huge, hard, and swollen tight as a drum, that gave him his diagnosis.

"When was the last time he ate, madam?"

"A few hours ago," she said tightly, holding Tommy against her skirts and clutching his hand. "Oh, sir, is he going to—"

"Any vomiting?"

"Well, yes, he tried ... I made him a big plate of meat and potatoes for supper, then he drank his whole bowl of water, went outside to run and play with Tommy—he does that every night and he's such a gentle old dog and all the little ones in the neighborhood love him so much—oh, sir, is he going to live? Please, tell us he's going to live—"

Tommy broke from her side, fell to his knees beside the dog, and wrapped his arms around its big neck. "Oh, Homer ... Oh, Homer, please, don't die! Please, please, *please* don't die ..." Sobbing, the boy looked imploringly into Colin's grave face. "Please, mister, don't let him die. *Please* ... You won't let him, will you?"

Colin opened his bag and took out his spectacles. "I'll do what I can, Tommy. Now, you do *me* a favor and go stand with your mama, all right?"

The little boy's throat worked, and he ran to obey.

Colin put on his spectacles and once more returned his attention to his patient.

Commotion surrounded him. Traffic stopping in the street ... carriage wheels grinding against worn cobblestone ... running footsteps, windows sliding open in the rooms above his head, someone shouting, the hollow clatter of a horse's hooves. Colin never raised his head, intent on the dog, and the dog only. He passed his hand over its abdomen as the crowd pressed close, some unwashed and rank with sweat, others heavily perfumed, all of them blocking out sunlight, air, thinking space—

"Give the fellow some room, folks!" a man shouted, from somewhere above. "Clear away, get back. *Back* ..."

The dog stared glassily into space through half-closed eyes, whimpering through its nose in pain.

"Do you know what ails him, sir?" the woman asked, tightly.

"Gastric dilatation. Bloat, if you will."

"Bloat?"

Colin was already eyeing the hugely swollen abdomen, silently praying that the stomach was not twisted up inside; if it was, the animal was as good as dead. But the woman didn't have to know that. Not yet, anyhow.

As gently as he could, he answered, "There's a large amount of gas trapped in your dog's stomach, madam—if it is not released, he'll die." His hands still resting on the mastiff's side, Colin twisted around, looking up at the anxious faces until he found the man who'd summoned him. "Sir? If you'll please restrain Homer for me while I attempt treatment ... Yes, like that. Just put your hands on his neck and shoulders. Good."

Little Tommy hid his face in his mother's skirts, crying bitterly. Colin's chest constricted. He glanced at the woman, and she stared beseechingly into his eyes with that frozen plea he was all too familiar with, that blind faith and hope and trust that the animal lover bestows upon the one person in the world who might be capable of saving their beloved pet.

"Please do your best, sir," she said quietly. "For my son."

There was no time to waste. Reaching for his bag, Colin

9

hurriedly searched its depths for the small bottle of rum, a cloth, and the trocar, a short needle that was Homer's only hope of survival. He lifted the instrument out, keeping his face perfectly blank and his features composed for the sake of the mastiff's distraught owner. He'd used the fine needle on sheep—but never on a dog.

There was no other choice.

Palming the mastiff's distended belly, Colin found its highest point. The dog tried to roll into an upright position, but Colin held him down, his voice gentle and soothing. As the crowd went hush-silent around him, he poured rum onto the cloth and cleaned the area. Then he leaned over the dog so the little boy could not see what he was about to do—and pushed the needle straight down into the hard, swollen stomach.

Behind him, the woman gasped.

The needle pierced the stomach wall. Fluid, sunset-colored and fetid, shot from the top of the trocar, spattering his cheeks, his brow, his spectacles; he blocked out the sudden, overpowering stench and the alarmed murmur of the crowd, aware of only the malodorous fluid bubbling out of the trocar and the pent-up gas escaping the dog's stomach in a frenzied hiss.

At his side, the man was staring at him in shocked horror.

Please, God, let the stomach wall be healthy, Colin thought, desperately—for if it were not, the organ would burst inside the abdomen and the resulting peritonitis would surely kill poor Homer.

The moments crept by.

The crowd held its collective breath.

He laid his fingers against the inside of the dog's hind leg, checking its pulse once again. Counting. Feeling his helper's gaze upon him, searching his face for some sign of encouragement, hope, promise.

Come on, big fellow, he thought, holding the needle in one hand

and stroking the dog's heavily muscled neck with the other. *Don't bow out on me now. Come on, Homer ... make little Tommy happy ...*

He shut his eyes, oblivious to the bits of gravel driving into his knees, the sunlight against the back of his neck, feeling only the dog's ribs moving steadily beneath his palm, up and down, up and down. Long moments went by. The crowd around and above him had gone deathly silent. The hiss of the escaping gas dropped in pitch, then faded out, and gently, Colin withdrew the needle.

He risked a glance up and saw some fifty anxious faces, all staring down at him, all expecting nothing short of a miracle, and he was suddenly terrified of failing them all.

Just as he had failed the many men who had died that night he'd made the single worst decision of his life.

He looked away—and it was then that he saw her. A petite young woman, refined and elegant, sitting astride a deep-chested bay stallion and staring directly into his eyes. Her hair was stuffed beneath a wool cap, breeches molded her shapely thighs, and only the fine arch of her brows, the clarity of her skin, and the hint of a bosom beneath her coat belied the fact she was not the lad she appeared to be. Her head was high and her dark eyes were smiling, as though she secretly shared his success; she gave the faintest of nods, and in her gaze he saw more than just blind faith in his abilities—he saw complete, unflagging confidence that he would succeed in saving the dog.

Suddenly flustered, Colin's gaze shot back to his patient.

And then, beneath his hand, he felt it. The slowing and strengthening of pulse and the return of spirit, the defiant rush of blood, of promise, of life, through veins and arteries and heart.

He forgot the woman on the horse.

"Yes!" he said through clenched teeth, bending anxiously over the dog as the crowd closed in and their shadows fell over the both of them. "Come on—what's your name, big fellow?—Homer. Come on, Homer," he urged, stroking the dog's thick neck and gazing intently into its half-shuttered eyes. "Come awake for me, Homer ..."

The dog whimpered and stirred. Its foreleg jerked, the huge paw scraping the cobblestones, its whimper becoming a harsh cry deep in its throat as full consciousness began to return, and with it, pain. The crowd murmured excitedly, their voices rising in a sudden, thunderous din; the little boy's sobs caught, held—and then the mastiff's eyes opened, and it lifted its huge, noble head to regard the man who had just saved its life, its dark eyes looking deeply, gratefully, into those of the veterinarian.

Colin smiled.

The dog's tail thumped once, twice, on the cobblestones.

And the crowd went wild.

"*Home-e-e-e-e-e-r!*" Tommy shrieked, tearing himself from his mother and plunging to his knees at the mastiff's side.

His head ringing with that elated screech, his ears filled with the cheers of the crowd, Colin stood up and passed a wrist across his brow. People were clapping him on the back, congratulating him, jabbering excitedly amongst themselves. He took off his spattered spectacles and turned to speak to Tommy's mother—but her fond gaze was on her son, who was bent over the dog, sobbing into its fur, embracing it and hugging the big body ecstatically.

"Oh, Homer!" Tommy cried, sobbing happily. "Oh, Homer, Homer, *Homer!*"

Colin dropped the spectacles into his pocket, wiped his face with a handkerchief, and gazed down at the happy pair as the boy's mother moved to stand beside him. "I think," he said with a helpless grin, "that Homer here will live to eat many more atrociously huge meals—though I would advise against them."

He looked up then, toward the woman on the bay stallion—but the spot where they had been was empty.

His guardian angel was gone.

❧

"I WANT THAT MAN."

Daniel and Simon, walking on either side of Shareb-er-rehh's hooded head as they hurried away from the cheering crowd, came to such a simultaneous stop that the action might've been choreographed. The two grooms stared up at her.

"What do you mean, you *want* him?"

Lady Ariadne St. Aubyn tugged her cap down over her brow and urged the stallion on. Again, she relived that silent drama: the veterinarian down on his knees in the street, his dark blond head bent over a mastiff, the dog's tongue hanging out to rest lifelessly upon the cobblestones. Again, she saw the concentration in that intent, handsome face, the hair falling unheeded over his brow, the blood spraying his spectacles, and he never flinching, never faltering, never losing that expression of purposeful intent. The steady hands, the muscles beneath his rolled up sleeves, the horror she'd felt at seeing that needle plunging into the dog's swollen abdomen—

"My lady?"

And the dog. Coming back to life as though raised from the dead. Lifting its massive head to look up at its savior, and the humble gratitude in its dark eyes before the happy shrieks of the little boy, the thunderous cheers of the crowd, had drowned everything out.

She would never forget it, not as long as she lived.

"I said, *I want* him," she repeated, glancing behind her. There was no one following them, but even so, she couldn't help but feel nervous and vulnerable out here in broad daylight where anyone might recognize her... or, Shareb-er-rehh. Though a hood covered his noble head, and leather cups concealed most of his wide, intelligent dark eyes—the right one ringed with white and giving him a perpetual look of curiosity and coltish wonder—she was taking no chances. The stallion's blood was impeccably blue, his existence the result of four decades of careful planning, his worth—as the last and only male heir to his heritage—beyond value.

A horse like Shareb stood out.

A horse like Shareb would be easily recognized.

The sooner they were out of London, the better.

"I need to get Shareb-er-rehh to Norfolk, and I need an escort who is capable of ensuring his health along the way. I want you two to follow him, find out who he is and where he resides, and report back to me. We'll need to convince him of my need for his services in as discreet a way possible—*without* telling him of my identity or the bounty on my head."

"But my lady, what if he refuses?"

'Do what you must to convince him. I cannot take no for an answer." She gave them both a stern look. "You both have served my family well, but don't make a muddle of this."

"But my lady, *we* can escort you to Norfolk, keep you from harm, make sure your brother doesn't recognize or find you along the way—"

"Yes, but you cannot cure a sick or injured horse. That man, obviously, can." She reached down and nervously touched the stallion's neck. "It's not wise for me to tarry out here in the open, so I'm off to my hiding spot. Report back to me in an hour, and don't forget Shareb's pastry and ale. I wish to leave London tonight—*with* the veterinarian."

※

NIGHT HAD long since fallen outside the livery where Colin ran his practice. As was his habit, he strode the length of the barn, carrying a lantern and looking in on each horse before closing the place up for the night. A small office and two stalls at the stable's far end were his to use in exchange for veterinary care for the owner's horses, and now, both of those stalls were empty—the last one on the left, painfully so.

He looked at it for a long moment, his fingers tightening around the lantern's wire handle. Poor Old Ned, who'd served him so faithfully these past three years ... sickly, in pain, and chronically lame, he was one animal Colin had *not* been able to save.

"I miss you, old boy," he murmured, gazing sadly at the empty feed bin, the empty water bucket, the empty confines of the stall. Around him, the other horses abruptly stopped munching their hay, listening. He reached out and ran his fingers over the door's worn edge, where a few white hairs still clung. "Miss you like hell." Then he turned away and continued on, the chronic ache in his right leg warning him of impending rain.

The past weighed heavily on him tonight, despite the day's triumph. Ned. Orla. And other memories ... memories that had nothing to do with horses, and everything to do with the life he'd once led. A life of glory, of honor, of distinction, of pride.

Of loss.

He took a deep and steadying breath, the quietness of the stable making him feel all the more alone. It was best not to think of the past. There was nothing to be found there but pain.

But the animals around him sensed his sorrow, and every horse in the stable turned its head to watch him as he passed, their quiet, soulful eyes dark with love and adoration that Colin never noticed. The livery's owner had long since gone home, the two stable hands off for the night to drink themselves into a stupor at the Blue Rooster. As usual, they had invited Colin to join them; and as usual, he had politely declined. It wasn't that he didn't like people; he just wasn't a gregarious man, a trait that he'd first become aware of back in his Royal Navy days, when, alone in his cabin and cut off from the rest of the ship, he'd found a haven in isolation where others of his rank had often complained of finding it a self-imposed prison.

He reached out to stroke the nose of a stout gray gelding whose head hung over a stall door. Better not to think of those years. Nor, of the disgrace that had ended them forever, toppling him from the pinnacles of public and military acclaim to spend his life in forgotten obscurity, bringing shame on his family's name, and condemning him to nightmares that would probably haunt him for the rest of his life. He might as well have just disappeared off the face of the earth, really. And yet, the man he had been still remained, and the parallels between the two, vastly different careers were not lost on him. Once, he'd been a hero. And sometimes—like today, he thought with a little smile, as he remembered the mastiff coming alive under his hands, the boy's tearful shriek of glee—he still felt like one.

Giving the horse a last fond pat, he continued on, his limp more pronounced than usual, remembering that beautiful, elegant woman sitting astride the stallion.

Watching him.

Sharing a smile with him.

What had *she* thought?

He'd probably never know. Just as he'd never know who she was, nor why she had concealed her gender, nor why she'd been staring at him so intently.

He hadn't been able to get her out of his mind all day. Surely, such obsessions were a direct result of spending too much time with animals instead of people. Perhaps he *should* have joined the two stable hands for a wet or two at the local tavern, just for a change of scenery ...

He completed his nightly tour, the straw and dirt sighing beneath his boots. For a moment he stood listening to the sounds of a happy, healthy stable—horses munching their hay, the occasional swish of a tail across a sleek haunch, the stamp of a foot, the rattling of a bucket. All was as it should be. Satisfied, he stepped into the small office where he treated the occasional dog or cat that found its way to his mainly-equine practice, intending to retrieve his bag and his nightly dose of educational reading.

He stopped in surprise. A man stood there, a stained hat clenched between his stubby fingers.

"Can I help you?" Colin asked.

The man put out a thick, broad hand. "Name's John McCarthy. Just wanted to stop by and thank ye for savin' that dog today—he belongs t' me son, ye know. The wife baked ye a loaf of bread f'r yer services; I put it there on the table."

Setting the lantern down, Colin returned the handshake. He thanked the man and heard himself making some inane comment about what a good patient Homer had been.

"I know ye don't remember me," the farmer went on, the lantern light gleaming off his balding head as he gazed in wide-eyed wonder at the vials and jars of salves, pills, and powders that competed for his attention on the wall-shelves. "But I came to the talk ye gave last week at the lecture hall, the one on lameness in the horse. Enjoyed it a real lot, Mr. Lord. Thank ye for leavin' out all those eee-ses and oh-ses so that us plain folk could know what ye was talkin' about."

Colin nodded, smiling in amusement as the man screwed up his brow and peered at a bottle of pills whose cobalt color he seemed to find particularly attractive.

"I, uh ... I'm sorry to be botherin' ye, 'specially at this hour when ye probably want to go home and eat yer supper, but ... well, I was wonderin', Mr. Lord, if ye might suggest a remedy for me little mare. She's got a cold—you know, runny eyes 'n' nose an' the whole lot, and I've already had her bled once. It didn't do no good, sir, and I was just wonderin' what *you*, bein' one of these new *vet-rinarians*, think I ought t' do."

"Do you have her with you, Mr. McCarthy?"

"Well, er, no ... figgered she was best left at home since she was feelin' so poorly."

Overhead, rain began to drum softly upon the roof, and Colin felt his leg throbbing right along with it. Leaning against the examination table to take the weight off it, he bent his head, raking a hand through his hair and pushing it back off his brow.

"F'rgive me, Mr. Lord. Ye look tired—I can come back in the mornin'—"

"No, no, I'm fine, really." Colin looked up and gave a reassuring smile, his mind drifting back to the woman. The memory of that pixie face would put off any hopes of a peaceful night's sleep, as surely as the pain that was plaguing his leg. "About your little mare ..."

"Do ye think I ought t' get her bled again, Mr. Lord?"

"Absolutely not."

"But the farrier said—"

"I *know* what the farriers say," Colin said, with more sharpness than he intended. "*And* the cow leeches, *and* the surgeons, *and* my own colleagues, even. Phlebotomy is the accepted treatment for everything from colic to pneumonia. But it is cruel and unnecessary, and I don't believe in it. Cover your little mare with a blanket instead, give her a hot bran mash, get her away from your other stock so she does not infect them, and rest her from her work for a day or so."

McCarthy stared at him for a moment, mentally digesting the information. Then he nodded, slowly. "Blanket, bran mash, and rest," he said, counting off on his fingers. "No bleeding."

"No bleeding."

He pumped Colin's hand, beaming with gratitude. "Thankee, sir. Much obliged. And what do I owe ye for yer good advice?"

"Not a thing. Just your promise that you won't have her bled. And please, if she doesn't improve, send for me and I'll come take a look at her, personally."

"I'll do that, Mr. Lord." Smiling, the farmer clapped his hat down atop his balding pate and reached for the door. "Thanks again ... and I'm sorry for botherin' ye."

"You're not both—"

But he was already gone, his cheerful whistle and heavy footsteps following him as he pulled open the door and disappeared into the rainy night. For a moment, Colin stood leaning against the examination table, listening to the gentle tap of rain against the roof. He could smell it as it came sweeping through the open window on a feathery gust of wind, and the fresh, earthy scent of springtime; damp dirt and grass, blossoming flowers, clean, newly washed air. He looked forward to a refreshing walk home in the damp.

Another trait, left over from his years at sea. He liked weather, in all of its many facets and moods.

He was just retrieving the key to his bookcase when the door opened once more, admitting two young men who had a look of nervousness and secrecy about them.

"Are you Mr. Lord?"

"I am." He pocketed the key. "What can I do for you?"

"We, uh … we have a horse, and we need you to, er, come look at him." said the taller of the two.

"Sick?"

"Well, not really," said the other one. "But he might *get* sick."

"Yeah, you never know, he just might."

"And even if he doesn't get sick, La— I mean, our employer wants to know if you'd accompany us to Norfolk—"

"To make *sure* he doesn't get sick."

"And to cure him if he does."

"But he's not sick, now."

"And he never *gets* sick."

"So it would be a really easy task."

'Very easy."

"You really wouldn't have much to do."

"So will you come with us?"

Colin just stared at them. The taller one flushed, his gaze darting toward the door. The other was nervously picking at a thread in his coat; both had the look of trapped animals about them.

"Let me get this straight," Colin said, trying to keep the impatience from his voice. "You want me to accompany your employer to Norfolk to make sure his horse doesn't get sick?"

"Yes, will you?"

"It would be an easy job!"

"And you'd be well paid!"

Colin bent his head to his hand as he kneaded his tired eyes. "How much?"

"Well, we really don't know, that would be between you and—and our employer."

"And where is this employer?"

"At the moment? At the moment, um, well, I don't really know, but I'm sure we can find him."

"He's, um—he's in hiding."

"Hiding," Colin said flatly.

"Yes, hiding."

Colin felt the last of his patience waning. His stomach was growling, he was tired, and he wanted nothing more than a meal, a bath, a few minutes with a book, and bed.

"Gentlemen, I have had a long day," he said. "If you have a horse that is truly sick, then by all means, come and seek my services. In the meantime, if you will excuse me—"

"But Mr. Lord, you must listen, must hear us out!"

Colin was already guiding them toward the door. "I believe I have heard enough. Good night, gentleman."

"You won't come with our employer to Norfolk?"

"No."

"But—"

"I said, good night, gentlemen."

And with that, he opened the door, saw them out, and shut it behind them, wondering what the devil that had been all about. It must be the lateness of the hour, he thought. Or perhaps it was the full moon. He shook his head, unlocked his bookcase and selected the second volume of Delabere Blaine's *The Outlines of the Veterinary Art* and Bracy Clark's recently published *A Series of*

Original Experiments on the Foot of the Living Horse—the former for its discussion of laminitis, the latter for its theories regarding elasticity of the foot, complete with an anatomical and physiological dissertation long and complicated enough to keep him well distracted into the wee hours of the morning. Heavy reading, but certainly easier to rest on than thoughts of that petite beauty who'd been watching him earlier. Tucking the books beneath his coat, Colin reached for his bag.

He was just turning when out of the corner of his eye, he saw a shadow slide past the window.

His head jerked up and he stared at that ominous black square for a long moment. The rain suddenly seemed louder, the room darker, and unconsciously, his hand went to his hip. But there was no longer a sword there; that had been part of his former life, though the instinctual motion remained.

Frowning, the lantern in hand, he moved toward the door, his gaze on that black window and his suspicions aroused.

He pulled the door open and stared out into the rainy night.

Nothing.

Let it go, Colin. You are no longer an officer on watch, with the responsibility of a man-of-war and some eight hundred men resting on your shoulders. You're just a humble London veterinarian. Get used to it.

Feeling a bit foolish, he picked up the bread that the farmer had given him and, blowing out the lantern, set it on the floor. For a moment he stood listening, all alone in this room with only his thoughts, and two years of warm memories played out within its walls—of saving, healing, and helping those poor, gentle creatures who could never voice their complaints of just how much it hurt.

He pushed open the door and stepped out into the cool spring night. Rain tapped against his face, moist wind kissed his cheeks. He locked the door and pocketed the key, thinking, still, of *her*.

He had just turned when there, in front of him, were the two men he had just sent from his office. The taller one had a pistol, and he was pointing it directly at Colin's heart.

"If you wish to rob me," Colin said flatly, "I'm afraid I can offer precious little with which to reward your efforts." And then, looking the man straight in the eye, he calmly reached out, palm up, fingers beckoning. "Even so, I suspect the only thing you might actually steal from me is my patience with the two of you. Give me the pistol."

"Simon, don't give it to him!"

"I said," Colin repeated, giving the taller one an implacable stare, "give me the pistol. *Now*."

He saw the resolve wavering in the other man's face beneath his tone of command; and then, slowly, and with cool, unflappable intent, Colin reached out, took the pistol from the other man's suddenly nerveless hand, and, removing the flint so that the weapon could not be fired, handed it back to him. The man stood staring at him, slack-jawed at his audacity and total lack of fear.

"Forgive me for depriving you of both your dignity and your flint, but violence is not necessary, and neither of you look as though you should be playing with guns. And now, since you have finally succeeded in arousing my curiosity, perhaps we should all go and meet this employer of which you speak?"

Chapter Two

L ady Ariadne waited restlessly in the darkened street. What was taking them so long?

She was terrified.

A part of her vast inheritance was sewn into Shareb-er-rehh's saddle blanket, but the thought of having it stolen from her by thieves was not the only cause of her fear.

It was the veterinarian.

What if he recognized her as the most wanted fugitive in London? What if he didn't wish to leave his veterinary practice to escort her to Norfolk? What if he refused the money she was prepared to offer, and turned her in to the authorities instead?

As though sensing her distress, Shareb-er-rehh moved forward, shoving his head against her arm and rubbing hard. She threaded her fingers through his mane, trying to calm her racing heart. Moonlight was infusing the mist now and making it look ghostly and ethereal; shadows crept from the trees, stretching across the street and reaching for her, and from somewhere off in the night, she heard two cats fighting, their angry, drawn out wails winding through the darkness before ending on a high screech of synchronized fury.

She tried to take comfort in the stallion's presence. He stood quietly beside her, his mane, singed by the fire, trimmed sparse and short. His scorched tail had been chopped, racehorse style, to the level of his hocks. The blinkered hood enclosed his expressive head, the saddle blanket covered part of his back, and weighted leg-bandages threw his long, fluid gait off enough to disguise it. No one would know who—or what—he was. But Ariadne was still nervous. She couldn't risk Tristan or anyone else tracking them down by Shareb's description.

Or, she thought, looking ruefully down at her masculine attire, her own.

Clenching her fists, she tilted her face up to the moon that now sailed through the silver clouds.

Oh, Papa ... why did you bequeath Shareb-er-rehh to Tristan? Didn't you know that he doesn't care for him the way I do, that he will sell him to pay his debts? Were you so caught up in your dreams of creating the Norfolk Thoroughbred that you were blind to the weaknesses of your only son? Sudden tears stung her eyes, as she thought of her father—the man that she had loved from afar, the man whose attention she had spent her life trying to gain, the man who was always too busy, too preoccupied, too involved in other things, to spend time with a motherless daughter who was starved for love and affection. Even now, Ariadne was not unaware that, in trying to keep Shareb safe, she was *still* trying to gain her father's attention ... even if he was now in a place from which he could never again give it.

A tear slipped down her cheek for all that had been—and for all that could have been. And yet, had her father truly loved Shareb, either? Had Papa thought of him as anything more than a possession, as he had thought of her?

She reached into her pocket, unwrapped the last piece of pastry she'd been saving, and broke off a chunk of it. Hearing the crackling of the paper, Shareb-er-rehh immediately perked up, nosing her hand and lipping at her fingers. She put the treat on her palm, and felt his velvety lips brushing her skin. Only his quiet munching, and the sound of water dripping from the leaves above her head, broke the stillness of the night.

That—and now, something else.

Shareb-er-rehh heard it, too. Crumbs peppering his whiskers, he jerked his head up in mid-chew and stared off toward the increasing spill of light from the veterinarian's door as it was opened from within, every muscle in his big body tense, his eyes gleaming like jet in the moonlight.

Ariadne caught her breath. There was Daniel and Simon—and the veterinarian walking purposefully between them, headed their way.

FOR SOME ODD reason that he couldn't explain, Colin wasn't surprised to find the same young woman who had piqued his curiosity and plagued his thoughts from the moment he'd seen her sitting astride that same stallion, waiting for him outside in the street.

No, not surprised at all.

"Colin Lord," he said, taking off his hat and bowing. "And whom do I have the pleasure of addressing?"

"How gallant you were today, saving that little boy's dog as you did!" she said hurriedly, ignoring his question. "I commend your persistence, your skill, and your knowledge. I have never seen anything quite like it in my life. You were magnificent. Simply brilliant!"

Magnificent?

"Where did you learn such a thing, sir? You must be appropriately educated."

"Veterinary College, London. I graduated from there, and did an apprenticeship with Delabere Blaine— "

"Ah yes, the Veterinary College. My father, God rest his soul, had great faith in the future of the veterinary art and gave much money to support that institution. Always said it was a pity that France had a veterinary college before England did ... After today, I can certainly see why he harbored such belief in your profession. Your knowledge far surpasses that of the common farrier and I think you'll do quite nicely." She smiled nervously, and glanced over her shoulder down the darkened street. "Are you ready to leave, Mr. Lord?"

"Leave?"

"Why, yes, leave. I trust Simon and Daniel told you that I have need of your services, and that there is no time to be lost. We must be on our way, and immediately."

"To be fair, Madam, your two lackeys here were not entirely forthcoming or persuasive in their attempts to convince me to accompany you. I understand that you want something from me—"

"Yes, but I am willing to pay handsomely for it."

"And I also assume that you are the 'employer' whose whereabouts were unknown to your two friends here."

"Well, yes, but—"

"They said something about Norfolk, sick horses, and payment. Pray, madam, do not keep me in suspense."

She was obviously not accustomed to such direct and relentless questioning, and he saw her pause for a moment before she finally tightened her mouth, stood up, and pulled off her cap. In the lantern's soft glow her hair tumbled down, gleaming rich and red and lustrous, like a warship's new copper. She drove a hand through it, obliterating the flat imprint left by the cap and making the glossy tresses spring and bounce to life around her shoulders. For the first time, he saw her features in all their glory —the impudent little nose, the high cheekbones, the saucy tilt to her perfect mouth. Her skin was the color of his mother's finest china, her eyes alight with piquancy. She was more lovely than he'd imagined, and he suddenly found it too hard to breathe.

"What?" Her eyes sparkled, and he caught the challenging, almost teasing, note to her tone. "Have you never seen a *lady* before?"

"Not ... garbed so charmingly."

It was a bold reply, and he saw her brows shoot up, the quick burst of color in her cheeks before she quickly turned her back on him and moved to stand beside the stallion, her hand stroking the horse's muzzle with rapid, nervous movements.

"You have aptly demonstrated your knowledge of dogs, Mr. Lord," she said, her hand moving faster now. "Tell me ... what do you know about horses? Say ... racehorses?"

"Thoroughbreds?"

"*Racehorses.*"

Thoroughbreds, he thought. "Well, they have four legs, a mane and tail—"

"I am dead serious, Mr. Lord!"

He sighed. "Really, madam, I'm tired, hungry, and not in the mood to go into a lengthy discourse about the merits of the various breeds, nor the illnesses to which each of them are predisposed. What do you want me to tell you about thoroughbreds? That the lot of them are a sick and fragile collection, cruelly forced to run themselves to death for the amusement of humans?"

One copper brow lifted, ever so slightly. Her eyes gleamed, a hint of a smile touched her mouth, and she shot a triumphant glance at the two silent youths. Her hand encircled the stallion's muzzle, and still watching him, she rested her cheek against the side of its face. "Sick and fragile, Mr. Lord? How so?"

"Are you testing me?"

"As a matter of fact, I am. Answer the question, please."

He shrugged. "I worked with racehorses at Newmarket for a bit—I saw broken-winded animals, many with bones too fragile to withstand the rigors those poor beasts were asked to endure. A deplorable lot, really."

"Enough, Mr. Lord. You have satisfied my curiosity, and now it is time for us to leave."

"What?"

"Will you accompany us, Mr. Lord?"

"You haven't even told me what—"

"Because if you're not, I can go find another veterinarian to give the three thousand pounds to."

"Three thousand *pounds?*"

"Yes. It is what I will pay you to accompany me to Burnham Thorpe in Norfolk. I wouldn't expect you to know where it is, of course, but—"

"On the contrary, madam," he said. "I ... had a friend who hailed from there." A shadow crossed his face as he remembered that friend—dead now these past four and a half years and sleeping forever in the crypt of St. Paul's, not far from where he now stood.

"Well! Such a small world, is it not? Burnham is just a tiny village tucked up in the corner of Norfolk, near the sea; probably no one in England had ever even *heard* of it until Lord Nelson put it on the map."

The pain in Colin's heart increased, and memories of the state funeral, the national grief, the outpouring of love and gratitude from a grateful England toward the man who had rid the seas of Bonaparte's fleet at Trafalgar, were as near as if he'd lost that same friend only yesterday. *Lord Nelson.* Admired by so many, but loved by those who had had the honor of knowing him.

He would be forever grateful that he had had that honor... .

"So are you interested in earning three thousand pounds, Mr. Lord?"

His head was spinning. Three thousand pounds was more than his practice made in an entire year. Three thousand pounds would enable him to buy his own establishment, perhaps even one in the West End of the city. Three thousand pounds would more than fund his research on equine laminitis. Three thousand pounds ...

"I think, madam—"

"You'll do it, then?"

"—that before I agree to anything, you should tell me just who you are, and why this need for such haste."

Silence. She was looking uncertainly at the grooms, as though hesitant to reveal her identity; then, she raised her chin, her shoulders went back, and she faced him resolutely. He saw her chest rise and fall on a deep, steadying breath, almost as though she was bracing herself.

"I am Lady Ariadne St. Aubyn," she announced, "daughter of the late Earl of Weybourne."

He looked at her blankly, then glanced at the grooms. "Forgive me, but ..."

Her eyes widened. "You don't know who I am?"

"No. Should I?"

She glanced at the two young men; all three exchanged fleeting, relieved smiles. Then her shoulders relaxed, and he heard her release her breath as she met his questioning gaze. "I'm a fugitive, Mr. Lord. The whole of London is after me, and probably East Anglia as well."

He looked at this lovely elfin creature and grinned. "For what, stealing male clothes and going about dressed as a lad?"

"No, for stealing my own horse and fleeing the clutches of my horrid brother."

"Oh. How nice. So you wish to involve me in a family dispute."

"For three thousand pounds, I should think it wouldn't matter *what* I ask you to involve yourself in."

He grinned. "Are you implying that I might want for money?"

"Well ... your clothes do not suggest to me that you are a wealthy man."

"Yes, well, I wouldn't want to wear my everyday velvets and silks for crawling around in cow manure and performing rectal exams on—"

"*Really*, sir!"

"Let's get straight to the point, shall we?" he murmured, a bit annoyed by her presumptuousness. "In exchange for these three thousand pounds, you wish me to escort you to Norfolk and look after a horse."

"Yes. Not just *any* horse, but the Fas—"

"*My lady!*" cried the two grooms in unison.

Her eyes flashed to them and she raked a hand through her coppery hair, looking flustered and blown off course. "Yes, a, er, horse, Mr. Lord. He's not ill, but he has great ... sentimental value, and I'm terrified that something will happen to him ... unfortunately, my wicked, horrible brother Tristan—he's the new Lord Weybourne, you know—wants Shareb-er-rehh as much as I do. He's even posted a reward for the return of this horse. *My* horse. A sister-brother dispute, is that not so, Daniel?"

"Yes, my lady. A sister-brother dispute."

Colin looked at her suspiciously. There was more here than met the eye, but for three thousand pounds he was hesitant to dig too deeply.

"So, is it *this* horse you want me to look after, then?"

"Yes. Shareb-er-rehh, His name means 'Drinker of the Wind.'"

"And just what is so valuable about this animal that you're willing to pay me so much money to protect him?" Colin asked, stretching out a hand toward the stallion. The animal flung its head up with violent force; its ears swept back, and thick white teeth gleamed savagely in the darkness.

"I wouldn't get too close," the young woman warned. "He's very protective of me and quite jealous besides."

"Yes, well let's pray he never requires any medical attention," Colin said, dryly.

"No, I doubt that he shall. But to answer your question, sir ... my father, the sixth earl, had a life-long interest in breeding horses. He—"

"*My lady!*" Daniel and Simon cried once more.

"Yes, you two, I *know*." Her eyes flashed, and she was looking mildly irritated now. "In any case, Mr. Lord, my father devoted his entire life to developing a ... very special breed of horse. Superior in intelligence, and ... other things. Shareb-er-rehh is the last surviving male to represent it."

"And just what is so special about this breed?"

She looked away. "It is, um ... renowned for its ... high-stepping gaits."

"I see."

"With the exception of one mare, who is in the possession of Lord Maxwell of Norfolk, the rest were all lost to a mysterious illness two months ago." Her eyes grew sad, and she looked down at her toes. "Four decades of careful breeding, Mr. Lord. My father's legacy. Wiped out, just like that."

"And you don't know what this 'mysterious illness' was?"

"No. All I can tell you is that the horses went out of their minds, and had strange convulsions and behavior just before they died ... thank God my father got Shareb-er-rehh out of there and down to London before he could catch it, as well." She turned to him, her eyes haunted and bleak. "What do you think it might have been?"

"I'd have to see the clinical signs and examine the animals," he said, evasively.

"A guess, then?"

He shrugged. "Could be one of many things. Moldy corn disease, perhaps."

"Moldy corn dis—"

"Aye, sometimes the corn goes bad and upon ingestion, proves fatal to the horse."

"Oh."

"But you say there is one mare left?"

"Yes, just one. My father gave her to Lord Maxwell—he also resides in Norfolk, you see—and her name is Gazella. She is the *real* reason that I must get Shareb-er-rehh to Norfolk—so that they can be bred, a foal can be got, and the horses that were my father's legacy, preserved." Her eyes grew angry and she turned away to stroke the stallion's neck. "But my wicked brother Tristan cares naught for our father's forty years of dreaming and planning! All he cares about is catching up to me, claiming Shareb-er-rehh as his own, and then handing him over to his creditors in order to pay off his immense gambling debts!"

"Aaaah. So now I understand your desperation to get to Norfolk," Colin mused, rubbing the back of his neck.

"Can you help me, sir? Will you travel with us to Norfolk, look after Shareb-er-rehh, protect us from Tristan and any other threat to my stallion's well-being?"

"Well, I—"

"Though Tristan, of course, inherited the title and the estate, my father did not, I can assure you, leave me destitute. Not by any means. I'll pay you well for your trouble, Mr. Lord!"

He nodded, thinking. "You say that this animal is superior for its high-stepping gaits. Yet his build—from what I can see of it— is extraordinarily lean and rangy."

"He's ... been off his feed."

"Sick?"

"No, just ... stressed."

"Forgive me, but your stallion does not *look* like a fancy gait-horse," Colin said dubiously, wishing the animal would let him get close enough for a more careful examination.

She tossed her head. "*That's* because he's in disguise."

"In case your brother happens to see and recognize him?"

"Of course."

"Of course," Colin said, smiling.

"Just as *I* am in disguise, for the same reason."

"And just how much is your brother offering for the horse's return?"

"Ten thousand pounds," she said unthinkingly.

"Aaah. So, ten thousand pounds to return him to your brother —" he pushed the hair off his forehead and left the heel of his hand against his brow, gazing sideways at her as though in deep thought— "and yet, only *three* thousand pounds to get him to Norfolk? I daresay, it would be a most unwise business decision on my part if I were to settle for a mere three thousand pounds when I can more than triple that amount by simply turning you over to your brother."

She stared at him, stunned and open-mouthed with horror.

"Furthermore," he mused, "such a course of action would require far less work on my part, and I would merely have to travel across town as opposed to all the way up to Norfolk—"

"Why, you rotten scoundrel! I wouldn't have thought you were a devious man!"

"I am not a devious man. Merely a practical one."

"Fine, I'll pay you *five* thousand pounds!" she snapped.

"Twelve would be nice."

"Six!"

"Twelve."

"Eight!"

"*Twelve.*"

"I am *not* giving you twelve!"

"Very well then. I'll settle for the ten offered by your brother instead. Come with me, my lady—"

"Daniel! Simon!" she cried, panicking. "Don't just *stand* there!"

The two youths exchanged nervous glances, unsure what to do. "But my lady, that stallion is worth far more than—"

"Never mind what he's worth!" Ariadne cried, cutting them off before they could do more damage. Dear God, could this situation get any worse? "A fine lot of help *you* two are!"

"Sorry, my lady," they said in unison.

She glared at the veterinarian. He merely stood watching her, an infuriating, amused, calmly assured little smile playing about his lips. "Very well, Mr. Lord," she seethed, already beginning to suspect that he was cut from the same cloth as her worthless, money-grubbing brother. "I'll pay you twelve thousand pounds, you cunning blackguard! But let me tell you, I think you're *despicable*."

"Thank you. But actually, I would rather you tell me I'm a shrewd businessman. 'Twould be far more flattering, I think."

She clenched her fists at her sides.

"So, do we have an agreement then?" he asked, lifting a brow.

"Yes, we have an *agreement*."

"Splendid. I suppose we should get started right away, then. But first, let me pack some clothes, hang a sign proclaiming my absence, and collect my medicines and surgical instruments."

She swung herself up onto the stallion's back. "Very well, but let me tell you, Mr. Lord, I am in great haste to get this horse to Norfolk and will not wait long for you."

"Which leads me to one last question, my lady."

She spun around in the saddle, her eyes flashing. "What?"

"Just what sort of refuge do you expect to find once you reach Norfolk?"

"Oh, did I not tell you? The mare belongs to Lord Maxwell." She glared down at him. "He's my *betrothed*."

Chapter Three

A riadne, waiting in the dark street just outside, was growing increasingly frustrated.

Already, she regretted the rash decision that had put her in the position in which she now found herself. She did not quite know what to make of Colin Lord. He angered her, with the way he had shrewdly outsmarted her. He confused her, with an attitude of command and authority she would not have expected in such a gentle healer. And he unnerved, annoyed, and flustered her —with his patient ways, his smiles of private amusement, and, the way he had looked at her. *Especially*, the way he had looked at her. Directly. Appreciatively. Too hard, and for far too long.

She suddenly felt hot all over.

Just who did he think he was?

His eyes had been no less keen upon studying Shareb-er-rehh, and she knew he would have liked nothing more than to strip off the blanket and hood and see the animal beneath. Thank heavens he had not discerned the truth about what the stallion *really* was. *Guit horse?* Imagine! Well, it was safer to let him—and everyone else—believe such rubbish. It was only a matter of time before the veterinarian realized that Shareb-er-rehh was no gait-horse at all, and the less he knew, the better.

With a start, she realized Daniel and Simon were talking to her.

"My lady, we *insist* on coming with you to Norfolk," Daniel was saying, and she wondered that his throat wasn't raw from repeating the same words so many times in the last two hours. "You don't even know this—what d'you call him, Simon?"

"Veterinarian."

"*Veterinarian.* You don't even know him, my lady—he may take liberties with you, he may steal the stallion, he may do you dreadful bodily harm—"

"Or worse," Simon said, evasively.

She looked at them, puzzled. "Or worse?"

The two young men exchanged glances. "Never mind, my lady. Suffice it to say that you cannot travel alone with a *man*—"

"Oh. And so you wish me to travel alone with *three* of them."

"Yes, but—"

"Listen, I appreciate your concern, but you will remain here in London, at Weybourne House in case Tristan comes looking for me. And if he does, you must tell him I've gone to be with—who can I think of who lives in the opposite direction? ... ah yes, with Lady Chadwick and her family at Greenvale Manor in Milford, Hampshire. Yes, tell him that."

Lud, what was taking that veterinarian so long?

"But what is Lord Maxwell going to think, when you show up on his doorstep wearing a coat and breeches with another man in tow?"

Ariadne raised her chin and pretended to study the detail of a window ledge, fifty feet away. "I should hope he'll be grateful that I've gotten Shareb-er-rehh to him in one piece. Now, go. And Godspeed."

"But my lady, please—"

"Go!" she cried, keeping her gaze fastened on the window

ledge so they wouldn't see the glimmer of tears in her eyes. Another part of her life, gone. The horses, her father, the servants who had shared her childhood, even, quite likely, her reputation ... one by one, they were all being taken from her by fates that seemed to have no end to their cruelty.

She heard the two grooms sigh, and then walk dejectedly off into the darkness.

Ariadne stared straight ahead, swallowing hard and rhythmically stroking Shareb's sleek neck as she fought to regain her composure.

Just think of getting Shareb to Norfolk. That's all that matters. Tristan will never be able to get Shareb once you reach Maxwell's protection ...

Maxwell. Yes, she was eager to see Shareb to safety, but the idea of marriage to this man that Papa had chosen for her, this man whom he, in his wisdom, had thought would "tame" her wild ways, settle her down, be able to "manage" her, this man that she barely knew and was just a little bit afraid of...

The idea of delivering Shareb to Maxwell was one thing.

The idea of delivering *herself* to the man was quite another.

Colin Lord's door opened, and the veterinarian, with a small, curly-haired mongrel twirling about his heels, came out. Her escort and protector had changed into a serviceable coat of navy-blue; a simple waistcoat, a clean white shirt and a muslin cravat gave him a dash of panache and elegance, and buckskin breeches tucked into military style riding boots emphasized the long, muscled leanness of his legs.

She frowned, though, as she noticed that he seemed to favor one of those legs.

Probably kicked by a horse, she thought.

However, her vulgar admiration for his masculine splendor, and her curiosity over how that slight limp had come about, were quick to turn to annoyance—especially in light of how he'd neatly turned the tables and gotten another seven thousand pounds out of her. *The blackguard.* She watched impatiently as he locked his door, positioned a sign upon it that took him a full minute to arrange until it hung to his exact satisfaction, and stooped to pick up the large trunk he had set on the steps. As heavy as it looked, he never staggered under its weight, and lifting it to one broad shoulder, he called for the dog and came toward her.

Barely breathing hard, he set the chest down and picked up the dog, fondly ruffling its ears and holding its squirming body out toward Ariadne.

"Lady Ariadne, meet Bow. Bow, meet Lady Ariadne."

"*Bow?*"

"Aye, Bow." He grinned, still holding the salt-colored mongrel toward her and waiting for her to make a response. The animal's pink tongue slid out, and its button eyes fastened on Ariadne. "As in the forward part of a ship."

From her lofty perch atop Shareb-er-rehh's back, she stared in disbelief down at the veterinarian.

He regarded her with a patient, imperturbable expression.

"Mr. Lord, what do you think you're doing?"

"The task you're paying me for, my lady," he said, tickling the dog's fat pink stomach and setting it down.

"And just where do you propose to put that trunk?"

"It's not a trunk." He stepped back, and she looked down to see that indeed, it was not, but a heavy wooden chest emblazoned with, of all things, a beautifully engraved drawing of a ship, and letters picked out in gold that spelt, HMS *Triton.*

"Dare I ask what it *is* then?" she asked, with mounting ire.

"A sea chest. It goes everywhere with me, and has many senti- mental memories attached to it. But lest you think I'm toting useless frippery, I'll have you know that this chest contains medic- inals and surgical instruments, as well as several changes of clothing."

"I hope you've considered just how you plan on bringing it

along," Ariadne said sharply, "because I can't imagine that you intend to carry it."

"You're absolutely right. I have no intention of carrying it." He looked up at her, studying her as though he thought *she* was the addle-pated one. "Come, follow me."

Hoisting the chest to his shoulder once more, he turned his back and strode off, the little dog yapping at his heels. Miffed at the way he was giving orders when this was *her* venture, annoyed that she was losing control of this situation, and even more annoyed that she found herself admiring the way his shoulders filled out that blue coat, Ariadne angrily sent Shareb-er-rehh trotting after him.

"I'll have you know, Mr. Lord, that I quite object to your high-handed ways. And I'll thank you to remember your station in life, and how you address your betters. Furthermore, may I remind you that you are working for *me* and I'm the one giving orders here!"

Ignoring her, Colin suppressed a grin and easily balanced the sea chest atop his shoulder. *I know more about giving orders and ensuring that they're obeyed than you ever will,* he thought. But it was best to let her remarks go by the board. Favoring his bad leg, he led the way around the back of the building to the little court-yard, her peppery words stinging the air behind him, the stallion following in his footsteps and mincing like a fop. She was lying about the beast, that was for damned sure. Even for a gait-horse, it had a strange and singular way of moving, throwing its feet high and strutting like a damned peacock.

Well, she must have her own secrets, and for twelve thousand pounds, he wasn't going to pry too deeply.

Reaching the tarpaulin-covered chaise he'd brought over from the livery with the intention of repainting it, he set the trunk down and looked up at his employer. From her perch atop her steed's back, she was staring down at the shrouded lump, and frowning.

"And what, pray tell, is *that?*"

"A chaise."

"And what do you intend to do with it?"

"Why, harness your fine steed to it." He saw the color rushing into her face, and added, "It will enhance his disguise. No one will suspect a carriage horse as being a fancy riding hack, will they?"

"Now see here," she began, "Shareb-er-rehh is the bluest of bluebloods. He can*not* be made to pull a chaise—"

"My dear lady." Colin had more patience than cold treacle, but it was beginning to wear quite thin. "We have between us, your belongings, my sea chest, Bow, and over a hundred miles between here and Burnham. In case you have not noticed, we also have only *one* horse, with no time to hire another. I personally don't care if he's a pet or the most valuable stallion in England, he is still a horse, and I'll be damned if I'm going to walk all the way from here to East Anglia."

Ariadne drew back in surprise. The veterinarian's anger was the quiet type, restrained but effective, the kind that was all the more intimidating because one was unable to discern its depth. Beneath her, Shareb-er-rehh stiffened, as though he had understood the animal doctor's logic—and, his words.

"But—" she began.

"But what?"

Her mouth tight, she looked out past the soot-stained buildings that even now, were starting to gain shape and color from the blossoming pink and gold dawn. "I don't want him pulling a chaise," she said mulishly. "He's never had to do such a thing and I'm ... I'm afraid."

"Of what?"

"That he'll get scared and hurt himself."

"He's not going to get scared, and he's not going to hurt himself."

"Just because you know how to save dying dogs doesn't mean you know a thing about my horse!"

"He's not going to get scared, and he's not going to hurt himself," the veterinarian repeated, with deliberate patience.

"But he's never pulled a chaise, he's never pulled anything!"

"He can learn."

"He'll balk. He'll shy. He'll refuse to budge."

"Then I guess we won't get him to Norfolk, will we?"

She glared at him,, rankled by his quiet but firm authority. He gazed calmly, implacably back—Lord, she was starting to loathe that particular look—awaiting her answer.

"I can see right now that this is going to be one miserable journey."

"Only as miserable as you choose to make it."

"Know something? I'm beginning to wish I'd never hired you."

He shrugged and began stripping the tarpaulin cover from the chaise. "It is not too late to change your mind."

"What, and have you go running straight to Weybourne House to tell Tristan that I'm still near at hand? Oh, no. You know too much as it is, and you're coming with me whether you like it or not, Mr. High and Mighty Animal Doctor!"

"And *you* are going to hitch that horse to this chaise whether *either* of you like it or not, Your Spoiled and Sassy Ladyship."

"How dare you insult me so!"

He merely grinned, leaned insolently against the side of the chaise and gazed calmly up at her.

And as the first fingers of daylight breathed color into the morning, she saw that his eyes were a clear, unusual shade of lavender shot through with gray.

Beautiful, arresting, keenly perceptive, eyes.

She wasn't supposed to notice things like that. Not when her future belonged to another. She jerked her gaze away, staring at the shoddy stone and brick buildings instead.

"Very well, then," she snapped. "Finish uncovering the thing."

Out of the corner of her eye, she saw him touch his brow as though in salute, turn, and resume where he had left off. The temptation was too much, and despite herself, she slowly twisted her head to look at him, ready to jerk her gaze away in case he straightened up and caught her watching.

For a lowly commoner, Colin Lord possessed no small degree of charm and dash, and he issued orders as though doing so came second nature to him. She didn't like the way he was already taking over command of this venture. She didn't like the feelings he evoked in her, didn't like the fact there was something about him that didn't quite ring true, didn't like the hot prickle of sensation that swept her blood every time their eyes met. There was no reason he should affect her so.

None at all.

She watched as the fat little mongrel sidled close to her master's legs, cocking her head at the sound the night's rain made as it rolled off the tarpaulin. Yapping, she dove at the droplets trickling to the ground, inciting a burst of laughter from her master before he playfully shooed her away.

Losing interest, the tiny creature came up to the stallion. Then she went down on her forepaws before him, barking happily and looking up at Shareb-er-rehh with sparkling, mischievous eyes. Her tail waved madly; Shareb pricked his ears and took a step forward, blowing softly through his nose. Then his head went down, the reins slipped through Ariadne's fingers, and the mighty stallion touched his nose to the little dog's.

Bow, the veterinarian had called it. Part of a boat. What kind of a name was *that*?

"Your chariot awaits, Lady Ariadne."

Startled, she raised her head to look. The chaise, a white, two-wheeled contraption with a collapsible top and a red leather seat, was barely large enough for two people. Ariadne gauged the size of that seat, and felt suddenly uneasy. She'd have to sit closer to this man than propriety, her liking, and her own betrothed status would permit.

Yes, beautiful, unusual eyes. Broad shoulders, a handsome face, and a very well-made form.

His hand rested on one wheel, and it was then she noticed the ring on his left forefinger. She wondered if he was married.

If he, too, was promised to another, had a sweetheart, someone whom she loved.

Stop it, Ariadne!

He leaned over to pull a harness and bridle from just beneath the seat. Beneath his coat, she could see the muscles stretching taut across his more-than-capable shoulders. Sudden warmth coursed through her. Did Maxwell have shoulders that looked like that? After all, she'd never really thought to study them—

"Well?" he said, holding the tack and looking expectantly at Shareb-er-rehh.

"What I don't understand," she said loftily, "is that you have a chaise but no horse of your own to pull it."

"I *did* have a horse to pull it."

"Well, why don't we hitch *him* to the chaise, then?"

"Because he died three days ago."

"Lovely. You're a veterinarian and your horse *died*. Oh, I feel supremely confident now about hiring you to look after *my* animal, truly, I do."

He had been reaching into the chaise to wipe a bit of dampness from the seat; she saw his back go stiff, and he turned around slowly, *too* slowly, and met her gaze with that direct and unnerving stare of his. "My horse," he said softly, "was twenty-nine years old."

Ariadne swallowed hard and she looked down at Shareb's mane, her cheeks flaming. Twenty-nine years was a long time for a horse. He must've looked after the animal quite well indeed.

Unable to meet his eyes, she murmured, "I'm sorry, Mr. Lord. That was very unkind of me."

"Yes, it was. "

She bit her lip and glanced at him. He merely stood there, the harness and bridle slung over one arm and a little smile playing across his face to soften the awkwardness of the moment. She tried to smile back, and felt small and insignificant in the face of his gentle patience.

"Friends?" he murmured, raising one brow.

She looked down, feeling terrible. "Friends."

"Very well then. Let's get our equine nobleman hitched up to the chaise, shall we? It will be dawn soon, and I think it best to get out of London before the city awakes."

She nodded, dismounted, and holding the bridle, watched worriedly as he approached Shareb, the mass of leather straps and buckles hanging over his arm. Sure enough, the stallion took one look at the harness, flung up his head, and backed away.

"He's not going to let you put that thing on him, Mr. Lord."

But the veterinarian murmured softly and stretched out his hand toward the horse.

Shareb took another step back, broke out in a hard sweat, and turning his blinkered head, gazed beseechingly at his mistress.

"Oh, Shareb ..." Ariadne caught the cheekpiece of his bridle and pulled him toward her. Giving the animal doctor a long-suffering look, the horse lowered his head and buried his face against his mistress's chest, keeping only his ears on Colin while Ariadne murmured and consoled. "It's all right," she crooned, threading her fingers through his mane. The small ears remained pointed at Colin. "That big, bad horse doctor is not going to hurt you ..."

"This big, bad horse doctor thinks it's getting late."

"He doesn't want to pull the chaise. Look at him. He's sulking, Mr. Lord."

"He's not sulking."

"Well, what do you call it then? Look at his face. He's *sulking*. I told you this was a foolish idea."

"Have you a better one?"

"Well no, but ... "

"Then stop delaying and let's get him harnessed. Unless, of course, you don't really wish to reach Norfolk before the decade is out ..."

"Mr. Lord, you are the most irritatingly practical man I have ever met!"

"And you, my lady, are the slowest moving fugitive I have yet to encounter. Now harness the horse while I hold his head."

"*Me*, harness a horse? I haven't the faintest idea how to harness a horse. Even on those rare instances when I did any driving, a servant always did it. I'll hold his head and *you* harness him."

"No, *you* harness him and *I'll* hold his head."

"You're giving orders again, Mr. Lord."

"Indeed I am. Here."

"I don't like it when you give orders. *I'm* running this adventure!"

"No you're not, you're financing it. Now harness the horse and let's get this escapade underway."

She had no time to protest further before he was thrusting the tack at her. Their fingers accidentally touched, and the heavy mass of leather fell to the ground with a thud.

Simultaneously, they both bent to pick it up. Brows rapping painfully, they jumped back and away from each other, he letting loose with a curse and she coming up with the harness.

"Sorry," she said, blushing.

"No, no, 'tis my fault. Are you all right?"

"Of course I'm all right, I have a very hard skull. Father used to tell me that all the time, you know—"

"And no doubt, he was correct," he said, ignoring the sudden burst of angry color across her cheeks. "And I see that you have consented to harness the animal after all. They say that patience is a virtue, but I far prefer obedience. Especially when it comes to dealing with spoiled young noblewomen."

"*Spoiled?*" she retorted, drawing herself up to her full height.

"You'll watch what you say to me, sir! And I'll tell you right now that I prefer my servants to display a reasonable amount of respect. Had I known you were such a boor I would never have hired you!"

"I am not a boar, I'm a man. Boars have tusks."

"What?"

He plucked the breastpiece and neck strap from her suddenly nerveless hand, shook it out, and directing her to put it over Shareb's head, grinned innocently at her. "So, for that matter, do walruses."

"You are unforgivably impossible! Stop teasing me!"

"Am I?"

"You are, and I order you to stop it!"

"And I order *you* to put that harness on that horse under my tutelage, or I shall go back inside, have my breakfast, and allow you to figure it out by yourself."

They faced each other, she holding the leather straps and glaring angrily at him, he merely looking at her with little crinkle-lines of amusement fanning out at the corners of his eyes and the side of his mouth turning up in a lopsided, boyish smile that did dangerous things to her heart.

And Shareb-er-rehh—pricking his ears, arching his neck, and sniffing curiously at the strange leather in her hands—was no help at all.

Sputtering and fuming, Lady Ariadne St. Aubyn began to harness her horse.

§

"REALLY, Tristan ... I expected more from you than miserable excuses."

He gripped the edge of the table, hard, and leaned forward over his white knuckles. "They are not excuses, milord—"

"Sit down, Tristan."

"But you must believe me!"

"I said, sit down."

Sweating and terrified, he obeyed.

Clive sat regarding him calmly, one dark, hypnotic eye fixed unblinkingly on his face, the other, blinded long ago and now an eerie milky blue, making him want to shudder. A signet ring glowed dully on one long finger, every hair was in perfect, impeccable place and, dressed in his habitual black, he had never looked more sinister.

"I suppose I should've known better than to expect so much from one who seeks to pay off the gambling debts he owes me by amassing even bigger ones."

Tristan sank a little lower in his chair, and only that fixed, one-eyed stare held him upright and kept his suddenly nerveless body from sliding right down beneath the table.

"But I'd been so lucky at the card tables, I really didn't think—"

"No, you are far too young and stupid to think. Which is why you find yourself in this predicament, isn't it, Tristan?"

He was terrified; fear curled around his kidneys and squeezed his heart within his chest. "I'll come up with the money I owe you, my lord, I swear it!"

Clive leaned back in his chair, his face without compassion, pity, or soul. "Ah ... and what brilliant plan have you now, my young friend?"

"I'll ... I'll ask my father for my inheritance."

The earl regarded him with bored impatience. "And what shall you tell him, Tristan, when he asks you for what purpose you need the funds? Hmm? I suppose you might just come right out and tell him you owe me some money ... to the tune of twenty-one thousand pounds."

Tristan went white. He swallowed, his Adam's apple cutting into his crisply starched necktie, the thick lump of fear catching in his throat and hanging there. He clasped his hands beneath the table and forced his breathing to remain steady. His creditor was playing with him like a cat with a mouse.

"I suppose if you were a truly callous and enterprising young man, you could rather ... shall I say, force your inheritance."

"You mean ... k-kill my father?"

Clive took out a cheroot, tapped it, lit it, and sat regarding Tristan through a lazy cloud of smoke. "Now, did I say that ... Tristan?"

He stared into that black eye, unable to speak.

The earl smiled darkly. "Did I?"

"No, sir, you did not. But—"

"Come up with the money, Tristan." Clive tapped the ashes from his cheroot with studied elegance. "You fancy yourself such an enterprising young man ... I'm sure you can manufacture some clever scheme in which to do it." He sat back in his chair, that one eye blacker than the devil's soul. "Because you see, Tristan ... if you do not come up with the money, I can promise you that this Season in which you've brought about your own ruin... ."

The earl smiled, evilly, and the blood ran cold in his veins.

... Will be your last."

❧

Will be your last ... will be your last ... will be your last ...

The words seemed to be in step with the mare's steady trot, repeating themselves over and over and over in his mind.

Will be your last ... will be your last ... will be your last ...

Two months ago that dreadful meeting had been, and even now the memory made Tristan's mouth go dry with fright. With every mile the mare put behind her, with every person and beast they passed as he sought the Norfolk Road that would take him out of London and bring him home to Burnham—*please God, let me get there before* she *does*—he felt that fear returning, its black tentacles curling around his spine and squeezing the air from his lungs.

For somewhere out there, was Clive ...

Waiting.

Will be your last.

It had been all too obvious that his creditor had something far more dark and ugly planned for him than mere debtor's prison.

And what good would his inheritance, vast as it was, do him? Five months shy of his twenty-first year, he was too young to claim it anyhow. His hands began to sweat on the reins. He should never have told his father about his predicament, should never have expected the old man to react in any way but how he had, should never have put it past Ariadne to steal the one and only means he had of saving his own life ...

And maybe her own as well.

He gazed bleakly ahead through the mare's ears, watching them twitching back and forth, her creamy mane rippling on the light wind.

If only it was Shareb-er-rehh I had with me, not some common mare ... if only I had Shareb-er-rehh... .

But he didn't have Shareb-er-rehh.

Ari did—and she already had a good head-start on him.

He thought again of Clive's slow, saturnine smile of evil and foreboding, and urged the mare faster, into a canter.

He had to stop her.

But the rolling, triple-timed beat of the mare's hoofbeats made those final words even louder.

Will be your last ... .

Chapter Four

Her Ladyship managed to harness her own horse with surprising skill, and Colin didn't know which of the two nobles—the girl, or her equally high-bred nag—seemed more put out by the procedure. It was all he could do not to chuckle with mirth when he directed her to free the stallion's tail-hairs from the crupper, an action that made her cheeks go pink with embarrassment and Shareb-er-rehh's head to jerk up with indignation.

Finishing, she turned, folded her arms across her chest, and stared at him with haughty triumph.

"Satisfied, Mr. Lord?"

He eyed her long and hard, until her composure began to falter. "Should I be?"

"Indeed you should. I have finished harnessing him."

He grinned and held out the driving bridle to her. "No, you haven't."

Her mouth tightening, she snatched the bridle and turned her back on him. Suspecting a conspiracy, Shareb-er-rehh eyed it with malice, backed up, and reared. Colin instinctively moved forward, but Lady Ariadne brought the stallion down with a quick yank on the reins.

Gripping the bridle's cheekpiece, she put her face as close as she could to the horse's blinkered head and stared into his dark eye. "I don't like this any more than you do!" she hissed, but in a voice that was clearly intended for Colin to hear. "Now, be good and stop your fussing!"

Instantly the big beast quieted, albeit with a surly look in his eye that belied his seemingly good manners. Then his mistress reached up, deftly removed the hood and bridle, and gave Colin his first full view of the stallion's face.

His breath caught in his throat. The head was beautiful, classically sculpted, broad across the forehead with a white blaze starting just between the dark, intelligent eyes and widening as it spilled downward so that it encompassed nearly all of the horse's muzzle.

"Handsome animal," he said, stretching his hand toward the stallion.

Shareb-er-rehh lashed out and nearly amputated his fingers.

"Loves compliments, doesn't he?"

"He loves his *dignity* even more."

"Yes, I'm sure he does. But he'll have to make do without it until we get to Norfolk. Please proceed."

"I have never been treated so insultingly in my life."

"And I've never had the liberty of having my horse harnessed and bridled for me. I find I rather like it."

She shot him a murderous glare, hooked an arm around the stallion's poll and gently coaxed the bit into his mouth. Shareb-er-rehh stood chomping the metal, working it between teeth and tongue and eyeing Colin with as much malevolence as did his mistress, but otherwise making no further protest as she pulled the bridle into place. Her tiny fingers buckled the throatlatch, pulled the stallion's forelock free from the browband, ensured the blinkers were adjusted over each eye. Then she walked briskly around the lathering animal, taking off her cap and tossing her hair over her shoulder as she swept past Colin in what could only be a deliberate attempt to tempt and taunt her human companion.

Her efforts found their mark. Colin caught the scent of lavender, and with it an engaging blend of soap, horses, and femininity. Heat flashed through him, riding a wave of desire.

She went to the stallion's head, turned, and eyed him with feminine triumph.

"I really think that we should make an effort to get along, if this trip is to be at all pleasant," she announced.

"I'm glad we are of like mind."

"Therefore I expect you to show me a modicum of respect."

"And I would desire the same."

She smiled.

He gave her the same unflappable stare that had once placated his admiral.

And she turned quickly away, stroking the stallion's nose and blushing furiously. "Furthermore, I've been thinking that *Mister* Lord simply will not do. It is far too ordinary, and not indicative of the great miracles I believe you are capable of performing with regard to healing animals. Therefore, I shall call you 'doctor' instead. Yes, *doctor*. Besides, if I go one hundred miles having to address you as 'Mr. Lord' I shall wear out my tongue!"

"That would be a blessing," he murmured, picking up his trunk and shoving it under the seat of the chaise so she wouldn't see the twinkle in his eye.

"I beg your pardon?"

"I mean, that would be an unusual form of ad*dressing*—" he looked up and gave an innocent grin—"me."

"Oh. I thought you said something else."

"I would never insult my lady so."

"I should hope not. So, do you like your new title, Doctor Lord?"

"You flatter me, Lady Ariadne, but veterinarians are not regarded as doctors."

"Indeed they are not. But you are *my* veterinarian and if I want to consider you a doctor, I will." Her eyes sparkling, happy that she'd gotten the upper hand in at least something, she put her hands on her hips and made a small circle around him, immensely pleased with herself and reminding him of a happy queen who'd just raised one of her subjects to the peerage. "Besides, you rather *look* like a doctor, especially when you wear your spectacles, as you were doing yesterday when you saved that poor dog. By the way, where are they? You haven't forgotten them now, have you?"

"No," Colin said, his concentration swinging from her to the task at hand as he picked up the shafts of the chaise and brought the vehicle directly up behind the horse. The big animal stiffened and turned, regarding him warily. Already, the dark eyes were rolling, the ears back, the nostrils flaring with trepidation. The horse was no idiot, and obviously suspected what was to be asked of him. Colin tossed a blanket into the chaise. They'd be damned lucky if they weren't all killed.

"Good. You rather look like a University graduate, all brainy and highborn with them on ... I do hope you shall wear them often for me, just so I'm reminded that I have indeed purchased myself a veterinarian worthy of my stallion. I mean, at twelve thousand pounds you had better be worthy!"

"Perhaps next time you should shop around for a bargain," he said drolly, as he directed her to back the horse into the shafts.

"Are you sporting with me, sir?"

"Me, sport with you?" He widened his eyes and gave her his most innocent smile as he fastened the traces. "I would not dream of it. You are *far* too important a personage to make sport of, and I would be less than a gentleman if I were to insult you so."

"Good." She raised her chin and regarded him with a cool hauteur that was effectively destroyed by the mischief in her eye. "Because I would take great offense, I think, if you were to make sport of me without my knowing. That would be unforgivably rude and impertinent behavior on your part."

"Oh, yes. Unforgivably."

They stared at each other, both trying not to grin. Then her chin came down a notch, and he saw the helpless sparkle in her eye, the deviltry in her expression.

"So, are you going to wear your spectacles or not?"

"I wear them for reading."

"You weren't reading when *I* saw you in them."

"I wear them during surgery, too. Or, for anything that requires strict attention to detail. Or when I'm tired. Or when—"

"Surgery!" She clapped a hand across her chest and went a bit green. "Do you mean ... *cutting* things?"

"Not 'things.' Flesh. Skin. Muscle—"

"How utterly *ghastly*. Pray I shall never have to see anything more disconcerting than what you had to do to that poor, bloated dog yesterday! Imagine, stabbing it in the belly with a needle—"

"You should have stayed a bit longer," he couldn't resist adding, with a teasing grin. "The stomach tube procedure that followed was even more impressive."

She blanched. "*Stomach tube?*"

"Aye. A long, snakish thing of wire wrapped with leather. One must push it down the esophagus and into the stomach so as to relieve the excess—"

"Never mind, Dr. Lord, you may talk of such things *after* we eat breakfast! Which reminds me, would you like a blackcurrant tart?"

As though on cue, the stallion's ears shot forward and he craned his neck and stared at his mistress' pocket. Odd behavior, Colin thought, frowning. The little noblewoman reached into her coat, pulled out a thick wedge of paper-wrapped pastry, and pushing aside Shareb-er-rehh's questing muzzle with her elbow, offered it to Colin.

He took it and thanked her, not realizing how hungry he'd been until the sugary, flaky pastry filled his mouth. The stallion eyed him flatly, one ear forward, one back; then it banged its head against Lady Ariadne's shoulder, hard, at the same time that Colin felt paws against his knees and looked down to see little Bow, begging, drooling, and staring at him with desperate eyes. Hungry as he was, he broke the pastry in half, gave the bigger piece to the dog, and when he glanced up, noticed the stallion was munching something and regarding him with haughty triumph.

He frowned. Dear God, he hoped she hadn't fed pastry to the horse ...

Early morning traffic was beginning to clatter past on the street beyond the buildings, and overhead, two chaffinches flitted amongst branches dressed in green. It was apparent that if they ever wanted to get out of London, he'd have to get this venture underway. He made one final check of the harness, lifted Bow into the chaise—

And saw his employer giving something to her horse.

"What are you feeding him?"

"Pastry." She smiled lovingly at the stallion as it lipped the last crumbs from her palm. "A blackcurrant tart, to be precise."

"I forbid it."

She stiffened, her chin coming up. "Dr. Lord, you'll not *forbid* anything. Shareb *likes* pastry and ale—"

"*Ale?*"

"Yes, *ale*. Are you hard of hearing? Or do you forbid that, too, *Doctor?*"

"As a matter of fact, I do. As your horse's veterinarian I cannot allow him to have pastry and ale, no matter how much he enjoys them. Surely he can subsist comfortably well on hay, bran, oats and corn, like any other horse—"

"Dr. Lord, you don't understand. Shareb-er-rehh is not 'just any other horse' and he deserves special treatment. Besides, I've been feeding him pastry and ale since he was a little colt. Now please, be reasonable ... you're already forcing him to pull that dreadful chaise. The least you can do is allow him some small recompense to atone for this grievous assault on his pride."

Another wedge of pastry on her palm, Ariadne turned her back on him, held out her hand to the stallion once more—

And felt her wrist caught in the veterinarian's grip.

"I said, *no*."

He was no longer teasing her, and his tone was hard and commanding and brooked no argument. She froze, staring at his fingers. How small and fragile her wrist looked, caught in that broad, masculine grip; how white and dainty her skin was, how tiny her bones in comparison to the breadth and strength of his hand. She felt the warmth of his thumb against her pulse, the calluses of his palm against her flesh, and once again saw the mastiff, and he leaning over it, these very same hands coaxing it back to life ...

Her head jerked up and she stared straight ahead, her mouth set. "Dr. Lord. I did *not* give you permission to touch me."

He didn't let go.

Her voice rose. "Did you hear me, sir? Kindly remove your hand from my wrist."

The pressure only seemed to tighten and tension crackled between them. "No more pastry," he ordered softly.

She set her jaw. Her breathing quickened, and a pulse began to beat in her ears.

"Your promise. *No more pastry*."

Ariadne took a deep, steadying breath, slowly turned her head, and glared angrily up at him.

He was so close that she could see the starbursts of gray radiating from the lilac depths of his irises, feel his breath against her brow, sense the solid, unbending strength of his will. She noticed a curious, vertical dimple-line faintly clefting his chin, strands of bleached gold running through the fair hair that tumbled over his brow, the long, pale crescents of his lashes, the firm shape of his mouth.

His mouth ...

Smiling coyly up at him through her lashes, Ariadne touched her forefinger to the corner of his lips.

"You have very beautiful eyes ... Dr. Lord."

Her remark, combined with that single touch, was enough to stun him into shock, which was precisely what she'd hoped to accomplish. Quickly jerking free of his grasp and pressing home her advantage, Ariadne pushed the pastry into his palm, making sure her fingertips lingered against his skin a second or two longer than was necessary. His mouth hardening, he snatched his hand away, dropped the confection, and ground it into the dirt with the heel of his boot.

"Really," she said, dark eyes flashing with laughter and triumph, "I think you are over-reacting."

"Get in the chaise."

Shareb-er-rehh flung up his head and flattened his ears.

"But—"

"I said, *get in the chaise.*"

Giving him a victorious grin, she raised her brows and climbed delicately up into the vehicle. There she sat, head bent, her lips twitching as she made a great pretense of straightening her sleeve.

Colin, his blood pounding, set his jaw. Well, she might've scored a hit, the little imp, but she wouldn't win this battle.

No way in bloody hell.

Did he have beautiful eyes?

"You know, Dr. Lord, I think this is going to be a very exciting adventure, don't you?" she said airily, coaxing Bow into her lap and behaving as though the contact between them had never happened. "And oh, how funny it will be, that the whole countryside will be searching for a highborn lady dressed in the height of fashion when the real Lady Ariadne will be sneaking past under their very noses disguised as a boy! Isn't it grand, Dr. Lord? Am I not clever? And what do you think my Maxwell will say when he sees me thus?"

"I don't know your Maxwell. I have no idea what he'll say."

"Well, what would *you* think, Dr. Lord, if it was *your* betrothed who showed up on your doorstep dressed in a man's clothes?"

"I'd think she had the wrong doorstep."

"I'm serious! What would you think?"

"I suppose I wouldn't care how she was dressed, as long as I loved her and she arrived safe and sound."

"Have you ever been in love, Dr. Lord?"

"Briefly."

"Have you ever *wanted* to be in love?"

"About as much as I wanted scurvy," he lied, walking to the stallion's head and taking a firm grip on the reins just below its chin.

"Be serious, sir! This is important business we're discussing. You are a very handsome man, you know. Why, if our stations were equal, and Papa hadn't betrothed me to Maxwell, I might even take a fancy to you myself."

"And why is that?"

"Why is what?"

Backing the horse up with one hand on its chest, he impaled her with his direct gaze, trying to put her off-balance as she had so successfully done with him. "Why would you take a fancy to me?"

"I—" Color swept through her cheeks. "Dr. Lord, that is *not* a very polite question to ask a lady."

"Regardless, I have asked it, and should you decide not to answer, 'twill be you who is being impolite."

"Very well then," she said, a bit huffily. "I would fancy you because ..."

Her face went crimson, and she looked away.

"Yes?" he goaded, pleased to have turned the tables on her at her own game. "Because why?"

Her chin shot up and she stared straight ahead. "I have no wish to further this conversation."

"A pity. And here I thought I was going to be enlightened as to why a beautiful young heiress might take a fancy to me. Such a cruel and unfair world, this! Never mind."

"Dr. Lord?"

He was hard-pressed to contain his grin. "Yes, my lady?"

She was still staring ahead, spine as straight as a frigate's main-mast, hands fisted between her knees. "I think it's time we leave."

Chapter Five

Shareb-er-rehh, however, had other ideas.

Ariadne was quick to recognize the alarm and indignation in the stallion's eyes. "Really, Dr. Lord, I think this is a very bad idea. You're asking for trouble, I tell you."

"He'll be fine."

"No he won't. Look at him, you can see how angry he is. He gets very unpredictable when he's angry—"

Colin tried again to urge the stallion forward, but the horse only hunched his back and froze, one hind leg coming up with dangerous intent. Ariadne couldn't prevent her smug smile; but then the animal doctor called a firm command and this time, Shareb-er-rehh moved ahead, not smoothly, not confidently, but in jolting, frightened rabbit-leaps that made his mane and tail snap out in the wind with each violent motion and nearly dislocated Ariadne's head from her neck.

"You are right, he possesses very unusual gaits," the veterinarian observed dryly. "I should think he is a most uncomfortable animal to ride."

"Very—funny—*Doctor* Lord," she managed, between the erratic jolts.

"How on earth do you sit to such motion?"

"Years of practice."

Ears flattened, Shareb moved forward, his head and neck at an unnaturally high angle, his lips pulled back in an angry grimace, his mouth dripping foam. Despite the fact that blinkers hid his eyes, Ariadne knew the dark orbs were wild and ringed with white.

But he was moving, and Ariadne had to admit grudging admiration for the veterinarian's skill. Pulling a chaise was a lot to ask of an untrained horse, especially one who had been bred to do something entirely different.

Yes, I am *glad I chose* him *to be Shareb's doctor*, she thought, despite her earlier views to the contrary. *There is something about him, something I cannot quite put my finger on ... something more than his gentle strength, his quiet demeanor, his dry humor. He is smart, strong, and sensible, and I feel safe when he is near.*

Now that was an odd notion. Safe?

Safe. But how long before she dared trust him enough with the truth about what Shareb *really* was?

Gait-horse, indeed!

The jerky, jolting motion began to ease off as Shareb-er-rehh found his stride, and his confidence, and soon the stallion's head had returned to its proper angle and the powerful hindquarters were churning in a fast trot. The veterinarian guided him out of the little courtyard, and shaking his head, Shareb moved into the street, his hoofbeats echoing loudly against the buildings that rose up on either side.

"Why, this is actually *fun*! Imagine, Shareb-er-rehh, pulling a chaise! My goodness, I never thought to see the day—can you believe how well behaved he's being? And here I thought we'd both be killed by now! Give me the reins, Dr. Lord, *I* want to try driving him!"

Such boundless delight was infectious. Colin chuckled, the wind on his face, buildings and glimpses of the silvered Thames passing in a blur as Shareb-er-rehh's fast, ground-eating trot sped them through London. As he'd predicted, his charge wasn't so hard to manage, after all.

The horse was one thing.

Her Ladyship was quite another.

His mouth still tingled where she had touched it, her comment about his eyes still rang in his head, both awakening some unexplored part of his soul that responded to the attention and wanted more. He was unused to having a woman, especially a lady, behave so boldly toward him, and he wasn't quite sure whether he liked it or not. Well, he thought he must like it, but he was unsure how to respond to it. Maybe the little flirt was just trying to upset his even keel. Maybe she was just trying out her own feminine wiles on someone she perceived as "safe." Or maybe she was calculatedly paying him back for winning the upper hand with regards to the twelve thousand pounds, or even harnessing the stallion. He didn't know. But what he *did* know, was that if she persisted on tormenting him so, he would see no recourse but to give her a taste of her own medicine.

And had no reservations about doing so.

Now, her thigh was a hair's breadth away, her piquant face too close to his own as she gazed eagerly into his eyes, waiting for his answer. Such scrutiny was enough to send the blood pounding through his heart at a clip that, coupled with her childlike joy at breezing along through the streets of London, was totally disarming.

Now, he felt the pressure of her hand over his, her fingers against his knuckles as she playfully tried to pry the rein free. "Please, Dr. Lord, let me drive, it's *my* turn!"

"Not yet."

"Why not?"

"Let's put the city behind us, first. Then you may drive all you like."

"Now see here, he's *my* horse and I'm sure I can handle him!"

"Fine." He shrugged and handed her the reins. "Take him, then."

Shooting him a triumphant glare, she raised her chin and took the reins loosely in her hands. But her smugness was quick to change to worry as she realized her folly. Shareb-er-rehh immediately stepped up his trot. Her hands tightened around the reins. Shareb pulled harder. Her hands became fists. The stallion shook his head, fighting her. Her teeth sank into her bottom lip. Her knuckles went white, and she planted her feet against the floorboards as the stallion's brute strength began to pull her straight out of her seat—

"Fine day, isn't it?" Colin mused, leaning back in the seat and pretending an interest in the tangles of ivy that choked the wall of a passing house.

"Lovely," she managed, through clenched teeth.

"Got any more of that pastry?"

"There's a man for you, always thinking of his stomach."

Colin grinned. Most of the men he knew put other needs before their stomach's, but he kept the remark to himself out of respect for her gender, her innocence, and her status. And as for such "needs" ... he was all too aware of a tightening in his breeches at the closeness of the female who sat beside him. Damn him if he wasn't getting hard.

They weren't even out of London. How on earth was he going to survive this trip to Norfolk?

He glanced over at his employer. Her cheeks were flushed with wind and the effort of holding the horse back, and her mouth was tight with determination. The stallion shook his head, trying to take the bit in his teeth and run.

"Having problems?" he asked, raising a brow and enjoying her obvious distress.

"I told you he was not a carriage horse. And I have no wish to drive a horse while you sit there and enjoy the scenery. Not that the scenery in this particular area of the city is particularly enjoy-able, mind you. Here, take him back."

Colin, grinning, pulled the sack of pastry out from beneath the seat. "I think I'd much rather eat my breakfast."

She all but stuffed the reins in his hands. "I said, take him back!"

"And how do you expect me to eat if I am to hold the reins?"

"I don't particularly care how you eat! Next you'll be asking me to feed you!"

Firmly taking the reins, he brought the stallion back under control. "Now, there's an idea ..."

She stared at him, eyes beginning to glint with deviltry. Or malice. It was impossible to tell which.

"Very well then, Dr. Lord," she purred. He raised a brow, wondering what she was up to as she took the sack, opened it, and peered within. "Let's see ... we have apple ... plum ... black-currant—"

"Plum's fine."

"Plum it is, then."

She reached into the bag and pulled out a thick, sugary wedge of pastry oozing globs of fruit filling. A mischievous smile curving her mouth, she held the pastry up to his lips. "Open your mouth, sir—"

Colin had no choice but to comply, and opened his jaws exag-geratedly wide so as to avoid having her fingers touch his lips.

The chaise hit a bump and they did anyhow. Sweet, sticky fruit and flaky pastry jammed against his teeth, and with them, her fingers.

An electric charge rocked him at the contact.

She blushed, and laughed. "Oh! Well, let's try that again. Open up, good doctor! Say, *aaaaah*!"

God, help me, he thought, every cell in his body beginning to throb, to ache, to burn.

He shut his eyes, briefly, and again opened his mouth. This time she got enough of the pastry in that he was able to get a bite of it. One of Shareb's ears was straight back, listening, and immediately the horse slowed its pace.

Colin rapped the reins against the powerful hindquarters.

"Another bite, Dr. Lord?

"Just one," he managed, swallowing, "then give the rest to Bow."

She held the pastry up to him once again, her gaze fastened on his mouth, her fingers touching his lips. He caught the scent of horse sweat on her sleeve, the hint of lavender wafting from her skin. Her eyes sparkled with humor, as though she knew just how difficult she was making his life, as though she knew just what she was about. In all probability, he thought wryly, she did.

God help you, young lady. You can't rattle me that easily.

"Has anyone ever told you that you have very beautiful eyes, Dr. Lord?"

Colin nearly choked on his pastry.

"You're a very handsome man, you know. And I think you should smile more often, as it is such a direct contrast to that intent look you usually wear. Are you sure you don't have a lady friend? Or two? I cannot imagine that you spend your life all alone."

"This conversation is most inappropriate."

Ariadne felt her lips twitching helplessly, for she'd discovered the chink in this stoic, unflappable man's armor, and, still smarting over his high-handed attitude, she was determined to press home her advantage. "Don't you like it when a lady pays you a compliment?"

He didn't answer, merely directing his gaze straight ahead, a nerve twitching along his jaw.

"Well?"

He turned his quiet, direct stare on her, letting it rake heatedly over her face, down her neck, and to her bosom, where it lingered long enough to make her feel as though she wasn't wearing anything at all. Her throat went dry, and her face felt suddenly hot and damp.

"As a matter of fact," he said slowly, raising his gaze back to hers, "... I do."

Coloring furiously, Ariadne looked away.

"So ... no more compliments?" he said, lifting one brow in warning.

"You'll get them when you deserve them," she snapped. "Drive on."

He shrugged, leaving her to squirm uncomfortably on the seat and wish there were ten miles separating their thighs instead of a mere two inches. She was uncomfortably aware of his male power and heat, the scent of his clean clothes and body, the way the sun slanted down through his eyes and found the purple in them.

Five minutes passed. Ten.

She rubbed at her palm, raw where the reins had chafed it. The chaise hit a dip in the street and the doctor's thigh bumped her own.

She moved over, trying to get away.

He glanced at her, watching her with a look of high amusement.

"Conversation," he said mildly, "can go far to make a long and boring trip into one that is a lot more interesting."

Conversation. Yes, that would take her mind off of how close together the seat forced them to sit.

And how that closeness was making her feel.

"How long do you think it will take us to reach Norfolk?" she ventured.

"Given the superb condition your animal is in and the speed with which he seems to enjoy traveling, I shouldn't think it will take long at all. In fact, we ought to be able to put a good fifteen or so miles behind us by the time we stop for the night."

"Twenty!"

"No. Let's not push him too much. Fifteen, and a good night's rest at an inn for him."

"And maybe a bit of pastry, Doctor?"

He shook his head. "No pastry."

"But you feed it to your dog!" she protested, picking up the little mongrel that had been crouching under the seat and setting it atop her lap. "Why is it that Bow can have pastry and Shareb cannot? That's not fair!"

"The digestive systems of dogs and horses are two different things," he returned. "What is good for one is not necessarily good for the other. Can you not substitute something healthy—an apple, a carrot—instead?"

"Shareb doesn't *like* apples and carrots. He likes *pastry*."

"And I suppose Shareb is used to getting anything he wants?"

"But of course. He is Royalty, as far as horses go."

"Persist in feeding him pastry and some other nag will succeed him to the throne."

"Dr. Lord, you are most impertinent!"

He looked over and down at her and smiled. "And *you*, my lady, are a bit too used to having your own way."

She gaped at him, shocked that he dared speak to her so.

"As is," he added, with a twinkle in his eye, "your horse."

"Really, sir! You do not know your place, do you?"

He laughed, quite impulsively for one she had thought rather reserved, and the action lit up his face like morning sunlight coming up over the sea. In that moment, Ariadne thought him quite handsome indeed, and felt an aching, overwhelming urge to lean against him, to laugh with him, to let down her guard and enjoy him for the man she perceived him to be. Uncomfortable with the feeling, and still keenly aware of his long, hard, thigh, she pointed her chin at the clouds and refused to look at him.

"Well, you cannot blame me," he said softly, his eyes fond.

"I'm having the devil of a time thinking of you as the grand lady when you've garbed yourself as the lowliest of stable hands."

She turned to him, her eyes gleaming conspiratorially. "It *is* a clever disguise, is it not, Dr. Lord?"

"Very clever." He nodded to a passing carriage driver. "But it didn't fool me."

"Well, no matter. The important thing is that I deceive my brother. The authorities. Reward hunters." She touched his sleeve and leaned close, peering inquisitively up at him. "Do you think anyone will believe that I am a man, Dr. Lord?"

The stallion's ceaseless pulling making his arms ache, Colin turned his head to look at her. Her eyes were bright, sparkling, and hopeful; her red hair bouncy and webbed across the flushed cheek she had turned toward the wind. There was no way, no way in hell, that that lovely face could be mistaken for anything other than what it was.

Strikingly, delightfully, female.

"No," he said, sobering. "They won't believe it."

Something in his gentle, intelligent eyes touched her soul, and taken aback, Ariadne looked away, fiercely stroking the little dog as she tried to get her suddenly-racing heart back under control. Swift color caught her cheeks, and she was thankful for the cooling breeze against her face. Why was it that every time she tried to unnerve the veterinarian with her coy flirtations, he turned the tables and made *her* feel flustered and uncomfortable?

Keenly aware of his nearness, she looked off at the passing scenery. Already they were into the country; just ahead was a grove of trees, and beyond, a little pond with a flock of quacking mallards breaking its early morning surface and leaving a long crescent of ripples in their wake.

"I wouldn't worry too much about your disguise," her companion murmured, his voice holding a note of humor. "I can assure you that for the moment, you're safe."

"The problem of my disguise, Dr. Lord, is not what is distressing me."

"I'm here if you would like to share a confidence."

"Oh, no, I could never!"

"Well, if we are to be together for the duration of this trip, we might as well be friends. Friends do those things, you know. Share confidences."

"You have not shared any of yours with *me*."

"What would you like to know?"

She looked pointedly at him. "You said you have never been in love—"

"I was jesting."

"Well, have you?"

"That's a rather personal question, don't you think?"

"Perhaps. But you were the one who suggested we share confidences."

"Well, I used to fancy an Irish girl."

"Did you, now!" She leaned conspiratorially close, though only Shareb and Bow bore witness to their conversation. "What was her name?"

He was grinning, remembering. "Doesn't matter."

"Oh, come now, Doctor, of course it matters!" She lowered her voice and pressed close, resting her fingers on his sleeve and peering up into his face. "Tell me her name!"

"Orla."

"Were you in love with her?"

"Well ... yes, I suppose I ... admired her from afar."

"You loved her. Admit it."

"Yes, I loved her. I admit it."

"Why didn't you marry her?"

"You ask very personal questions, my lady."

"I know, Father used to say that I talk too much. But since I'm paying you so much money I should be able to ask you all the questions I like, don't you think? So tell me about this Orla. If you fancied her, why did you not marry her?"

His smile faded. Something in his face changed, and a shadow darkened his eyes. "I—was forced to change my career."

"You have not always been a veterinarian?"

"No."

"What were you before?"

"A man who was paid good money to kill people."

"Come now, Dr. Lord! Tell me the truth!"

"That is the truth. And I've no further wish to discuss it."

"But—"

"I *said*, I do not wish to discuss it."

She stared at him for a moment, then her mouth snapped shut and she sat quietly beside him, her hands stuffed between her knees and her feelings obviously hurt. Colin felt a wave of remorse. He hadn't meant to be sharp with her, but her playful queries had brought back memories that, he realized, still had the power to bring him pain. A lot of pain. Not that *he* was still ashamed about the inglorious way his career had ended, but there were others who most certainly were, his father and Uncle Elliott included, and he suspected that this aristocratic, temperamental young pepper-pot who placed such value on class wouldn't under-stand any better than the others—save his own mother—had. For some, unfathomable reason, the idea of her pitying and scorning him filled him with sadness and despair.

"Dr. Lord?"

"Forgive me," he said, shaking his head and looking at her blankly. So much for her temporarily sulkiness. "What did you say?"

"I said I'm sorry. I didn't mean to upset you."

He just gave a pained smile and watched Shareb's muscled hindquarters, his mind still far away. But she wasn't the only one calling him back to the present; his leg was stiffening up, and there was nowhere, really, to stretch it.

She must have noticed his discomfort.

"How did you hurt your leg?"

He just shot her a sidelong glance, and didn't answer.

"Well, I did notice that you're trying to make it comfortable, and unless I miss my guess, failing miserably. You walk with a limp. What happened to you?"

"Really, Lady Ariadne, I think your father was correct. You talk too much."

"Are you embarrassed about it?"

"No."

"Did one of your patients kick you?"

"No."

"Then tell me what happened."

"Why are you so keen on knowing?"

"Nosiness. A desire to post it in the *Times*. So that I can hold it against you and blackmail you with the knowledge. Why do you *think* I want to know? Because I suspect that it burdens you more than you'll admit, and I just thought it would relieve your mind to talk about it."

"I see."

"So are you going to tell me about your leg?"

Cocking his head as though in deep thought, he frowned and stared straight ahead. "My leg. A long extremity consisting of muscle, tissue, skin and tendons enclosing one femur, one patella, one—"

Ariadne couldn't help herself. She leaned over and playfully cuffed his shoulder, and they both burst into laughter, defusing the tenseness of the previous moment.

"Don't make me laugh when I'm trying to be serious!" she protested.

"Of what concern is my poor leg to you?"

"I want to know how you hurt it!"

"I broke it."

"How?"

"I was shot."

"With a *gun*?"

"No, with a cannon."

"A *cannon*?" She clapped a hand dramatically to her breast. "Were you in the War?"

"Aye."

"Well, of course! Why didn't I think of that before? I know the Army employs veterinarians—I mean, with all those horses in the cavalry, *somebody* has to know how to care for them!—but I had no idea that you were a military veterinarian, although that does explain your fine posture and that irritating way you have of issuing orders ... I'm sorry, Dr. Lord, that I'm so nosy. I hope you don't regret telling me, now."

"I wasn't in the Army."

"Well, what *were* you, then?"

"Something I'm not, now. Something I don't want to think about, as the memories pain me. Let's talk about something else, if you don't mind."

"Such as?"

"Your stallion. He's no gait horse, is he?"

Her mouth fell open; then, quickly recovering, she flushed nervously and waved off his question. "Oh, Dr. Lord, the less you know about Shareb, the better. Trust me on that. But he is a smart horse, don't you think? Look at him, pulling us in this little chaise as though he's done it all his life. He is a wonderful horse, isn't he? The finest in all of England!"

Colin raised a brow.

"I know you can't see much of him, with the saddle cloth and leg bandages, but you'll just have to take my word on it. I know my horses, as they were my father's passion and now his legacy, and this one does not have an equal in all the land. Maybe, even, in all the world. Why are you smirking, Mr. Lord?"

"What happened to 'Doctor?'"

"Oh yes, that's right. You rather enjoy that, don't you?"

"Well, it is a bit unkind of you to bestow a title on me and then take it away."

"You're quite right, it *is* unkind. So tell me more about this Orla of yours. Did you ever kiss her? I've always wanted to be kissed. Maxwell kissed me once just once, but it was just a chaste peck on the cheek, and I've always been curious to know what a *real* kiss felt like."

"I'm sure you'll find out soon enough."

It wasn't appropriate, this conversation, and Colin didn't like the direction in which it was headed. Best not to think about kissing and this pretty young woman beside him. Best to think, surely, of something else. He turned his attention back to the horse, wishing he'd thought to use a different bit, something a little stronger, as this one was doing little to curb the stallion's relentless pulling and his shoulders were going to be on fire by the time they stopped for lunch—

"Dr. Lord?"

He knew the silence wasn't going to last.

"Yes?"

"I have a confession to make."

"I'm a veterinarian, not a priest."

"Father always told me that I was too wild, too hard to control, and that is why he betrothed me to Maxwell, because Maxwell, he said, would be able to rein me in. But I don't want to be reined in, Dr. Lord."

He risked a glance over at her. Her eyes were sparkling with mischief.

"What do you want, then?"

"It is very wicked, what I want. And you must promise not to tell anyone."

"I think I should have used a different bit on this horse... ."

"And *I* think I should like the chance to kiss someone else before I end up with Maxwell, just to see what a real kiss might feel like since his was so dull."

Colin felt suddenly too warm inside his clothing, and at the end of the reins, Shareb-er-rehh suddenly began to fidget and tried to break into a canter.

He pulled the horse back as it began to fight him. "And your confession?"

"Well, I know it is dreadfully wrong of me, my being betrothed and all, but... ."

Shareb began blowing hard, shaking his head—

"... I would very much like to know if *you* might kiss me, so that I might know what I'll be missing by marrying a man who seems to lack a certain ardor."

Shareb-er-rehh exploded into a full gallop.

"Whoa!"

"Good heavens, Dr. Lord, what's wrong with him?"

"Whoa! Easy!" A flock of pigeons burst skyward at the stallion's approach and Shareb went sideways against the shafts, stumbled, and recovered, hurtling down the street at breakneck speed. "Whoa, boy, *whoa!"*

With all of his strength, Colin managed to get the horse slowed down to a fast trot, then, after much fighting and coaxing, a panting, complete stop.

He blew out his breath, sat back on the seat and turned his furious glare upon his white-faced companion. "Is that your big secret? The fact that you want someone to kiss you?"

"Not 'someone.' You."

"The answer is no. A solid and resounding no, and I don't want to hear another word about it, is that understood?"

She blinked, and he saw the corner of her mouth twitching in a helpless little grin.

Colin put his elbows on his knees and his forehead in his hands, fingers splaying up through his hair as he damned himself, damned her, damned his impulsiveness in agreeing to this madcap adventure. Sir Graham in all his fury had never been able to rattle him, even Lord Nelson, firing questions at him that time like a warship's broadside, had not rattled him, even facing the French fleet and that damned Spanish battleship in the fight that had nearly carried off his leg had not rattled him, but this little sprite, this ninety-pound bit of flirtatiousness and fluff, had him so flustered and aback that he couldn't even think straight.

He was doomed.

Chapter Six

They continued on in heavy, awkward, uncomfortable silence.

Ariadne knew she should feel contrite, and her question hadn't been entirely innocent. It also hadn't been dishonest, because this kind, unassuming man with the gentle eyes was, indeed, someone she was feeling an increasing attraction to, and the idea of stealing a kiss from him before she was forever tied to the decidedly dispassionate Maxwell was, well ... exciting in a forbidden sort of way. Still, she hadn't counted on the veterinarian's reaction nor, for that matter, Shareb's.

Why had the stallion flown out of control?

Shareb was an intelligent horse, but she was pretty sure he didn't understand much English. No, her words had rattled the doctor, and that anxiety had gone straight down the reins and to the horse.

She sat there, pondering it, as the miles passed beneath them and the sun rose higher and higher.

"Nice day it's turned out to be," she said, trying to make benign conversation.

"Aye."

"Good that it isn't raining."

"Indeed."

"Dr. Lord, are you aware that you seem to have a way with animals?"

"So I've been told."

"That was odd, how he behaved back there ..."

"Yes, well, something probably spooked him. Nothing more."

"Nothing spooked him, and you know it. And I also find it very strange that he didn't kick you when you were showing me how to harness him. He would have kicked anyone else, you know. And he's behaving admirably well for a horse who has never been driven. What do you say to *that*, Dr. Lord?"

He gazed ahead, negotiating a turn in the road. "I'd say that Bow probably told him to behave."

"I'm serious."

He shrugged, the sunlight glinting off the brighter strands in his hair. "Animals like me, I guess."

She thought of the effect he had on Shareb—and wondered suddenly, shamefully, what feelings those strong, capable hands would evoke if they were laid on *her*.

Oh, dear God, what is the matter *with me? Please, help me to stop thinking such thoughts. Handsome as he may be, he's not for me.*

Shareb-er-rehh had settled into a comfortable trot once more, his small ears back, listening.

"Do you think we should stop for lunch soon, Dr. Lord?"

"We'll give it an hour, then look for a place."

He was obviously not receptive to conversation, and Ariadne found herself wishing she had a book, or embroidery, or something to occupy her. The silence loomed like an uncomfortable hole between them begging to be filled with something. The awkwardness was all but unbearable.

She could not know that her companion was also wishing for something; not to preoccupy his hands, but his thoughts, which were focused most acutely on his companion.

So, she wanted him to kiss her. Maybe it had been out of a genuine desire to see what she would be missing by marrying this man her father had chosen for her. Maybe it had been just a way to get under his skin, for he knew she was still piqued by the fact that he'd taken over this venture that she had previously controlled. Still, though—why? Did she lack feeling for her future husband? She certainly didn't behave like a woman in love with the man she was supposed to marry... .

It doesn't matter to me. I shouldn't care. I don't *care. My task is to get her to Norfolk, deliver her to this fellow who doesn't kiss her, turn around, and go home. That is all.*

But suddenly, that didn't seem to be quite enough, and he found himself feeling increasingly troubled by the whole situation.

Marriages in the *ton* were arranged all the time. Love had nothing to do with those agreements; they were made based on money, land, favors, power. Why should he care?

I don't.

He shot a glance at her from the corner of his eye. She had gone unnaturally quiet, and for some reason, he found that he didn't like the peace and serenity of the silence as much as he had thought he might. Her bald honesty—unusual in a lady of the *ton*—was quite startling, and, coupled with her air of self-importance, amusing. But her vivaciousness, her energy ... it fueled something in him, touched something deep inside him, buoyed him in a way that, well ... was rather nice, and he found himself rather missing it.

He couldn't help himself.

I don't care.

"So when is the wedding to this man who doesn't kiss you?"

Sure, I don't.

"Not for another year at least, as I'll have to complete a period of mourning for my father before I can marry Maxwell."

Maxwell. That bloody name again.

"But maybe that's a good thing," she mused. "It will give me time to ... well, to get to know him better. I know it's the done thing, a father arranging his daughter's marriage, but you know, we women have feelings too, and he is not the man I would have chosen for myself, had I had a say in things." She looked down, gently stroking Bow's soft fur. "I only went along with this to make Father happy. And if I never come to love Maxwell, and he never comes to love me, I will spend my life wondering what it is that I have missed." She glanced over at him. "Wondering what a *real* kiss feels like."

Bloody hell, Colin thought.

"Don't ask me to show you," he said, directing his gaze up and past Shareb's churning hindquarters.

"After your reaction back there?" She gave a little laugh, and her chin came up again in an attempt to reclaim some of her pride. "Not to worry, Dr. Lord. Besides, even though I might like it, Maxwell most certainly would not."

"No, I can't imagine that he would."

"He's a very dangerous man, you know. If you even so much as *looked* at me with any passing degree of interest, he would call you out. It would not be wise to insult him. He is expert with both sword and pistol, had gained a reputation as a deadly duelist, and I would fear for your life if he were to suspect that you had behaved in a way that is inappropriate."

"Then he's going to be overjoyed that we're to spend the next hundred miles alone, pressed against each other, and talking about kissing."

Her chin came up another inch. "I have to believe that he will make a fine husband."

"Yes, of course. He certainly does have good credentials, doesn't he? I mean, not everyone is so competent with sword and pistol. It is a commendable, fabulously useful talent, one that every husband ought to have."

"Yes, yes, I quite agree—" She paused, frowning as she caught him trying to hide a grin. "Dr. Lord, are you teasing me?"

"I might be."

"I think you're just jealous because *you* don't have Maxwell's talent."

"Yes, I am quite inept with both sword and pistol," he lied.

"It *will* be a good match. We have a lot in common. Besides, he's very knowledgeable when it comes to judging horseflesh. In fact, he has Black Patrick, the fastest racehorse in England, in his stable. That is to say—" she glanced at Shareb-er-rehh, then quickly away— "the fastest *tried* racehorse in England. Oh, and he's rich, but that doesn't matter, because so am I."

"So, he has lots of money, a fast horse, and can kill people in duels. Sounds like a prime catch. I wish you every happiness, my lady."

She went silent.

"So, how did you come to meet him?" he ventured, at length.

She shrugged, pulling Bow's long, silky ear through her fingers until the little dog was all but smiling. "He was an acquaintance of Father's. A business associate, and a Jockey Club friend, as well as a distant neighbor. Quite a bit older than me. Someone who could *control* me, rein in my wild ways—or so Father said." Sudden tears sparkled in her eyes, and she pulled herself up on the seat with false bravado. "I just have to tell myself that he knew what he was doing. That Maxwell will make me a fine husband."

Wordlessly, Colin reached out and touched her hand. But she quickly snatched it away, holding Bow close to her chest and hugging the tiny dog more fiercely than was comfortable for her. Bow never protested, only tilting her head back to lick the girl's chin.

It was obvious that if she was grieving, she wanted no comfort.

And really, he shouldn't have thought he could give her any. She was out of his realm, beyond his reach, *taken*. Her life was a neat and tidy package, cut to pattern by others and sewn up by herself. He should be happy for her. But still, there was a part of him that couldn't help but think, *If only I'd met her when I was the man I once was, I could have had a chance at her.*

But he was no longer that dashing hero, and never would be again.

No, he was only an animal doctor of modest means, and she, a high society beauty who would despise and pity him if she were to learn of his fall from grace. He could not have her. Better not to let himself even think it could be otherwise.

It couldn't.

He sighed and redirected his attention to the stallion, watching the countryside passing by as the animal's long strides put the miles behind them.

"You've grown awfully quiet, Dr. Lord."

"Forgive me." He grinned. "I was trying to think of a way to polish up my skills with sword and pistol before we reach Norfolk."

She looked at him, saw the cajoling light in his eye, and laughed. "Is that all?"

"That, and thinking the sooner we part company, the better. You're not good for me."

"Not good for you? Is this another one of those pastry-dictates?"

He shot her a confused look.

"What I mean, is—" She shrugged, for her words had made perfect sense to her—how can I not be good for you? I make you laugh, don't I?"

"Yes, and you talk about kissing me and you put images in my head that have no business being there. I am a man, Lady Ariadne, a man with normal, healthy, appetites, and spending time together may very well inflame something that is better left dormant."

"Do I inflame you, Dr. Lord?"

"Lady Ariadne, *please*."

"Well, do I?"

"You make my head ache. That's what you do."

"I can kiss it and make it better, you know."

"You're a damned flirt," he said, but not unkindly.

To his surprise, she let loose a peal of high laughter, and put her hand on his arm. "Yes, Dr. Lord, I suppose I am. Now what do you say we start looking for a place to stop for lunch? My stomach's growling and I'm sure yours is too."

Chapter Seven

The stallion came up lame several miles later.

Colin felt the sudden lurch of the reins through his hands, the quick stumble before the horse recovered himself. He pulled back to get the animal to halt, but Shareb-er-rehh only shook his head, fighting him and staggering a few last steps before finally answering the pressure on the bit. He stopped, shuddered, and dropped his head dejectedly as the two humans leapt simultaneously from the chaise.

"Shareb!" Ariadne cried, racing to his head.

The stallion raised his foot and held it up beseechingly, his eyes large, wounded, and hurt.

"Shareb! Oh, Shareb, sweetheart! Dr. Lord, his leg!" She was close to tears. Shivering in pain, Shareb put his face against her chest.

Colin put one hand on the stallion's hot and sweaty shoulder, and ran the other down the long foreleg.

"That bandage is going to have to come off."

"Oh no, I can't take it off, it's on there to conceal—"

"Hold his head then, and *I'll* take it off."

She bit her lip, about to protest. Colin knelt down, his

shoulder close to the stallion's, his hands quickly unwrapping the thick, unnaturally heavy bandage.

He removed it and looked up at her, his gentle eyes suddenly angry. "Why the *devil* do you have weights wrapped in this bandage?"

The stallion shifted his weight, regained his balance, plaintively raised his foot once more.

Sheepishly, she looked away. "To ... disguise his gait."

Colin made a noise of disgust and flung the hot, damp bandage to the grass at the side of the road. The stallion's leg was long, fine, and straight, the bones strong and well-formed. It was the leg of an aristocrat, but all he was concerned about was locating the injury. He checked the carpus, ran his hands down the long cannon bone, palpated the flexor tendons in search of a blown tendon.

Nothing.

"What is it, Dr. Lord?" she asked anxiously, hovering over his shoulder. Her voice sounded perilously close to tears. "Is he all right?"

He palpated the splint bones.

Nothing.

Searched the joints for swelling.

Nothing.

"Dr. Lord? Please, tell me, is he all right?"

"So far," he answered, and moving his hands down to the stallion's white-ringed fetlock, gently picked up the animal's foot.

"What are you doing?"

"Looking for a nail, a stone, or a bruise on the sole."

He pressed his thumb against the tough triangle that made up the hoof's frog. The stallion didn't flinch. He examined the hoof wall; aside from some caked mud, it was strong and healthy.

Gently, he let go of the stallion's hoof.

Shareb stamped it down on his toe, hard.

"Ouch!" Grimacing, Colin pushed hard on the animal's

shoulder to get its weight off his foot. The stallion stumbled, and drove his head into the cradle of his mistress's arms. One ear remained on Colin, and he had the strangest feeling that the animal was laughing at him.

"Oh, Dr. Lord, I knew it was a bad idea to hitch him to that dreadful chaise, now he's lame, he's injured, and what if he's broken something and has to be destroyed—"

"He's fine," Colin said, wryly. He grasped the bridle and tried to pull the noble, cunning head around so that he could stare into the stallion's dark eye, but Shareb jerked away, his ears flat back.

"He's not fine, he's in pain! His leg hurts, Dr. Lord, and you must do something!"

"I can't find anything wrong with him to do anything *about*, my lady."

"But he's *lame!*"

"I can see that." Colin stared at the stallion's leg, then, frowning, walked around to look at it from the front.

"Well?"

He straightened up, and stared into the stallion's eyes.

Shareb turned his face away, and hid it against his mistress' chest.

"There's a coaching inn just up the road," Colin said. He unhitched the stallion and picked up the shafts of the chaise. "You lead him. We'll stop, give him a rest, have something for lunch. If he's indeed injured, I should find some swelling by the time we return."

"What do you mean, *if?* Of course he's injured, look at him!"

But Colin didn't reply.

He was beginning to suspect that Shareb-er-rehh was a hell of a lot smarter than he'd given him credit for.

And—after looking at that long, aristocratic leg—not at all the *gait-horse* her Ladyship proclaimed him to be.

THE COACHING INN, a rambling, whitewashed building with a sway-backed roof, was nestled in a bed of daisies, grass gone to seed, and shrubbery through which two robins chased each other with merry abandon. Roses made pools of scarlet against the walls and sills, and a sign in front swung gently in the breeze, proclaiming the establishment to be the "Hungry Horseman."

"Oh, good," Ariadne said, breathing a sigh of relief. "It has windows."

Pulling the chaise while the horse limped along beside him, Colin followed her gaze. An ancient hound slumbered on steps splashed with sunlight, and a mare with one hind leg propped beneath her was tethered just outside. Upon noticing Shareb-er-rehh, she turned and whickered softly.

Up went Shareb's head, and his ears along with it.

"Windows," Colin said, as the stallion began to prance and blow and arch his neck. "I should think the food would be of more importance than the windows."

"Oh, no, Dr. Lord. It *has* to have windows. I have to be able to see Shareb-er-rehh from inside. What if someone should try to steal him?"

"I daresay they'd lose their fingers in the attempt."

"Oh, stop!" she said, playfully. "I told you, he's a very sweet horse, just angry because you denied him pastry and ale. Now come. Let's get something to eat. My treat, of course."

She went on ahead of him.

"Uh ... my lady?"

"Yes?"

"If you wish your ruse to succeed— " Colin rubbed his jaw, and looked thoughtfully at her shapely legs. "Try to not walk so ... well, try to walk like a man."

"Like a man?"

"Your hips, my lady. They—tend to swing a bit."

"Very well then." She let go of Shareb's reins. "Shall I walk like this?" Apishly hunching her shoulders and letting her arms hang stiffly at her side, she walked awkwardly toward the stairs, where she turned and shot him a look of high amusement.

"Never mind," Colin said, putting the shafts of the chaise down and taking the stallion's head. Stiffness clawed through his leg as he led a protesting Shareb-er-rehh a safe distance away from the mare and looked for a place to tether him. "This is never going to work."

"Yes it will, I shall make it work." She glanced at Shareb-er-rehh, and her face lit up with excitement. "Look, Dr. Lord! Shareb's not limping any more!"

"Yes, war wounds tend to disappear when there is a fair lady to impress."

His comment went right over her head. "We'll stop here for a nice, leisurely meal and maybe when we come out, Shareb will be all better. Come along, Doctor!"

Colin tied the stallion, casting a dubious glance over his shoulder to check the animal one last time as he went to join Ariadne. Shareb-er-rehh caught his glance, and lifted his left front leg to show that he was still lame.

But the horse had erred.

It had been the *right* that had supposedly been injured.

Colin grinned.

"Think he'll be all right, Dr. Lord?"

Colin turned his back on the horse, and passed the mare as she perked up her ears and swung her rump toward the stallion in saucy invitation.

"Aye, my lady. I'm sure of it."

THE CEILING WAS THICKLY BEAMED and ancient, the walls painted in shades of oxblood and hung with prints of foxhunts and racehorses. Laughter came from a group of locals near the hearth, but the two travelers preferred instead to take seats beside the window where Ariadne could keep an eye on her horse. There, they lunched on steak and mushroom pie, thick, crusty bread, cheese, and a flagon of rich, foamy ale. Or rather, Ariadne did. Halfway through the meal, she noticed her companion's appetite had not led him to touch the beef.

She stared at him in puzzlement. "Is the pie not to your liking, Doctor?"

He offered a rather sheepish smile. "I do not eat meat."

"Why not?"

"It's animal flesh. I ... I just can't. Not anymore."

She frowned a bit, studying him. Then she put down her fork and knife, propped her chin atop the heel of one hand, and stared long and hard at him. "You are a very unusual man, Dr. Lord."

He shrugged, broke off a piece of cheese, and ate it, grinning at her all the while.

Her gaze went to his unfinished glass of ale. "I see you don't drink much, either. What sort of an Englishman are you, anyhow?"

"A sober one."

"Indeed."

"My tolerance for alcohol is remarkably low," he added.

"Really? Mine's not. Hand me your glass, Dr. Lord. Better yet, be a gentleman and order me another."

She swept up his glass, shot him a challenging glance, and raised the drink high. "To ... friendship."

"Aye." He picked up his cheese and smiled. "To friendship."

She laughed, and downed the ale in three unladylike gulps. Their gazes met, and she blushed prettily. "You know, Dr. Lord ... I'm really enjoying your company. I take back my earlier words, about wishing I hadn't hired you to be my veterinarian. I'm very glad that I did, even if you *can't* figure out why Shareb is lame. Now, if you don't want it, may I have your beef?"

He looked at her, one brow raised, and she grinned in embarrassment.

"Well, if I'm to dress like a man, I might as well eat like one."

❧

THREE MILES AHEAD OF THEM, Tristan, Lord Weybourne, sat in a similar public house, nursing a cider and staring gloomily into the clear, amber depths of his glass. He, too, had positioned himself near a window, where he could watch the traffic passing on the Norfolk Road and be on the lookout for the bay stallion.

The bay stallion.

All that stood between him and total ruin. And all that carried Ariadne to a nightmare she couldn't even begin to imagine.

His mind wandered back over the years, to the time when Father had brought him to see his first race. He had never forgotten the thrill of seeing those mighty steeds galloping toward the finish line, thundering past with such force that he could feel the vibrations rocking his chest while the crowd went wild with excitement around him. Maybe the fever had started then—Papa certainly must've seen it, for he'd turned, looked steadily into his eyes, and warned him about the allure of the racetrack. But he hadn't listened, of course. After all, he, Tristan, had picked the winner of three out of four of those races. He had a talent. What did Father know, anyhow?

And as he grew older, spending his mornings observing the Norfolk Thoroughbreds galloping around his father's pastures, and his weekend afternoons stealing off to the races at Newmarket, it came to him that such a talent should not go to waste.

Age and maturity had not cooled the fever. He had found friends to share his interest, older, equally high-bred friends who didn't mind that he was the youngest of the lot. After all, he was the future Lord Weybourne. He was bored, he was titled, and he knew horses. And the races! He would win some, lose some, win a little more, gamble a lot. And the fever had spread—to the gaming tables, to the boxing matches, to the cockfights. He couldn't remember when it had begun to worry him. Maybe when he'd begun to realize that he was losing more than he was winning. When he knew he was in trouble.

And still, he could not stop.

Too proud, too ashamed to confess his dilemma to his father, he had gone to Clive Maxwell for help ... again ... and again.

And now he was in over his head.

He should've listened to Father, dear, wise Father, who had spent his life developing a horse that could outrun anything but the wind. His father had known more about racehorses than Tristan would ever know. Oh, how foolish he'd been! If only he'd gone to him before the debts had mounted, maybe things would've turned out differently. Maybe his father would still be alive; maybe Ariadne wouldn't be on the run with the last of the Norfolk Thoroughbreds; and maybe he wouldn't have a death threat hanging over his head.

He put his hands over his face, remembering his father's horror when he'd told him about Clive, and just how evil the man really was. And now Ariadne was involved, and heading for her own demise as surely as he had engineered his own.

God help him, he had to stop her. It was too late to save himself—but not his sister.

Picking up his cider, he gazed bleakly out the window, scanning the passing horses for Shareb-er-rehh's glossy bay coat. A damned common color, even if the horse himself was uniquely spectacular. But in the past quarter of an hour, no less than seventeen bay horses had passed, three in the last two minutes alone. One had been a smart, glossy-coated hack. Not Shareb-er-rehh. Another had been a stout Shetland pony hitched to a cart, with an old farmer at its head. Not Shareb-er-rehh. The most recent was a rangy, deep-chested, high stepping carriage horse with bandaged legs and a light blanket over its back, pulling a chaise with a man and his young son in it.

Definitely not Shareb-er-rehh.

Swearing in frustration and rising anxiety, Lord Weybourne put his head in his hands and ordered another cider.

TRISTAN WAS NOT the only one reflecting on the past, and thinking about his late father.

Some miles away, his sister was doing much the same thing.

They had been back in the chaise for an hour now, and the late afternoon sun slanted down through the trees and dappled Shareb-er-rehh's glossy rump as they trotted along the Norfolk Road. Sweeping green hills bright with crops climbed away to the right and opposite, fenced pastures dotted with sheep and cows met the eye for as far as it could see, until the horizon finally dropped handfuls of clouds upon the distant rises.

It was easy, with the sun slanting down and her belly full, to let her mind drift, to daydream, to think of days and times past... .

To remember a day when she was eight, maybe nine years old, lonely, bored, missing her mama, who had died some months before. Her nanny was a cold, detached woman, and she didn't see much of her father, who always seemed to be wrapped up with horses, and grooming Tristan to take over someday ... which meant she didn't see much of Tristan, either. There was nobody else in the nursery to play with, and Nanny always had her nose in a book, leaving her to her own devices.

The loneliness had been intense.

When Father had come in that evening from the stables, she had gone to him and begged him to play a game with her, and he had smiled rather distractedly and promised that he would, after he had dined. But he had broken that promise, claiming that he was too tired by the time he had finished his meal, and perhaps he was. Perhaps he always was, because he had not been a young man when his two children had been born, and the energy that might have been his as a youth, was certainly not there as a widowed man in his late fifties with two young children who were both starved for his affections.

Yes, he had broken his promise to play a game with her. It had been one of many promises to spend time with her that he had broken, and eventually, Ariadne realized that asking or even begging for his attention would never get it.

But behaving badly, would.

Behaving badly, as she had done when she had mounted one of Father's prized horses during an afternoon soiree and, in a reckless attempt to prove to him that she, like Tristan, could be a part of his world, gone tearing across the front garden in front of all the guests. But all that had resulted from that mad escapade was a flower bed shot through with hoofprints, horrified guests—and a father that had been so embarrassed that she'd seen even less of him.

Behaving badly, as she had done on the day she had turned sixteen. Father had thrown a party for her, invited all the neighbors—and had then forgotten to show up. Her hurt and humiliation had been such that she'd had a little too much wine, grown a little bit too loud, and caught the attention of Sir Thomas Dovecote's eldest son (not to mention Sir Thomas Dovecote, himself), which had resulted in Father's pained disapproval.

Behaving badly, showing just a little too much ankle during those balls and soirees of her first season, and reveling in the newly-discovered fact that, while Father might never had had time for her—indeed, nobody did—such was not the case with the young men who had begun to swarm around her, hanging on her every word, filling her dance card, competing for her notice, and willing, all too willing, to give her that which her father had never had time to give her.

Attention.

It was heady, exhilarating, and a drug she could not get enough of.

Outrageous flirtation had netted her not only the attention of titled and rich suitors, it had also netted her—finally—the attention of her father.

But even that had blown up in her face, for all that had come of it was a hastily arranged marriage to a man she barely knew, a man who was twenty years her senior, a man who was as wrapped up in horses as Father had been. "Maxwell has a firm hand, and maybe he can control you when I cannot," Father had explained, distractedly. "Besides, he has more interest in carrying on the legacy of the Norfolk Thoroughbred than you and Tristan combined. You will marry him."

Behaving badly... .

It had not done her any favors then, and it probably wouldn't do her any favors now, but beside her, Colin Lord had grown quiet, lost in his own thoughts, and Ariadne was becoming increasingly restless.

And, bored.

She wondered what his reaction would be if she behaved just a little bit ... badly.

"Really, Dr. Lord ... I think that if one has to work, they should have a job like yours. Your day must be so very interesting, treating sick animals and saving their lives. I mean, all you had to do was *touch* Shareb's leg, and the limp went away, just like that! I think you are wonderful."

He shrugged. "Your praise is appreciated, but I did nothing to heal your horse's lameness."

"Do you think it was the bandage, then? The weights?"

"No, I think you have a confoundedly smart horse who has no desire to pull a chaise."

"You mean, the lameness was all an *act*?"

"Aye, and a very good one, at that. Even had me fooled—til he forgot which foot was supposed to hurt."

"Oh, no, Shareb would *never* do something deceitful like that! He's an angel."

"Yes, and so was Lucifer."

"Dr. Lord, *really*. I would expect you to exhibit more loyalty and respect toward your patient! And to compare my sweet and innocent horse to the Devil ... That is unkind." She raised her voice and called, "Isn't it, Shareb?"

As if in agreement, the stallion tossed his head.

They continued on for another quarter mile, and the doctor's reluctance to be drawn into a conversation about Maxwell, combined with her full stomach and an overindulgence of ale at the coaching inn, began to weigh on Ariadne's eyelids. She looked up at him, wondering what he had *really* done to cure Shareb's poor, hurt leg. Surely, he must have worked some sort of magic. First the dog, then Shareb... .

And that shoulder of his, so very close to her own, was looking pleasantly inviting.

Lud, she was as drawn to him as animals seemed to be. But why? He was an uncommonly handsome man, her animal doctor, but she could have had her pick of handsome men before Father betrothed her to Maxwell, and none of *them* had made her heart beat just a little bit faster in her chest, as this man did.

"Dr. Lord?"

"I am beginning to dread that tone of voice... ."

"I think I ate and drank too much back there, as I am just getting so-o-o-o sleepy... ." She yawned prettily, and eyed that safe, solid shoulder. "Perhaps if you tell me about what your own horse was like, it will help me to stay awake. Was he as special to you as Shareb is to me?"

A shadow darkened the veterinarian's eyes, and he smiled wistfully. "Yes. He was ... very special."

Ariadne said nothing, trying to keep her heavy eyes open and her mind off his shoulder. She wondered very much if he would mind if she leaned against it and went to sleep.

"What was his name?"

"Ned."

"Ned. What a gentle, simple name." She yawned, again. "I'll

bet he was much better suited to pull this chaise than my Shareb is."

"Yes, I'm afraid he was. Much easier on my arms and shoulders."

"Is Shareb still pulling?"

"Pulling?" The veterinarian grinned. "I'm beginning to suspect this animal is not a riding animal, but a plow horse. He is devilishly strong and hard on the bit."

She tightened her hands in her lap, grateful that he hadn't hit upon the truth of what Shareb *really* was. Especially, since they'd taken the weights out of the bandages and Shareb's stride had returned to the long, fluid trot that was putting the miles behind them with tell-tale speediness. She figured their secret was still safe, though.

That is, as long as the doctor never saw him in a full gallop... .

"I'm sorry," she said. "Do you want me to drive for a while? I promise to try harder this time to control him."

"No. I'm fine, really. Sit back and enjoy the scenery."

She tried, but could not, for the scenery that was two inches from her body was far more interesting than that of the surrounding countryside. Emboldened by the ale, feeling liberated without her identity and the clothes that would have proclaimed it, she gazed up at her companion's face, the sweep of sunlit hair that fell over his forehead, the shape of his nose and the intent keenness of his eye. Though he was a commoner, his profile was nothing short of aristocratic.

"Dr. Lord?" The motion of Shareb's powerful trot jouncing the chaise was making her all the more sleepy.

"Yes?"

"I think I should not have had so much ale."

He looked down at her, suddenly concerned. "Are you ill?"

"No, merely tired. I mean, I usually do take a nap in the afternoon, because I keep very late hours—Town hours, you know—but between this sunshine, the motion of the chaise, a decided lack of sleep and now, the ale ... well, I hope you can forgive me if I am not quite awake."

"There is nothing to forgive."

"Even if I use your shoulder as a pillow?"

He just turned and looked at her with that flat, indiscernible stare that said more than a thousand words.

"I know, it is most inappropriate ... but there is no place in this little vehicle in which to lay down, and I am so very sleepy."

"We could stop at an inn, if you like."

"No, no, we shall do that tonight. I want to put London—and my brother—well behind us. Besides—" she covered her mouth, trying to keep her yawn to ladylike proportions— "that's not what I asked you. I asked if you'd mind."

"Not at all," he said, a bit tightly.

She smiled her thanks, curled her arm around Bow, and carefully lowered her cheek to the veterinarian's shoulder. He stiffened, the muscles beneath bunching with tension, but there was no place for him to move, nowhere for him to go, nothing he could say or do, really, that wouldn't make him look petty and ungentlemanly. He had taken off his coat, and his shirt smelled of soap and clean wind. Ariadne closed her eyes in contentment. But her face had no sooner touched the soft fabric when the chaise hit a bump, painfully smashing her teeth together. She tried again, settling her cheek against the hard muscle and closing her eyes. *Ahhhh...* . She smiled, and sighed ...

And began to sink into slumber.

The chaise hit a rut and her cheek slipped from his shoulder. Blinking in annoyance, she stared gloomily ahead, growing more perturbed by the moment.

And then the doctor's arm went around her shoulders, pulling her close to his body and coaxing her head down into the cup of his shoulder. Ariadne closed her eyes, feeling his warmth and strength surrounding her, hearing his heart beating beneath her ear, knowing that he would keep her safe while she slept and never let anything happen to her.

Suddenly, all was right in the world.

She felt her body twitch, grow heavy. And then, with a sigh, she smiled against his shirt, rested her hand against his knee, and went to sleep.

THE TRAFFIC HAD THINNED out the further they got from London, and they passed nothing more than a team of draft horses that Shareb ignored, a fast-trotting mare who elicited enough of the stallion's interest that Colin had to touch him with the whip to keep his mind on business, and an old shepherd who, with the help of a faithful dog, was bringing home his flock for the evening. The sunlight was rusty, the shadows long and reaching by the time Colin finally decided to start looking for a place to spend the night.

His employer was still asleep, her cheek nestled in the cup of his shoulder, her little hand lying innocently across his knee. For the hundredth time in the last hour, he looked down at her, and felt his heart skip a beat.

She fit within the circle of his arm as though she'd been made to it. Her cap was perched loosely on her coppery hair, and she smelled sweet and warm. She did not snore. She did not twitch. She merely lay there against him, soft and lovely and painfully beautiful.

Damnation, how I envy you, Maxwell!

He could not take his eyes off her. His chest tight with feeling, he looked down at the top of her nose and fair cheek, and after a moment of long, careful hesitation, bent down and kissed her brow.

Her skin was smooth and sweet and soft. He shuddered, looked up—

—and saw two pretty girls standing at the side of the road with their ponies, giggling and pointing at him.

"My son," Colin said, blushing furiously.

Their high laughter followed him.

"Bollocks," he swore.

Shareb-er-rehh snorted.

"Yes, you would think it's funny, damned horse!"

Lady Ariadne stirred, stretched, and opened her eyes. But she did not lift her head from Colin's shoulder. "What's so funny?" she murmured, sleepily.

"Nothing."

"I don't talk in my sleep or anything, do I? Or God forbid, drool. That would be quite ghastly and embarrassing, drooling."

"You did not drool. And if you talked in your sleep, you spoke to yourself, because I did not hear you."

"Mmmmm." She closed her eyes, and belatedly, Colin realized he still had his arm around her back and shoulder. He leaned back and tried to pull his arm away.

"Dr. Lord ... please don't. I'm so comfortable ..."

"This is unseemly."

"Only if I deem it so. And I don't. So please, let your arm stay where it was."

He sighed, allowing her to take his arm and pull it about her like a blanket. Tightness coiled in his loins, and he mentally counted off how many days, how many more hours, he would have to put up with this sweet torture.

He looked down at her, but she was asleep once more.

"Heaven help me," Colin said, and drew her close.

In a few days, she would belong to Maxwell.

But for the moment, she belonged to him.

Chapter Eight

"I'm sorry, sir, but I 'ave only one room left. Ye might try Mrs. Downing's place back up the road a mile or two—sometimes she 'as a few extra rooms, and would probably be able to take ye in. On second thought, yer horse—be it a mare or a gelding?"

"Stallion."

"Oh, then forget *that*," the innkeeper muttered, waving his liver-spotted old hand in dismissal. "Won't put up a stallion, Mrs. Downing won't. Husband got killed on one and she won't 'ave one in her stable. Says they're too wild and unpredictable." He straightened up, put a hand on his hip and with a twisted grimace, jerked the crick out of his back, allowing Ariadne to see beyond him and into the tavern. It was dark, gloomy, and low-ceilinged, with great beams and rafters darkened by centuries of pipe smoke; quite ordinary as taverns went, with lanterns cutting swaths of cheer through the smoky gloom, maids rushing around with plates of food, groups of men engaged in lively conversation. The pungent scent of smoke and greasy meat hung in the air like a fog. "Well," the man said, impatiently. "I have one room left, take it or leave it."

Ariadne saw her companion reach up to palm his brow and

rake his hand back through his hair, making it stand on end before it tumbled haphazardly back into place. The veterinarian was tired—she could see it in the faint lines around his eyes, the grimace of pain he'd tried to hide when he'd stepped down from the chaise and, walking up to the door of this coaching inn, all but dragged his leg behind him.

"Thank you, but I think we'll continue on and see what's up the road a bit," he said, rubbing the back of his neck and turning to leave.

Ariadne caught his arm.

"Nonsense," she said, counting out some coins and pressing them into the innkeeper's hand. "This is the third coaching inn we've tried tonight, and yours is the only room to be had. My poor ... brother is very tired. We'll take the room."

"But—"

"Now *Colin*, don't argue with me. I'm right this time, and you know it. Sir? If you'll be so kind as to show us where your stable is so we can tend to our horse?"

"Let me get the ostler and 'e'll take care of 'im—"

"That is very kind of you, but we would prefer to do it ourselves," Ariadne said.

The innkeeper knotted his receding brow and regarded them thoughtfully, then dropped the coins into his pocket. Turning, he cupped his hands over his mouth. "Meg! Guests! Show 'em where the stable is, would ye?" He turned back to them. "Take care of yer horse, and by the time ye get back in I'll have a good supper on the table, waiting for ye."

A serving maid, wiping her hands on her apron, sauntered around the corner, looking over her shoulder and laughing at something someone had said back in the kitchen. She was buxom and pretty in a rustic sort of way, with yellow curls tumbling about her shoulders and blue eyes that were alive with humor.

She shot a ribald report back to the unknown person in the kitchen.

And then she saw Colin Lord.

The narrowing of the eyes, the sudden, silky smile, the passing of the tongue over the full lips—Ariadne saw it all, and was filled with a sudden, unreasonable, sense of irritation.

"Right this way ... gentlemen," the woman said huskily, casting a long, assessing look at Ariadne's companion. Then she picked up a lantern and glided past him, looking coyly over her shoulder to make sure he was following.

Totally unaware of and completely oblivious to the serving maid's interest in him, the veterinarian merely removed the spectacles he'd donned earlier in an attempt to rest his tired eyes, pinched the bridge of his nose, and followed the woman out of the inn.

"Methinks you have an admirer," Ariadne said, a bit more sharply than she intended, as he put the spectacles back on.

"I beg your pardon?" He stopped and looked at her, his eyes confused behind his glasses.

Ariadne jerked her head toward the serving maid, who was several strides ahead of them and rolling her hips exaggeratedly as she walked. "I sincerely doubt that brazen display is for *my* benefit!"

The doctor frowned, looking more confused than ever. "Oh. Her. I hadn't noticed."

Ariadne grabbed his arm and yanked him forward. "Never mind. I swear, Dr. Lord, you're as blind as a bat sometimes!"

They followed Meg outside, and across the drive to the darkened stables. The wind had become gusty, the summer air heavy and charged. As they approached the stable, a cat melted out of the darkness and wound itself around Colin's ankles, mewing plaintively and gazing up at him with adoring, feline eyes. He reached down to pick it up while Meg unlocked the door.

"Looks like rain," Meg grunted, wrestling with the latch. Then she spotted the tortoiseshell cat in Colin's arms, and her eyes widened with surprise. "Well, would ye look at that! Gemma 'ere never goes to anyone, 'specially strangers!"

"Dr. Lord has a way with animals," Ariadne said, flatly.

"I should say he does," Meg murmured, letting her gaze wander up and down his body in a heated caress that he, still petting the cat, never even noticed. "Bet he's got one with the ladies, too."

That comment caught the veterinarian's attention. He looked up and, despite his fatigue, managed a broad, engaging smile that had Ariadne bristling in annoyance and feeling like a third wheel. He stood cradling the cat in his arms as the servant dragged open the door, then, giving the feline a last fond rub behind the ears, carefully put it down and went to get the stallion. The cat ran after him, following worshipfully at his heels, meowing, and nearly tripping him.

"What happened to yer brother?" Meg purred, leaning against the stable door while they waited for Colin to return with Shareb-er-rehh. "Such a pity, that limp."

"He was in the War."

"Fine lookin' man. Too bad he's a cripple."

Ariadne stiffened and bestowed a withering glare on the other woman. "He is *not* a cripple. He's capable and confident and I'll thank you not to demean him so."

"Don't get so huffy, little boy, I was merely making an observation," the wench said, her voice a husky, sultry thing that grated on Ariadne's nerves. "In fact, ye can tell yer handsome sibling that I rather fancy him ... limp or not."

"Yes, well, you can fancy him all you wish, but he's taken. He already has a lady friend."

Now why on earth had she said *that*? The other woman laughed, obviously unfazed.

"Is that so? Well, I'm sure he won't mind ... another."

There was nothing that Ariadne, in her role as "little brother," could say without drawing suspicion to herself, and so she raised her chin and bit her tongue and dug her nails into her palms to keep her angry retort at bay. She hated herself for feeling so possessive about something—or rather, someone—who didn't belong to her. She had no claim on Colin Lord. For heaven's sake, he was just a servant! Yet why did she feel this red shaft of jealousy?

Shareb's smart hoofbeats heralded his approach out of the darkness, and Colin had barely gotten him into the stable and unhooked from the chaise before the skies opened up in earnest, the rain hammering against the roof at such a volume that talk was impossible. As the other horses turned their heads to watch his arrival, Shareb-er-rehh's sulky attitude immediately vanished, as though he'd been humiliated by pulling the vehicle and had just been released from a terrible burden. He whinnied softly, and each horse in the stable stared at him as he passed, tail high, neck arched, nostrils flaring with self-importance.

Ahead, Meg walked with the lantern, leading them down the gloomy aisle, occasionally glancing over her shoulder to smile invitingly at Dr. Lord. She had regarded Shareb-er-rehh's over-sized saddle cloth and bandaged legs rather dubiously, and Ariadne hoped that the disguise did not call suspicion down on all of them.

She saw the veterinarian watching her from above Shareb's withers, the lantern light gilding his fair hair.

"Go inside, little brother. I'll see to the horse."

And leave him to Meg? "No. I'll stay and help."

He merely grinned, causing her to suspect that he knew exactly why she chose to stay.

It was infuriating.

Meg paused outside an empty stall, and jerked her head to indicate it for the stallion's use. As Dr. Lord led Shareb inside, the woman let her eyes rake appreciatively over his back, his face, his form. Again, Ariadne felt the hot lance of jealousy.

She raised her chin. "We have no further need of your

services, save for supper and a good breakfast in the morning. Good night."

Meg looked startled, then indignant, at Ariadne's unexpectedly haughty tone. "My, such airs," she commented, and giving the veterinarian a last, inviting look that he never noticed, turned on her heel and strode angrily out of the stable.

Ariadne went into the narrow stall. Her companion was removing the harness, looking down at Shareb's sweat-dampened hide, and smiling a private grin.

"Care to tell me what you find so funny?" she snapped.

"Not really."

She reached up and straightened the saddle cloth into which was sewn more money than he'd ever see in his lifetime. "Here we go, more secrets."

"Forgive me, my lady, but you seemed almost ... jealous."

"What, of that overblown rose? Hardly!"

"She didn't look so overblown to me. In fact, I thought she was rather pretty."

"I'm sure you could do much better."

"You really think she fancied me?"

"Well she did issue you an open invitation to her bed. Maybe you ought to take her up on it, might do you some good."

He raised one brow; then, his eyes twinkled, and his mouth turned up in that helpless, crooked grin that she didn't know whether to love or hate. Ariadne swung away, her face flaming, and busied herself with unbuckling the harness. "Very well, then," she admitted, sullenly. "Maybe I *was* a little bit jealous. I mean, angry. But I disliked that woman, and I disliked the way she was looking at you. She had no right."

"And you do?"

"I'm ... *paying* you!"

"Oh, that's right. You own me. How dreadful of me to have forgotten."

"Dr. Lord."

"Yes?" he said, innocently.

"Mind your impertinent manners."

He grinned, tied the lead rope to a ring bolted to the wall, and put the harness in the chaise. "Yes, my lady," he said in an exaggeratedly grave, deep voice. "Anything you say, my lady." He scowled down at her until her frown faded to a helpless smile, then offered his elbow with a gallant flourish. "Come, let Shareb and Bow have their suppers and let us go have ours, and perhaps after a good night's sleep we'll both feel better in the morning."

"Oh, how *do* you put up with me?"

"With patience and delight," he said honestly, and then, before she could question him on such a remark, he led her out of the stable and through the rainy darkness.

SUPPER WAS a fine steak and kidney pie served with roast potatoes, parsnip, and swede, accompanied by a loaf of hot, freshly baked bread, creamy butter, a wedge of aged cheddar, and plenty of ale to wash it all down. Respectful of her companion's aversion to eating flesh, Ariadne traded her vegetables for his slab of pie. She held off on the spirits this time, and when Meg brought deep dishes of apple cobbler topped with cream for dessert, she set her mind to thinking up a way to sneak her portion out to the stable so she could give it to Shareb-er-rehh.

God forbid if the stallion didn't get his nightly dose of pastry and ale. He'd be an absolute demon come morning.

She pretended to toy with the cobbler, and shot a quick glance up through her lashes at the veterinarian. His face was golden in the glow from the lantern, his hair rumpled, but tired as he looked, those clear, keen eyes of his were alert and awake.

And on her.

He smiled, and looked at her from over the rim of his tea cup. "Don't even think about it."

"Think about what?"

"Bringing that cobbler out to the horse."

She widened her eyes and with a guilty little laugh, plunged her fork into the crumbly topping. "Be serious, Dr. Lord, do you think I could just put it in my pocket? What a mess it would make, with all this cream and sticky juice." She smiled innocently up at him. "Why, I'd soil my clothing!"

He looked at her for a dubious moment before sighing heavily and shoving his half-finished cobbler away. Then he took off his glasses, rubbed his eyes, and sat staring down at the table, too tired to trade banter with her.

"Dr. Lord?"

He looked up. "Yes?"

Ariadne took a bite of her dessert and dabbed delicately at her mouth. "Is it past your bedtime?"

"It's been a long day."

Both of them looked down at their dessert bowls, thinking about the bedroom that awaited them upstairs, and neither quite willing to bring up the subject of sleeping arrangements. A minute dragged past. Two. Ariadne glanced up and saw that the doctor's head was drooping, his beautiful, long lashes starting to slip down over his eyes, and that he was fast on his way to falling asleep in his chair.

"Dr. Lord!" she said, sharply.

He jerked his head up, blinking.

Ariadne got to her feet. "Despite the fact that both of us feel rather awkward about this situation—"

"Well, one of us does, anyhow—"

"I see no reason to delay it any longer. Come, let us go upstairs. If we both sleep with our clothes on and don't share the bed, there is nothing unseemly about it."

But Colin wasn't thinking about the unseemliness of the situation. He was thinking how lovely and desirable his companion looked, and wondering how the devil he would be able to pass a night with her in the same room, not just *any* room, but a damned bedroom, for God's sake. He rested his elbows on the table, then reached up to knead his aching nape, trying to massage away the stiffness caused by Shareb's ceaseless pulling.

She was already on her feet, beckoning him with a practiced motion of her hand to rise and follow her. Too tired to protest, Colin got up, threw down his napkin, and limped painfully after her. They passed the landlord's old dog, sprawled before the hearth, and headed for the stairs, she marching like a general and he all but dragging his leg behind him. The other patrons had long since gone to bed, and each step creaked loudly beneath them.

At the end of a short corridor was their room, and with no small degree of trepidation, Ariadne pushed open the door. The chamber was small, cozy, alarmingly intimate—and dominated by the bed.

She swallowed hard, trying to maintain her bravado and poise, and glanced at her companion. But he'd already turned and was headed toward the door.

"I think it best if I sleep in the stable."

She sidestepped so he couldn't pass. "No, no, Dr. Lord, *I* should."

"Nonsense. You're an earl's daughter, for God's sake, you can't be sleeping in a stable."

"The good Lord not only slept in a stable, He was born in one. If He can sleep in a stable, then so can I. You stay here, and take the bed. You're far more tired than I am."

"No, I must protest. As a gentleman, I insist that you take the bed."

"As your employer, I insist that *you* do."

"You hired me to look after your horse. Therefore, *I* will sleep in the stable with Shareb and Bow, and I'll hear no more argument on the subject. Good night, my lady. I shall see you in the morning."

He strode past her in a gait that belied the pain his leg must be causing him, leaving her staring after him with her jaw agape. In his wake, the room suddenly felt lonely, empty, and cold, and Ariadne waited just long enough to hear his tread on the stairs before she went marching after him.

"Dr. Lord," she announced, watching his broad back as he went down the stairs, "you'll not have the final word about this!"

"I just did."

"You just *think* you did! I shall not let the matter rest here, do you hear me? I won't!"

She ran down the stairs after him. He pushed open the door and went out into the rainy night, letting it slam back in her face.

She jerked it open. "Dr. Lord!"

He turned and wagged a finger at her. "Go to bed!"

"Don't you tell me what to do!"

"I'm telling you, and you'll do it." He turned and kept walking, his boots sighing over the wet grass.

She hurried after him. "Fine, be that way! We'll *both* sleep in the stable, then!"

He pulled open the door of the stable and stormed past their chaise, the stalls, the cat that was curled sleepily atop a bale of hay, until he was just outside Shareb's stall. Taking off his coat, he tossed it to the straw, sat down on it, and thrusting out his legs before him, leaned his back and head against the wooden door.

"You can't sleep like that," she said, standing above him with her hands on her hips.

"Watch me."

He shut his eyes and turned his face away from her.

She squatted down in front of him and pulled off his glasses.

He would not open his eyes.

"Lady Ariadne, *please*. You are beginning to anger me."

His tone was tense and hard, unlike anything she had heard him use yet, and it cut her to the quick. The playful smile faded from her lips and Ariadne, brought up short, could only remain unmoving, torn between going quietly away or standing her ground. But oh, God help her, she had no wish to go back to that lonely, upstairs room. She wanted to stay here, in this warm, cozy stable, where the scent of hay, grain, and horses lent it a homely, comforting ambience that would be sadly lacking in that small upstairs chamber. She waited for an apology from the veterinarian. None came. Hurt, and feeling suddenly unwanted, rejected, she sat down in the darkness beside him, her shoulder and hip a mere two inches from his. He made no sound, and she could feel the tension emanating from him. It was too late now to retreat back to the bedroom. Childlike, Ariadne wrapped her arms around her knees and squeezed tightly, trying to keep her emotions under control.

"Dr. Lord ... I don't want to be alone, up there in that tiny room, when the only two souls left in this world who are dear to me are sleeping out in a stable. Besides ... I feel responsible for you and your well-being—"

He chuckled without humor. "*You*, responsible for *me*?"

"Well, yes—"

"Imagine that."

She hugged her knees in the darkness, feeling suddenly cast out, lonely, and foolish. Tears stung the back of her eyes, slipping down her cheeks and falling softly atop her kneecaps. She bent her head and squeezed her arms tighter, willing herself not to cry.

And then, unexpectedly, he reached out in the darkness, pried her clenched fingers out of her upper arm, and clasped her tiny hand within his own.

Ariadne froze, her hand a rigid block of wood within his.

She felt his thumb caressing the inside of her palm, the warmth of his fingers covering the back of her hand. She trembled inside, unsure of whether to jerk her hand away or not and feeling suddenly trapped and panicky. Over and over his thumb moved, the motion no longer invasive, but now calming, now soothing, until she wanted to bury herself against him like a little child and release her pent up sobs. But she could not do such an unspeakable thing and so instead, she held his hand, gingerly at first, then as though it was a lifeline, and sat listening to the rain tapping gently against the roof, the hoot of an owl somewhere off in the night. It was dark, but no so much that she, just turning her head, couldn't see the dim profile of her companion's face. His eyes were open and he was staring into the nothingness.

His glasses were beside her hip. She folded them and set them carefully on the straw a safe distance away. "I'm sorry, Dr. Lord. I didn't mean to ... anger you."

"It is a difficult situation in which we find ourselves."

"I just can't bear to be up in that little room all by myself. I have spent too much of my life alone ... neglected ... a burden, I think, upon my father, who had little interest in anything outside of horses."

He remained quiet, just staring into the darkness.

"I don't want to be alone, tonight."

"Then by all means, stay, my dear."

My dear. The words sent a flood of warmth through her, and she hugged herself even harder, wanting to cry at the impossibility of the situation in which they found themselves.

"I like it, that you called me that," she whispered, shyly.

"Called you what?"

"'My dear.'"

"Forgive me," he said, his eyes slipping shut. "I must be more tired than I thought. We both know there is nothing 'dear' about you at all, now, don't we?"

"If you're trying to goad me, it will not work. I know by now that you're just teasing."

"Mmmm." He smiled without opening his eyes. "And as I am very tired, you will also know that I'd be quite happy if you'd go visit Shareb and allow me my rest."

"And if I remain quiet, instead?"

"We're talking impossibilities here, I take it."

"I'll consider it a challenge."

"Very well then. Stay if you like."

She had no intention of leaving, of course. She did not want to be alone. She enjoyed the way he teased her, goaded her, and made her laugh. He did not ignore her, as Father had done. He was not preening and primping and competing for her, as so many shallow suitors had done. With his direct glances and ability to see through her foolishness, his firm but quiet way of reining her in when she got just a little bit too full of herself, he was a refreshing change of pace, and she liked that. In her world of rules and seriousness, his dry humor was intoxicating.

He shifted a bit, trying to make his leg comfortable, and she remembered the serving maid's mean comment. *Cripple.* A fierce sense of protectiveness rose within her and for once, she cursed her genteel upbringing. Had she been the lad she was masquerading as, she would've slapped the chit across the face.

"Does your leg pain you, Dr. Lord?" she murmured, suddenly concerned.

"I knew the silence couldn't last."

"Just answer this one question and I shall be quiet."

"Leg's fine," he said, and in the darkness, she could see that he'd closed his eyes and tilted his head back against the door. "Or, as good as can be expected given the weather. In truth, 'tis my shoulders that are on fire."

"From Shareb's pulling?"

"Aye. He's a strong horse, that one."

She said nothing, only holding his hand in the darkness. Gradually, she found herself thinking of that hand itself, and growing acutely aware of the rough texture of the palm, the warmth of the skin, its sprinkling of fine hairs and the shape of the knuckles. She wondered if he was making similar observations about *her* hand.

"I'm sorry about that," she said.

"Why?"

"Well, he's my horse, and I feel rather guilty... . I suppose we should be thankful he even consented to pulling the chaise, considering he's never done so before and surely did not enjoy it. Beneath his dignity, you know. But then, as I've said, you *do* have a way with animals, Dr. Lord, and perhaps that is why he behaved as well as he did."

He said nothing, only the sound of his breathing disturbing the quiet of the stable. She pulled her hand out of his and of its own accord, it crept up to touch his shoulder. The muscles there were rock-hard beneath her fingers.

"Can you sleep, Dr. Lord?"

"I ... don't know."

She innocently misinterpreted his comment as referring to the pain in his shoulders when in truth, it had more to do with the proximity of her body to his—and the effect it was having on him.

"You're an animal doctor," she said quietly, her hand still lying against his shoulder. "If someone brought a horse to you that was stiff and sore, how would you treat it?"

"Liniments, a good rub down, and a warm blanket."

"Oh." Ariadne was glad of the darkness; it concealed the sudden trepidation that must've been written all over her face. She cleared her throat, and even though he couldn't possibly see it in the darkness, she felt her face going hot with color.

Liniments, a good rub down, and a warm blanket.

She couldn't. No. It wasn't proper ...

He sighed and stretched his leg, drawing his breath in sharply.

She couldn't!

He pulled the leg back up, trying to get comfortable.

God help her. "I ... may not have liniment, but I ... *can* give you a —a, uh—rubdown and a blanket."

He was quiet for so long that she thought he mustn't have heard her. Then she saw him turn his face toward her in the darkness, one brow raised. "You would do that, for me?"

"I would ... if you do not tell Maxwell, that is," she added, hurriedly.

He was silent again. *Too* silent, as though her words had made him angry. At last, he let out a heavy sigh, eased himself down, and stretched out on his stomach in the hay, the side of his head resting atop his crossed wrists. "Very well, then," he murmured. "Be about it, then."

"You'll, um—" She stared at those broad shoulders, curled her hands into fists, and bit her lip— "have to instruct me on what to do."

Hay rustled as he positioned himself more comfortably. "I suppose you've never kneaded bread dough?"

Her silence was answer enough.

"Never mind," he said quietly, fondly, and folding his coat into a pillow, propped it beneath his forearms.

"No, I won't 'never mind,'" she retorted, suddenly feeling quite foolish—again. "You're hurting, and I can't bear the thought of you tossing and turning in pain all night." She moved closer, sitting as close to him as she could get, until her thighs were pressed right up against his torso and the heat of him warmed the entire side of her leg. Panic—and something else—rocked her. She swallowed hard, and with an effort, found her voice.

"You'll tell no one about this, will you, Dr. Lord? If anyone were to learn of it, I'd be shunned and banned from polite society."

"My lady, I fear that your actions over the past two days will have already accomplished such a banishment," he pointed out. "But if it will make you feel any better, your secret is quite safe with me."

"You promise?"

"I give you my word on it."

"V-very ... well, then."

He smiled, and relaxed.

Waiting.

Taking a deep breath, Ariadne stretched shaking hands toward that strong, broad back.

And knew—the moment her fingers touched his shoulders— that she'd made a mistake. She felt his warmth, his strength, the sudden gallop of her heartbeat. Oh God. She shouldn't be doing this, it was wrong, wrong, wrong!, but she couldn't stop, not now, not when her hands were already on his shirt, her fingers already probing the stiff muscles beneath the fabric, her palms skimming hesitantly, confidently, boldly, now, over the span of his shoulders. Blindly, she shoved away thoughts of wrong-doing and concentrated on her task, kneading the soreness from his muscles, marveling at the feel of them and telling herself over and over that she was only tending to a friend while her face flamed and her heart pounded and the breath came hot and harsh through her lungs—

Maxwell's face reared up in her mind.

"Mmmmm, that feels good," the veterinarian murmured, just when she would've snatched her hands away. Guilt flooded her, to be replaced with admonition for behaving like such a frightened ninny, and with renewed determination, Ariadne bit her lip and continued her ministrations. She was no coward! And she would prove it—if not just to Colin Lord, then to herself.

Her fingers strayed, moving up his spine, his neck, until the ends of his hair brushed her knuckles. Gently, she stroked the thick, silky locks that followed the curve of the back of his head, enjoying the feel of them against and through her fingers. Again she thought of Maxwell. Again—angrily this time—she shoved the thought of him aside. Then the veterinarian made a contented, sighing sound and Ariadne promptly forgot Maxwell, her station, and any guilt of wrongdoing because suddenly all was right in her world and nothing else mattered, nothing at all. Shutting her eyes, her fingers trailing through his hair, she listened to the rain beating gently against the roof while the stable slumbered around them.

"Is that better?" she asked, knowing, just by the way he had relaxed beneath her hands, that it was.

"Yes ... yes, much," he murmured, and she could see the faint smile just touching his lips. "I think I could go to sleep, like this."

"I thought that was the idea." Her hands drifted down, found the powerful muscles of his shoulders. They seemed to be carved from stone, and as she began to knead them with her fingertips and sides of her thumbs, he winced, as though in pain. She nearly jerked her hands back. "Does it hurt?" she whispered, not daring to call up her voice for fear he'd hear its hoarse trembling.

"Yes, but in a good way. You're doing quite well for someone who has never given a rubdown before."

"If so, it's only because I *have* watched the stable hands giving them to the racehorses after a hard workout—"

She winced and sucked in her breath at the errant slip of her tongue, but in his fatigue, he never noticed. But did he notice other things? Her rapidly beating heart? The hot dampness of her hands, the nervousness that must be apparent in her voice? Thank God he couldn't see her face. *I'm not doing anything wrong!* But if she wasn't doing anything wrong, then why did she feel so hot and flustered? So nervous, quivery and skittish? She swallowed hard, bearing down on the heels of her hands, her fingertips, putting her weight into the gentle massage and pushing at the stiffness she felt beneath her fingers until he gave a slight groan of pain.

"I'm sorry!" she gasped, easing up on the pressure.

"Don't be, my lady. You could never hurt me."

For a long moment she said nothing, merely gazing down at the back of his head, his ear, and her hands, lost amidst the folds of his shirt where it spanned his broad and powerful shoulders. Then, gently placing the heels of her hands against the knots of muscle, she leaned down until her lips were inches from his ear and whispered, "Ariadne."

"Sorry?"

"Ariadne. It is my name. I give you permission to use it." She gave a nervous little laugh. "In trade for your permission for me to use *your* Christian name, as well."

She felt the sudden threads of tension in his shoulders, heard the slow release of his breath. He was so close that she could easily lean down and bury her lips in those silky locks.

"Ariadne," he said, his voice muffled against the coat as he tried the sound of it out on his tongue.

"Colin," she returned, doing the same.

"Such is a pretty name," he murmured, and she could just see that his mouth was turned up in the softest of smiles, his lashes lying against his cheeks. "I like it."

"A bit difficult to say though, don't you think?"

"Ah-ree-ahd-knee. The young beauty who led Theseus out of the maze with the ball of string."

"The very one."

"Dare I dream I am Theseus?"

Something hitched in her chest, but his was a question best left unanswered. It was obvious that he was growing more than fond of her, and she had no desire to lead him down a path that would only be a dead end. That would be cruel, and she was beginning to care for him far too much to hurt him so.

And yet ...

"You have a nice name too ... Colin. It may take me a while to get used to calling you anything but 'doctor,' but I will manage." She sighed and smiled, keeping her hands moving in gentle, firm circles over his back, shoulders, and upper arms. And nice arms they were, too: strong and well-formed, with a natural grace and beauty of definition. Unbidden, she thought of what it would be like to go to bed every night held safely within them, with those beautiful eyes looking up at her in the darkness and her name—*Ariadne*—a gentle, whispered caress on his lips.

It occurred to her that even in the short time she'd spent with this man, she already knew him better than she did Maxwell, the man she was supposed to marry.

Would that it were you, Colin, instead.

A deep, blooming ache gripped her heart—for some things, of course, could never be, and should not even be thought about.

Thank God he could not see the sudden moisture in her eyes. She smoothed his hair back from the side of his brow, over and over again until his eyes drifted shut, his breathing grew rhythmic, and his lashes lay heavily against his cheeks once more. He would make a good husband for some lucky woman, she thought, with no small degree of wistfulness and pain. And a good friend, as well. How very special he was, this kind, gentle man whom animals loved and trusted. Maybe it was time *she* dared to trust him, too ...

And tell him the truth about Shareb-er-rehh.

Tomorrow.

"Sleep now, good doctor," she whispered, as she felt the last stiffness fading from his body, until she felt him slipping away beneath her hands, until she knew she had brought him beyond pain and into sweet, peaceful slumber. She gently pulled his coat out from beneath him and spread it over his back. Then she gazed down at him, a huge lump filling the back of her throat as she put her lips beside his still cheek.

"Dr. Lord?"

Nothing.

She smiled then, listening to his quiet breathing, letting her hand rest on the side of his head. Then—very slowly, very carefully—she closed her eyes, leaned down, and buried her lips in his hair.

It was sweet-smelling and clean, like silk against her face.

She took a deep, shaky breath, and pressed the softest of kisses against his temple.

"Good night, my sweet friend."

Chapter Nine

B linding sunlight, glancing off the waiting guns, off the broad deck, off the waves that separated HMS Triton from the enemy battleship as she bore steadily down on them with deadly menace. They were vastly outnumbered, but beside him, Admiral Sir Graham Falconer—a man he would have followed to hell and back—stood with smiling confidence, despite the fact the odds were stacked heavily against them. And then the first salvos were exchanged, the decks trembling beneath the might of the flagship's broadside, smoke pouring back in through the gunports. Within seconds, the sparkling sunlight dimmed beneath acrid smoke, and the world became nothing but the violence of sound, of spars and sails crashing down to the deck around them, of yelling men, shouted orders, metal flying, and controlled chaos. Around them men began to bleed, to fall, to die. I want more speed out of the starboard gun crews! Colin shouted to his first lieutenant, and was just turning to speak to Sir Graham when he was slammed hard to the deck, there to lay sprawled against a gun carriage. He tried to get up, but there was nothing but blinding agony somewhere below his kneecap. Tried again—and woke up on the surgeon's table, the admiral's anguished face above him, and all the while the deafening thunder of the flagship's eighty guns booming around and above him, each one making the ship shudder deep in her bones as above, the fighting continued.

"The leg will have to come off, Sir Graham," the surgeon said gravely, already picking up his saw. "The risk of it turning gangrenous is too great—"

"You take that damned saw to his leg, Ryder, and so help me God you'll find yourself wishing you'd never met me. Now set it, damn your eyes!"

"But sir—"

"I said set it!"

Colin heard himself groaning, then there was nothing but Ryder, pouring rum down his throat until he was choking and dizzy ... Ryder, pulling off his shoe and throwing it down ... Ryder, grasping his ankle, bracing his own foot against the table and hauling on the fractured bone, the screams of his own agony ringing in his ears until he'd finally passed out... .

Colin came awake to the sound of rain tapping against the deckhead above. He lay there in the darkness, waiting for his servant to come in and tell him the ship's position, its course, the direction and strength of the wind. Blinking, he sat up—and with the slipping away of the dream and the return of consciousness, felt the heavy plunge of his spirit at the cruel realization he was not in his cabin aboard HMS *Triton*, but was land-bound, and the sound he heard was nothing more than the dull tattoo of rain against a roof.

He wondered if he'd always come instantly awake at four in the morning, wondered if the memories would ever go away, wondered if he'd ever be able to get the sea out of his blood.

And suddenly realized just where he was—and whom he was with.

She lay beside him, deeply asleep—as most people were, at four in the morning—her spine pressed intimately into his chest, her hand caught in his, her breathing soft and slow in the darkness. His blood ignited, bringing on an erection made all the more excruciating by the fact that it was already pressing into the softness of her backside. Taking a deep, unsteady breath, Colin carefully pulled his hand out of hers and eased away from her.

He stood up, trembling, aching, needing, *wanting.*

Dear God. Dear God, please give me strength... .

His head bent, the heel of his hand pressed to his forehead, he stumbled down the long, dark aisle, pulled the door open, and turned his hot face up to the cool, drenching rain that poured out of the night.

"God help me," he said aloud, his fists clenched, his body rigid, the water streaming down his cheeks. He shook his head and squeezed his eyes shut, baring his teeth in pain. "I just can't resist her much longer. I beg of you, help me, give me strength, take this temptation away ..."

The rain came down harder, beating like shot against his upturned face, soaking his hair and plastering it to his scalp. Water ran down his neck, his nose, pummeled his brow and cheeks and eyelashes.

He began to walk, away from the stable, away from *her.* His breeches pressed against his arousal, making each step an exercise in discomfort. He heard the door creak behind him and little Bow came racing out, streaking ahead of him through the darkness after a barn cat.

Walk, and it won't hurt as bad. Walk, and put her out of your mind. You cannot have her. She's promised to another. It's not to be, damn it, the wind blows from a different quarter.

He walked faster, head bent, the rain streaming down his cheeks, dripping off the tip of his nose, beating against his bare head and soaking the back of his neck. Gravel crunched, then mud squished, beneath his boots as he crossed the drive and headed up the footpath that traversed the hills, coming down heavily on his good leg and mercilessly abusing his bad one. The latter screamed in protest and he walked faster, damning the fates that had made him look up the other day and see *her* sitting so coolly astride that damned horse, the fates that had thrown the two of them together and would only rip them cruelly apart in the end.

You cannot have her.

She belongs to another.

And she would never want you, if she knew what you had done.

Oblivious to the pain in his leg, oblivious to the coming dawn, he pushed himself, hard. He didn't see the dog racing off into a wet tangle of blackberry bushes after a hare, didn't smell the musky fragrance of blossoming wildflowers and wet grass, didn't hear the birds coming awake around him, nor notice the sky to the east lightening with the approach of dawn. He could only think of *her* back there, asleep, could only relive the sweet bliss of drifting away beneath her touch last night only to wake up with his rock-hard erection pressing into the softness of her backside.

Didn't she know what she was *doing* to him?

He passed a field, gray and misty beneath the still-dark skies, where several cows stared at him as he passed. One of them raised its head, let out a long, lonely, call, and began to walk after him, separated only by the fence. Sure enough, the rest of the herd began to follow, all stumbling along placidly through the mud, swishing their tails, and trailing in his wake.

He kept walking, too full of anguish to notice them, his chest so tight with distress and emotion that it hurt just to breathe. He thought about leaving her, and returning to London. He thought about how many other women there were in the world, and lamented the fact that he'd never met anyone he'd desired as much as he did his copper-haired employer. For five years he'd been a recluse, throwing himself into his new career as emphatically as he had his old one; for five years, he'd felt his purpose in life was to ease suffering, a small atonement for the lives he had taken or destroyed in the name of war; for five years, he had avoided entanglements for fear that women would reject him as a ruined hero.

And then he had met Lady Ariadne St. Aubyn. Her charm, her bubbly playfulness, her carefree attention to him made him aware, in painful, striking clarity, of all that he had been denying himself.

You can't have her, he told himself with the stoic practicality that had saved him from crushing despair after the courts-martial. *She belongs to another, and there is no sense pining for her. There are other women out there. She has merely opened a door, shown you that there is more in life than just being the finest veterinarian you can be, that you need someone to love and be loved by as much as the next person ...*

Then why didn't he tell her about the court-martial? Why did he hold back when she wanted to know about his old life? After all, he'd long since accepted and come to terms with what had happened to him—it was others, who could not.

He trudged along through the wet grass, the fragrance of clover and damp earth filling his senses. Oh, how he wanted to share with her the pain he'd felt when his former career had come to its abrupt and untimely end; how he wanted to tell her what had really happened, so she might know that once he'd been a hero, and worthy of her. But he couldn't. Because she, like his peers, like his former friends, like the rest of the world, would only pity and despise him, and he couldn't bear the thought of that bright smile fading away when he revealed what he had done. She was young. She was class-conscious. She had not yet learned, might not ever learn, given her privileged spot in the room of life, that it was the person inside that counted.

He might have fallen from glory, but he was still the same man he had been.

A better one, probably.

The rain began to let up, the droplets fading to cool mist against his face. A flock of geese winged overhead, and still, he pressed on. He thought of Orla, and tried to recall her dark hair and wise eyes that had seen too much, but her face was lost to time and all he could remember was the little pirate ship, the all-women crew of which she had been a part, and their lady-captain, his cousin Maeve, who'd found her own true love in the arms of Sir Graham himself.

They were painful memories. Especially when he considered what had happened after he, Colin, had brought them all back to the Caribbean ... and the storm had hit, changing his life forever.

Now, Orla was an ocean away, far beyond his reach. But even the brief flame he had felt for the Irish girl was nothing compared to the raging fire that burned in his heart and blood at the mere thought of Lady Ariadne St. Aubyn.

He ought to leave her. He ought to run, to flee, while he still had a heart beating within his breast.

Has anyone ever told you that you have very beautiful eyes, Dr. Lord?

He raked a hand over his wet face.

You're a very handsome man, you know.

He ought to get as far away from her as he could, and as quickly as possible.

You have a very nice smile, too.

Yes, far away ... and fast.

He dug the heels of his hands into his eyes, pressing hard. He couldn't leave her, of course. He was a man of honor, had given his word to stay by her side, to protect her and safeguard the well-being of the stallion. He could last just a few more days, couldn't he? Besides, what he felt for the lovely heiress was nothing more than infatuation borne out of his own loneliness. It would go away, as soon as he saw her safely to Burnham and returned to London.

It had to.

Soaked to the skin, he walked until grey light revealed the patchwork-fields and hills, the fences and hedgerows and the muddy, rutted path on which he walked. He whistled for Bow, and turning, strode back the way he'd come, resolved to be strong where *she* was concerned, resolved to put some distance between them for the sake of his own heart, resolved to be practical about the matter, as he was about everything else in his life, and not let a bit of whimsy fill him so full of anguish.

The world had awakened during his absence. He heard the old sheepdog barking in the drive long before he came down the last hill and saw the coaching inn in the distance, people already moving in and out of the barn, travelers coming and going, and Meg hauling twin buckets from the well and carrying them into the inn. A curl of smoke rose from the chimney, and his stomach growled at the thought of breakfast.

His employer was nowhere in sight.

A pair of matched grays hitched to a fine carriage stood in the drive, their coats streaked with rain, their eyes on Colin. As he passed they, like the cows, tried to follow him. A groom pulled them back. With Bow at his heels he slipped into the barn, his gaze helplessly drawn to that place where he and Ariadne had spent the night. But there were people up and about the stable now, horses being led in and out, and the place where he had slept and dreamed and ached for a woman he could never have was marked by nothing more than a flattened patch of straw.

Passing their chaise, which had been pulled over to the side of the aisle, Colin peered into Shareb-er-rehh's stall.

The stallion was gone.

A rush of fear and alarm swept through him and he whirled, only to collide with Meg.

"Ah, Mr. Lord! Your little brother asked me t' give ye a message—said the horse needed exercise and he was going t' take him out for a gallop. Said he'd be back in an hour."

"Oh." Colin sighed with relief. "Thank you."

Touching his arm, Meg tilted her face up at him. "An hour ain't so long, you know." She winked. "But long enough to take a little *ride* of our own. What do ye say, handsome?"

Colin smiled, his mind groping for a suitable but polite excuse to decline. Though it would probably do him a world of good to take a tumble with Meg, he just couldn't do it. Didn't *want* to do it. He shook his head, and made some excuse that sounded implausible to even his own ears, leaving Meg to stare at him as though he'd grown a third eye, the corner of her mouth twitching with good humor.

"Ah, Mr. Lord. 'Tis heartier fare I'm offering ye, but maybe there's some truth that the way to a man's heart is through his stomach. Maybe next time, hmm? Come, follow. Uncle Rodney's serving breakfast, and that's the least I can give ye."

He followed her out of the now-busy stable, passing horses being brought out and harnessed, the matched grays, and an old, sway-backed bay gelding that had just been driven into the little yard. Its coloring and markings mirrored Shareb's, but any similarity stopped there. The animal's head was lowered, its nose hanging near the ground, its eyes half-closed and its entire body broken and defeated.

"Hello, boy," Colin murmured, and put out his hand to touch the drooping head.

Unlike the fiery Shareb-er-rehh, this sad, gentle creature took a weary step forward and placed its muzzle in his palm. Its sides expanded in a deep sigh, and it was then that Colin noticed the cruel sores beneath the harness, the rawness about the animal's mouth. *Oh, God*, he thought, his heart constricting, and laid his hand against the old beast's rain-soaked neck.

You have healing hands, Delabere Blaine had once told him, upon noting the eerie way that animals behaved around him. But even healing hands could do nothing to take away cruelty and the pain of abuse.

"Hey, you, there! Git away from my horse, ye hear?"

Colin looked up as a fat, pox-scarred man waddled toward him, a cowed-looking gun dog trailing at his heels. Out of the corner of his eye, he saw Meg standing on the inn's steps, hands on her hips, head cocked, watching. Not wishing to make a scene, Colin gently stroked the gelding's thin neck and said mildly, "You might try a little kindness where your horse is concerned. He'll perform far better for you."

"I'm kind as the day is long," the man puffed, glaring hatefully at the poor old gelding. "But my luck with animals is the devil's own. Damned dog here won't hunt, damned horse ain't no better. Paid enough money for 'im and 'e's sick. Won't go. And here I gotta be in Norwich day after tomorrow an' this animal ain't fit for nothin' but dog food. Damned farrier's supposed to be along any minute t' have a look at 'im. I'm tellin' ye, though, if he can't do anything for the stinkin' beast I'm sending 'im off to the knacker's!"

"Mr. Lord?" Meg called saucily. "Coming?"

Colin's worried gaze remained on the gelding. He touched the soft white and pink muzzle and felt the animal's breath against his fingers. "Perhaps I could help," he suggested, keeping his tone steady and mild in an attempt to defuse the owner's ill temper. "I'm a veterinarian."

"A what?"

"Veterinarian."

"What the hell is that?"

Colin smiled, and stroked the gelding's neck. "An animal doctor."

"There ain't nothin' you kin do that me own farrier can't," the man growled. "I don't need no university-educated know-it-all telling me how to treat me horse."

Colin sighed. Maybe, just maybe, one of these days he'd learn that he couldn't fix the world. "Have your farrier treat him, then. But if my advice means anything to you, try putting a pad of sheepskin right here—" he gently lifted the saddle of the harness and indicated a raw spot, just behind the gelding's withers— "to keep the leather from chafing his back. He has harness sores, and they hurt. No wonder he won't go for you."

The man stared at him, and wordlessly, Colin gave the poor animal's nose a last stroke. But as he turned and walked away, the old horse let out a long, plaintive whinny, trying to call him back. The sound tore at Colin's heart. Steeling himself, he kept walking. The gelding whinnied again.

You can't fix the world.

Meg was holding the door open for him, and as he stepped inside, a notice displayed boldly across its front caught his eye and pushed thoughts of the old horse to the back of his mind.

WANTED: Any information leading to the whereabouts of Lady Ariadne St. Aubyn, daughter of the late Earl of Weybourne, who disappeared on Sunday last... .

"Bloody hell!" he said under his breath. "She *wasn't* exaggerating!"

"What?" Meg asked.

His smile was quick and false. "Oh—uh, nothing. Friend of mine told me about this—um, this fugitive, but I suppose it's such a singular story you have to see something like this in order to believe it, eh?"

"I suppose. Whole countryside's talkin' about it, though. Can ye imagine? Ten thousand pounds to return the girl—an heiress, no less!—an' the stallion to her brother. Must be one valuable nag indeed... ."

Sudden sweat ran down Colin's back, his heart pounded in his ears, and it was all he could do to retain his composure as he followed Meg into the inn. It was a far different scene than it had been last night, with patrons laughing and drinking and sitting elbow to elbow at the dark, polished tables. Smoke and the nauseating scent of frying pork clogged the air. Finding a chair, Colin stared desperately out the window, where green hills dotted with sheep rolled away to the horizon.

He fisted his hands beneath the table. *Come back, Ariadne. We have to get out of here,* now.

Meg set a plate before him, and a pot of tea. He shook his head, waved them away. "No, no. Ale. Strong, dark, with plenty of bite to it. Ale."

"Mr. Lord, are you quite all right?"

He raked his fingers down his face. "I'm fine. Bad night. Didn't sleep well. Take this away, please, I can't eat it."

"But it's fresh bacon, surely—"

"For God's sake, woman, take it away and bring me a plate of eggs and toast instead!"

Forgetting the teapot, she hurried off, leaving him to sit there in his soaked clothes. By the time she returned Colin had gotten his composure under control once again. He guzzled the ale, shoveled the eggs into his mouth and sopped up the yolks with the toast. Something touched his feet, and he looked down to see the tortoiseshell cat slamming its torso against his ankles and purring in delight.

He waited until Meg's back was turned, then scooped up a bit of egg yolk on his finger, put his hand beneath the table, and let the affectionate feline lick it off.

The door opened, and *she* walked in.

He grabbed her sleeve as she approached, hauling her so close that her startled face was mere inches from his. "Where on earth have you been?" he demanded, beneath his breath. "We can't stay here, not now—"

She stared at him, properly affronted. Then, with that casual, haughty elegance she could command at the bat of an eye, she shook him off, moved around the table, and sat down across from him, her eyes sparkling with humor and the love of what surely, to her, must be the ultimate adventure. "Really, *Doctor*, do you think I did not know? They were banging that notice onto the door at an hour unfit, even, for the roosters. Made enough racket to wake the dead. Now where's that foolish maid? I could go for some tea and toast."

He glanced over his shoulder then leaned forward, hoping no one had recognized her. "Ariadne, keep your cap on and your head down. Don't meet anyone's eyes. Just sit there, don't say a *word*, and for God's sake, keep your coat closed!"

"Really, Colin, I have no plausible reason to open it."

"Plague take it, it's not funny!"

"No, the situation is not." She reached over and touched his wrist. "But your concern, is." Grinning, she picked up his cup and angled her head toward the untouched pot of tea.

Rolling his eyes, Colin picked up the pot and filled the cup with the steeped brew, keenly aware of her eyes on his face.

She grinned, and raising the cup delicately to her lips, lifted her hand in an imperious motion for Meg to bring her some toast. "I have been on the run for several days now. I have seen these notices all over London. I expect to see them all the way to Norfolk, and with, I'm certain, increasing frequency." She smiled sweetly, and leaned back as Meg set toast, butter and a pot of marmalade before her. "But I know, the shock of seeing one for the first time is rather distressing, is it not? By the way—"

She reached into her pocket, and grinning, came up with his spectacles. "Look what I found in the hay this morning."

The memories came flooding back.

"Sleep well, Dr. Lord?"

So, they were back to *this* again. She, virginal and shy by night, bold and flirtatious by day. He couldn't keep up with her, let alone understand her.

"Lady Ariadne—"

"I watched you sleep, you know."

He tried to scowl, but she merely grinned, her eyes sparkling.

"You made a charming sight. I hope you don't mind. I've never watched a man sleep before."

"Let me guess," he said wryly, picking up a piece of toast and buttering it for her. "*I'm* the one who drools. Who talks in his sleep."

She laughed, opened his glasses, and leaning over the table, slid them onto his nose. "To be honest, good Doctor, I really didn't notice. And if I did, I am not so sure I would embarrass you by telling you."

"Marmalade?"

"Yes, please. And lots of it, if you don't mind."

He spread the jelly thickly over the toast, then handed it to her. Still grinning at him, she took a bite out of it, crunching happily and studying him pertly from across the table. His heartbeat began to quicken, and he suddenly felt hot all over. She was the only person he'd ever met who could reduce his composure to pudding; not even his admiral, not even Nelson had been able to shake him. But this girl—this playful, saucy, flirtatious little noblewoman—she could reduce him to a bucket of guts without even trying, just by paying him too much attention in all the right places.

Wishing he could ignore her, knowing he could not, he picked up his mug and brought it to his lips.

"I wish I'd met you before Father promised me to Maxwell," she said baldly.

He nearly choked on his tea.

"Oh, Colin, you are so refreshing after the pampered blades of London! So artless, and totally unaware of yourself ... really, there's no need to glare at me as if I were an errant child, because you really are a lot of fun and I quite enjoy your company. You know, I might even keep you on as my personal veterinarian after I get married so that—"

"How was your ride?" he said tightly, trying to change the subject.

"My ride?"

"Yes, your ride. Meg told me you took Shareb-er-rehh out for a gallop."

She grinned and stretched her hands over her head, totally oblivious to the pain she had just caused him with that single word—*Maxwell*—, totally unaware of the charming sight she made in her shirt, cap and breeches. "Ah, it was exhilarating! Shareb-er-rehh is all set to go, happy as a lark this morn because I gave him some pastr— I mean, breakfast, and now the sun is starting to break through the clouds, and you know something, Dr. Lord, I think it's going to be a positively beautiful day!"

Just then, a terrified, inhuman scream split the air.

Colin jumped to his feet, nearly upsetting the table, his face paling.

"Lud, what on *earth* was that?!" Ariadne gasped, clapping a hand to her chest.

But the veterinarian threw down his napkin and heedless of the angry protests, shoved his way through a group of milling patrons in his haste to reach the door. As he charged outside, the other diners rose to their feet, their chairs scraping and silverware hitting their plates.

"What is it?"

"Dunno. Something going on outside!"

"Cor, what a bloody awful sound—"

Ariadne ran to the door to see what the commotion was all about, but the other patrons were there before her. Again came that chilling scream, and she felt the hair rise on her nape and her blood running cold as she shoved her way through the other people and halted in her tracks on the doorstep just outside.

Her hand went to her mouth in horror.

In the space of a moment, she saw it all. An old, broken-down bay horse, harnessed to a cart and screaming in terror as a man beat it about the ears with a stick and another man, holding a bucket and some sort of knife, tried to get close to its neck.

And the veterinarian. *Her* veterinarian, striding angrily down the lawn towards the frightened animal, his fists clenched and his back stiff with rage.

"Colin!" she cried. Then, she broke from the crowd and raced headlong across the lawn after him. "*Colin!*"

He never stopped, his angry, hitching stride carrying him toward the horse at a speed she would never have thought him capable of attaining. Breathless, she caught up to him and grabbed his arm. His jaw was set, his eyes hard and furious behind his glasses.

"Colin, you can't just interfere—"

He shook her off, shoving his way through the small group that surrounded the horse until he reached its head.

"I beg your pardon," he ground out, with barely suppressed fury, "But may I offer a bit of advice here?"

He caught the gelding's bridle, and Ariadne saw the poor, suffering animal turn its face against his chest in grateful relief.

"What the hell do you think you're doing, you blighty bugger?" the farrier cried, raising the scalpel as Colin came between him and the horse. "Get out of here and mind your own business, I've got work to do!"

Cradling the gelding's head in the curve of his arm, Colin turned blazing eyes on the farrier. "There is no need to practice phlebotomy on a horse with the mere complaint of harness sores. Leave him be."

People came running from the inn, and soon there was a small crowd surrounding the horse. An awed murmur rippled through it like lightning through thunder clouds.

"Who the hell are *you*?" the farrier persisted.

Filled with pride and admiration, Ariadne stepped forward. "He is Colin Lord, London veterinarian, and if says the horse doesn't need to be bled, he doesn't!"

"Well, *I* say he does, and I damn well ought to know!"

"He does *not* need to be bled! No animal does!" Shielding the gelding's face from the enraged farrier, the veterinarian turned to the horse's shocked owner. His voice was shaking, unsteady with rage. "Look, Mister—please. Let me treat him. For God's sake, I won't charge you a damned penny—"

The farrier flung his bucket down in the mud. "You questioning my skills? You think I don't know what I'm doing? Who the hell do you think you are, to just come in here and tell me how to do my job? Huh? You tell me, you bastard!"

The crowd stirred uneasily, anticipating a fight.

"Tell me!"

"He's going to hit him," whispered a man standing near

Ariadne, jerking his head toward the farrier. "You can't push John Beckett too far, I tell you!"

"Nah, he won't hit a lad with specs," another hissed back.

"Ye want to make a bet? My money's on Beckett."

"And mine's on the veterinarian!" Ariadne cried. "Don't let him hurt that poor horse, *Doctor* Lord! You hear me? Don't let him!"

Her shrill cry sent the farrier over the edge. Scalpel raised, he went for the gelding's jugular, and from her close vantage point, Ariadne saw it all.

The perfect composure of the doctor's face. The absence of hesitation as he stepped protectively in front of the gelding. The quick, upward flash of his fist.

And the farrier, crumpling to the wet gravel, his nose spraying a fan of blood.

Colin stepped back, shouldering the horse away with him.

"Huzzah for you, Colin!" Ariadne shouted, caught up in the moment and jumping up and down as the crowd went wild around her. "Give the blackguard what he deserves!"

The farrier stumbled to his feet, one hand covering his bleeding nose. "You hit me!" he roared, flinging down the scalpel. "Damn yer eyes, ye bloody hit me!"

"Yes, and I'll do so again if you so much as come near this animal with that scalpel." Still holding the gelding, Colin turned to the shocked owner. "Sir, please. I'll buy the beast from you. The dog, too. How much do you want for them?"

"Well, I—"

"Twenty pounds? Thirty?"

"You bloody HIT me!"

The farrier hurled himself at Colin, and in the space of a heartbeat, Ariadne saw her veterinarian draw a breath—no, it was more a sigh than a breath—glance heavenward in a plea for divine patience, and then whirl to drive his fist into the farrier's jaw with such force that the man's head rocked back, his knees buckled, and he fell sprawling on his back in a fresh pile of dung.

And this time, he did not get up.

The crowd, shocked, went dead silent as Colin turned calm, patient eyes upon the horse's owner. "Sir? You were saying?"

"T-t-twenty pounds," the man stammered, backing away. "Twenty pounds and they're yours."

Colin smiled. "Done."

Chapter Ten

They did not linger at the inn.

In moments, the old bay gelding was harnessed and being backed into the shafts, someone, at Colin's request, had found some sheepskin to protect the animal's sores, Shareb was being tied to the chaise, both dogs were loaded, and they were hastily on their way, the milling knot of people on the lawn growing smaller and smaller with distance behind them.

Dr. Lord, it was obvious, was eager to put as many miles between them and the inn as quickly as possible.

"You were *magnificent* back there," Ariadne gushed, "Simply magnificent! I would never have guessed you could fight like that, being such a quiet and gentle person, but my goodness, that awful man deserved everything you gave him and I'm so proud of you! How anyone could be cruel to such a kind old horse as—what did you say his name was?"

"Thunder."

"Thunder, is beyond me. Just think of what would have happened to that poor horse if we hadn't come along in time."

Her companion cast a quick glance over his shoulder, oblivious to the way Ariadne was smiling up at him, and she wondered if her own eyes reflected the same worshipful adoration toward him that those of animals did. At the moment, she didn't care. At the moment, she was just a little bit in love with Colin Lord, maybe even more than just a little bit, and who wouldn't be, after seeing what he'd done back there?

"You're a hero, Colin."

His face looked pained.

"And I'm so glad you gave that man what he deserved. But, do you think that having Thunder along is going to complicate things for us?"

"Actually, it should be to our benefit," he said, finally relaxing as it became apparent that they weren't being followed. "Every money-hungry reward hunter from here to Norfolk is on the lookout for a bay horse and a young, flame-haired woman. Thunder may be a complication, but he is a necessary one."

"How?"

"No one is going to be looking for *two* bay horses, similar in size and color—"

She laughed. "Dr. Lord, how can you even *compare* such an animal with Shareb? They are night and day! At least Thunder seems to enjoy pulling the chaise, which should put Shareb back in good humor."

"So stop complaining."

"I'm not."

"You are."

"Dr. Lord, sometimes you are too high-and-mighty for your own good. Acting better than you are. Such behavior is highly inappropriate."

"And how would you like me to behave?"

"Appropriately."

"And what is appropriate?"

She sniffed. "Suitably subservient."

"Yes, your Highness."

"Don't get smart."

"Of course not, your Highness."

She laughed and playfully swatted him with her cap. He couldn't prevent his lips from twitching. Then she coaxed Bow into her lap, and moved her feet so that their other new acquisition, the gun dog—whose soulful brown eyes were gazing reverently up at the doctor—had a place to lie down.

"And what are you going to call your new dog? Stern?"

"What?"

"If that one's Bow, then is this one Stern?"

"Why don't you name him."

She looked at the dog; unlike the horse, he appeared to be nobly bred, with a beautiful head through which an off-center blaze ran, and plenty of muscle under his short white coat with its brown ticking. He had the look of an aristocrat about him, and he needed a suitable name.

"Marcus," she announced. "We'll call him Marc."

"Aurelius?"

"Antony."

Colin, grinning, reached down to scratch the dog's ears, and glancing at his employer, saw that she was leaning back in her seat watching him.

Not just watching him. *Studying* him, with admiring, worshipful eyes—just as she'd been doing ever since he'd stepped in and rescued Thunder from the farrier. It was unnerving. Disconcerting. And, if he were honest with himself, flattering, because her perky energy, her bubbly spirits, drew him like water to a sponge. God help him, how was he going to endure this all the way to Norfolk? He looked away, pretending indifference, but out of the corner of his eye he saw her still watching him from beneath her cap. He could see her red locks, her pouty mouth, the bored, restless look in her eye that spelled trouble.

She sighed.

He didn't say anything.

She began drumming her fingers against her knee.

"Would you like to drive?" he asked, trying to think of something to amuse her.

"No." She sighed again. "I would not like to drive. I would like to talk about ... last night."

"That's unfortunate, because I would not."

"Don't be a prude, Colin. It's not as though anything *happened*."

She drew her legs up, turned on the seat, and then startled him by lying back until her shoulders were against his thigh, her head in his lap.

Colin went stiff.

"My lady, this is *not* appropriate," he said, his light humor vanishing.

"What, do you mind so very much?"

"It's not that I mind, but—"

"Then what is the trouble?"

"You're betrothed."

"Yes, but I'm not doing anything wrong. Besides, I am most comfortable, you're a very handsome man, and I enjoy looking at you."

"You shouldn't enjoy looking at me, you belong to somebody else."

"Not yet I don't. Until I'm married I may look at anyone I please. And right now, I find it immensely pleasing to look at *you*. It's unfortunate that you don't like to look at *me*."

"What makes you think I don't?"

"It's obvious."

"So, I behave within the confines of propriety. There is nothing contemptible about that."

"No, but how utterly *boring*. So, good doctor, are you saying you do like to look at me?"

He merely turned that patient, unflappable, stare upon her that said more than words ever could.

"Well?" Ariadne pressed, her eyes sparkling.

"Any attraction I feel for you is a useless emotion."

"So. That doesn't mean you cannot have it. Are you attracted to me, Colin?"

"Ariadne, this conversation is doing neither of us any good—"

"I don't see the harm in it. Because right now, you see, I'm not feeling very pretty, garbed as I am in a man's clothes and watching what's left of my reputation fade away with every mile we get closer to Norfolk. It's reassuring to hear that someone finds me attractive, especially someone who, I must say, is the hero of the hour."

Her companion just looked straight ahead, his eyes bleak.

"You *are* a hero, you know."

"And you are a flirt. Sit up, Ariadne, and act like a lady."

"I cannot act like a lady when I'm masquerading as a man."

"If you were serious about your masquerade, you wouldn't be lying here with your head in my lap."

"I *want* to lie here with my head in your lap, and look up at your face, silhouetted against the blue sky and clouds, and watch the sunlight dry your hair and slant down through your eyes, watch it throw the shadow of your lashes over your cheeks and the shadow of your head over mine."

"I suppose you get everything you want."

Ariadne looked up at him, her handsome hero and savior of animals, this man she had gazed upon long into the night, this man who filled her head with wicked thoughts of kissing and touching and, well, other things a lady should not be thinking about, this man who could make her skin tingle and her heart race with just one glance from his oddly beautiful eyes.

Wicked, wicked, Ariadne. She—*oh, admit it!*—wanted him to touch her. Wanted him to kiss her. Wanted ...

She sighed in despair. "No," she said, softly. "I *don't* always get everything I want."

He kept his gaze straight ahead. "Do you want this marriage to Maxwell?"

She didn't answer, merely gazing up at the underside of his chin with sad, suddenly wistful eyes, noting the tiny gold bristles picking up the glare of the sun.

"Do you?" he repeated, his voice tight.

"I ... well ... well, yes, of course I do. Why wouldn't I?"

She saw his lashes fall as his eyes closed, briefly. "I don't know. It's just that as your friend, I thought it my duty to warn you that marriage is not a commitment to be entered into lightly."

"No. Indeed, it is not. But I am an heiress, and my father promised me to Maxwell. I have to marry him. It's what he wanted."

"Yes, but is it what *you* want?"

He bent his head and turned his clear gaze on her, and the look of raw longing and desire she saw there went straight to her heart. The color faded from her face, and she suddenly felt confused, afraid, trapped. Of course she wanted to marry Maxwell! Didn't she?

Yet why, suddenly, did the thought fill her with panic and doubt? Why did it make her feel helpless, unhappy, and trapped?

"All brides get cold feet," she snapped, unable to look him in the eye. "I suspect it's quite normal."

He looked back up, a shadow darkening his eyes and his jaw tight with what could only be anger. She sensed him mentally withdrawing from her, pulling within himself, and as it had last night, the feeling left her scared and lonely. Rejected.

"Colin?"

"What?"

"Did I say something wrong?"

"No."

"You're being short with me. I don't like when you become aloof and distant."

He stared straight ahead and did not respond.

"Your eyes are just as beautiful when you're angry, you know."

"Stop it, Ariadne."

"No, I won't stop it. Unless you give me just a *tiny* smile."

"I said, *stop it*."

"A teeny, tiny smile... . Come now, Colin! Show me that crooked grin."

But he didn't respond, only looking away with eyes full of pain, and Ariadne was reminded again, as she had been so many times in the past, how her outrageous remarks and slightly risqué behavior had never gotten her the attention she craved, but had only landed her in trouble, again and again and again.

Including this marriage that she did not want. This marriage that was supposed to put firm reins on her increasingly wild behavior, according to Father after Maxwell, himself, had proposed it.

Bad behavior. No, it had never worked in the past.

So why, then, do I keep doing it?

"Colin," she ventured after some moments had passed. "What are we going to do about our arrangements tonight?"

"I don't think we should be sleeping near each other. Last night proved that."

"Well, we can't very well sleep apart. You're supposed to be protecting us. So therefore we have to sleep near each other, don't you think?"

"We'll cross that bridge when we come to it."

"I wish we would come to it now, because I very much enjoyed sleeping together last night. I felt so ... so *safe*, Colin. As though nothing could ever happen to me as long as you were near."

"We weren't *sleeping together*."

"Well, we were sleeping *next* to each other."

"And don't let appearances deceive you," he added. "I'll do my best to protect you and Shareb, but I am not infallible."

"Oh, Colin, stop being so self-deprecating. I saw the way you laid that farrier out cold. You were magnificent, wonderful! And you fight remarkably well for a healing man. Did you learn how to do *that* in the War, too?"

"You might say that."

"Did you get in fights very often?"

"Often enough."

"Fistfights?"

"No."

"What kind, then?"

"I'd rather not talk about it."

"Why not?"

"Ariadne, *please*."

"Well, I cannot imagine what the big secret is... ."

"Yes, and it's better that you don't. I find it painful to discuss. Talk about the weather if you like, ask me questions about my career as a veterinarian, but do not query me about my past."

His hard tone forbade further prying. What was the big mystery? What had happened to him that was so upsetting that he refused to discuss it? Ariadne finally sat up and gazed thoughtfully over at him. His eyes were distant, dark with remembered anguish, and she had a sudden, unexplainable urge to take him in her arms and comfort him.

That, of course, would be very bad behavior. Very bad behavior, indeed, and she knew he wouldn't welcome it. Instead, maybe she could cajole a smile back onto his face. Or at least a little grin. Anything was better than the sad, wistful look in his eye.

"Colin?"

"What?"

"Can I tell *you* a secret, then?"

Her conspiratorial tone raised a reluctant smile from him. "I suppose you will whether I wish you to or not."

Her eyes were dancing. "I kissed you good night last night, you know."

He sighed and kept his gaze between Thunder's ears, but his grin was spreading.

"Did you know that?" she asked, playfully. "That I kissed you?"

"I was not aware of it."

"Are you ready to hear my *real* secret?"

He dropped his brow to his hand and shook his head.

"Last night," she said, watching his face, "I kissed you. That is not my secret, because I already told you. But Colin, I—I have a confession to make. Maybe it started when I first saw you, down on your knees on the cobblestones and saving that poor dog. Certainly, it has grown stronger, this fondness I have for you, with every kind thing that you do, with every witty thing that you say, with ... well, with just being around you. And I know I'm not supposed to want this when I'm engaged to be married to Maxwell, but since I have yet to speak my vows I see no harm in it—"

"Ariadne, *what* is your point?"

She smiled, suddenly nervous, but knowing it was too late to back down. "I still want you to kiss me."

"You want me to kiss you."

"Yes, that is what I said."

She could sense the tension flowing into his body, could see his knuckles growing white, his jaw hardening with vexation.

God help her, she'd just committed more bad behavior, and this time, it hadn't even been intentional. She was just being honest, just trying to cajole him out of his sadness, and oh, dear God, instead she'd made him angry.

"Colin?"

He was breathing hard, his eyes bleak, angry and helpless. His tension communicated itself right down the reins and Thunder picked up his pace. Behind them, Shareb-er-rehh broke into a trot to keep up.

"Colin?"

She lifted her hand and grabbed the reins, pulling back on them. The old horse faltered and came to a halt.

"Plague take it," the veterinarian said, and bent his forehead to his hand. "Must you do this to me? Must you torment and tease me and put me in a state of —"

"All I want is a kiss. A simple, harmless, ki—"

He looked at her then, turning such a look of pure fury and desire on her that she wanted to melt right down into the floorboards. She had pushed him too far.

And now, he was going to teach her a lesson.

"A simple, *harmless*, kiss," he murmured with dangerous softness, and she felt her flirtatious grin freezing in place, her heart beginning to beat a panicked tattoo within her breast as he reached out and grasped her wrist.

"I'm sorry, Colin, I was just t-teasing—"

"I've had it with your teasing, Ariadne. One of these days you're going to push somebody too far. It's about time you learned that kissing can be about as *harmless* as setting a spark to gunpowder!"

He pulled her close, and then, before she could protest, cry out, or even raise her hand to slap him, his mouth came down hard upon hers. She knew him as a gentle man, one of quiet patience and strength, but there was nothing gentle about him, nothing patient as his tongue thrust between her lips and plunged into her mouth, one hand sliding up behind the back of her head to anchor her tight, the other moving toward her breast. Whimpering in shock, she tried to pull away, backwards, sideways, anywhere, but there was nowhere to escape. His tongue invaded deeper. She couldn't breathe. Couldn't think. She opened her eyes, saw only his cheekbone, his hair, the too-close crescents of his lashes, and then his hand had found her breast, his fingers stroking the nipple through her light coat, rubbing and kneading the sensitive bud until her shock gave way to need and desire, until dampness began to flood the hot junction of her legs, until she began to push upwards, into the sweet force of his mouth, his tongue, *him*—

And then, with no warning, he released her and left her reeling.

Shaken, Ariadne fell back, her eyes wide, her pulse beating in her ears as she stared dazedly up at him. She put a trembling hand to her breast, trying to calm her pounding heart.

"C-colin?"

He impaled her with a glare that was hot, dark, and full of warning. "That is just a taste of what happens when you push a man too far," he said hoarsely, snatching up the reins. "You wish to taunt and tease me? Well, keep at it, then, but I'll not answer to the consequences. Do you understand me, Ariadne?" A muscle jumped in his jaw. "*Do you?*"

"Yes," she breathed, staring fixedly at his mouth and swallowing hard. "I ... understand."

He looked at her for a long, hard moment. She gazed back, wide-eyed and contrite. Unconsciously, she licked her lips, savoring the taste of him, and with a sudden curse, he leapt from the chaise and hauled Shareb's tack out from beneath the seat, bridling the stallion and all but flinging the saddle onto his back before tightening the girth with such quick, sharp, movements that the horse swung fiercely around and struck him, hard, with his teeth.

He gasped, and grimacing, clasped a hand to the shoulder, shutting his eyes in pain.

"Colin!" she cried, leaping out of the chaise.

"Stay in the chaise," he said hoarsely, breathing hard and leaning his brow into the curve of his arm. "Just stay in the bloody chaise, don't move, and for the love of God, don't *ever* ask me to kiss you again."

Chapter Eleven

Ariadne came to her senses just as he swung stiffly aboard Shareb-er-rehh.

"Colin, *don't*!"

Too late.

With a shrill cry, the stallion exploded up and outward, his body twisting, writhing, and coming five feet off the ground before his back heels kicked out in a savage, jarring thrust that sent the animal doctor halfway over his neck.

"Shareb!" she screamed, racing forward.

The stallion hit the earth and reared straight up on his hind legs, higher, higher—

"*Shareb!*"

—and began to go over backward.

Horrified, Ariadne saw it all. Colin, falling from the horse, rolling out of the way a split second before Shareb's big body crashed down into the dirt, and Shareb—landing on his back, his legs flailing, his frightened squeals piercing the air, before he lunged to his feet and stood there, shaking and trembling and blowing hard through his nose.

Ariadne loved her horse—but it was the man on the ground that she ran to.

"Colin! Colin, are you hurt?"

He was lying on his back in the road, his lips parted, his eyes staring up at the stallion. His face was pure white.

"*Colin!*"

As she fell to her knees in the dirt beside him, he moved his head and looked dazedly up at her. "I ... guess that was a bad idea."

She burst into tears, cradled his face in her hands, and buried her forehead in the warm curve of his neck. "For God's sake, he nearly crushed you, you could've been killed, don't you know he has never been ridden by anyone but me, will not tolerate another soul on his back, for heaven's sake, Colin, *he could've killed you!*"

"Kind of you to warn me beforehand," he muttered, ignoring the hand she stretched toward him to help him up. He got painfully to his feet. Then he brushed the dust from his clothes and turning his back on her, limped toward the stallion, leaving Ariadne with her hand still outstretched and her face going crimson with shame and embarrassment.

Shareb saw him coming and shied away, his eyes wild, angry, frightened.

"Easy, there. Easy ..."

Colin put a hand out to the shuddering beast. Again, Shareb tried to shy away, but not before he managed to snare one rein. The stallion reared high once more, legs pawing the air, hooves flashing dangerously close to his head. Colin jerked down, hard, and Shareb plunged to the earth, shied, and nearly tore the bit out of his mouth.

"*Easy!*" he repeated, firmly, and laid his scraped palm against the animal's hot, lathered, neck.

Instantly, the horse quieted. His head drooped, his sides heaved, and he stood there, trembling and shuddering and refusing to look at the man who held him.

Colin heard his employer coming softly up behind him. She wouldn't look at him either, but merely patted her horse, her dusty face streaked with tears and her skin a bright pink. "He's embarrassed," she interpreted, meekly. "He's sorry."

He, or you? Colin wondered.

Shareb lifted one front leg in agreement.

"Yes, he looks very contrite," Colin snapped, his voice cold and angry. He was still shaking inside, and his knees felt like pudding. Keeping his hand on the horse's glistening hide, he passed the reins to his tiny employer. "Hold his head while I make sure he didn't injure himself."

"But what about you?"

"I said, hold him."

Her throat tight, Ariadne took the reins and watched quietly as he stroked the stallion's neck a few more times to steady him. Guilt and shame filled her. The fall had hurt the animal doctor; she could see that in the tightness around his mouth and the way he was dragging his leg, but he, kind soul that he was, was too concerned about the horse to give a thought to his own injuries. She bent her head, and kicked at a stone poking out of the dirt. She should never have asked him to kiss her, should never have tried to satisfy her own curiosity and wicked longings, should never have flirted so shamelessly nor pushed him as far as she had. She glanced up, watching him, her eyes remorseful as he ran gentle hands down Shareb's fine legs, limped painfully to the stallion's far side, and repeated the process there.

"Colin, are you hurt?"

He was kneeling down, inspecting Shareb's uplifted foot. "I'm fine. Though I daresay your saddle didn't fare as well."

"I don't care about the saddle. I care about *you*."

He didn't look up, though she saw a muscle ticking in his jaw as he carefully examined the stallion's foot. He was vexed with her. Not just vexed, but furious.

He stood, raked his hair back over his brow, and, laying a

calming hand on the stallion's throat, gazed levelly, angrily, into her eyes.

"You shouldn't care about me, Ariadne. You shouldn't care a damned bit about me, because you and I are on different paths and the two of them shall never mesh."

"I care about you as a *friend*."

"Be that as it may, your behavior transcends *friendship*."

"But it is totally harmless—"

"You *think* it's harmless. You think it's flirtatious and funny that you have my desire at your mercy, and my insides so twisted up I don't know if I'm coming or going. You know I'm attracted to you, but I dislike your little game. You may think it amusing, but you are not the one having to suffer the pains of deprivation, you are not the one being teased and tempted, you are not the one who has to exert all the will in your body not to do something you'll later regret."

"Colin!"

"Now get in the chaise, and I don't want to hear another word about it."

"But I was only—"

"*Get in the damned chaise!*"

Her face hot with shame, she glanced away—and at the side of the road, saw a flock of sheep lining the perimeter of a stone fence, gazing at the animal doctor with wide-eyed, ovine adoration.

She stared in astonishment.

The veterinarian turned his head to follow her gaze. The animals pressed themselves against the fence as though trying to get closer to him. One let out a soft bleat, then another, and then the rest of the flock followed suit, until the whole group was bleating and baaing.

"Colin?"

He was still gazing at the sheep, beginning to smile a little.

"*Colin!*"

He turned then, shook his head as though to clear it, and looked away. Ariadne stared at him. Again, she sensed the eerie pull that animals felt toward this gentle man, and had a sudden, strange feeling of standing on the fringe of a circle she could never be a part of. Again, she saw him falling from Shareb's back, and the thought of him lying dead, his neck broken, his body crushed, sent a shaft of terror straight through her heart. He was becoming very dear to her, this man. If anything had happened to him ...

Swallowing her injured pride, she reached up with both hands, smoothed his hair back from his temples, and thumbed away a smudge of dirt from his cheek.

"You're hurt, aren't you?"

His eyes suddenly desperate, he caught her wrists in his hands and took a step backwards. "Don't touch me, Ariadne. *Please*."

"But you're hurt."

"I'm fine."

"No, I saw Shareb get your shoulder when he bit you. Let me see it."

"I said, I'm *fine*."

Ariadne got the message. With a sigh, she pulled her hands from his, her heart hurting.

"I'm sorry, Colin. You have asked me not to touch you, and so I shall not." Trying to regain some of her dignity, she turned her head so she wouldn't have to meet his gaze. "I should not have asked you to kiss me. You are a man and men are weak and unable to help themselves. Besides, if anyone were to find out that we kissed, I would be ruined. I deserved to be set in my place and I thank you for doing so."

She raised her chin, trying to command hauteur and failing miserably. Her hands were trembling, her nerves quaking, and she had the awful feeling that he could look into her eyes and read every one of her wicked, wanton thoughts ... and know that she had actually enjoyed the kiss, which, surely, had not been his intent at all. She looked down, pretending a sudden interest in the fabric of her sleeve, and felt tears welling up in the back of her sinuses. "I suppose I shall go straight to Hades for admitting this, but I think I feel drawn to you just as these animals are. That's all it is, isn't it? Animal attraction. Nothing more. I am helpless against it. Just like Shareb, just like Thunder, just like—" she gave a little laugh and jerked her head to indicate the flock of sheep— "like those stupid beasts over there."

Her nose was beginning to run, now, and her sleeve was blurring beneath the gathering tears. She set her jaw in an effort to keep from crying. A long moment passed. And then she heard him clear his throat, and his hand, so warm and strong, reached out to take hers.

"Ariadne."

She passed a knuckle beneath her eye. "What?"

"There is nothing to forgive."

She sucked her lips between her teeth to still their trembling and looked up at him. Her heart ached with guilt, with confusion, with a mad wish to touch him, hold him, and yes, kiss him. But she could not tell him that, could never tell him that. Instead, she sniffed back the tears and accepted the handkerchief he pressed into her hand. "Oh, Colin ... I—I know you probably don't think you're an attractive man, but ... but you are, and maybe some of the things I've done have been because I could not help myself. I did not do them out of a devious wish to torment and tease you."

"I know."

"Do you?"

"Of course. You're ... young. But no good can come of it, Ariadne. You said it yourself. We are as alike as—" he grinned, more handsome than he had a right to be, and she felt her chest constrict with a raw, unfulfilled ache that twisted her heart like a dishrag— "the digestive systems of the dog and horse."

"Oh, Colin... ."

With a forgiving little smile he held out his arms, and she

went into them, their hard, gentle strength pressing her close to his heart. She shut her eyes over a film of tears, the clean scent of his shirt and skin filling her nostrils, his heart beating beneath her cheek. *I don't want Maxwell,* she thought, desperately. *Dear God help me, but I want you.*

But that was impossible, and as she sensed the stiffness in his stance, she realized she'd stayed within his embrace a second longer than what either of them might've considered proper.

"Your shoulder," she said, shakily, pulling back and pushing a stray lock of hair out of her eyes. "I'm sorry, I hope I didn't just hurt you—"

He grinned, trying to lessen the awkwardness of the moment. "Not that you could. That fool horse of yours, on the other hand …"

"I think you should let me look at it. I feel horribly guilty—I mean, if it weren't for me, Shareb would never have bitten you."

"Shareb has been itching for an excuse to bite me since we first met. Don't blame yourself."

"Let me look at it. If only to satisfy my own conscience."

He frowned, but her hands were already at the closure of his shirt. She tilted her head back and looked up at him. "Please, Colin?"

He shrugged in answer and looked away, his eyes dark with pain.

With trembling fingers, she undid the top buttons of his shirt. She drew it down and off his shoulder, her hands tender, gentle, shaking, barely grazing his skin as they moved over his collarbone and to the bruised area.

He shut his eyes and drew a ragged breath, and beside them, Shareb twisted his neck and watched.

"He says he's sorry," Ariadne said quickly, trying to take their attention off what she was doing.

"Does he, now?"

"Yes. He says he's not *happy* about having to apologize, but since you did not punish him for trying to kill you he thinks he should act with reciprocal gentlemanly behavior."

Colin looked at the stallion.

Shareb bared his teeth.

"How magnanimous of him."

"Yes, I rather thought so, myself."

"And what does Thunder think of all this?"

"Oh, Thunder doesn't think," she said, dismissing the old gelding with a casual wave of her hand. "He's just a horse."

"And Shareb is not?"

"Well of course he is, but he's *special*."

He looked down at her, his eyes soft. "All of God's creatures are special, no matter what their looks, their character ... or their breeding."

No matter what their looks, their character ... or their breeding.

Roses bloomed in her cheeks, and his gentle reprimand made her feel small and mean. He didn't mean that statement, she knew, to apply to just horses. It was meant to apply to people as well.

She glanced at the old, broken-down horse. It had dark, soft eyes, and was gazing at her with infinite sadness.

Lud, it was uncanny, the way the animal was looking at her. Almost ... accusingly.

"You are correct, Colin," she agreed, and unable to face the gelding's mournful eyes, turned her attention to the doctor's shoulder. She felt his breath in her hair as he bent his head, trying to see the spot where Shareb had struck him. Her fingers began to tremble madly, and she heard the old horse take a step or two forward, as though it wanted to protect its savior.

Ariadne pulled the shirt away—and knew she'd made a mistake as soon as his chest was bared to her gaze.

She saw the soft, sparse hair there, light brown and tickly against her fingertips. She saw slabs of muscle, sharp and defined across his chest, flat and tapered where they embraced his ribs.

She saw his chest rising and falling with his breath, saw the pulse beating at the base of his throat—and saw the purple bruise in the cup of his shoulder where Shareb's teeth had broken the blood vessels.

She looked up at him, her eyes very wide. "Ouch," she said.

He smiled, tentatively, though she sensed the tension in his body, the emotions that raged through him at her soft touch. "Ouch."

She held his gaze for a long moment. Then, she lifted her hand, put her lips against her palm, and turning it outward, pressed it tenderly against the injured area.

"Ariadne." He shut his eyes, shuddered, and took a deep, steadying breath. "You ... said you would not touch me."

"This is my way of kissing it and making it better."

He opened his eyes, and in them was a desperate plea. Whether it was for her to keep her hand there or remove it, she did not know. Did not *want* to know... .

Softly, she said, "I can feel your heart beating, Colin. Tha-dump, tha-dump, tha-dump." Her thumb grazed his chest, and she saw its wide expanse grow shimmery behind the tears that sprang up in her eyes all over again. "A few more inches, and Shareb would have crushed you and silenced that heartbeat forever. You have become very dear to me, Colin. I don't think I could've borne it, if Shareb had fallen atop you."

"Indeed, I don't think I could have, either," he said wryly. "He outweighs me by about sixty stone."

She looked up and found him perusing her with amusement. The depth of naked desire she saw in his face unnerved her, and recovering herself, she snatched her hand away from him, closed his shirt and fumbled with the buttons. Every fiber of her being wanted to go into his arms and beg him to kiss her once again; every part of her ached to be close to him. The pain of denial was real, and unbearable. How unfair, this attraction for a man she could never have and should never want.

"Come," she said, giving a false little laugh to disguise the ache. "You ride in the chaise and I'll ride Shareb. That way, I won't be tempted to touch you and you won't be tempted to touch me in return, and nothing can happen between us, right?"

"That is the wisest idea you've had all day," he said, his gaze lingering on her face for a long, searching moment. Then he turned abruptly and climbed back into the chaise. But as he picked up the reins and clucked for Thunder to move, his countenance mirrored the raw agony she felt in her own heart at being away from him—and she cried inside at the fates that had separated them by class and circumstance.

Tristan, Lord Weybourne, pushed open the door to the coaching inn, shoved his way through the crowded, smoke-filled room, peeled off his gloves, and threw himself down at the nearest table. His throat was dry with road dust, his stomach churned with emptiness, his fine clothes were damp with sweat, and he was nursing a headache of thunderous proportions.

Putting his elbows on the table, he bent his forehead to his hands and kneaded his aching temples.

"Hello, handsome."

He looked up, and into the face of a buxom serving maid.

"Name's Meg," she said brightly, tucking a yellow curl behind her ear. "What'll it be today, luv? A good pint of ale? Something to fill yer stomach and stick to yer ribs?"

"Ale, and whatever's on the menu."

She nodded and wound her way through the patrons, deflecting a groping hand here, saucily responding to a jibe there. A moment later she was back, a plate in one hand and a foamy mug in the other. "Should've been here a few hours ago," she said, setting the food before him. "Missed all the excitement, ye did!"

Tristan didn't bother responding to her attempt to draw him into conversation. His mind was elsewhere.

The woman persisted. "'Twas quite the scene, I tell ye! Some fellow calling himself a veteran—" she frowned, cocked her head, tapped her tooth with a long nail— "vettanar — Oh, never mind, it don't matter none. Animal doctor! Aye, that's what he was, an animal doctor. Had breakfast here with his little brother, then went outside an' laid John Beckett out senseless! And all for bleedin' a horse. Can ye imagine?"

"No," Tristan said flatly. He lifted his mug, closing his eyes as the cool, foamy liquid slid down his parched throat. By his calculations, Ariadne was probably a third of the way to Norfolk by now. Pain and terror washed through him at the thought, and he felt a fresh wave of cold sweat break out along his spine. By God, he had to catch up to her and that horse before—

"Oh, 'twas something to see, it was! Such a quiet and gentle-looking man, who would've thought he had such fire in him? Some people, ye never know ..."

"No, I suppose you don't. If you'll please excuse me—"

"Had a fine lookin' horse with him though, and now he has two. Matched bays, though the broken-down old gelding he saved from the bleedin'—now what did he call it? A flu-bottomy. Aye, that's what it was, *flu-bottomy*—can't hold a candle to that fiery stallion he came in with. Gorgeous horse. Simply gorgeous."

Something clicked in Tristan's brain. He set the mug down and looked up, his eyes narrowing. "Fiery stallion?"

"Oh, aye. Grand looking animal, though ye couldn't see much of it beneath all the trappings they had on it. Legs all bandaged up, blanket on its back, and the strangest hood on its head, covering most of its face an' little cups over its eyes. Big chest, though. Long, long legs, rather like a racer's—"

Rather like a racer's.

Tristan's hand shot out and grabbed the maid's arm.

"Did it have a white blaze down the front of its face?"

She knuckled her brow, thinking. "Well, now ... aye, as a matter of fact, it did. Couldn't see much of it, though, what with that hood they had on him, but aye, I do recall 'e had a white muzzle—"

"How tall?"

"Oh, maybe sixteen, sixteen an' a half hands?"

"His eye—" Tristan was gripping the maid's arm almost cruelly. "Was his right eye ringed with white?"

"Oh, don't know about that, luv, 'twas dark last night when they got here and what with all the excitement this morn, I really couldn't tell ye. Only caught a good look at the horse this morning; the little brother was up at dawn and took it out for a hard gallop. Runs fast, that horse. *Real* fast. The laddie came back and fed it a piece of apple pie and then—listen to this!—shared a mug of ale with it. Imagine, a horse that craves apple pie and *ale*! I've never seen the like—"

Tristan leapt to his feet, grabbed his hat, slammed a coin down on the table, and nearly knocking over an incoming traveler, ran for the door. "Which way did they go?"

She folded her arms and pointed up the road.

"North. Toward Norfolk."

Chapter Twelve

After spending eight miles alone in the chaise, with only the two dogs for company, Colin found that physical separation from the little noblewoman was no release from temptation or torment, and as storm clouds began to sweep in from the west and low, angry rumblings of thunder sounded from far off in the distance, he felt the weather's growing turmoil reflected in his own heart.

Granted, he did not have to suffer the exquisite anguish of having her leg bumping against his with every movement of the horse, didn't have to counter her bald compliments, didn't have to inhale her sweet scent or fight the impulse to kiss pretty pink lips that seemed to always be smiling at him, laughing at him, teasing him, but torture could—and did—come in many forms, all of them equally painful. It came in watching her sitting astride that stallion of hers with all the elegance and dignity of Joan of Arc. It came in gazing at the taut curve of her buttocks, and watching the play of her muscles beneath her breeches; it came in listening to the sound of her laughter, fantasizing that her smile really *was* for him, and biting back the unreasonable jealousy he felt every time she mentioned the name *Maxwell*.

"I am damned," he muttered, tearing his gaze from her back and glaring over Thunder's tail and plodding haunches. "Damned and double-damned."

Bow put her paws on his chest and licked his face, and one of Thunder's ears went back, listening. Even Shareb-er-rehh, walking just ahead of them, turned his head, the white ring around his right eye lending him an expression of high amusement.

"Colin?" His employer pulled the stallion up, allowing Thunder to catch up with them. "Did you hear me? I do wish you could coax some speed out of that horse. We'll never get to Norfolk at this rate."

"Thunder is old, tired and sore. I don't wish to push him."

"Yes, well if he ends up being responsible for Shareb's loss and my capture, don't expect that twelve thousand pounds."

Overhead, thick, dark clouds were sliding in over the hills to the west, the late afternoon sunlight painting slivers of orange against their ominous black bellies. A gust of wind rustled the leaves of a nearby oak tree, and from off in the distance came the low rumble of thunder.

Colin raised a brow at her petulant words and slanted her a chastising look. Immediately, her face went pink with embarrassment. "I'm sorry, Colin—there I go, sounding mean again. I hope you can forgive me, but the deprivations of this adventure are contriving to wreak havoc on my nerves."

"Of course."

"Don't you think we should find a place to wait out the storm, and possibly stay for the night?"

Colin's leg was throbbing incessantly. He reached down, kneading the deep ache with his fingers as she rode just beside the chaise.

"Colin? Did you hear me?"

"Yes, of course. I was just thinking, that's all."

"About what?"

"About ... tonight's sleeping arrangements and what to do about them."

"Oh." Her cheeks reddened a bit, but the familiar sparkle lit her eye. She reached down to poke his shoulder with her crop. "You mean you're not going to let me soothe your aching muscles and play with your pretty hair again, Doctor?"

"We already discussed that. No touching."

She ruffled his hair with the end of her crop. "I wouldn't dream of it."

Grinning, he deflected the whip with his elbow. "And what do you call that?"

"You didn't say I couldn't touch you with my crop."

He shook his head, torn between exasperation, desperation, and desire.

"Or," she continued, kicking her foot free of the stirrup iron and resting her toe on his shoulder, "my boot."

"Stop flirting."

She smirked. "I'm not."

"You are."

She put her foot back in the iron and gaped at him with exaggerated shock. "Really, Colin, that is *not* gentlemanly, to accuse a lady of such a thing! Although it is, of course, true. I cannot help but flirt, though I suppose I shall probably roast in the fires of hell for my wickedness."

As if in answer, a long, low rumble issued from the incoming clouds, and Ariadne instantly sobered. She frowned, looking at the green pastures as they grew dark and silent with the approach of the storm. Even the air seemed tight with tension, and now, a gust of wind drove across the land, pulling ripples from the surface of a small, nearby pond. Little Bow whined and hid her face in the cup of Colin's shoulder.

"Yes, I think you're right," he said, cradling the shivering little dog to his chest and soothing her with gentle fingers in her fur. At his feet, the newly-christened Marc pressed close, also growing uneasy, and making him wonder if the dog was gun-shy as well as unwilling to hunt, which would certainly explain his former master's eagerness to be rid of him. "We'd best look for a place to stop now, before the storm is upon us."

"Not a coaching inn, I hope! Oh, how I despise them, someone will surely recognize Shareb and me, I just know it. And my horrid, degenerate, wastrel of a brother ... he's out here, Colin." She waved her crop to indicate the darkening hills, the road ahead and behind them. "He's out there, and he won't stop until he finds me."

Again, the thunder rolled, deep and dark and ominous.

"Yes, I've been giving considerable thought to the problem of Shareb-er-rehh's disguise. To be safe, I think it's time to alter it a bit, just in case any of the people we've encountered have put two and two together and realized he's the horse the whole country-side is searching for."

"Alter it? How?"

"With some mud or grease to cover that white blaze of his. And maybe some dye around his fetlocks, to conceal the white coronets and stocking and make his legs appear solid black."

"Dye? *Mud*? On my noble Shareb?" She gave a little laugh. "Oh, Doctor, that would be horribly degrading for him—"

"He'll survive."

"But—"

Another long, warning growl of thunder came from over the hills, and the sky went the color of ink. Raindrops began tumbling down and gusts of wind drove Shareb's mane over Ariadne's fists. The stallion began to snort and blow, nervous about the approaching storm.

"Don't look so woeful," Colin chided, "it will only be tempo-rary. But in order to get that horse safely to Norfolk we must constantly alter his disguise. After all—" he gestured to the empty road behind them, and the black clouds that were bearing down on them— "you don't know who may be tracking us."

She nodded, seeing the wisdom of his decision.

"Very well then, Doctor. Let's be about it, then."

THEY FOUND a printer in the next village. While Ariadne waited anxiously outside, Colin—ignoring the raised brows of the proprietor—purchased a large quantity of black ink, which the kindly, but perplexed man supplied to him in a wooden bucket. Carefully placing it on the floor of the chaise, Colin jumped in and sent Thunder hurrying on, hoping to find refuge before the storm hit.

Refuge came in the form of a pub up the road, which had a barn and stables attached.

Hurriedly making arrangements to stable the horses, Colin returned to the darkening paddock where Lady Ariadne waited with a fretful Shareb-er-rehh and the two nervous dogs.

"Time to get this disguise in place," he said cheerfully, trying to banish both the darkness of the day—and the darkness in her face. It was obvious she was none too happy about putting ink, or mud, on her beloved horse. Well, he wasn't either—but some things were for the best.

"And just how are we supposed to get ink out of Shareb's fetlocks, once we get him safely to Norfolk?" she asked, sulkily, as Colin led the horse beneath the shelter of a lean-to and placed the bucket in the dirt beside him.

"I have a special soap in my trunk that removes just about anything."

"Yes, and it will probably remove his hair as well. I'm warning you, Colin, that if Shareb suffers any ill effects from this—"

"Ariadne," he said tersely, "What is more important? Keeping Shareb safe or keeping his blaze pristine white?"

"Well, keeping him safe, of course ... ."

She looked hurt, and Colin immediately felt the stab of guilt for raising his voice, but why couldn't she just trust him, just a little?

He removed the leg bandages and looked at Shareb's long legs. A true bay, the horse's black stockings started at the knees and hocks and ran down to the hooves—where they were broken by distinctive bands of white in the form of tiny coronets on the front legs, and on this right rear one, a half-sock. All would have to go, so that the legs appeared totally black. He dipped a rag into the ink and touched it carefully to the white anklet.

"I promise you, Ariadne, it *will* come out. Now, please hold him, would you? I don't like the way those ears of his are coming back ..."

"Yes, and *he* doesn't like the indignity of what you're doing to him."

"Too bad," Colin said, working the ink into the white half-stocking. "He'll just have to suffer until further notice."

COLIN HEARD the fiddler long before he and Ariadne, trailed by the two dogs, entered the pub, and its haunting melody was enough to make him forget all about his current troubles.

Inside, the room was teeming with travelers, all laughing and drinking and hoping to escape the deluge that was about to pour out of the heavens outside. A fire crackled in the hearth, a game of backgammon was in full swing with a dozen people clustered around one table, and the air was thick with the pungent scents of smoke, sweat, and grease. The din was so loud that he couldn't hear himself think.

But still, he heard the fiddle.

Didn't *want* to hear the fiddle—

"Oh, listen!" Lady Ariadne exclaimed in delight. She pointed to the old man who sat in a stool near the hearth, the fiddle against his cheek as he pounded out a rollicking old sea chantey. "Isn't he grand?"

Colin pushed the hair off his brow, his hand shaking. The music went straight to his heart, settling there with a deep, raw ache that spread to the farthest reaches of his very soul. He didn't have to see the tattoo on the old salt's arm, didn't have to spot the out-of-fashion queue hanging down his back, didn't have to recognize the chantey he pulled from the willing old fiddle, to know the man had been a sailor.

Pain swept through him and memories that, even after five years, were still too fresh and raw to be delved into. *She*, walking just behind him, was never aware of it. But the old fiddler was. He looked up after finishing the tune, and as the tavern erupted in applause, cheers, and loud calls for more, his gaze caught Colin's and something deep and unspoken passed between them.

The old man knew. Maybe it was in the way that Colin walked, maybe it was in his military bearing, maybe it was just the look on his face as the two stared at each other; maybe the old man had seen him piped aboard some ship five, maybe ten years ago, with ceremony and respect, and remembered his unusual lavender eyes and blond hair, though it had been paler then from the constant bleach of the sun, or maybe he simply sensed a kindred spirit who would never again feel the freedom of sea and wind and sky but would never stop longing for it. Nevertheless, he *knew*, and as Colin passed, the old man touched his forelock in a gesture of respect.

"Evenin', Cap'n," he said, soberly.

Colin gave a brief nod, and hoped the man's words had been lost on his companion.

They had.

"Dr. Lord, I find this establishment most disagreeable!" she hissed, pressing close to him. "It reeks of sweat and smoke, the din is horrific, and I'm worried about Shareb."

As if to punctuate her remark, thunder rolled from the

heavens outside, though the brunt of its roar was lost amidst the noisiness of the tavern.

"Yes ..."

"Colin?" She caught his sleeve and peered up at him. "Are you well?"

He gave a pained grin and turned his back to the fiddle, wishing he could turn his back on the memories it evoked, as well. "Yes, I'm fine," he assured her. "And stop worrying about that damned horse."

"I cannot help it!"

"Do you want me to go out and hold a parasol over him to shield his noble head from the threatening raindrops?"

"Oh, very funny. I *still* think he should've been put in their stable, not out in a paddock!"

"You heard the man, the stable is full. He'll be fine in the paddock, and there is shelter for him. Besides, we shan't tarry long here."

"Colin, I do wish you'd tell me what has upset you so—"

"I'm not upset."

"You are. I can see it in your eyes, even though you're trying hard to hide it. Is it anything I've done? I mean, I have been so very good, and have not even flirted with or touched you for the past hour."

He looked down at her. Her bright eyes were worried, her piquant little face distressed. "No, Ariadne," he said, softly. "It's not you. It's just ..."

"Just what?"

He guided her toward a table near the fire. "Ghosts from my past."

He slid behind a group of travelers involved in a dispute about the benefits of horse versus cow manure as fertilizer, and onto a bench seat along the wall. Outside, lightning flashed purple through the windows and glazed the rolling hills as the storm moved closer and closer. Bow jumped up into his lap, trembling, and against his feet the gun-dog, Marc, pressed, beginning to pant in fear. And still, came the strains of the fiddle—haunting, sad, and bringing back too many memories.

Too much guilt.

She took the seat across from him, perching on its edge with stiff-backed, ladylike grace, and stared at him.

He looked at her and raised a brow.

"I worry about you," she said. "You are so very ... aloof, sometimes. And when your eyes look sad, I can't help but be sad, too." She reached out and touched his hand. "I'm sorry if I hurt your feelings with my remarks about Thunder slowing us down. I know he is very special to you, and I should never have said that."

He smiled, helpless against her natural charm. "You have done nothing wrong. Don't trouble yourself over me."

"Truthfully, I think you are very brave for stepping in and saving the animal as you did. You have won my eternal and undying admiration."

Her words brought the smile into his eyes at last. "Eternal and undying."

"Forever."

"Ariadne?"

"Yes?"

"I suggest you slouch a bit, as you are attracting the attention of the poor fool sitting ten feet behind you."

"Oh!"

Her eyes glinting with conspiracy, she slid down in her seat, tucked a lock of red hair up under the cap, and duplicating him, lazily placed her arm over the back of the adjacent chair. "Better?"

"Much."

"Lud, next you'll be telling me to belch and scratch!"

"Well, come to think of it, it probably wouldn't be a bad idea ..."

"Dr. Lord!" She grabbed up a napkin and playfully tossed it at him. "What an utterly heinous suggestion!"

He laughed, enjoying her exaggerated shock, and she laughed right along with him. Their gazes met, held, and the unspoken attraction that passed between them caused them both to look away. Colin cleared his throat and wiped up a ring of moisture with the napkin; Ariadne thrust her hands into her lap and glanced out the window.

He followed her gaze. Thunder, being a gelding, had been safely turned out with the other horses who had arrived too late to be given space in the stable, and stood happily munching hay with a crowd of mares whose allure he was totally oblivious to.

Too bad the same couldn't be said of that damned stallion.

Shareb-er-rehh, confined to a small paddock with a lean-to shed, had thoughts for nothing *but* the mares. His head high, his nostrils flaring, and his tail flung jauntily over his back, he made a magnificent sight as he galloped back and forth along the fence that separated him from the other horses. As they watched, he let out a long, piercing scream, skidded in the dirt at the end of his short space, wheeled, reared, and raced back the way he had come.

"Oh, look at him, Colin!" Ariadne said, nose pressed to the window. She paid no attention to the maid who brought them tea, a pitcher of milk, and cakes. "He's showing off for those mares!"

Lightning flashed down, splitting the sky and washing the paddock and buildings in violet. The clouds grew darker.

Blacker.

The rain would come down, any minute now ...

"I'm afraid, Ariadne, that it is not just the mares he is trying to impress, but a rival for their attention." Colin sniffed the milk to ensure its freshness before pouring some into each of their teacups, then pointed toward another paddock, opposite the stable. "Look."

There, also confined, was the real reason for Shareb's challenging display; a huge, glossy red-chestnut steed with fire in its eye and fury in its stance.

Another stallion.

Colin sipped his tea, thankful for the fence that separated the two horses.

"Yes, but look at Shareb! Isn't he beautiful? It's the desert blood in him, you know. He wants to fight. He is pure fire, pure magnificence. Everything a horse should be."

Desert blood?

Lightning flashed down again, and the two stallions screamed threats and challenges to each other across the small field that separated them. Inside that field the mares lifted their heads and began to mill nervously.

Thunder kept on eating.

Now the red stallion began to prance and pace the length of his fence, calling insults to Shareb. Shareb responded with a shrill scream. Then his ears swept back, he galloped across his paddock—

And a brilliant flash of lightning forked out of the clouds.

The timing couldn't have been worse. Colin saw it all: Shareb, bolting sideways as the resulting crack of thunder split the sky just overhead, wheeling, then plunging straight for the fence, where he paused for only the briefest of seconds before leaping the tall enclosure like Pegasus on the wing; then, without breaking stride, he tore across the grassy field and bore down on his rival at a speed that nearly burned the grass up beneath his hooves.

"Stallion fight!" shouted one of the patrons, and everyone ran toward the door on a mass exodus.

Colin was already on his feet and racing from the tavern. With Ariadne hot on his heels, he charged toward the paddocks, knowing he'd never make it in time. Shareb's challenging scream split the air, and he saw the stallion hurl himself straight into the chestnut's fence, heard the horrible crash of breaking wood and the other horse's enraged squeal as it rose to meet Shareb's attack. There was the awful sound of heavy bodies slamming together, hooves hitting flesh, squeals and screams and angry whistles, and over it all, the boom of thunder at close range.

"Get that damned bugger off my horse!" a balding man cried, running past them with a pitchfork. "So help me God, I'll kill him!"

He paused, drew back his arm to hurl the pitchfork—and faltered as a tiny ball of salt-colored fur flung itself at him.

Bow.

But Colin had no time to grab his pet, no time to warn Ariadne back, no time to respond to the enraged man's cries as he tried to fend off the little dog. The stallions were fighting with savage, murderous fury, and the chestnut was getting the worst of it.

"Colin!" he heard Ariadne cry, "get them apart!"

He raced past the mares. Their heads were thrust over the fence as they happily watched the two stallions fighting over them, and he could almost hear them cheering on their favorite. Grabbing up a broken piece of fencing and heedless of the danger, he dove between the two enraged animals, brandishing the wood like a club.

The chestnut, already losing the fight, bolted away to the side, his neck streaming blood where Shareb's teeth had found purchase. Colin threw down the board and made a wild lunge for Shareb's halter—but the stallion's blood was up, fire was in his eyes, and without breaking stride, he turned, crashed back through the fence, and with lightning glowing against his flying body, galloped out of the broken paddock—

—and straight toward an elegant gray horse just entering the yard, whose handler screamed and dived out of the way as Shareb charged toward them.

In horror, Colin realized the newcomer was a mare.

There was nothing he could do to stop it, and he saw it all. The mare, flinging up her head in alarm as the mighty stallion bore down on her at a speed Colin would never have believed had he not seen it with his own eyes; her handler, fleeing for his life; and Shareb, teeth bared, neck outstretched, earth, grass and thunder flying from his hooves.

Shareb gave a piercing scream, nipped the mare's rump as he galloped past, and tail high, thundered out of the yard and down the road at a speed so intense it was almost frightening. The mare, whinnying like a barmaid in love, went charging off after him, lead rope flying.

"Colin! Colin, *do* something!" Ariadne cried, her jacket flapping open as she raced up to him with Bow in her arms and Marc racing ahead.

But there was nothing that he could do. The stallion was gone. The landlord was barreling toward them, already screaming for recompense for the damage to his fence. And now the first drops of rain were beginning to pelt the earth, gathering in force, frenzy, and fury, and Colin found himself stuck with a geriatric gelding, two frightened dogs, and some thirty men who were all staring at Ariadne's distinctively lovely chest.

He turned, and looked bleakly at Thunder.

The gelding was still munching his hay.

"Time to go," he said, and spinning Ariadne around and shoving her toward the barn, ran to get the horse.

Chapter Thirteen

The long legs. The unusually deep chest. The sloping, powerful hip, the great lay-back of the shoulder, and the speed.

Especially, the speed.

After witnessing that blistering display of pure lightning out of the courtyard, Colin now knew the truth. Shareb-er-rehh was no high-stepping riding horse. He was no carriage horse, pleasure horse, or lady's pet.

He was a racehorse.

A damned *fast* racehorse.

And now, an hour and a half after he'd made his blazing escape, he was still missing.

With Colin leading Thunder and Ariadne walking on the gelding's other side, they trudged through the drizzle, Colin tracking the stallion by his fading hoofprints, Ariadne gripping Shareb's lead shank like a nun with her rosary beads, both of them huddled in their coats and neither of them saying much. Marc ran on ahead, chasing a rabbit, while Bow, her fur wet, tangled and muddy, trotted at Colin's heels; every so often she, like Colin, shot a worried glance at Lady Ariadne. The little noblewoman's face was white and strained, and only the dictates of her breeding and upbringing prevented her from giving in to the tears Colin knew lurked just beneath the surface.

It was that same threat of tears that kept him from confronting her.

No gait-horse at all, but a racehorse.

It hurt and angered him that she had lied to him. That she had not trusted him. Who did she think she was fooling? How long had she expected to keep a horse like that hidden under a disguise?

But the raw misery on her face was enough to do him in, and for now, he'd hold his tongue.

She paused for the tenth time in as many minutes to cup her hands over her mouth and call the stallion.

"Shar-e-e-e-e-e-eb!"

Colin stopped, too, listening to her voice echo emptily over the green hills. Only the rain answered, coming down harder now and obliterating the awful silence.

"*Shar-e-e-e-e-e-e-eb!*"

Nothing.

"Come, Ariadne. Let's keep moving."

Ignoring him, she called the stallion one last time, her voice rising in desperation and cracking under the strain; then she wiped at her eyes, jerked her chin up, and trudged along beside him.

"He's gone, Colin," she said miserably. "Someone must have stolen him and turned him in for the reward. If he was out here, he would have come to me."

"Now, now," Colin said soothingly, walking just to the side of the long, muddy puddles that pooled in the wheel-ruts. "We still have another two hours of daylight. And rain or not, *I'm* not ready to give up."

She shot him a watery look. "Oh, Colin... I don't know what I would do without you."

"You'd still be dilly-dallying in London," he teased, trying to coax some humor back into her. Bravely, she tried to smile, but he saw her face crumple, and she looked quickly away before he could witness her loss of composure.

They continued on. A black-and-maroon mail coach thundered toward them, its wheels spraying great arcs of muddy water as it tore through the puddles, the scarlet-clad guard clinging for dear life to the back of the coach; then the vehicle was past, the team of horses that drew it sending up great clods of muck from their galloping hooves.

Silence, and the sound of the rain once more.

Colin stole a sideways glance at his companion. The lead shank drooped from her hand, her feet dragged in the mud, and her eyes were vacant and staring. Gone was the piquant vibrancy of her personality, the sparkle in her eye, the saucy, snappy spirit that had so captivated him.

"We'll not find him tonight, Colin," she said bleakly, pointing at the empty road ahead of them. The mail coach had obliterated most of the stallion's tracks, and what was left of them were fading, the edges cut by his shoes growing blunter and blunter as the rain hammered them into mud. And then, as though nature itself was against them, the skies opened up and the rain came down in cruel, slashing torrents that ran like tears down Ariadne's cheeks. Maybe they *were* tears; at this point, it was impossible for Colin to tell.

Moments later, all that was left of Shareb-er-rehh's tracks were washed away into puddles of mud.

Ariadne stopped and bowed her head against the rain, her shoulders slumped in defeat as the torrents beat cruelly down on the back of her head and neck.

For Colin, it was too much. Blinking against the deluge that slashed his face, he took off his coat, tenderly wrapped it around her head and shoulders, and fashioned a sort of hood out of it to protect her from the rain as she stared miserably up at him. Then he took Thunder's bridle in one hand, drew the noblewoman into the protection of his other arm, and half carrying her, ran as fast as his bad leg would allow to a grove of oak trees.

There they stood, relatively sheltered by the canopy of leafy branches above their heads, the two dogs huddled around their feet. Around them, the rain came down in torrents, then white sheets of fury, beating against the earth with such force that steam began to rise from the grass. The drumming roar obliterated all sound, and instinctively, Ariadne huddled closer to the veterinarian, seeking shelter beneath his arm.

She looked up at him. His hair was plastered to his head and curling loosely at its ends. Water dripped down his brow, clumped on his lashes, trickled down his cheeks. His wet shirt clung to his body, emphasizing the muscles of his arms and chest.

Even soaked, he was beautiful.

He sensed her staring and glanced down, an encouraging little smile playing about his mouth. She smiled hesitantly back, and moved closer to the steamy warmth of his body. He made no protest, merely watching the mad torrents bombard the earth around them and keeping his arm wrapped securely around her shoulders. A part of her wished he would keep his arm there forever, and closing her eyes, she laid her cheek against his wet shirt. It occurred to her that she had not had to resort to flirting, to *bad behavior* as Father would have called it, to gain his attention. It occurred to her that his kindness wasn't just for animals, as her father's had been, but for others, as well.

For her.

Somewhere out there in the rain was Shareb; but sheltered by Colin's body, comforted by his presence, Ariadne's fears began to subside, and as she'd done when she had first seen him saving the mastiff from bloat, she relinquished her fears and placed all her trust in him. They would find Shareb. The doctor would make sure of it.

❦

SHE OPENED HER EYES. The roar of the rain faded to a dull thrum, then individual spatters against the leaves, leaving the exhausted earth to catch its breath in gratitude.

Colin's arm was still around her shoulders. She knew she should step away now that the rain had tapered off and his gallant protection was no longer necessary. But she did not move, and neither did he, and at last, the rain was only a soft, lulling drip as it trickled from the leaves overhead.

From somewhere nearby a songbird called, then another.

And still, Ariadne did not move.

She laid her palm against his chest, then her cheek against the back of her hand, and stared off over the green, green hills. Beneath her hand, she felt his heart beating.

"Colin."

He cleared his throat. "Yes?"

"You are very kind, giving me your coat as you did."

He leaned his head back against the tree trunk, letting the rain drops splash against his upturned face and smiling with the enjoyment of the sensation. "Oh, I think any gentleman would have done the same."

"I know plenty that would not have," she returned. She studied the intricate weave of his shirt, thought of the strong body it clung to, listened to and loved every precious beat of his heart. God help her, but she wanted to peel the wet shirt off of him and bury her lips in the hair that sparsely covered his chest; God help her, but she wanted to stand on tiptoe and kiss the damp skin at the base of his throat; God help her, but if she never saw Maxwell again, she really wouldn't care as long as she could be with Colin Lord.

I don't want to go to Norfolk. I don't want to marry Maxwell. I want this *man.*

"Colin?"

She felt his heartbeat quickening beneath her palm. "Yes?"

"Do you think it's wrong, that we're standing here as we are, with your arm around me and me enjoying every moment of it?"

"You're not the only one enjoying it, Ariadne."

She colored a bit, and looked earnestly up at him. "*Is* it wrong, Colin?"

"I don't know anymore. Wrong it may be, but if feels *right*."

"Yes.... I daresay that is what I was thinking, too. That it feels right." She sighed, and inhaled deeply of his clean, wet, male scent. "You are very dear to me, Colin. I only wish ..."

His arm curled around her back, and she felt his gentle hand against her shoulders, pressing her body closer to his. "You only wish what?"

"I wish that ... things could be different, I guess. That you were Maxwell. I—oh, Lud, I know that sounds terrible, but I don't know any other way to put it."

He said nothing, only holding her tightly and allowing her to continue. Rain dripped from the trees, and the grass sparkled in the brightening, late afternoon sunlight.

"That one kiss he gave me, " she said softly, remembering. "It was out in the garden at Lady Andrea's soiree. We stepped out for a breath of fresh air after a particularly strenuous round of dancing. He put his lips against my cheek, and he kissed me. But do you know something, Colin?" She looked up at him, her eyes confused, sad. "It didn't make me *feel* anything."

He gazed down at her, his face troubled. A drop of rain fell from the leaves above, hit his eyelashes.

"I would have thought that since Maxwell is to be my husband, that his kiss should have made me feel happy, thrilled, eager for more. But it didn't. It was—cold." She stared into his face, her eyes wide, desperate. "The kisses of your future husband are not supposed to make you feel cold, are they, Colin?"

Carefully, he said, "I shouldn't think so."

She laid her cheek against his wet shirt and stared dismally off over the darkening hills. "I suppose that if I had nothing to compare Maxwell's kiss to, I wouldn't be so worried. Perhaps this whole matter would not trouble me so much if I hadn't kissed *you*. When *we* kissed, it was entirely different from when I kissed Maxwell. With you—" she blushed, and gave a sad little smile—"it was ... different. I wanted more."

Beneath her cheek, his heart was beating fast. Faster. He swallowed hard, and as she pulled away to look up at him, he gazed down at her, his eyes holding hers for a long, searching moment, before his hand came up to gently caress her cheek.

"Yes," he said, softly, and she shut her eyes as his lips grazed her forehead. "So did I."

"I'm sorry, Colin. It may be horribly vulgar, but I have always been one to say exactly how I feel. I don't mean to embarrass you."

"No, no. I am not embarrassed. Actually, I'm ... rather flattered."

She pulled back and looked up at him. "Flattered?"

"Well, of course. It is not every day that a lonely old sod like me hears a beautiful lady confess that she finds his kisses exciting."

"You're not an old sod! For heaven's sake, you're what, twenty-five? Twenty-eight?"

"Thirty-three."

"Well, you look younger. It's the spectacles, I think, even though you don't wear them very often. Or maybe it's your youthful face, or your teasing grin. Plus, you're not paunchy like so many other older men—"

"For God's sake, Ariadne, I'm not an older man!"

"Well, I didn't mean it *that* way," she said, quickly. "How is it that here I'm trying to tell you that I enjoyed your kiss more than I did my future husband's, and we get into a row about older men?"

"Truly, I don't know. But what I *do* know is that if your future husband were to see you standing here with your cheek against my chest, he would be inclined to call me out."

"Oh, no, Colin, I would never let you duel over me. I'm not like some of those other women who like to have men fighting over them. If you ever got hurt—"

He sighed, his eyes twinkling. "First she thinks me an older man. Now she doubts my prowess with sword and pistol. Dear God, what will it be next?"

Ariadne laughed and drew back, still keeping her arms wrapped around his waist. "Oh, Colin. You always know just what to say to make me feel better. You have made me laugh in one of the darkest hours of my life."

"Well then, before that hour grows any darker," he said lightly, as the green faded from the hills and the shadows grew long, "shall we use what time we have left to try to find that confounded stallion of yours?"

He offered his hand, and she took it. It was warm, strong, comforting, and hers fit within it as though the two had been made for each other.

The thought hit her with sudden alacrity.

Made for each other.

Shareb-er-rehh was out there somewhere, perhaps in danger, perhaps gone forever. But there was something she had to say to the veterinarian before they did anything. Something she had withheld from him, something she could keep to herself no longer. She squeezed his hand, looked up into his handsome face, and knew it was time to tell him the truth.

"Colin," she said, and held her ground as he grasped Thunder's bridle and tried to move out from beneath the tree.

He paused, raising one brow in question.

She gazed up and into those clear, intelligent eyes that had so entranced her from the very first, and wondered how she had ever been able to keep anything from him. Why she had ever wanted to. Then, taking both of his hands, she drew a deep breath.

"There is something about Shareb-er-rehh that I have not told you."

"I know," he said, gently, with a little smile. "He's no gait-horse, is he?"

She shook her head, still holding his gaze.

"I didn't think so. In fact, if I were to make one guess, based on his build, his carriage, and what I saw today, I'd say he's a racehorse."

"He's more than a racehorse, Colin. *Much* more than a racehorse."

"What is he, then?"

She looked him straight in the eye. "The Fastest Horse in the World."

Chapter Fourteen

"The Fastest Horse in the World."

He was gazing at her with a patient smile, the sort a parent might bestow upon a child who'd just said they'd seen a fairy queen sitting on their pillow.

"That is what I said."

"Granted, my dear, the horse is obviously a Thoroughbred, but that is an extraordinary claim."

They trudged through the pasture, the wet grass brushing their knees, Thunder between them, and the two dogs leading them back toward the road.

"No, Colin, you're wrong. Shareb-er-rehh is *not* a Thoroughbred. At least, not a Thoroughbred as you might know them."

Overhead, the clouds began to break up, and patches of bright blue sky peeked through.

Ariadne gazed off over hills dotted with sheep and cattle. "My father was a very wealthy man. He had the money to pursue many interests, most of them eccentric, but his life's passion was horses. In particular, racehorses. He was an active member of the Jockey Club, and he devoted his life to a project that he had begun long before he and my mother were even married—specifically, a quest to develop a superior racehorse."

Ahead, the road beckoned, a flat, brown ribbon of mud wending through the green pastures. "Do you remember the famous, immortal, and unbeaten Eclipse?" she asked. "Well, Father bred two swift little mares—one, he'd imported from the Orient and the other was a gift from a Bedouin tribe leader whom he befriended when he went there to study their horses—to Eclipse. Then he bred the finest of *their* fillies back to him. Surely, you know the benefits of selective inbreeding. Well, it took my father decades of meticulous planning to see the embodiment of his dream, but see it he did. Fifteen years ago, he produced the very first Norfolk Thoroughbred, an animal similar to our English Thoroughbreds, but one with more intelligence, more heart, more fire—and more speed. They are the fastest horses in the world—and Shareb-er-rehh is the last surviving stallion."

Colin gazed down at her, and saw the truth—at least, as she believed it—in her eyes. Fastest horses in the world or not, only a timepiece could tell. But after seeing Shareb-er-rehh's blistering display of speed, he wasn't altogether inclined to challenge her claim.

"Is he faster, then, than Black Patrick?" he asked, thinking of the mighty and undefeated King of Newmarket.

"Shareb has never been raced. But he *is* the Fastest Horse in the World, Colin. Trust me on that."

"And he is the last stallion?"

"Yes. And Gazella is the last mare. Because Father gave her to Maxwell as a betrothal agreement, she was not in the barn when that strange illness claimed the rest of the stock. Shareb-er-rehh was the only horse to survive both that and the fire. And if something happens to him ..."

"The Norfolk Thoroughbred will be no more."

"Yes." She sighed. "Now you know why I must get him to Maxwell's before my brother can catch up to me. Tristan has no regard for our father's dream, and is in debt to the tune of thousands. Shareb-er-rehh is his only means of paying off his creditors —and to that end, he'll sell him off without blinking an eye."

"How much is the horse *worth*?"

She shrugged. "I don't know. Nobody knows. But the Duke of Leighton once offered my father three hundred thousand pounds for one of our stallions, and he wasn't nearly as nice, nor as fast, as Shareb."

They had reached the road. Ariadne climbed over a small fence and stood there in the mud, gazing off at the wide vistas that rolled away on all sides of them. She cupped her hands to her mouth and called the stallion, throwing her head back and letting the wind carry her voice off over the hills.

Nothing.

She let her hands drop to her sides and stood looking up at him in defeat.

"Colin—I know I should trust in you, but I just don't know where to go from here."

"I have an idea," he said, and held out his hand for the stallion's leather lead shank. Wordlessly, she handed it to him, her brow creased in a frown as he squatted down and called little Bow to him.

Even Thunder pricked his ears, curious.

"Really, Colin, what is Bow going to be able to do—"

But the veterinarian was holding out the lead shank to the dog, who approached it and sniffed it furiously.

"Go find," Colin ordered. "Go find Shareb."

Cocking her head, the little dog yapped and regarded her master with bright, button eyes.

Again, Colin held the rope out to the dog. "Bow, *find*!"

"Rarf! Rarf!" Bow cried, and like a white cannonball, streaked off the road and over the adjacent field; Marc looked at her for a moment in confusion and then, wondering what he was missing, charged off after her.

"Let's go!" Colin cried, and leaving Thunder safely ground-tied, grabbed Ariadne's hand, ducked beneath the fence and ran as fast as he could after the dogs.

Running beside him, her hand caught in his and her legs flying through the wet grass, Ariadne felt exhilaration and hope race through her for the first time since the stallion had escaped. Her cap bounced on her head and she swept it off, stuffing it in her pocket as she tried to keep pace with her companion. Wind drove against her flushed cheeks, dried her wet hair, filled her lungs.

"Hurry, Ariadne, or we'll lose her!"

"Rarf! Rarf, rarf, rarf!" came Bow's voice as the dog paused to wait for them at the crest of a hill. Then, barking, she turned and disappeared from sight, only her excited yaps marking her flight as she raced headlong down the other side, Marc running easily beside her.

"Colin, *wait*! I cannot keep up!"

But laughing, he only gripped her hand harder and pounded up the hill after the dog. Higher and higher they climbed, the breath roaring through their lungs, their hearts pounding—and then, as they reached the crest of the hill, Ariadne looked down and saw a flat, fenced-in field, a barn, and a rambling old brick house. In the paddock was a herd of mares. They looked sleepy, sated, happy—

And in their midst, preening himself like a proud rooster, was Shareb-er-rehh.

"*Shareb*!"

Gripping Colin's hand, she raced down the hill—and lost her footing.

She shrieked as she landed hard on her backside, dragging the veterinarian down with her. Down the hill they went, sliding in mud and grass, laughing with delight and Marc racing alongside, barking, until they both ended up at the bottom looking and feeling like two children who'd just been given a sled and a snowy slope on which to try it out.

Ariadne came to a stop first, and giggling hysterically, gazed up into the veterinarian's mud-splattered face. He looked more than a little shocked, more than a little embarrassed.

"Oh, Colin, you *found* him!" she cried, and tears of happiness raced down her muddy cheeks. "Never, ever, will I doubt you again!"

"Oh, no, it was Bow who found him."

"And *you* who thought of setting her on Shareb's scent!"

She laughed until her sides hurt. Colin smiled hesitantly, then, as he saw the absurdity of their situation, and the amount of mud that covered them both, he too began to chuckle, until they were both giggling and guffawing uncontrollably.

"I feel like a pig that has just spent the day in a pen of muck!" Ariadne cried, reaching out to wipe away a spatter of mud from the doctor's nose. "And look at you! You sure don't look like any University graduate *now*!"

"Forgive me, my lady, but *you* don't strike me as any nobleman's daughter! Perhaps you should maintain that coat of mud and even your brother will never recognize you!"

"Oh, Colin! I haven't had this much fun since I was a little girl and Tristan and I put earthworms in Nanny's bed!"

With the herd of mares watching them, and Shareb-er-rehh shaking his noble head as though disdaining their childish delight, they both erupted in laughter once again. Then, Ariadne looked into her protector's clear, beautiful eyes, and her laughter stopped abruptly.

As did his.

The moment was as fragile and precious as a raindrop poised at the edge of a spring leaf. Neither moved. Ariadne saw only the intense color of his eyes and the shape of his mouth, heard only her racing heart and the sound of his breathing. She drew a deep and shaky sigh. Then, his hand came up to clear the damp hair from her brow, his knuckles grazed her cheek, her jaw—and, heeding the gentle pressure, she moved her head toward his.

"Kiss me, " he said softly. "That is—if you want to."

She swallowed hard, and looked deeply into his eyes. "Yes, Colin. I want to."

Closing her eyes, she tilted her head back and sighed as he touched his mouth to hers. This time, there was no punishing savagery, no angry lesson in manners. This time he kissed her slowly, deeply, carefully, giving her time to savor the warmth and firmness of his lips, the taste of his mouth, the wondrous sensations that began to pulse through her blood. An involuntarily shudder swept through her; a helpless moan escaped her lips. Her hand came up to encircle his nape, her fingers splaying up through his wet hair, pressing against the back of his head and pulling him toward her. His tongue moved against her lips, touching, licking, tasting, until her mouth opened under the gentle onslaught. Oh, the sweet taste of him, the feel of him, the heat of his breath against her cheek, the bold touch of his hand upon her knee! His fingers moved up and down her leg, then her arm, and the sensation of her wet shirt sliding over her own skin, and his hands touching her so intimately, was enough to send shock waves of sensation driving through regions of herself she hadn't known existed.

She pulled back, feeling drugged, feeling helpless, feeling like she wanted to drown in the fathomless depths of those beautiful purple-grey eyes.

"Colin ..." She reached up, and with a shaky hand, smoothed the hair off his brow. "God help me, but every bone in my body goes to water when you kiss me. It's wrong, I know it's wrong, but I want more—"

He eased himself down on one elbow, his hand roving over the curve of her hip and down her damp breeches. She shuddered, loving the feel of that hand against the outside of her thigh, wishing there was no fabric to separate her flesh from its questing warmth. His eyes were troubled, and as she touched his muddy shirt to feel his heartbeat beneath, he looked up at her.

"I share your feelings, Ariadne," he said. "And never have I wanted a woman as much as I want you. But you are a lady, and even if you were mine to claim, I would not have you out here in the grass for all the world to see." He grinned then, making her want to kiss the water droplets from his lashes, his brows, his cheeks. "Especially, with you garbed as a young boy. What would people think?"

She giggled, her face growing hot. He smiled back, and plucking a blade of grass, touched it to the bottom of her chin.

"Oh, Colin, I do not care what people think—"

Shouts and hoofbeats interrupted them and they looked up to see a horse and wagon arriving at the house. Colin lunged to his feet, pulling her up with him just as a farmer, waving his arms and yelling furiously, came charging toward the paddock.

"Hey! That your horse? Get him away from my mares!"

It was obvious, however, that Shareb-er-rehh had already had his way with the ladies. Craning his head to give his attacker a smug, amused stare, he waited for the man to get close; then he wheeled on his hind legs and in a lazy, ground-eating canter, flowed across the field toward Ariadne, neighing happily.

She ran toward him, her arms open.

Ears pricked, the stallion bore down on her, tail flying behind him like a banner. Colin caught his breath, for it didn't look as though Shareb was going to stop. But at the last moment he planted his feet, skidded in grass and mud, and nearly plowed into his mistress. She threw her arms around his neck and as the horse rubbed his head up and down against her chest, laughed happily.

"Oh, Shareb, I missed you so!"

"Ariadne, I think it best to leave before—"

"Oy, that your horse? If he bred any of my mares I'm holding you two personally responsible!" the farmer raged, puffing and panting as he reached them. "This is private property and ..."

Suddenly the farmer's brows snapped together, her head darted out like a chicken's, and he stared at the horse, his eyes bugging out as he realized that the water dripping down the stallion's brown face was washing away mud and ink and revealing a bright white blaze ...

And that the high voice, the fine-boned face, and the obvious breasts beneath the loose coat belonged to a woman.

"My God! You're—*you're the fugitive the whole countryside's looking for!*"

Everything happened at once. The farmer ran toward them; Ariadne made a desperate lunge for Shareb-er-rehh's back, and the man's fingers caught her coat and tried to drag her down. She kicked out, savagely, her boot connecting with his elbow—and then Colin was throwing himself at the farmer, trying to give her time to escape. As Shareb reared up and wheeled away, she saw him slip on the wet grass and lose his balance, the farmer's fist crashing high up on the side of his cheek.

"Colin!"

"Get on the horse!" he yelled, even as the farmer swung again, that huge, ham-fisted hand arcing toward his head. She screamed —but again, she had underestimated her gentle protector. He deflected the blow with a quick, upward thrust of his arm, and bunching his fist, slammed it into the farmer's belly hard enough to send the man, retching, to the grass.

And now a crowd of people were charging up the hill after them, waving their arms and yelling at the top of their lungs.

"Run!" Colin shouted, swatting Shareb across the rump. "Here come the reinforcements!"

Shareb reared beneath her, nearly spilling her from his bare back. "No, Colin, I'll not leave without you!"

"Go!"

"*No!*"

Shareb hit the earth, rose again—and as he came down, Colin vaulted up behind Ariadne as the horse shot away from the oncoming crowd. Beneath him, he felt the powerful churn of mighty, hardened muscles gathering speed, the raw power that the stallion had not even begun to tap. He leaned forward, his arms embracing Ariadne on either side, and managed to grab a hunk of the stallion's sparse mane in both fists.

"Where should we go?" Ariadne yelled.

Beneath them, Shareb found more speed, his hooves thundering over the ground, the wind beginning to scream in their ears, both dogs barking and yapping behind them as they tried in vain to keep up.

"Back to get Thunder!"

There was nothing to do but hang on for their lives. Ariadne, leaning forward, dug in with her knees, feeling the veterinarian's hard chest against her back, his thighs embracing hers, and Shareb's mane whipping her face as his legs pounded beneath them. The stallion was flying across the pastures at a full gallop, fast enough to pull the tears from her eyes, fast enough to leave anything or anyone who might be chasing them floundering in his hoofprints. She looked down and saw that her companion's hands were white against the black depths of Shareb's mane, and knew that he was terrified.

But she alone knew that the stallion was not at full speed.

Far from it.

"Easy, Shareb!" she cried, terrified that he'd hit a hole and snap a leg. "Slow it down!"

But he only stretched his neck, flattened his body, and went faster.

Down the hill they tore and up another one, racing through the gathering gloom and decidedly back in the direction from which they had come. The sensation of the stallion's flowing muscles beneath her, coupled with the memory of the veterinarian's burning kiss and the hot press of his body against every tingling inch of her back, arms, and thighs was enough to make Ariadne breathless and faint.

And there was Thunder, ahead in the distance.

"Pull him up!" Colin shouted, just behind her. "Pull him up or he's going to go right through that fence!"

"Shareb, whoa!"

The stallion shook his head and blowing hard, kept running.

"*Whoa!*"

The roar of the wind in Colin's ears lessened in pitch, and he felt the horse beginning to slow. The great muscles beneath him stiffened, and Shareb-er-rehh broke to a canter, then a plunging, hopping series of jumps until at last he came to a halting stop ten feet from where Thunder stood. Then, as though wishing to discharge an unwanted passenger, he reared high, and Colin slid off and over the stallion's rump, his legs promptly giving out beneath him.

The little noblewoman's laughter bubbled around him. Even the stallion swung around to regard him with amusement. Far off over the hills, Colin heard little Bow's frantic yapping as she hurried to catch up to them.

Ariadne slid from the stallion and reached down to help him up.

Her eyes were sparkling with triumph.

"*Now* do you believe he's the Fastest Horse in the World?"

Chapter Fifteen

W hether Colin believed it or not was of no consequence, because at that moment Bow and Marc came racing over the furthest hill, two horsemen a half-mile behind them.

"Time to test that claim!" he said, clipping a lead rope to Shareb's halter, looping it around his neck and quickly fastening it on the other side of his head as makeshift reins. In one easy, fluid movement, he seized Ariadne around the waist and tossed her up on the horse's back. Her eyes were bright with excitement, her skin glowing. "There's a pond five miles up the Norfolk Road—I'll meet you there as soon as it's fully dark. Now, prove to me that this confounded nag of yours can indeed run a hole through the wind!"

Laughing, she sent the fiery steed galloping off over the dark-ening pastures. Colin stared after her, a little smile playing about his mouth, a dreamy look in his eye—then, his heart leapt to his throat as he saw Shareb-er-rehh heading for the tall hedgerow that separated the fields. The mighty racehorse paused only long enough to gather himself, then flowed over it like a dolphin arcing over the waves.

And then he was off, pounding over the hills with his tail streaming behind him

THE MOON WAS HIGH, fading in and out behind tendrils of cloud and mist by the time Ariadne finally dared to creep out of the copse of trees where she had hidden, and venture back onto the road. The night was spicy with the scent of grass and flowers, the air a gentle whisper of a breeze, but the relative quiet did nothing to calm her nerves. Now, as she guided Shareb with her knees, weight and the rope, she found herself jumping at every shadow, freezing at every sound of a distant, barking dog.

For the first time since undertaking this adventure, she was alone.

Colin is out here. Just another mile or so and you'll come to the pond. He'll be there, waiting. You know he will... .

But what if he hadn't been able to divert the pursuers? What if he *wasn't* waiting at the pond? What if he—like her father all those times he'd promised to spend time with her but never bothered to show up—let her down?

She didn't know what she'd do, then.

Just as she didn't know what she was going to do about the situation with Maxwell.

Maybe it didn't bear thinking about ... at least, not yet.

But like a persistent toothache the problem was there, and Ariadne knew that no matter how much she tried to ignore it, it was not going to go away.

Beneath her, Shareb-er-rehh moved like silk, his ears up and his long neck stretched before her, his shoes grinding against little stones in the road. But Ariadne was not thinking about Shareb-er-rehh, nor her pursuers, nor her brother. She reached up and touched her mouth, tracing the shape of her lips as *he* had done with his tongue in the farmer's pasture. Oh, how warm and wonderful that kiss—the memory alone was enough to make her blood burn and little tingles race up and down her spine.

Oddly enough, she felt no regrets. Only, confusion.

Father had arranged the union between herself and Maxwell in an attempt to "rein in" her wildness, and put paid to the increasingly scandalous behavior she had employed in a futile attempt to get attention. But she also knew that the match was also, as so many were between the aristocracy, meant to further and build upon the acquisition of property, though in this case, it hadn't been land or other holdings that would seal the betrothal, that would complete her dowry—it was the Norfolk Thoroughbred. The union had been Maxwell's idea, and Father had embraced it. She had never had a choice in the matter, really, and had told herself it was all for the best—perhaps not for herself, but for the future of the Norfolk Thoroughbreds, whose legacy would be kept alive by Maxwell's own passion for racehorses. The match was a brilliant one, everyone said, and the earl was older, steady, wealthy, and everything she should want in a husband.

Perhaps everything she *would* want in a husband.

If not for Colin Lord.

Now, she could barely even recall the details of Maxwell's swarthy face, could not remember quite how tall he was, or what his lips had felt like that one time that he'd kissed her. She could only recall his eyes, one of them dark and penetrating, the other milky-blue with blindness, and how there was something about him that had made her more than just a little bit afraid.

He could be, she knew, a dangerous man.

And a dangerous enemy if ever she crossed him.

The wind blew softly through the branches overhead, and she shuddered.

Best to put Colin Lord and any romantic notions where he was concerned right out of her mind. No matter how attractive she found him, no matter how much she was beginning to fancy him, he was not for her and never would be. That fact alone effectively cut off any thoughts of marriage. And even if Ariadne was willing to suffer being ostracized from the society in which she had been born and raised for giving up an earl in favor of a commoner, there was still Maxwell. *A dangerous enemy indeed*, she thought, and shuddered to think how he might retaliate if she were to break off their engagement. At the very least, he would probably refuse to give the beautiful Gazella back to her. And if that happened, Shareb-er-rehh and Gazella would never be paired, the heir that was so desperately needed to carry on the Norfolk Thoroughbred would never be gotten, and Father's legacy would die with him.

She could not allow that to happen. Even with her father not yet cold in his grave, she realized she was still seeking his approval. She *had* to marry Maxwell, or the Norfolk Thoroughbred would be no more.

Tears of frustration, hopelessness, and despair welled up in her eyes, and so absorbed was she in her thoughts that Ariadne never saw the pond where she was supposed to meet the veterinarian. Now, lifting her chin and swiping away her foolish tears—*be realistic, you cannot have Colin Lord!*—she remembered passing a tiny depression in the ground that was barely more than a mudhole some distance back, but the only movement there had been caused by several mallards, some moorhens, and a pair of swans whose plumage had glowed white in the gathering gloom.

Had they come further than five miles?

The road made a gentle bend, and from out of the night came the sounds of racing water. Surely, if there was a brook it would lead into a pond? Guiding Shareb off the road, Ariadne urged him down the hill to its banks, following the stream and allowing him to pick his way through the high grass.

Sure enough, there was a pond, silver beneath the clouds and moon. Shareb dropped his head to drink while Ariadne gazed off into the night. Moonlight glinted against grass that was bent and waving in the wind, and she could just see a grove of trees hugging the eastern horizon, dark against the gently rolling hills. Only the rush of the brook and the distant sound of lowing cows broke the stillness of the night.

Shareb's head jerked up and he gave a soft, inquisitive whinny.

"Colin?" Ariadne called, her voice a half-whisper.

Silence.

Maybe this was the wrong pond. Maybe she ought to retrace their steps, or continue up the road and see if there was another one. But no. What if Colin had been detained by the reward-hunters? What if something had happened to him? And what if poor old Thunder had broken down? If nothing else, the gelding's stride wasn't even comparable to Shareb's, and neither was his energy level.

But there was also a darker, more troubling thought.

Maybe Colin wasn't coming.

Maybe he, like Father, had other interests, and was even now on his way back home to London.

She slid off Shareb-er-rehh, her bottom sore and her legs stiff and wobbly after being astride him for so long. She would not allow her mind to go in that direction. Instead, she thought of her immediate discomfort, and what to do about it. What she wouldn't give for a hot cup of tea right now—and, a bath. Mud caked her clothes, and her hair felt lank and unclean. And that pond, still beneath the night sky, looked dreadfully inviting …

Biting her lip, she glanced back in the direction of the road, but the slope of the hill blocked her view of it. Then she gazed at the pond and, unbuttoning her shirt, pushed through the tall weeds and grasses until she reached the water's edge.

She pried off her boots. Around her the darkness pressed, big and deep and silent. She paused, listening to the grunting chorus of a frog, and the lonely sound the breeze made as it whispered through the reeds and sent tiny ripples skating across the pond. She put her foot in the water. Then, the other. Again, it struck her how helplessly alone she was, and her heart began to beat fast and hard.

"Shareb!"

The horse lifted his head, a tuft of grass hanging from the side of his mouth. In the darkness, she could just see the tell-tale white ringing his right eye.

"Keep a watch for danger," she murmured, and he looked at her blankly before dropping his head once more.

A big help *he* was. Oh, dear God, *where* was Colin?

I will not be afraid, she thought, as the night seemed to grow blacker, deeper. *He'll be along shortly. He is not Father, and never will be. Try to have just a little faith in him...*

Leaving Shareb to his grassy meal and trying not to think about how empty her own stomach was, Ariadne waded further into the pond. The water was warm, still, and unhappy about being disturbed. Deep mud sucked at the soles of her feet, slimy weeds swished against her ankles, and she shuddered in revulsion of what insects and other ... *creatures* ... must lurk in the water in which she was about to bathe. Again, she paused, listening to the night. If only *he* would appear to smile at her in that wry, private way of his, teasing her and watching her with unspoken admiration in his eyes ...

Had Maxwell ever looked at her like that?

She turned and glanced behind her, her eyes straining to pierce the darkness. But the little slope behind the pond was empty, and the breeze sounded lonelier than ever.

Shivering, Ariadne bit her lip once more, desperately trying to quell the growing voice of doubt, and waded farther into the pond. There, she washed herself as best and as quickly as she could, and as she trudged out of the water, squeezed her arms against her drenched clothing in a futile attempt to dry herself.

Miserable in her wet, scratchy clothes, she lay down on the bare grass and folded her arms beneath her head. Above, the stars looked down, and the utter vastness of the night sky only reminded her how alone she was. She turned her head. Beneath her forearm something was crawling, and shuddering in revulsion, she got up and moved a few feet away. Tufts of grass were lumpy beneath her arms, and the earth was hard and silent. She moved to press her ear against it, yearning for the quiet vibrations that might signal Thunder's approach.

Nothing, but the frogs, and the quiet burble of the brook.

And the darkness.

She thought of Tristan out there in the night, hunting her down like an animal. She thought of Maxwell, and wondered why she felt a ripple of foreboding at the memory of his face. She thought of Colin Lord, and how much she yearned for that gentle healer she could never have. And then she thought of her father, and the wonderful horses that had once cavorted around the pastures of Burnham Thorpe. A father that she would never see again in this lifetime, a father so consumed by his life's passion that he hadn't had time for her ... but a father whom she had loved all the same.

Tears of silent grief began to roll down her cheeks and into her hair, and her chest convulsed on quiet, choking sobs. She put her hands over her eyes, trying to quell the sounds of her pain, to no avail. She cried until she had no tears left to cry, and when at last she opened her eyes, she saw Shareb-er-rehh standing protectively over her, his body huge against the starry sky.

Her father's horse.

Her father's horse—who loved her, it seemed, even more than her father himself had.

He lowered his head and she put her arms around his neck, her face against his jaw until her sobs finally quieted and the wind blew softly against her damp cheeks. She stayed that way for a long, long time.

The Fastest Horse in the World and a soaked, sobbing noble-woman. What a pair they made now.

Her cheek still pressed to the stallion's, she stared off into the night, wishing with all her heart for her veterinarian and the safety and comfort of his arms.

THE BAYING OF A HOUND ... Shareb's piercing, alarmed scream, and the earth shaking beneath his hooves as he galloped in a circle around her. At first, Ariadne thought she was dreaming; then, her eyes shot open and she sat up with a gasp, only to see three men standing over her with their muskets pointed at her heart.

She froze, the blood icing in her veins.

"So, what 'ave we here, eh?" one of them said coldly, with a triumphant look at his cohorts. In the moonlight his eyes were small and mean, tiny chips of flint in a fat, bejowled face that was all but dominated by the breadth of his bullish shoulders and great, barrel-like body. "A young lad or a *fugitive noblewoman?*"

"A ticket for a ten thousand pound reward, if you ask me," his companion snarled, cocking his musket. "Get up."

Shareb-er-rehh shot past again, his tail flying behind him as he tried to divert the men.

"Somebody grab that damned stallion before 'e falls an' breaks a bloody leg!" the huge bullock of a man shouted. "He ain't going to be worth nothin' to us then!"

One of them, a tall, reedy sack of bones with a broken nose, rushed off after Shareb, trying in vain to catch him.

Ariadne sat up, her heart pounding in her ears. "Really, sir, I don't know what you're talking about," she snapped, trying to sound appropriately indignant. "Do I look like a noblewoman to you?"

Again, Shareb galloped past, his eyes wild, his nostrils huge and wide.

The man thrust the musket against her ribs. "Get up."

Slowly, she got to her feet, her chin high, her stomach sick with fear, her legs like custard. She was shaking so badly she was afraid she would fall, and if she fell, they would probably shoot her and she would die right here, right now, never to be found again. But somehow, her legs managed to support her, and she glared defiantly at them, her eyes on their frightening faces, their long muskets, and the growling hound they must have used to track Shareb-er-rehh.

"Somethin' wrong with your legs, *my lady*?" the huge man said, with a sneer. "I ain't got time to waste chattin' when I could be collectin' that ten thousand pounds for yer return. "Now, *move*."

"My brother hasn't the money to pay you," she retorted. "He is in debt up to his ears, so you might as well just let me go and save yourself a lot of trouble!"

"Oh, he'll pay," the man growled. "I'm goin' to march you an' that horse right back to London an' make *sure* he'll pay. Now shut up an' move, or I'll make you sorry you ever met me."

"I'm already sorry that I met you, you disgusting heap of—"

Her remark was abruptly silenced by a sharp cuff across the mouth that split her lip and nearly knocked her down, and in that moment, Ariadne had no doubt whatsoever that if she tried to fight them they would kill her.

Dear God. Had they found and hurt Colin?

"Move!" the leader shouted, and shoved her forward with a meaty hand between her shoulders.

Her head high, her legs trembling, she turned and walked stiffly ahead of them, the musket pressing cruelly into the small of her back. Sweat prickled her scalp, ran like icewater down her spine. She had to do something.

In the end, she didn't have to. Shareb-er-rehh did it for her.

The stallion had been circling the field, leading his frustrated pursuer a merry chase; now, he saw the men forcing his mistress away and his savage, angry call rent the night. And though Ariadne could not see him, she could hear his hoofbeats, and knew the exact moment he moved out of his lazy canter and came charging across the field in thunderous fury. This time, he did not feint away at the last moment. Head down, ears back, he let out an enraged, stallion-scream—and came straight for the little group.

Howling in fear, the men dove for cover as the horse, teeth bared and neck outstretched, bore down on them like a demon straight from hell. The huge one dropped his musket and leapt headfirst into the pond; the other flung himself into the weeds, his musket going off in the process with a thunderous explosion of smoke and fire. Only the dog stood his ground, crouching low, racing alongside Shareb as the stallion swept past, then making a leap for the mighty shoulder. The hound glanced off the flying horse, connected with his hooves and fell back, shrieking and yelping in pain. A shot rang out and then Shareb was turning, his tail flying, his scream piercing the night as he came galloping back toward Ariadne.

She was already running toward him, and he slowed only long enough for her to make a wild, desperate lunge for his back. Her balance failed her, and she clung to his mane with one leg curled over his back and the ground rushing past beneath her.

Angry voices rang out behind them.

"Stop her! Damn it, *stop her*, that horse is worth ten thousand bloody *pounds*!"

Her fists wrapped in the stallion's mane, her leg hooked around his back, his flying hooves inches from her shoulders and head, Ariadne managed to pull herself up onto him as shots rang out behind her. Something whined past her ear, and she bent low over the outstretched neck, burying her face in the flying mane and feeling the wind ripping through her clothes, her hair, her—

"Go, Shareb, *go*!" she cried, driving her heels into his flanks. "Run, like you've never run before!"

Back went the stallion's ears, and he nearly exploded out from under her in a burst of speed that stole every bit of air from her lungs. Mighty muscles churned beneath her and Ariadne buried her face against his neck, urging him on with hands and voice.

"Run, Shareb! For God's sake, *run*!"

Behind them the hound set up a frenzied baying, but it could never catch them. Another shot rang out and pain exploded in her arm. She cried out and sank her teeth into her bottom lip, trying to hold back the sudden dizziness of terror, for blood was running hot and wet down her arm and she knew she'd been hit. Wrapping her fists in the stallion's mane, she bent low over his neck and hung on for dear life, knowing that if she passed out and fell, it would be all over.

"Go, Shareb," she whispered, the whipping mane stinging her cheeks. "Go ... find Colin."

The stallion lunged over a hill and hit the road at a blistering gallop, the rapid *ta-da-dump*! *ta-da-dump*! *ta-da-dump*! of his hooves beginning to fade to a dull roaring in her ears.

Darkness began to invade her vision and she buried her cheek in his mane, praying she could hold on, that she wouldn't fall when she lost consciousness. Her face bumped against the hard neck and her eyes began to slip shut, and the last thing she felt was the stallion, leveling out into that tremendous, ground-eating stride that was more a flight than a gallop, that fabulous, soaring gait that carried him over the earth faster than any domesticated creature alive. She never saw his ears prick forward, never heard his long, urgent whinny as he thundered down the Norfolk Road with his precious burden perilously balanced on his back, his tail streaming behind him and his dark eyes searching the night.

Shareb-er-rehh screamed again, the sound flowing out over the hills and to the stars above.

Looking for the veterinarian.

Chapter Sixteen

G*unfire.*

He heard it as a sharp crack in the distant night, and the blood ran cold in his veins. Moments later the baying of a hound echoed over the hills, and then—faintly at first, then growing louder and louder—the sound of a horse bearing down on them.

Fast.

In the darkness, Colin could just see the road ahead, ribboning away behind a low rise. The pounding hoofbeats grew louder and he cautiously steered Thunder over to the side, waiting for the animal to come charging around the hill and hoping it wouldn't run them down.

Louder and louder came that furious crescendo, the baying of the hound—

And then the steed burst around the bend.

It was Shareb-er-rehh, the moonlight glowing in his eyes, fire flying from his hooves.

Fastest Horse in the World.

Colin leapt from the chaise and ran out into the road, waving his arms to intercept the stallion.

"Whoa! *Whoa!*"

Shareb planted his front feet and nearly sitting back on his haunches, came to a skidding, sliding halt, the dirt spraying up beneath his hind legs and belly.

And then Colin saw the tiny burden he carried on his back.

"*Ariadne!*"

She tumbled off and into his arms. The hound's baying was furious, growing louder, and any moment the dog was going to burst around the bend and God only knew what it was leading.

Colin wasted no time. The unconscious woman in his arms, he slapped Shareb-er-rehh hard on the rump. The horse understood perfectly, and with a shrill whinny charged off down the road, his tail streaming behind him. He'd no sooner vanished around the bend when the dog burst into view, baying furiously, a trio of mounted horsemen in hot pursuit.

Colin leapt into the chaise, put Ariadne beneath a blanket on the floorboards, and leaning over her with his elbows on his knees, urged Thunder into a slow, plodding trot.

The hound streaked past, followed by two of the riders. The third paused, breathless, his jowly face dark and angry. "You see a horse go by with a rider on its back?"

Colin raised a brow and kept Thunder walking. He scratched his head. "Horse? What kind?"

"Bay one, a stallion, white blaze down its face!" the man shouted, fighting to keep his own winded mount under control.

"Oh, aye," Colin said slowly. "Saw one go past about ten minutes ago, though I don't think it was the one you're looking for. Little white mare, she was. Definitely no stallion—"

"The hell with ye!" the man yelled, and drove his heels savagely into his frightened mount, sending the protesting animal charging off down the road to join his companions.

Colin waited for the pounding rumble of their hoofbeats to recede; then, with Bow huddling fearfully on his lap, Marc sitting on the seat beside him and Ariadne's body pressed against his toes, he steered Thunder off the road and deep into the darkened pastures.

"Faster, boy," he called, urging the old gelding on. The horse tucked his head and pulled a quick trot out of his long-forgotten repertoire of gaits, and the chaise creaked, bounced, and rolled over the dips and rises.

They followed the perimeter of a broken fence. Colin heard water rushing ahead, and saw a flat, bubbling brook cutting through the starlit field. At his feet lay Ariadne's limp, warm body, and its very stillness caused his heart to pound and cold sweat to break out along the length of his spine. Urgently, he steered the gelding down the bank and into the water to cover their scent, then back up the other side and into a grove of trees. There, he pulled him to a stop, leapt from the chaise, and sliding his arms beneath the blanketed noblewoman, gingerly lifted her.

"Ariadne," he whispered, cradling her to his chest. "Oh, sweetheart ..."

He peeled back the blanket, and his heart breaking, pressed his lips to her brow. It was pale and cold in the darkness.

"Colin?" Her voice was the faintest of whispers; then, her head fell back against his arm, her hair tumbled over his wrist, and she was still and silent once more.

His face grim, his eyes bleak and worried, he carried her swiftly toward the grove of trees, little Bow whining worriedly at his heels, Thunder following along behind him with his nose at Colin's arm.

Please, God, let her be all right. He found a flat spot in the grass, set her and the blanket down, and knelt beside her.

The two dogs milled about, panting, as he laid his fingers against her cheek. Her face was white in the gloom, her lips parted, her little hand lying at her side with the palm turned upward. Colin swallowed hard. Then, he gently peeled the blanket back—and there, black and ugly in the moonlight, was a huge stain spreading over her left sleeve.

Wordlessly he got up, went to his sea chest, and got his surgical instruments and spectacles. With precise orderliness, he lit the lantern, and laid out forceps, tweezers, a scalpel, bandages, and a small bottle of rum.

He had never performed surgery on a human before, but he shoved aside his misgivings and concentrated on the task at hand. Lifting her tiny wrist, he pressed his index finger to her pulse and found it to be steady and strong. Then he pulled the lantern close, rolled her gently onto her side to expose the injured arm, and with two quick, steady slices, slit the sleeve from wrist to elbow, then elbow to shoulder.

His patient moaned and gave a little sob, and he gently laid his hand against her cheek, smoothing the fragile, dewy skin and feeling something thick and burning rising up in his chest.

Please God, help me to help her... .

He leaned down and tenderly kissed her damp, tangled hair.

"Colin," she whispered, opening her eyes and looking dazedly up at him. "I'm so scared... ."

"You're going to be all right," he murmured, close to her ear. "Just lie still and think of happy things. Clouds floating over the sky. Birds singing on a sunny morning. Kittens, sleeping in the sunshine."

He pulled back, peeled the wet, bloody fabric from her arm, and with gentle fingers, examined the injury.

Given his former profession, Colin had seen enough gunshot wounds in his life to recognize what he saw now, and hot rage pounded against his temples with such force that he had to sit back and press his fingertips against them to quell it. He shut his eyes, briefly, until his emotions were once again under control. Then, he peered down through his glasses, pulled Ariadne up and into his lap, and with businesslike efficiency, went to work.

The wound was an open, gaping hole, still trailing a bloody

thread of crimson. He put his fingers against its perimeter and pushed, hard. Blood bubbled out and trickled down the white flesh of her arm, and the girl made a sobbing, wrenching noise deep in her throat.

Instantly, Bow was there, licking her face.

"Be brave, my little Ariadne," he murmured, wishing desperately that he wouldn't have to cause her further pain, wishing he could take it on himself and thus spare her the agony of what he had to do. "It's going to hurt."

"A lot?"

"Maybe, sweetheart. Just ... hold onto me, alright?"

She whimpered, terrified and dazed, one hand reaching out to grasp a handful of his shirt like a child with a toy. "Am I going to die, Colin?"

His skilled fingers pushed against the wound, forcing more blood out of it to cleanse it, and dimly, it occurred to him that what he was doing was probably the closest he would ever come to phlebotomy. He moved his fingers a fraction of a inch, and sure enough, he felt it—something hard just beneath the skin and buried in the superficial fibers of her bicep.

"No, my love, you're not going to die," he said, trying to sound cheerful and chiding in the hope of calming her. "Besides, who would pay me the twelve thousand pounds if I were to lose you?"

"Oh, Colin—" Bravely, she tried to laugh, but the sound came out as a hitching sob of fear, and he enfolded her tiny hand within his own large one, his fingers gently stroking her forearm until she stopped trembling. Then he pressed her hand to his lips, not noticing the way her eyes fastened on his in wonder, trust, and ... something else.

My love, he had said. Maybe he had not been aware of his own words, but Ariadne was.

He rambled on about sunshine and kittens, detaching that part of his mind from the part belonging to the professional, competent surgeon she had first seen on his knees in the street.

But Ariadne wasn't thinking about kittens. She was looking at his face; the hair tumbling over his brow, the planes of his cheeks, the glint of moonlight off his spectacles, the intensity of his gaze. She thought that maybe if she concentrated on him, she wouldn't feel the pain as much. But feel it she did, and when she cried out at the first touch of the scalpel, she saw the muscle twitch in his jaw, the flash of anguish in his beautiful eyes.

My love, he had said.

She closed her eyes and drifted off, feeling herself floating ... sinking down beneath dark, gentle blankets... .

"Colin?" she murmured.

His hand was warm and gentle against her cheek, smoothing the wet hair away and stroking her skin to soothe her. "It's only a flesh wound, with the musket ball still caught inside. If you can just hold on for a few minutes longer, we'll be all through."

"Shareb-er-rehh—"

"Has led your pursuers a merry chase, and I have complete confidence in his ability to lose them. Now be still, love, and think of all the little foals he shall some day sire... ."

"Yes, little foals... ."

Colin reached for his tweezers and gently palpated the muscle, trying to pin down the exact location of the lead fragment. There. Right ... *there*.

Balancing her in his lap, he pulled the lantern close to her arm, bent his head, and knitting his brow in intense concentration, put the tweezers against the wound.

The girl's eyes flew open, her teeth catching her bottom lip hard enough to raise blood.

"Little foals," he repeated softly, in a low, soothing tone. "Little foals, kicking up their heels and running alongside their mamas—" he touched the tweezers to the lead ball once more, trying to see what he was doing in the lantern's meager light— "little foals, with little feet and little faces, little foals with fuzzy little whiskers and long, long, legs like their papa's... ."

So intent was he on his work that he didn't quite notice the moment she lost consciousness, and it was only the distant thunder of galloping hoofbeats that brought him back to awareness of the present.

His head jerked up in alarm, and he was seized by an impulse to sweep up the girl and make a run for it—but as the hoofbeats grew louder and louder, he realized it was no threat at all, but Shareb-er-rehh.

The stallion burst over the furthest rise and silhouetted against the moonlit sky, charged along the rim of the hill before plunging down it and toward them. He lurched to a stop, tossed his head, and prancing with triumphant fire, came forward, his nostrils flaring and the breath rushing through his lungs.

"Did you lose them, boy?"

Shareb tossed his head as though to respond, and stepping forward, lowered his nose to his mistress' still body, his nostrils flaring at the pungent scent of blood.

"She's going to be fine," Colin said. Tweezers in hand, he raised his arm and pointed to a spot several feet away. "Now off with you, and let me work. Go chew on some grass or something."

Shareb put his ears back and eyed him flatly.

"Go!" Colin said, waving his hand.

The stallion squealed, trotted a short distance away, and stood staring.

Once more, Colin bent his head, the hair falling over his brow. He pushed it back with his wrist and hurriedly found the place where the lead ball was. Behind him he heard slow, hesitant hoofbeats approaching. They came to a stop, and heavy, hot breathing blasted the back of his neck.

"Go away, Shareb."

The breathing grew hotter.

"Go *away*, Shareb, I will not hurt her!"

But the stallion refused to move, and trying to ignore him,

Colin slid the tweezers beneath the ragged edges of torn skin and skillfully retrieved the lead fragment.

The girl never stirred. Shareb's head hung protectively over Colin's shoulder, and twice, he had to elbow the stallion away so that he could work. He squeezed more blood from the wound, pinched and stitched the edges shut, and cleaned the blood away with a piece of linen soaked in rum. Then he wound a bandage around the arm, tied it in a snug knot, and began to get up. His feet and legs had fallen asleep, and he stumbled as he set Ariadne down on the blanket, stood up, and passed a weary hand over his brow. His body aching with fatigue, he moved a little distance away and there, stood leaning against a tree.

Thinking.

Moments later, when he returned to the little group, he saw the rum bottle lying empty on the grass, and Shareb eyeing him innocently.

Colin was too weary to scold him. He looked at Thunder, dozing with one hind leg cocked beneath him, and the two dogs, both curled up on the blanket with Bow nestled against Ariadne's calves. Only Shareb-er-rehh was awake, the lantern light glowing in his dark eyes, and Colin wondered what was going through that canny, equine mind.

Mentally dismissing the horse, he sat down beside the girl, slid his arms beneath her, and wrapping her in the blanket against the cool night air, pulled her protectively up against his chest. Shareb eyed him for a long, decisive moment; then, he gave a great sigh, walked a few feet away, folded his long legs beneath him, and lay down. His tail flicked once, his sides heaved, and then he was asleep.

Around them, the night breathed, deep and silent at last. There were no hounds, no reward-hunters in hot pursuit, nothing but a clear sky, the distant hoot of an owl, and there, just above the treetops, a bat winging its way through the darkness.

His precious burden sheltered in his arms and held protectively close to his heart, Colin leaned back against the wheel of the chaise, and put his lips against her damp hair.

For a long, long, time he remained awake, staring bleakly into the night and aching for the woman he held so tenderly in his arms. Sometime between midnight and the wee hours, his head lolled against the wheel spokes, the spectacles slid from his nose, and the veterinarian joined his companions in exhausted slumber.

Chapter Seventeen

❧❦❧

Ariadne became slowly aware of several things at once. A burning ache in her arm that throbbed in time with her pulse. Damp, itchy clothes that clung to her skin. The lingering scent of a spent wick, a soft linen shirt against her cheek, the sound of deep, rhythmic breathing and a heartbeat thudding beneath her ear.

And warmth. Hard, encompassing warmth, beneath her face and surrounding her back and shoulders.

Enclosing her.

Protecting her.

She opened her eyes, and there, so close she had to adjust her vision to focus on it, was the pale, moonlit wedge of the veterinarian's chest.

Full awareness came quickly back to her, and bits and pieces of things she couldn't fully remember. Those horrible men, she remembered *them*, and the gunshot that had cracked the night the same moment she'd been hit. Shareb-er-rehh, calling on his extraordinary speed to bring her to safety; how she'd remained aboard him she didn't know, but she had a hazy memory of tumbling from his back and into the doctor's arms, and then, later, his soothing voice and comforting touch as he'd made her arm hurt more and told her to be brave.

And yes, his eyes... . She remembered his eyes, those beautiful, gentle eyes, the intense concentration behind his spectacles as he'd stared down at her arm and dug at her flesh with the same fixed purpose he had demonstrated when he had saved that poor, dying dog from bloat.

Colin ...

She gazed at all she could see of him; the base of his throat, and the wedge of skin just beneath her lips, where soft, wiry hair lay and a pulse beat rhythmically. She moved her head just enough to nuzzle his shirt aside and put her mouth against it. He smelled clean, of English wind and English pastures, hay, clover, and wild grasses.

Colin... .

She kissed that warm, beating pulse.

He did not stir, and gingerly, Ariadne tried to push herself out of his protective embrace. It was no easy task, with his arms locked loosely around her, but she felt the call of nature and had no choice but to answer it. Holding her breath, she moved back another inch, and the arm that weighed down her shoulders slid off and thumped heavily to the blanket.

She froze. He made a soft, unintelligible noise, but did not wake.

She stood and looked down at him. He lay with his back propped against the hard spokes of the chaise's left wheel, his head at an uncomfortable-looking angle to his body and his lashes making long, sweeping crescents atop his cheeks. Moonlight gilded his hair and turned it silver.

He had not abandoned or forgotten her after all, but had come for her.

He had saved her.

He had saved all of them.

"You are beautiful," she whispered, her heart in her throat. "I think ... I could love you."

His spectacles lay upside-down on the grass beside his hip, and carefully picking them up and folding them, she put them on the seat of the chaise. The movement sent pain winging the length of her arm and wincing, she hesitantly touched the area. A bandage bound the wound, tight enough that it felt snug and secure. Her eyes filled with tears of adoration, and as she gazed down at her handsome, gentle savior, sleeping like a babe in the starlight, she felt her heart constrict, then overflow with something so powerful it did not even have a name.

In that moment, she *knew* that she loved him.

Knew that she'd loved him from the moment she'd seen him bending over that dying dog.

"Dear, dear, Colin ..." she whispered, kneeling down beside him and placing her lips against his forehead. She leaned back, just looking at him, and feeling the tears gathering in her eyes. "God help me, but I have fallen in love with you."

And then, suddenly, Maxwell, her betrothal, and the plight of the Norfolk Thoroughbred swept over her like a dark cloud.

She moved stiffly away and attended to her needs. The brook babbled quietly in the darkness, and kneeling on its bank, she splashed water on her face and tried to make sense of things. The stars reflected on the flat parts of the water, refracted into millions of bright sparkles on those broken areas where the brook tumbled over rocks and rises. She stared down into the depths, her heart aching with longing and despair and something she couldn't quite grasp, couldn't quite understand.

Colin ...

Bits and pieces of scenes came back to her. That hot kiss on the muddy slope, promising further, untold delights. His hand on her breast, sweeping up her thigh on a trail of fire. The long gazes, the accidental touches, the silent glances when the other wasn't supposed to be looking, and always, the constant awareness and underlying attraction they each had for the other. She thought of the sound of his voice, the taste of his kiss, that crooked grin and his helpless laughter when she said something outrageous. She was lost. But then, she had been, from the moment she'd first seen him and he'd glanced up and caught her with those striking, oddly beautiful eyes.

Just thinking of his kisses, the gentleness of his strong, warm hands—and the idea of them touching her here, there, and all over—was enough to melt her from the inside out and reduce her to a state of mindless need and want.

Lady Ariadne St. Aubyn got to her feet and stared resolutely across the darkened pastures that stretched away toward the pink rim of the coming dawn.

There was nothing to do but face the truth.

She loved Colin Lord, veterinarian.

Wanted him more than she had ever wanted anything in her entire life.

Head high, she turned and went back the way she'd come.

"Blowing a good one, sir," said his first lieutenant, as Colin, with difficulty, came up on the steeply heeling deck and noted the waves roiling, thrashing and building all around. He glanced up at the pennants, noting the strength and direction of the wind, and braced himself against the crutches, keenly aware that the officer had moved a bit closer to him, protectively, though he was trying to be discreet about it.

"Time to take in the courses," Colin said. "Get some cloth off her and let her fall off a few points so the seas are running under her counter. 'Twill make it more comfortable for those who are below, recovering from their injuries."

The order was conveyed, and men ran to the shrouds, others to the lines and braces. Above, the sky was turning a deep, ugly charcoal, almost green, and a gust of wind hit the mighty man o' war, heeling her over even farther, still. Desperately, Colin braced himself against his left crutch, the pain in his shattered leg radiating up past his kneecap, his thigh, and into his groin. Nausea flared in his stomach, and he bit it back, determined not to show weakness, determined to prove that he could still do this.

He lifted his gaze to the horizon, at the parade of building swells marching toward them, and there, he saw it, a sailor's nemesis, a rogue wave, huge, towering, and heading mercilessly toward them.

He shouted a warning, and felt the thing slam into the starboard hull and burst high, the giant spray of towering foam hanging suspended against that black cloud before the monster wave broke and fell streaming over the deck. The sheet of gray-green water came sluicing toward him, bursting through scuppers and crashing up against the boats in the waist, washing over men who, like himself, had seen it coming and grabbed onto anything they could hold. Colin had seen and survived many a rogue wave in his years at sea, but never on crutches.

The water slammed against him, and he never had a chance, no matter how great the strength in his arms, no matter how prepared he was for it. It swept the crutches right out from under him and he fell, hard, to the deck, there to lay gasping, helpless and humiliated, as the water rushed past him and poured out of the larboard scuppers, carrying him with it; then Lieutenant Pearson, his face pale, was there, grabbing his wrist before he could be swept over the side, and Colin knew then, that he was never again going to be able to inspire confidence amongst those who looked to him to lead them, if he could not even stand up... .

HE LAY SLEEPING where she had left him, a golden angel lacking only the wings and the halo. In the starlight, his hair was almost silver, and the effect was enough to lend him a sort of ethereal mystique that held her breathless and spellbound.

Ariadne knelt down before him.

It has been said that if you stare at a sleeper for long enough, he will waken. Squatting, she propped her elbows on her knees, her chin in her palms, and focused her gaze on his closed eyelids. But after five minutes of this, he still had not moved.

Growing impatient, she reached out and carefully touched his hair.

He flinched, but did not wake.

Her hand remained with the soft locks caught between thumb and forefinger; then her palm moved lower, tracing the warm, stubbly curve of his jaw and cheekbone. She put her hand against his cheek, and with a soft sigh, he leaned his face into it.

And then his eyes—beautiful, mystical, almost magical in the kiss of the starlight—opened.

He said nothing, only looking at her. There was no fogginess in his gaze, none of the customary adjustment most people must make from sleep to wakefulness. For a moment she thought he was going to kiss her; then, he seemed to remember himself, and reaching up, gently encircled her wrist with strong, warm fingers.

The moment was broken.

"Your arm—"

"My arm is fine."

He frowned, seeing her face. "Are you alright, Ariadne?"

Her eyes pooled with tears. Slowly, she shook her head.

He sat up, leaned against the wheel of the chaise, and patted the ground beside him. She swallowed hard and joined him, feeling very tiny beside him, feeling very foolish for making such a mess of things. Anguish filled her, and the tears slid unchecked down her cheeks. He was too gallant to call attention to them, merely pulling out his handkerchief and dabbing silently at her eyes until she had herself until control. Then he slipped his arm around her shoulders and pulled her close, and only her breeding and manners kept her from huddling against him and burying her face in the warm cup of his shoulder.

"I love you, you know," she said. Then she raised her chin and stared mutely out into the darkness. Her lip trembled, but her voice was firm with resolution. "I love you, Colin, have loved you from the moment I first saw you, I think, and I don't quite know what to do about it."

Sighing, he drew up one knee, lay back against the wheel of the chaise, and gazed wordlessly out at the coming dawn.

"Colin, did you hear me?" Feeling suddenly foolish, she looked down and began to twirl a clump of grass around her finger.

"Yes, sweetheart, I heard you."

"I ... don't know what to do about it."

"Yes—it, uh, well ... certainly does present a problem, doesn't it?"

"Yes, and it is all your fault, because I wouldn't even *be* in love with you if you'd only stop doing things to make me love you!"

The corner of his mouth lifted in a helpless grin. "Oh, well, yes. I really should have left you to bleed to death."

"And you should not have rescued Thunder from that heinous ogre, and you should not have saved that poor dog from bloat, and you should not show such patience with me, and—"

"Ariadne."

She sniffled and glanced at him, her eyes glassy with tears, her lower lip quivering. "What?"

He smiled, a bit sheepishly. "You are missing a beautiful sunrise."

To his surprise, she began to sob, and buried her face in her hands. "Oh, Colin ... I am *so confused.*"

He tightened his arm around her shoulders. "I know. I am, too."

"I don't know what to do ... what to say ... what to feel."

Again, he drew his handkerchief and gently dabbed the tears from her cheeks. "Neither do I."

"What do you think we ought to do about it?"

He looked up again, off into the gathering pink dawn, with eyes that were distant and sad. "Keep away from each other, I guess. It's ... safer that way."

"Is that what you want?"

"What I want, and what I shall have, are two different things."

"That is not what I asked you."

"Very well then." He turned to face her, his gaze holding hers in the faint light. "What I want is a beautiful young noblewoman who is promised to another. What I shall have, is the heartbreak of having to deliver her into the arms of somebody else."

She pulled her knees up to her chest, locked her hands around them, and propped her chin on her kneecaps. A lump rose in her throat, and she looked down at the ground, seeing it through a haze of tears. "Colin ... I'm not so sure I still want to marry Maxwell."

"Have you ever been, Ariadne?" he asked, gently.

She swallowed hard, feeling something thick and harsh catching in her throat.

"No," she whispered. "Not ... after having met you."

"You've only known me for a few days. Not so long as you've known Maxwell, and not long enough to consider giving up your future."

"You're too noble."

"No, merely practical. And older than you."

"You mean, wiser?"

He shrugged and gave a little grin. "Maybe."

Her eyes sad, she gazed at him, her cheek still lying atop her kneecaps. "You will make some lucky woman the perfect husband," she said wistfully. "You are the gentlest, yet strongest, man I have ever met, and you make all those London blades to which I am accustomed look like a bunch of whining sissies. You stand up for what you believe in, you defend what you think is right and just, you are ... a *man*."

His grin widened. "Yes, I was, the last time I checked—"

"Colin?"

"Yes?"

"Do you love *me*?"

He plucked a blade of grass, began knotting it around his finger, and slanted her a chiding look. "Do birds fly?"

"*Do* you?"

"Fly?"

"No, silly ... love me."

He tossed the grass aside and looked into her eyes, his gaze so full of feeling she thought she would drown beneath the force of its intensity. Then he gave a great sigh, took her hand, and turned his face to the dawn. "Yes, Ariadne. For all the good it does me, I do."

The words hung in the still air, and there was not even any breeze to sweep them away. They glanced at each other, he looking a bit sheepish by what he had just confessed, she gazing at him with a slow grin spreading across her face that lit up her entire countenance. Then, shyly, they both looked away from each other.

She looked down at her feet. "So now what do we do?"

"*You* need to think about whether you will go through with this marriage to Maxwell, and if not, how to end it."

"And you?"

"I think—" he squeezed his eyes shut and pushed the heel of his hand against his forehead— "I think I need to go take a walk."

He got to his feet, and left her sitting there in the grass by herself.

"Why?"

"I need to think."

"Why?"

He stood staring down at her. "Because if I *don't* think, I'll take action, and then both of us might—correction, both of us ~~will~~—regret it."

He turned and began walking away.

"But *would* we regret it?" Feeling rejected, Ariadne stared after him. "And would the 'action'—I presume that means lovemaking

—be so very bad, Colin? If we both want to do it I can't see why—"

He spun around, shoving his hair off his brow. "For God's sake, Ariadne, think about it! At the moment you're engaged to another man, and you need to make some major decisions before you can even think about marrying *me*—"

"I never said anything about marrying you."

"What?"

"I mean, I cannot marry you. That should be obvious."

He stared at her, shocked. "You would make love with me, then go off and marry somebody else?"

"Colin, I don't *want* to marry Maxwell, but I have to! The future of the Norfolk Thoroughbred depends upon it! Don't you understand?"

"No, I guess I damn well don't."

He turned and began walking angrily away.

"Colin!"

He kept walking, his shoulders stiff with fury.

Ariadne leapt to her feet and ran after him. She caught his arm, her fingers sinking through the soft cotton of his sleeve and meeting hard muscle before he spun around, his eyes flashing, his mouth hard. "Damn it, don't you know enough to leave me alone?"

And then, before she could shrink back from his anger, he shoved a hand through her hair, yanked her up against him, and slammed his mouth down atop hers. The kiss was hard, hot and punishing, his lips almost brutal, his tongue plunging deep within her mouth. He caught her behind the waist with his other hand and ground his hips against hers, and she felt his arousal against her belly, the heat of his body burning her through their clothing. Her head fell back beneath the onslaught even as she wrapped her arms around his neck and drove herself upward to meet his kiss, and she would've lost her balance if not for the hand beneath her head, the arm behind her waist. And then, like a storm blowing itself out, he became gentle, loving, the pressure of his mouth growing sweet instead of savage, the hand that crushed her head against his now gently cupping her skull, the thumb caressing her cheek.

He broke the kiss, and breathing hard, let his brow rest against the top of her head. For a moment neither moved, their hearts pounding and their bodies clinging to each other with desire and need. From somewhere off in the distance a crow called ... then, he gently cradled her jaw in his hands and lifted her head.

They gazed into each other's eyes—

And time stopped.

Her hands caught in his shirt front as they stared at each other across mere inches of space. She blushed and smiled nervously. He gave a slow, defeated grin. And then they sobered, their anger, hurt, and pride forgotten as their bodies began to respond to each other.

"Doctor Lord?"

He gazed down at her, his body catching fire where it touched hers. "Yes, Lady Ariadne?"

"Will you kiss me?" she asked, in the softest of whispers.

His eyes darkened, and Ariadne knew in that final, triumphant moment that he was hers. She watched the long lashes sweep down over his eyes as his head bent, his mouth neared hers and his warm breath feathered against her cheek ... felt his fingers thread through her hair and cup the back of her head; then, there was only the gentle pressure of his lips, the sweet thrust of his tongue ...

And nothing more.

She slid her palms up his chest and sank against him. The kiss went on, drawing her up and into its heat until her head was swimming and her flesh went up in fire. She heard herself moan somewhere deep in her throat, and then all thought, all reason, fled, and the only occupant of her universe was ... *him*.

Colin ... how I love you, adore you, want you, want—

Dimly, she felt his hand caressing her back, pulling her shirt out from her breeches and then sliding beneath the fabric to move down her spine... .

Lady Ariadne St. Aubyn sobbed deep in her throat, and began to melt.

Chapter Eighteen

Some distance away, Shareb-er-rehh came awake and raised his noble head. His ears went back and sulkily, he heaved himself to his feet. He heard the veterinarian's voice, his mistress's answering giggle, and jealousy—ripe, hot and searing—tore through him.

Nostrils flaring, he skulked past Thunder, who regarded him with a warning look in his old eye.

Not bothering to honor the gelding with even a glance, Shareb-er-rehh paused.

And then he spotted the doctor's sea chest.

One ear went forward, and he glanced stealthily off toward where *his* human was giving her attentions to the hated newcomer. He lowered his nose to the chest, lifted out the last remaining rum bottle, and managing to uncork it with his teeth, consumed every drop of the fiery spirits with a single, triumphant gulp. Then he raised his shod foot and began pawing through the chest.

Sharp pain burst in his shoulder and savagely, he whirled around to see what had caused it.

The old gelding stood there, his ears flattened in warning.

They glared at each other for a moment; then, defiantly, Shareb raised his front foot once more. The gelding bit him again, this time, hard, his yellowed old teeth tearing into Shareb's flesh and raising a trickle of blood.

Shareb lunged for the other horse, but Bow leapt between them at the last moment, barking furiously. Her small body hit Shareb squarely between the eyes. The impact was painless, but it knocked some sense into the stallion and with an angry squeal he galloped a short distance away, where he stood sulkily eyeing the other animals. They ignored him and frustrated, he reached for an overhanging tree branch and began to take out his wrath on it, instead.

Savagely, he ripped a spray of leaves and twigs from the branch and ground it between his teeth. He tore off another branch, began to chew—and suddenly found himself with a stick wedged across the roof of his mouth and braced hard against his teeth.

He shook his head, trying to dislodge it. The stick remained. He stamped his foot and angled his jaw and tried to twist his tongue around it, but the branch was stuck fast.

He broke out in a hard sweat and snorting, shook his head once more, furiously this time—but the ends of the branch only dug themselves in deeper, and suddenly the proud young horse knew he was in trouble.

COLIN LAY BACK in the grass, Ariadne atop his ribs and the dawn sky a crown of fire and fading stars around her face. She felt tiny within the cradle of his arms, her shoulders and bones fragile beneath hands that suddenly seemed big and clumsy. Fiercely protective instincts rose within him and he held her close, the need to take her, to possess her, so fierce that he was trembling with need and desire.

God help him, he hadn't wanted, hadn't *meant*, that is, to find himself in this position; wasn't he stronger than this?

No.

But it was too late now. Her slight weight inflamed him, her sweetness filled his senses, and now, she was passing her tongue over her well-kissed lips in an unconscious plea for more.

No. He could not do this. She was no dockside tart, no practiced whore, but a fine, well-bred gentlewoman who was still promised, and engaged, to another. He reached up to push her off of him—and found his hands pressing into her shoulders instead, his mouth seeking her lips.

There was no help for him.

None at all.

Cursing himself, and his weakness, he gently rolled her over until they lay side by side in the grass, staring into each other's faces as if seeing each other for the first time.

"I think you have the most beautiful eyes I have ever seen on a man," Ariadne murmured, touching his cheek. "I could get lost in them, and never find my way out. Never *want* to find my way out. Why, if you were to take my pulse right now, I'm sure you would not be able to count it, so rapidly is my heart beating!"

"Perhaps you should take mine instead," he said suggestively, his eyes glinting as he drew his finger down the slope of her nose and traced her lips.

"Why, I wouldn't know what to do," she said, blushing.

"I can show you ..." Propping his head on one hand, he offered his wrist and smiled lazily at her. "Put your finger right there, against the underside of my wrist," he instructed, watching her with amusement. "No, no ... higher."

"Right there?" she said, shyly, placing her finger where he had directed and feeling no pulse, but hot, hard, male strength.

"Up another half inch—aah, you have found it. My pulse."

"Yes ..."

"Can you count the beats, Ariadne?"

She felt herself going hot with anticipation at what was to come. Beneath her finger, his pulse was racing.

"You're blushing," he said teasingly, his eyes darkening with desire. "Perhaps your temperature is rising ..."

"Perhaps," she agreed, her own heartbeat matching his.

"Perhaps the good doctor should do something about it, quick."

"Yes ... perhaps he ... should."

"Perhaps—" he slowly pulled his wrist from her hand, his fingers drifting up to the base of her neck, where her own pulse beat like a butterfly's wings against the fragile skin "—what my lady needs is some cool air to ... revive her."

"Cool air," she agreed, as his fingers moved against the buttons that closed her shirt at the throat. She felt one button slide through the hole; another, and a cooling wash of air against her hot skin. His fingers lingered against the sensitive flesh, beginning to move downward toward her breast. A last, maidenly instinct swept in to save her, and she lightly slapped at his hand, bringing a rich chuckle of laughter from him. He did not make another attempt to undo her buttons, but simply lay there, lazily watching her with his head still propped on his hand, his eyes intense, clear, and beautifully violet.

And then his gaze shifted, looking down, and she saw one brow raise.

"A wonder, what that cool air does to ... *revive* things," he said, suggestively.

She followed his gaze—and saw that her nipples were taut, hard, and clearly visible in high relief beneath her shirt.

"Oh!"

Again, his hand came out, making a slow, lazy circle around her shoulder before drifting down toward her breast. But he did not touch her aroused nipple, merely let his fingers caress its perimeter through the fabric until the ache of pleasure withheld made her shut her eyes in bliss and yearn to shove herself against his hand. "Perhaps some more cool air is in order, to effectively revive this patient?"

"Yes, cool air ... I feel faint."

"Feverish?"

"Dizzy."

"Afraid?"

She opened her eyes, stared into his gentle, understanding ones.

"Yes."

He smiled and gently rolled her over onto her back, his mouth coming down to claim hers as his fingers undid the last button at her throat and slipped beneath her shirt to caress her skin. She was half-aware of shifting her body so that he could drag the shirt up and over her head; cool air tingled over her skin and her leg came up of its own accord to encircle his thigh. His kiss grew hot and demanding, his palm—strong, warm, hard with callous—dragging fire over her breast. His fingers found her nipple. She moaned deep in her throat and arced upwards, into him, helpless beneath the building heat.

He lifted his mouth, kissed the side of her jaw, her cheek, her neck.

"Still afraid?" he murmured, his breath hot against her skin.

"No, feverish," she said, burning up. "So hot ..."

"That is good, Ariadne ... because I am much better at treating fever than I am fear ..."

His lips were against the base of her throat now, kissing, grazing, tasting the delicate skin, even as he kneaded the erect nipple and made her gasp with longing. Her hand came up, her fingers splaying through his hair and pressing his head against her as his mouth moved lower and lower ...

His lips feathered over one breast, then closed over the aching bud, his tongue tracing wet circles as he drew the peak up and into his mouth.

"Oh-h-h-h-h-h... . Oh, Colin—"

He raised his head, cupped the side of her jaw, kissed her on the lips until she was mindless with desire. Then he gazed down at her breasts, slowly tracing a finger over one creamy mound, then the other. The skin was pink with the kiss of dawn, the nipples bright salmon and thrusting eagerly toward him. "I have always thought you were more than pretty, Ariadne ... but dear God, you are beautiful."

She blushed and took his hand. "And just think, now you can take *my* pulse, Colin ... right from its source."

Closing her eyes, she pressed his palm against her thundering heart, feeling the fire spreading out and into her breasts at the close proximity of his hand to them.

"Aaah, but I crave touching you," he said huskily, leaning down to kiss her once more as his hand moved away from her heart, only to cup, knead, and caress her breast once more. Heat burned through Ariadne's blood as his finger traced little circles around her softly puckered aureole. She moaned beneath the sweet torment ... forget his hands, she wanted his mouth, his lips, his tongue, on her—

He looked up, his eyes dark and searching. "Ariadne, do you have an awareness of what comes next?"

"I have my suspicions." She smiled tremulously, trying to show bravery, flippancy even, so that he wouldn't stop, *please God, don't let him stop*. "I should hope you're as good a teacher as you are a doctor, Colin. You'll show me, won't you?"

He just smiled. His mouth moved to her nipple once more, suckling, licking, tasting. Dampness began to pool between her thighs, and the heat that was centered there to stretch fingers of fire up through her belly.

"Oh ... that feels so, very, nice."

Her body was burning up. She put her hand around the back of his head, holding him down against her breast and arcing shamelessly up and into his hot mouth.

"I like that ... Don't stop."

Colin had no intentions of stopping. He felt her urging him on, tasted the sweetness of her breast and drove himself down into the very source of it, suckling the delicious pink nipple until she began to sob with pleasure. God help him, he was drowning in the feel, the scent, the taste of her and knew couldn't take much more of this. His heart was beginning to race now, his arousal pressing painfully against his breeches. He skimmed a hand down her belly, and such a tiny, flat belly it was, slid his fingers beneath her trousers and impatiently undid the buttons there; a moment later, he found the silken nest of damp curls and was stroking the moist flesh until she was writhing beneath him—

Take it slow. Make it beautiful for her.

His finger found her entrance, sank within it and pushed upwards, her hot sheath engulfing the digit with delicious wet heat all the way to its base.

She went momentarily stiff in his arms and made a little cry, and for the briefest moment he feared he'd hurt her—but no, she was pressing herself against him, gasping and urging him on with tiny, guttural whimpers.

He licked and nuzzled her breast, inflamed her with mouth and tongue and finger, wanting her, needing her, feeling the heat rising up and out of her until her skin was dewy and hot, until she was moaning and gasping beneath him, until she finally caught his head in her hands and gasped breathlessly beneath him.

"Oh, Colin, I ... am so full of feeling, I don't know where to put it all. It grows ... unbearable. I love you, Colin ... please, please don't stop ... I love you ..."

He had found her wet, inner wall with his finger, stroking it ceaselessly until he had her sobbing with the start of climax; he withdrew just before sending her over the edge, then concentrated on the hidden nub of her femininity. Bathed in wetness, it swelled and hardened as he kneaded it between thumb and forefinger. She cried out, digging her nails into the back of his head and neck as he took one of her breasts deeply into his mouth, all the while pressing and rubbing that secret part of her, inflaming her to a state of pleading, sobbing need and want until she was begging for something she didn't understand. He felt her beginning to spasm, and withdrew his hand to let her hang suspended on the shelf of ecstasy, wanting only to make the pleasure so fierce that she would never forget it for as long as she lived.

Gasping, whimpering, she groped frenziedly for his hand.

"Wait, love ... it will be better, if you take it slowly."

He sat up and began to unbutton his breeches, but Ariadne, delirious with need, thrust his hand away and did the task for him. A moment later he was free, swelling hard and stiff against her hand. She paused, uncertain, her pulse pounding in her ears, and looked up into his face.

"It's alright, dearest. It is part of me. Nothing more."

He leaned close and kissed her, and Ariadne felt him growing larger in her hand. She drew back and stared down at him, her eyes widening as she took in the size of his erection. For once in her life she went mute, and her gaze lifted, past the tapered waist and widening ribs, past the broad chest and up into the doctor's eyes.

His gentle eyes, regarding her with love and adoration.

"I'm still here," he said softly, in understanding, and touched his finger to the bottom of her chin. "Still the same person, Ariadne. It's alright to be afraid of ... well, the unknown."

"But it's ... *huge!*"

"Yes, it rather gets that way, when it's aroused."

"How on earth do you keep it safely hidden in your breeches? Do you have to tie it down?"

He had the good grace to actually blush. "I don't spend my every waking moment walking around in this state, Ariadne. Indeed, you have done this to me."

"So *now* what do I do with it?"

"Anything you like," he said, softly. Invitingly. Perhaps even a bit shyly.

She clamped her legs against the still-throbbing ache at their junction. Horrified, yet a little eagerly, she gazed up at him. Again, those kind and gentle eyes were regarding her, with patience, love, and understanding.

He is Colin, she reminded herself. *Colin! And he will never hurt me.*

She went bright red. "I'm sorry, Colin. I've seen s-s-stallions before, but never a man."

He began to look embarrassed, and for a brief, terrifying moment she thought he was going to button his breeches back up and leave her there, hot, desperate, and burning like a candle running out of wick in the deepest part of the night. She saw the hesitation in his eyes, the quick look of regret crossing his face.

Then he gave a guilty little grin and said softly, "I fear that in comparison to a horse ... I am sadly lacking."

He looked up at her and pursed his mouth, and he looked so dreadfully serious and comical all at the same time that she could not help but laugh.

He laughed too, banishing the awkwardness, and when she looked back down at him, that manly appendage was no longer frightening and strange, because it was a part of *him*.

"Touch me, Ariadne."

"You want me to *touch* it?" she squealed, horrified.

"Yes. It does not bite."

She was shaking as she lay back down in the grass and helped him to remove his breeches, stockings and shoes. His manhood was fully bared to her view, along with long, beautifully muscled legs sprinkled with golden-brown hair. One of those legs was marked by a gruesome tangle of raised, angry scar tissue, and Ariadne bit her lip as she imagined what agony the injury must have caused him. She reached out and put her hand over the puckered, scarred flesh, feeling the lumpiness of bone beneath that had never quite healed the way it should have. The doctor regarded her steadily. She swallowed hard, caressed the injured area as though she could smooth away the long-ago pain. He smiled. Then, Ariadne's curiosity over the male organ got the better of her, and hesitantly, she reached out and touched ...

It.

It jumped beneath her finger, and she gave a little cry.

"I hurt you!"

He laughed, and leaned over to kiss her. "No, no, you could never hurt me."

"But—"

"I know. Touch it again, Ariadne. It is only a part of me, and nothing more."

She reached out and gingerly laid her fingers against the blunted apex of the appendage. It was warm and surprisingly soft, as velvety as the hide of a newborn colt, the skin of Shareb's muzzle, the most elegant of silk.

He smiled, watching her.

Gently, she stroked the length of the strange, hard, organ, feeling it growing firmer beneath her touch, larger, stiffer, warmer, until it outgrew her hand and thrust harshly against her palm with every tortured stroke of her fingers. She looked down at its owner; he now lay with his eyes half-closed, as though in the deepest of pain. Anguish, even. She looked back down at his arousal, and felt a warm drop of liquid on the inside of her thumb. She smeared it over the blunted head.

"Oh, my, what fun—Colin, look what it can do!"

Gasping, he caught her hand, began to guide her away.

"Am I hurting you?"

"No. But you will soon put me over the edge with such handling."

"Edge of what?"

He slowly shook his head and eased himself onto his back, one arm gathering her close and pulling her down atop him until their mouths met once more. She felt his warm breath on her cheek,

231

his tongue exploring her mouth, and unable to leave it alone, put her hand around that hard, hot part of him.

"I'm warning you, Ariadne ..."

She kept stroking him, feeling a dawning sense of triumph and femininity as he groaned softly beneath her. Finally, his eyes opened and he gazed up at her with a faint smile and eyes glazed with passion. "Sweetheart, I ... want to make love to you."

He looked intently into her eyes, waiting for her answer.

She took a deep breath, her flesh, her skin, her very blood, on fire.

"Yes, Colin ... I would like that. Love me. Love me with all of your heart."

Gently pushing her hand aside, he moved over and atop her, one arm sliding beneath her head to pillow it, his hand caressing her breasts, her belly, and then, the silky junction of curls at her thighs. She went to butter as his fingers moved toward her hot recesses, spreading the inner lips apart and stroking her until she felt her own moisture flooding in fresh, hot waves against his fingers.

His eyes had gone deep and soft, his brow creased with concentration, his breathing thick and heavy. Under his intimate caress, she once again felt something huge and wonderful starting to build deep in the pit of her belly, beginning to burn, to ache, to make her squirm and sigh and gasp ...

"Oh, Colin, something's *happening*—"

And then he withdrew his hand, grasped that manly part of himself, and guided it to her cleft. Quivering, she felt it touching her flesh, parting it, felt her very insides stretching as he slowly slipped inside her.

It was not enough. She ached for his weight, ached for his body, ached for his touch and the feel of him against her. She ached to have him inside her, as far as he could go, ached for ...

"Ariadne, I dare not go any further," he said hoarsely. His eyes were clear as glass, intense, penetrating and brilliant; she thought he must be able to see right down into her soul. He cupped her face in his hands, kissed her brow, and breathing harshly, said, "It's going to hurt—"

"I trust you, Colin."

"Do you want this, Ariadne?"

"God help me, I do ..."

"Then hold onto me—tightly—and know that I love you, and that the pain will only last but a moment."

"Yes... ." She thrust upward, seeking him, her breath hot against his skin.

He lowered himself down onto his forearms to take his weight and kissed her fervently, his lips and breath hot against her temple, her cheek, her brow, her lips. Between her thighs she felt him filling her, stretching her to the point she thought she might break, and her breathing quickened as that searing, sweet ache grew stronger and stronger. He began to move within her, pulling back and then thrusting slowly back in. She felt her body expanding to accept him, felt him sliding into her, inch by glorious inch, until at last he came up against the fragile membrane that proclaimed her innocence.

He paused, head bent, the hair hanging over his forehead.

"I love you, Colin. Please ... Just make me yours."

He kissed her, held her tightly, and then, just when she thought that she would die for want of him, he drove himself into her—and made her a woman.

The pain was brief, brilliant, and blessed. She felt the warmth running between her legs and was thankful for it, and then there was only *him*, picking up and continuing the rhythm, going deeper with each long, slow thrust, until the brilliant sensation that had been building and building reached its pinnacle—

He gave one last, driving thrust at the same time Ariadne felt herself splintering apart. She cried out, arced up, clung to him and drove her nails into his back with the force of her first climax, her body convulsing out of control. Sweat sheened their bodies and she heard nothing but his groan of pleasure and the sound of her name tumbling from his lips, felt nothing but the blood shrieking through her ears and the sky flying, spinning, whirling, above her. She clung to him, sobbing with wonder and joy until the waves began to ebb, and at last fade away like the ripples in a pond. And then there was just the two of them, bodies entwined on a bed of grass with the stars fading and the dawn coming up in the eastern sky in a beautiful mantle of fire and gold.

Chapter Nineteen

For a long time, they lay together on the blanket, side-by-side, holding hands and watching the sun coming up.

"Oh, Colin, never have I dreamed that something could feel so good, so right ... how I want to be in your arms, forever."

For a long moment he said nothing. When at last he spoke, his words were flat and tortured.

"I don't think you would, Ariadne, if you only knew what disgrace I have suffered, just what I *am*—"

She turned and looked at him steadily. "What you are, Colin, is a kind, caring, and patient man."

"I am a commoner. Beneath you in station, unable to support you in the comfort and style to which you're accustomed."

"And I am an heiress. I don't need you to support me. Besides, I would love you whether you were a hero's son or a Chelsea veterinarian."

"I *am* a hero's son—and nephew, too, come to think of it. My father is Admiral Christian Lord, my uncle, his brother Sir Elliott. And I ... I am a humiliating embarrassment to them both."

"Why? Because you're an animal doctor? That is a noble calling, and you've proven to me over and over again these past few days that you're a hero, too." She turned over onto her side and gazed steadily into his eyes. "War is not the only way in which heroes are made, Colin. Do you think you're not a hero to that little boy whose dog you saved? That you're not a hero to Thunder and Marc? And to *me*? Sometimes everyday life presents ample opportunity to shine, as well."

"Ariadne, there are things about my past from which you would recoil if I were to confess them. Things that would make you ashamed of me. You see, I was once in the service of the king, but not the Army, as I allowed you to believe. I–I was in the Navy–"

"Is that where you hurt your leg?"

"Yes—"

"And why you left it? Because of your leg?"

Images flashed through his mind. The shipwreck. The court-martial. The newspapers—

"In part. But there is more. And if I were to tell you the whole story, you would turn away."

"Colin, why can't you trust me? There is nothing in your past that would erase or change the way I feel about you here in the present." She smiled and touched his jaw, wishing she could smooth away the anguish in his eyes, the lines of sorrow and tension around his mouth. "Besides, I trusted you with the secret of what Shareb-er-rehh really is. Don't you think it's time you trusted *me*?

He just gave her a bleak look and looked away. She reached out to touch his arm—and in that moment hoofbeats shook the ground and Shareb-er-rehh came bursting out of the nearby stand of trees, the dawn's light gleaming in eyes that were wild, panicky, and ringed with white.

Ariadne leapt to her feet, Colin right beside her as the stallion hurled himself toward them at a dead run.

A chill raced up Ariadne's spine, for she didn't need more than a second glance to know that there was something wrong with her horse.

Something dreadfully, seriously, wrong.

"Shareb!"

She ran forward and grabbed the stallion's neck as he plowed to a stop before her. The force of the action nearly knocked the breath from her, and she felt pain explode along her injured arm. She lost her grip and stumbled backwards, saw the sky above her as a brilliant splash of pink, orange and mauve—then there was only Colin's strong arms as he caught her, and made a wild grab for Shareb's head.

Screaming, the stallion bared his teeth and struck savagely out, just missing him.

"Colin, do something!," Ariadne cried, trying to get close to the horse. "He's sick!"

"Get back, Ariadne!"

"I will not, he's my horse and—"

But Shareb was clearly out of his mind with panic. Mighty hooves slashing the air, he reared, wheeled, and thundered off, shaking his head and making a pitiful, horrible noise that raised the hair on Ariadne's neck. He galloped a circle around them, his hide flecked with sweat, saliva flying from his mouth; then, the grass plowing up before his hooves, he came to a stop, blowing hard and staring at them as though recognizing them for the first time.

Ariadne stood frozen, her fingers caught, claw-like, atop her lower teeth.

Slowly, she turned to look at her companion.

He stood as still as a stone, one hand stretched entreatingly toward the trembling horse a short distance away.

Shareb shook his head and began to back up.

"Here, boy," Colin murmured, never moving. He stared deeply into the stallion's dark eyes, willing the animal to come to him. "Let's have a look at you."

"Oh, Colin, what's wrong with him—"

"Get his halter," the veterinarian commanded.

"But Colin, I— "

"Ariadne, get his halter," he said, again.

Blind with terror she ran to obey, feeling that same horrible, paralyzing nausea she'd experienced upon being told about the stable fire and her father's death. Frantically, she tore through their belongings in the chaise, trying to remember the symptoms that Father's other horses had shown just before they died, trying to think of anything that might help Colin save her beloved stallion—

There, the halter. Clenching it in her fist, she ran back to him.

He never turned, merely reaching out to accept the halter while keeping his gaze on Shareb. The stallion took a hesitant step forward, shaking his head. Thick, foamy blobs of blood-flecked spittle arced from his mouth, spattered on the grass.

"Come here, boy," the veterinarian murmured, so softly that Ariadne wasn't even sure he'd even spoken. She watched the horse take another step forward; saw the barely perceptible movement of Colin's fingers, beckoning the animal closer.

And closer ...

Shareb dropped his head in defeat and walked forward, ears drooping, body shaking, the drool running in little rivulets from his mouth. He stopped miserably before Colin, then lifted his head to look at the animal doctor with great, pleading eyes.

Colin hooked an arm around Shareb's poll and buckled the halter into place. Once more, the stallion dropped his head and gazed dejectedly at the ground, his breath coming out in great, labored breaths.

"Ariadne, please bring me my lantern."

She scurried off and found it, still in the grass beside the wheel of the chaise. With Bow and Marc trotting worriedly at her heels, she carried it back to the veterinarian, her eyes misty with hot tears that even now, were running down her cheeks.

Have faith in him, Ariadne. Remember the first day you saw him, and how he saved that dog. He is a healer. He can save animals. Faith, Ariadne, faith... .

But out here in a lonely pasture, with daylight strengthening and her beloved horse looking sicker than she'd ever seen him, it was not easy to have faith. She picked up little Bow and buried her face in her soft fur. The dog was trembling, and sensing Ariadne's grief and worry, twisted around to lick her cheek. The little animal's compassion was enough to bring on the sobs in earnest, and Ariadne pressed Bow's fuzzy ear against her eyes so that Colin would not notice her distress and be affected by it.

She peered through Bow's fur and risked a glance at his face, fully expecting to see grave concern there. But his handsome features were expressionless, his eyes intent as he murmured to the trembling horse, dragged his drooping head up, and ran a gentle, soothing hand down the stallion's long jaw. Thick ropes of spittle leaked from Shareb's mouth, slid to the ground and lay glinting upon the grass in the early morning sunlight.

The tears were running freely now, soaking Bow's ear, raising the scent of wet dog.

Colin. Please, please save my horse ...

Her arms locked around Bow, her body frozen with fear and grief, she rocked from side to side, watching as he bent sideways and forced the stallion's head high. Shareb squealed and fought him, shaking his head and sending more drool flying from his mouth. Ariadne bit her lip so hard that the coppery taste of blood burned her tongue. The tears came harder, streaming silently down her cheeks and filling up her throat so that she couldn't swallow.

Bow licked her face again, and Marc pressed himself against her legs, but there was nothing in her world but the veterinarian. She saw only his wheaten hair falling over his brow and picking up the first rays of sun, saw only the intense concentration in his eyes, saw only the skill in his strong, gentle hands as he pried open the stallion's mouth. *Colin*. He would make everything all right. He *had* to, because if he couldn't, no one could—

"Is he going to ... to d-die, Colin?"

"Oh ... I don't think so," he murmured absently, trying to peer into the dark depths of Shareb's mouth. "Really, Ari, you make a terrible assistant. Bring the lantern over so I can see what I'm doing, would you?"

She didn't like his calm insouciance, the jocular note in his tone, nor the fact he did not seem as concerned as he should be. Didn't he realize how priceless Shareb-er-rehh was? Didn't he sense the gravity of the situation? Pursing her lip, she put Bow down and did as she was told, holding the lantern up and wishing she could keep its bright glare out of the veterinarian's eyes as well.

"What do you see?" she managed, swallowing back the sobs and feeling the prickles of fear clawing up her spine.

"Teeth."

Teeth.

She watched as Colin turned his back, thrust his thumb between Shareb's lips right where a bit would have gone, and then she saw only the back of his golden-brown head, the play of muscles in his shoulders and at his nape as he forced the stallion's jaws wide.

"Eaaaayyuuuk," he murmured.

Raw terror lanced her. "What?"

"Slimy tongue," he said, flashing her a grin and pulling that thick, wet muscle sideways from Shareb's mouth. The stallion protested, and tried to fling his head up and back.

"Hold still, you confounded idiot," Colin commanded.

Shareb tensed, but did as he was told.

"Closer with the lantern, Ariadne, so I can see."

Her sore arm aching, she propped her elbow in her palm and held the lantern up.

Colin all but thrust his face between the stallion's jaws.

"Aha!"

"What?"

"Just as I thought... ."

"Colin, *what?*"

Somehow managing to restrain the stallion and hold his head up at the same time, the veterinarian held Shareb's tongue aside, thrust his hand between his jaws, and craning his neck, peered up into the stallion's mouth. "Our friend here has a foreign object—a stick, by the looks of it—wedged firmly across the dental arcade. Really, Ariadne ... I do wish you'd be more cautious about what you feed him."

"But I thought ... you mean—a *stick?*" She stumbled backward, feeling such an intense wave of relief that her knees went weak and she nearly collapsed. "You mean there's a *stick* caught up there?"

"Right across the roof of his mouth. Tie a string on each end and it would make a lovely bit."

A stick... .

He wiggled his hand within the stallion's mouth and triumphantly brought out a wet, chewed-up branch for her inspection. Grinning, he gave the horse a fond slap on the neck before taking the lantern from Ariadne's suddenly limp fingers, knowing, intuitively, that she would otherwise have dropped it.

"Really, Shareb ... I'm beginning to think you'd be better off with pastry, after all."

COLIN MAY HAVE ALREADY WON the undying love of the Earl of Weybourne's daughter, but with the removal of the stick from the roof of Shareb's mouth, he won the undying—and perhaps, unwelcome—devotion of the earl's horse, as well.

It was a devotion that proved to have mixed blessings.

Shareb-er-rehh followed him back to their little campsite. He followed him down to the brook and stood waiting patiently as Colin washed the spittle and flecks of blood from his hands. He followed him back to where Thunder waited, followed him as he carried his sea chest back to the chaise, followed him when he went to Ariadne and put his arms around her tiny shoulders.

It was as Colin felt the stallion's hot breath blasting against the back of his neck that his patience finally reached an end.

"Enough, Shareb. You've made your point."

Ariadne melted against him, her dark eyes sparkling with love, reverence and admiration as she gazed worshipfully up into his eyes. "You've made a friend for life, now, Colin."

"I think I'd prefer him as an enemy," he returned, wryly, but he was pleased with himself and happy that his initial diagnosis had proved correct.

Yes, sometimes he *still* felt like a hero ...

She laughed and buried herself against him. Her hair smelled like grass and wind, and she was so tiny that he was almost afraid to embrace her too tightly. But she wrapped her arms around his waist and gripped him with a ferocity of strength that belied any image of delicacy her small body conveyed.

He sighed and rested his cheek atop her hair.

"You're wonderful, you know," she whispered, as though he was a god and not just a mere human. "Every day, you do something to make me love you more and more. You don't know how grateful I am, that I chose *you*, Colin, to be my horse's veterinarian."

"Dislodging a stick is not terribly difficult, my dear. Certainly, not the most challenging problem of my career."

Her hand was sliding down his thigh, heading for his groin. "Then perhaps you need something *more* challenging."

"Such as?"

"Helping me think up a way to break off my engagement to Maxwell ... without losing Gazella."

"Obviously you think me capable of great miracles."

"Oh, you are far too modest! What am I going to do with you?"

He grinned, and said invitingly, "I can think of a few things ..."

"Can you, now?" She cocked her head and looked playfully up at him. "And what are they, my good doctor?"

He looked down at her, his eyes glinting.

"Hmmm ... ?"

She never gave him the chance to answer. Laughing, she slid her hand down between his legs, found his growing arousal ... and made him incapable of thinking of anything.

Anything at all.

Chapter Twenty

They reached the Burnhams three nights later.

It should have been a triumph—making it all the way to East Anglia from London without capture—but it was not. Ariadne had felt only dread and foreboding as she began to recognize landmarks, and their route took them on roads she'd known and traveled since childhood. Soon, she knew, she would have to confront Maxwell, and the thought, for some unexplainable reason, filled her with apprehension. She had begun this mad journey wanting only to get to Norfolk, beloved, familiar Norfolk. Now, with every mile that passed behind them, her heart beat a little quicker, and she grew more and more fearful. Even the landscape—which should have provided comfort and reassurance with its beloved familiarity—could not ease her restlessness, and she had felt tears of mixed emotion in her eyes at the sight of it. Sugar beets growing in endless, sweeping fields that were coffee-colored against the green Norfolk grasses; hard wedges of flint and stone peppering the dark earth, wind, windmills, the smell of the marsh, and always, the nearness of the sea.

The sea.

Her veterinarian sensed it too. She'd seen the change in him as they'd neared Burnham and the wind swept its salty scent across bent grasses and long, rolling pastures, saw the pain that darkened his beautiful eyes as a gull flew screaming overhead, and wondered at the cause of it.

He had his secrets.

She would find them out.

What was he hiding? What terrible, shameful thing from his past didn't he trust her with? Whatever it was, Ariadne had no doubt that Colin Lord was the man she wanted to marry. Not Maxwell, whom she barely knew. Not Maxwell, whom her father had chosen to curb her wild behavior and cement the future of the Norfolk Thoroughbred.

Not Maxwell.

But Colin Lord, who was far more suited to her than Maxwell would ever be. She didn't need someone to curb her wild behavior; she needed someone who grinned helplessly at her flirting and bold remarks and made her feel appreciated instead of foolish, someone who had patience and kindness, someone who was strong, intuitive and gentle, steady where she was volatile, wise where she was impulsive. He was everything she wanted in a man. In a husband. And even if there *had* been any doubts in her mind about him, they would have been eased by the way animals acted around him, for animals, she knew, were far better judges of people than humans could ever be. Shareb alone was a case in point; the way the stallion had forgotten his earlier animosity toward the doctor and now slathered all of his attention on him was almost nauseating. He was no different than any other beast who'd fallen under the veterinarian's spell.

And neither was Ariadne.

Now, ten minutes from Maxwell's estate, she twisted around in the saddle to gaze through the starlit darkness at him, following along behind her with Thunder and the chaise. Elbows resting on his knees, the reins held loosely in his fists, he looked preoccupied, gazing out toward the fields beyond which lay the sea—and heartbreakingly handsome as the wind ruffled his hair and sent his shirt sleeves rippling against his arms. She gazed longingly at those hands; he could reduce her to a puddle of honey just by touching her with them, could set her blood afire with the lightest of kisses, a mere sideways glance from beneath those beautiful long lashes. Oh, how she loved him. And she knew in her heart that she wanted nothing more than to be with him—forever.

But now, "forever" was a frightening uncertainty, for here, bordering the road, were the eight-foot high, ivy-choked stone walls that ringed Maxwell's estate, and the gates themselves lay just around the next bend. Soon now, Colin—if he wanted her as much as she hoped, prayed, he did—would have to make a decision.

A decision to trust her enough with whatever shameful secret he was harboring.

A decision to offer for her, himself.

Thunder stumbled on a rock, and the massive, cast iron gates loomed up before them, dark, skeletal sketches against the night.

"Is this it?" Colin asked, his voice oddly strained, flat.

"Yes."

He pulled Thunder up short. "Ariadne, I... ."

"Yes?" she said breathlessly.

They stared at each other, their thoughts and longings lying unspoken between them. Colin saw the hopeful expectancy in her eyes, saw that she had caught and was holding her breath, her hands tightly clenching the reins. He was no fool, and knew very well what she wanted, what her eyes begged him to do ...

Please ask me to marry you, Colin.

But he couldn't. What would her future be like if she consented to be his wife? How would she feel when the *ton* whispered behind her back and shunned her for marrying someone who had fallen so far from grace and glory? How would she feel when they snubbed her for breaking off her engagement with an earl, only to marry a lowly animal doctor?

She deserved better than that.

And, she deserved better than a disgraced naval officer who didn't even have the courage to tell her the truth about that awful night back in '05 that had ended his career with absolute finality. He liked being her hero. He liked her warm affection and declarations of love and the adoration in her eyes at the acts of healing and caring that came as naturally to him as breathing. But oh, what would her reaction be when she opened the Pandora's box of his past and saw the ugly things that lurked inside? That adoration would quickly be replaced by shock, pity, and disgust, she would go cold toward him, and then... .

And then she would turn away and no longer love him, because in her eyes, he would no longer be a hero.

"Colin?"

Veils of cloud drifted across the night sky, and a light wind sprang up, ripe with the scent of the sea.

Pain twisted his heart. He took a deep breath, his nostrils flaring, the old ache starting up deep within his soul. His eyes fell shut and he took another breath, sucking that precious scent deeply into his lungs until he wanted to put his head in his hands and weep with longing.

Five long years, and still ... oh, did it have to hurt so damned much?

And Ariadne. Looking at him. Waiting.

"Colin, are you well?"

Insects sang in the night around them. Far, far off in the distance, he could hear the sea running against the land, and knew the tide was coming in.

"I'm fine," he said, his voice sounding hoarse and raw.

He could feel her gaze upon him and knew she was worried. He heard the stallion's shoes against dirt and stone as she turned him and sent him back to the chaise, heard the squeak of leather as she dismounted, then the rustle of her clothes, the soft sounds her feet made as she came up to him. She leaned over the door of the chaise, and put her face close to his. Her scent invaded his senses, mingling with the tang of a sea he had not dared approach since—

"Colin, you're ill." Her hand was against his brow, soft, sweet, light as air.

He opened his eyes, raked a hand over his face and shook his head. "No, Ariadne. I'm ... missing something. Someone. We—we need to talk, I think, yes, need to talk, now, while there's still time and my courage is up to it."

The breeze rustled in the trees above them, in the star-shaped ivy that fought for space on Maxwell's old wall, through the long, bent grasses of the surrounding fields. A few strands of Thunder's tail skated over Colin's fist. Several feet away, Shareb-er-rehh lifted his head, his wide nostrils flaring as he, too, caught the scents borne on the wind.

Far, far off beyond the fields, beyond Ariadne's worried face, beyond the road that ribboned away into the night, Colin saw the distant, moonlit silver line of the sea that had once defined his life.

"I have not always been a veterinarian, Ariadne," he began hoarsely, not knowing how—or where—to start. *God, give me courage.* The wind blew harder, and he saw sails in the clouds above his head, sixteen years of sails, day in, day out, from the time he'd turned twelve 'til the day the Navy threw him out in the twenty-eighth year of his life; sails, stiff with salt and hard with wind, swelling above his head and reaching toward the skies, sails in rain, snow, sunlight, fog, battle, dawn, and darkness. The breeze whispered against his cheeks, his brow, and in it he could hear the memory of distant voices moving across time and space, the voices of junior officers passing his orders on down the line, the voices of seamen calling to each other from high, high in the tops. He shut his eyes, not wanting to remember. Wanting to escape the memories, the looming tragedy he had sensed as he'd begun to pace the quarterdeck of the mighty flagship, HMS *Triton*, the wind beginning to rise, the ship moving uneasily beneath his feet, and yes, even the coldness of brass and leather as he'd pulled out his night-glass and trained it aft on HMS *Cricket*, where his admiral, Sir Graham, had gone to join that ship's captain for a late dinner... .

His admiral, newly wed and the brightest star in the Royal Navy, for whom Colin would gladly have laid down his life.

Something welled up in his throat, and he suddenly couldn't speak.

A hand touched his arm. A voice stirred the hair near his ear, seemed to come from far away. "Colin, are you well?"

He heard the wind rising, growing stronger—

"Colin?"

Rain, beginning to pelt the decks, sporadically at first and then with the tattoo of a thousand drums, so deafening he couldn't hear himself think. He took shelter beneath the poop deck, growing increasingly uneasy as he waited for his admiral to return but no, the admiral was still aboard the frigate *Cricket* with Captain Young, and could not know of the sudden fear and foreboding welling up in the heart of his flag-captain: *Do hurry, Sir Graham. It's running a high sea and I don't like this at all—*

Was it that, with an unsteady, still-healing leg that would not support him, he no longer felt invincible? Had the weakness laid bare for all to see by the rogue wave that had swept the crutches out from under him, and humiliated him in front of his officers and men, robbed him of the steady confidence that had always been such a part of him? It was just a storm, one of many, nothing to be worried about... .

And then, through the howl of the wind and rain, he'd heard it —great booms of thunder as waves broke against distant, submerged rocks.

They had, in the darkness, come up against a lee shore.

It was every sailor's nightmare.

Chaos, shouted orders, all hands on deck as the mighty flagship had begun the desperate process of saving herself. And even now, Colin knew that he could have saved her. There had been room to wear the massive warship, to find sea room. Room for *Triton*, yes.

But not for *Cricket*, much farther in their lee, so much closer to the rocks—and doomed.

He had run, limping, to the shrouds, the rain pummeling his face and the wind shrieking like a legion of demons around him. Rain had streaked the lens of his night glass as he'd trained it on the helpless *Cricket* and saw there, a sight he would never forget: Sir Graham coming up on *Cricket*'s decks ... Sir Graham, who would die if Colin didn't do something ... Sir Graham, who immediately saw their predicament and rapidly signaled him to save *Triton*, and to leave *Cricket* to her fate... .

Colin had disobeyed that order.

New commands, directly opposed to those he had just given, a suicide mission if it failed. Beneath him *Triton* laboring and straining ... the horror if every man aboard as they watched *Cricket*, floundering helplessly, moving closer and closer to the breakers, driven toward certain death by the violence of wind and current; again he heard the shouts of her terrified crew, again he saw his admiral bravely clinging to shrouds that lay nearly vertical beneath the onslaught of the storm, determined to meet his death with courage and dignity ... and again, he made the decision that had cost him his career and in the end, the lives of so many—

Someone was shaking his shoulder. Blinking, Colin opened his eyes and stared at the woman for a long, uncomprehending moment.

Ariadne.

Her face was pure white in the darkness.

"I was calling you for the past minute ... Colin?"

A sudden, violent chill seized him, and he put his face in his hands and his elbows on his knees and sat there, unmoving. His face was slick with sweat, cold, clammy, as though coated in sea spray.

Dear God.

"Ariadne, it is time to tell you something you must know—"

At that moment Maxwell's giant black boarhounds, roaring with fury, came charging out of the darkness and hit the massive iron gates with such force that they clanged with the force of the great beasts' impact. Marc ran to meet their challenge, snarling at them through the gates while Bow dove beneath Colin's legs.

The shouts of a guard pierced the night. "Who goes there?"

The boarhounds' snarling was drowning out all sound. Defeatedly, Colin made a dismissive motion with his hand. "Go ahead, answer him, Ariadne."

"But you were going to tell me something—"

"Later."

"But Colin—"

"I repeat, who's there?" shouted the guard, and the hounds renewed their crazed snarling until little Bow was howling in terror.

The veterinarian turned away, his jaw hard in the moonlight, his eyes dark with pain. It was obvious he would not speak further to her of love, marriage, or whatever his shameful secret was, tonight.

If ever.

"Damn you," Ariadne swore beneath her breath, and leaving him sitting in the chaise, stormed back to Shareb-er-rehh. She grabbed the reins, swung herself up into the saddle and drove her heels into the stallion's sides. He snorted and balked, shying at a shadow that slanted across the road, then moving skittishly forward as though he had no wish to go near those tall, ominous gates.

Behind her, came the slow plodding of Thunder's hoofbeats as Colin sent him following after Shareb.

And there was the guard, holding a musket in one hand and straining to hold two snarling, snapping boarhounds in the other as he peered through the thick iron bars.

"I repeat, who goes there?" he bellowed.

Bravely, Ariadne urged the stallion forward.

"Lady Ariadne St. Aubyn," she announced haughtily. And then, aware of the veterinarian behind her, she spat, "Lord Maxwell's betrothed. Now do open the gate. His Lordship is expecting me."

✿

"Pay to the order of ... Colin Lord ... the sum of twelve ... thousand ... pounds."

"Really, my lord, *I* was the one who offered the sum to Dr. Lord," Ariadne snapped, as the earl waited for the ink to dry on the cheque while regarding her with a tolerant, sardonic lift of one brow. "I can pay my own debts, thank you."

"Ah, dearest," came the silky reply, "you are to be my wife. What is mine is yours, and what is yours, mine. If I want to pay your escort here for safely bringing you home to me, then that is my business, is it not?"

"You don't understand," she said, her face flushed and hot. "We—"

"Nonsense, my dear." Maxwell leaned back in his chair. It galled him to part with such a large sum of money, but once he was married to the beautiful heiress he would never have financial problems again. No more debts, no more threats on his life, no more fear of debtor's prison. But oh, to think that foolish, stupid, unthinking Ariadne had sacrificed her reputation in favor of getting the horse to him ... but then, he had to admit, the horse was worth far more than her reputation, anyhow.

And no one would ever have to know how she had got here.

No one *would* know.

Five feet away from her, the lout who had brought her here sat stiffly on the edge of his chair and regarded him in a way that was downright unnerving. A veterinarian, he had called himself. He was quiet and unassuming, but there was nothing benign about his lean, powerful frame, and the eyes that coolly took his measure shone with intelligence and perception. They made the earl uncomfortable, those eyes. Not just their unusual color. But the steady, watchful way they looked at him. Through him. As though the man knew those things that no one—except Maxwell himself—knew.

Ariadne, he could deal with. Colin Lord might pose a bigger problem.

The name struck him then. *Colin Lord.* He'd heard it before ... sometime, someplace. But where?

No matter. It would be only a matter of time before he placed it.

But he had a bigger problem than just Colin Lord. He had not failed to notice the way Ariadne had angled her body toward the veterinarian's, nor how he had pulled his chair possessively close to hers.

The slut.

Maxwell rose to his feet, consciously aware of his own height, and the image of power and sinister strength he conveyed.

The veterinarian rose to his feet, too. He reached out to take the check that Maxwell thrust toward him, and it was then that the earl saw the ring on the other man's finger.

Not just any ring, but one with an anchor on it.

In that moment, he knew precisely who Colin Lord was.

AS COLIN ACCEPTED THE CHECK, Ariadne felt as though someone had slammed a fist into her stomach and then left her to die. The blood drained from her face, and her fingers went cold. She started to get up but every limb in her body had frozen, and she fell back into the chair, staring at Colin in shock and betrayal while the flames crackled and popped in the hearth.

"I am in your debt, Mr. Lord, for safely conveying my lovely Ariadne to me," she heard Maxwell saying, and the casual, cultured tone of his voice finally invaded her shock. Feeling flooded back into her, and she managed to rise to her feet.

"H-he's a ... doctor," she heard herself say.

"Yes, of course," Maxwell murmured dismissively, and his eyes flickered over the veterinarian, giving away nothing. "Would you care to see the fabulous Black Patrick before you take your leave, *Mr.* Lord? The syndicate that owns him has stabled him here, in the hopes of breeding some of my fine mares to him. Surely you have heard of this wonderful horse? He is unbeaten, the fastest steed to hit an English turf since Eclipse." The earl reached out and cupped Ariadne's elbow, drawing her away from Colin. "Come, my dear—"

Colin had had enough. "I have something to say to the lady before you draw her away."

"Mr. Lord, she is my betrothed. Anything you have to say to her can be said in front of me."

"As you wish, then."

Maxwell stared at him with malice. Colin returned the look unflinchingly, then stepped toward Ariadne. The cheque lay like a diseased thing between his thumb and forefinger, making him want to shudder with disgust. Still holding Maxwell's gaze, he tore it neatly in half, balled the two halves in his fist, and tossed them into the fire.

Maxwell raised both brows.

Ariadne gaped, her eyes huge in her suddenly white face.

And Colin moved toward her, trying not to limp, and took her cold hand firmly in his own. It was not the way he had intended to propose, it was not even appropriate in manner, circumstance, or style—but desperate situations call for desperate measures, and he had no choice in the matter.

"Lady Ariadne—what I tried to say earlier—will you marry me?"

Her mouth opened and for one terrible moment he thought she was going to refuse him. She glanced at Maxwell, standing calmly beside the fire, his one eye as black as Hades, the other chilling in its opacity. She gave the tiniest of nods—and then threw herself into Colin's arms, her body shaking with relief.

She clung to him, and Colin looked up to see Maxwell staring at him with monstrous fury.

"I should call you out for this, Mr. Lord."

The fire crackled in the hearth. *Snap. Fizz.* A thump of a falling log, and then a shower of falling sparks.

Colin drew Ariadne beside him. "Pistols or swords?" he asked, mildly.

"Oh, I shouldn't think it would matter to you, *Captain*. I daresay you're quite skilled with both, are you not?"

Captain? Confused, Ariadne stared at the two men. What on earth was Maxwell talking about? Then she realized just what was happening, and horror swept through her.

"I will *not* have the two of you fighting like little boys over me!" she cried, stepping between them and glaring at them both in turn. "Colin, I give you my answer: *yes*. Maxwell, I give you my explanation: Dr. Lord and I have fallen in love. I cannot marry you when my heart belongs to another."

She saw fury darkening the earl's face, a faint quivering about his aristocratic nostrils. He stared at her—then turned his back and walked toward the fire, there to stand silently.

Ariadne's heart was too soft to tolerate the fact that she had just injured another so severely. She stared up at the back of Maxwell's dark, handsome head, the fringe of perfectly styled hair just touching his collar, the broad span of his shoulders beneath his coat. Maxwell was a proud man. She had just cut him deeply— and unforgivably. The least she could do was offer an explanation to this man she was supposed to have married.

Embarrassed, and feeling small and mean, she turned to Colin and took his hands in her own.

"Will you allow me a few moments to explain our situation to Maxwell ... in private?" she asked, silently pleading for him to understand.

She saw the uncertainty and distrust in his perceptive eyes, the hesitation etched in his features.

"Please, Colin?" She squeezed his fingers. "Just a moment?"

The earl remained standing at the fire, his back turned toward them and the burned, blackened bits that had been the cheque curling at his feet.

Colin pursed his lips and she could see the inner battle he was waging. He gave Ariadne a long, searching glance, and reached up to touch her cheek—then, without another word, he nodded and walked toward the door.

Her hands clammy, she anxiously watched him close the door behind him. And then she turned and found herself staring into the cold eyes of Clive, Lord Maxwell.

Chapter Twenty-One

A mere hour and a half after Maxwell's boarhounds had flung themselves at the big iron gates, another traveler appeared there, tired, hungry—and desperate.

Tristan, the new Lord Weybourne.

Splattered with mud, his fine clothes rumpled and dusty, the young earl sat astride his mare while the gatekeeper, holding the two growling dogs, opened the gate. Thank God for the darkness that hid his shaking hands, the sure pallor of his face. Carefully, he schooled his features into an expression of impatience and boredom, though his heart was thundering in his chest and his hands were sweating.

"My sister, the Lady Ariadne," he began, glancing down at the fresh hoofprints that cut the road up beneath him. "I have reason to believe that she is here."

"Yes, her ladyship arrived tonight," the gatekeeper said, straining to hold the boarhounds' collars and letting his gaze rake flatly over Tristan. "In fact, she is probably with my lord right now, as we speak."

Tristan shuddered. "I must see her. Immediately."

"Of course. Right this way, my lord," the gatekeeper

murmured, managing to raise his flat, hard voice over the vicious barking and growling of the boarhounds. He eyed Tristan coolly. "His lordship is ... *expecting* you."

Cold sweat broke out on Tristan's brow. He felt the customary prickle of fear threading its way up his spine at thought of confronting Maxwell, and his arms and hands went suddenly numb. *Think of Ariadne.* He urged the mare forward, and she shot nervously past the open gate.

He sent her into a gallop and flying down the long drive. Far ahead in the distance he saw the great stone manor house, black and foreboding against the night sky, its windows blazing with light.

Terror swept through him and he leaned low over the mare's neck, urging her faster and faster.

Ariadne was in there.

Dear God, don't let me be too late.

"Really, my dear ... you never fail to shock and surprise me."

Ariadne swallowed hard, suddenly, inexplicably, afraid. She gazed up into Maxwell's saturnine face, but she could read nothing there; the pain she had seen earlier was gone, replaced with a look of bored indifference, and only the tightness of his words and the way his hand clenched and unclenched the poker belied the sense of betrayal and rage he must surely feel.

Still holding the poker, he began a slow, studied walk, back and forth before the great marble hearth. The fire's light glowed eerily against his hair, the harsh planes of his face, the eyes that suddenly seemed bottomless and empty. The butler came in, was ushered back toward the door by the earl, who muttered something under his breath; then Maxwell turned and regarded Ariadne.

"You are throwing away your father's dream, you know, with

your insistence upon marrying this—this rabble," he said, noncommittally, with a glance at the door through which the butler had gone. "You are one of the wealthiest women in England. Do you think that a lowly animal doctor would really want you for your *looks?*"

That stung. "I should hope my *looks* are at least equal to my financial status, my lord," she replied coolly. "And as for my inheritance, I think it's obvious that *Doctor* Lord has no interest whatsoever in my money."

"Oh, yes, I'm sure he does not. Perhaps it is your horse that he wants then, eh?"

"Really, sir, I am trying to explain my feelings as a sane and rational adult. Please do not make this any more difficult for me than it already is."

He glanced at her, his eyes raking disapprovingly over her mud-splattered clothes, her ungloved hands, her loose and tangled hair. She felt suddenly unclean and barbaric.

"Difficult," he murmured, softly. "Here I have been worried sick about you while the whole countryside has been up in arms trying to hunt you down. You show up here looking like you just crawled out of a pasture, proclaim your love for another man, and do not expect me to be upset?"

"I had no intention of falling in love with Colin Lord. I sought him out because I needed an escort and someone to look after Shareb-er-rehh's welfare... ."

"And?"

"Well ... things just rather—happened, I guess." She felt her face flaming red, and the way Maxwell was looking at her made her feel suddenly foolish and ridiculous.

An urgent knock sounded on the door. Trailing off, Ariadne watched as the earl, carrying the poker behind his back like a whip, strode across the room to open it. The butler stood there, his face expressionless. He glanced at Ariadne, and then lowered his voice, murmuring something that she could not catch. Maxwell answered him, his words equally unintelligible.

"Thank you, Mr. Critchley," the earl murmured, and closing the door after the butler, turned to Ariadne. His eyes glinted, and a slow, triumphant smile began to curve his mouth.

"It would seem, my dear, that your affections for Mr. Lord are rather one-sided," he drawled, running his fingers almost lovingly over the poker.

"What are you talking about?"

"I left a check for fifteen-thousand pounds with Mr. Critchley in the hope of buying your beloved veterinarian off with it," he said smoothly.

Her fists clenched behind her back. "And?"

"It seems, my lady, that he has taken the money and run."

COLIN HAD NOT RUN.

In the darkened stable where Shareb-er-rehh and Thunder had been brought, he sat in the straw at the old gelding's feet, leaning his back against the animal's stout foreleg and cradling Bow in his lap. Although his hand ran rhythmically, soothingly, over the little dog's fur, she was trembling madly, her sclera white and framing huge, frightened irises.

Five more minutes, Ariadne, he thought, pulling out his watch. He gazed impatiently out the open door and toward the manor house. *Five more minutes, and I'm coming in after you.*

Bow trembled harder, almost nearing convulsions.

"Poor little dog," he murmured, gently stroking her ears. "Still not quite recovered from the terrible scare those boarhounds gave you, are you?"

Bow whined and tried to bury her whiskery face in the crook of his elbow. Nearby, Marc was sniffing in the straw, but now, the gun dog sighed and wandered over to Colin, licked his face once, and settled down against his bad leg, as though he knew it was troubling him and sought to relieve the pain. Something touched his hair and Colin looked up to see Thunder's muzzle there, velvety and smooth. The gelding blew softly through his nose, then lifted his head to regard Shareb-er-rehh.

Colin followed his gaze.

The mighty stallion stood tensely in his private box, ears pricked forward, black forelock falling rakishly over one eye, nostrils flaring wide and red. He was staring out the window and toward the great manor house. Every muscle in his body was rigid, and his sleek coat was dark with nervous sweat.

A tickle of foreboding swept through Colin. Something was not right... .

Suddenly, Shareb flattened his ears, his eyes glowing savagely in the moonlight.

"What is it, boy?"

Gently putting Bow on the straw beside him, Colin got to his feet. He brushed pieces of hay from his breeches, pocketed his spectacles, and approaching the stallion, ran his hand calmingly over the powerful hindquarters, the sleek ribs, the sharply angled shoulder and crested neck as he peered out the window to follow Shareb's intent gaze.

There, walking stiffly across the drive and toward the stable, was Maxwell's butler, a thin, crook-nosed man with a ring of pale hair encircling his skull. He stopped half-way across the little courtyard and waited while two stable hands melted out of the darkness and joined him.

Shareb began to blow and snort. One hoof struck angrily out at the wall and his squeal pierced the night.

Frowning, Colin watched as the butler punctuated words he could not hear with urgent gestures toward the stable, the manor house, the flat, Norfolk pastures that rolled away behind the stables. But Shareb must have heard them, maybe even understood them, for his squeal became a high-pitched sound of rage and he suddenly reared up, jerking angrily at his lead rope and slamming his hooves against the side of the stall, hard.

The butler cast a quick glance toward the stable; then he turned abruptly and walked back toward the house, the moonlight glowing against his pate.

Colin watched the man until the darkness swallowed him up. He put a hand on Shareb's neck, finding it hot and lathered. Something was going on, and he didn't like the feel of it. Ariadne had had long enough to explain their situation to Maxwell, and the sooner they collected the animals—including the lovely mare, Gazella—and got the hell out of here, the better.

With Bow trotting at his heels, he strode determinedly out of the box stall and the stable, never hearing Shareb-er-rehh's and Thunder's desperate whinnying behind him.

Never heeding Marc's attempts to wind himself around his feet and slow him down.

He reached the manor house and slammed his fist hard against the door. It opened, and the cadaverous butler stood there, smiling.

"Ah, Mr. Lord," the old man said archly, his eyes gleaming through years of cataracts. "We were wondering where you'd gone—"

"I want to see Lady Ariadne."

"But oh, she does not wish to see *you*."

"I beg your pardon?"

The butler smiled malevolently. "I'm sorry, sir, but the lady has come to her senses following her temporary lapse in judgment. She has decided to honor her betrothal to my lord, after all."

"What in God's name are you saying, man?" Colin demanded.

"That you are no longer welcome at Maxwell Hall. Good day, sir."

And then the big door was shut in his face, and Colin was left alone on the darkened steps.

❧

ARIADNE STOOD IN THE LIBRARY, the fire at her back and the darkness pushing against the tall, elegantly draped windows. She stared incredulously at Maxwell, her face white with shock while his last words echoed through her stunned brain.

It seems, my lady, that he has taken the money and run ... and run ... and run... .

"He wouldn't!" she cried, stalking to the heavy, olive-green drapes and yanking them aside. But there was nothing to see out there in the night, and letting the fabric fall back in place, she strode to the door, determined to find and confront Colin for herself.

A hand fell upon her shoulder, the fingers digging into her bones and halting her progress. She spun angrily around and found herself face-to-face with Maxwell.

"Unhand me!"

"Ariadne." The single word was spoken with a quiet, almost sinister finality, and the hand on her shoulder never wavered. She tried to wiggle free of it, but the fingers only sank further into her flesh, trapping her. "Can you not face the truth? Your veterinarian has more need of fifteen thousand pounds than he does a wife. Do not make a fool of yourself by running after him." The hand strayed, gently grazing the side of her neck, her cheek.

Ariadne stood frozen. She stared up at the earl's face, feeling horror, then hysteria rising up in her throat until she couldn't breathe and her world began to go dark. This was her past repeating itself all over again, her worst nightmare coming true. No. Colin wouldn't do this to her! He was not like her father, for whom money and horses and his own pursuits meant more than his only daughter! He was not like that, oh, dear God, he was not!

"But ... we love each other!"

The dark gaze grew warm, penetrating ... almost frightening, making her feel like a moth being drawn toward a hot fire out of

which there was no escape. "And you are Lady Ariadne St. Aubyn
—far too good for a disgraced *hero* the likes of Captain Colin
Lord."

Captain. That was the second time she'd heard that word
tonight..

"Disgraced hero? Captain? What are you talking about?"

One black brow rose. "You mean you don't *know*?"

"Know what?"

A slow, chilling smile lifted the earl's mouth, and he put an
arm around her back. "Why, my dear, it is no wonder he didn't tell
you, such a shameful scandal it all was ... You see, your veterinarian was formerly a naval officer who was court-martialed out of
the Navy. Five years ago it, was, if I remember correctly. 'Colin
Lord.' Ah, I knew that name sounded familiar—"

She stared at him, unable to speak.

"Don't look so shocked, my dear. The whole of England heard
about it, it was in all the newspapers. But then, you were too
young then to take notice, were you not?"

Ariadne found her voice. "A *captain*? Court-martialed out of
the Navy? For what?"

Again, that dark, satisfied smile. "A storm, it was. Against
orders, your dear lover made a foolishly heroic attempt to save his
admiral's foundering ship—and failed."

And failed.

So this was Colin's big secret, the thing that haunted him, the
terrible disgrace that he had hinted at but had been unable to
bring himself to relate. Relief and incredulity made her legs weak.
She put a hand on the back of a stuffed chair to steady herself,
while the world reeled around her.

"The Navy does not like to lose its ships, you know," Maxwell
said, smiling. "Damned expensive things to replace."

Ariadne pushed her fingers against her brow. It was all clear to
her, now. The sea chest. The strange little mannerisms, the
nautical references, even the name of his dog. At last, she knew

the reasons for the militaristic bearing, the air of authority, the visible pain she'd seen on his face when they'd heard that fiddler in the tavern, when they'd come into Burnham and the scent of the sea had lain so heavily in the night air.

Oh, Colin... .

No wonder he hadn't asked her to marry him. He was too ashamed of his past to think that she'd ever want him. Anger swept through her, and a desperate urge to go running after him. If he had left her, it had nothing to do with money, but with his own pride! And to think he'd been disgraced for trying to save his admiral?

"I'm going after him," she announced, and turning her back on Maxwell, strode, then ran, toward the door.

And found it locked.

COLIN MIGHT HAVE BEEN off the sea for five years, but his mariner's instincts—and skills—were still intact.

It didn't take him long to find a good, stout length of rope in the stable. An hour later, he was standing in the darkness outside the manor house, the rope in one hand, Thunder waiting patiently beside him, and the two windows that proclaimed the wakefulness of its occupant glowing golden between the drapes, two stories above his head.

He had no doubt that that occupant was Ariadne, and didn't believe for a moment that she had changed her mind about him. There was too much tension in the air, too much suspicious behavior on the part of the earl's servants, and his every instinct warned him that Ariadne was in grave danger.

Well, if they wouldn't let him into the house, then he'd just have to enter by his own means.

He gazed up at the imposing wall of ivy-choked stone that towered above his head. The breeze, ripe with the promise of rain, tickled the leaves of several nearby oak trees, making them shake ominously in the darkness. Bow whined softly and pressed against his ankle. He reached down to reassure her, gave Marc, who was also nearby, a scratch behind the ears, then looked up once again. The nearest handhold was a good ten feet up.

Too far to reach.

He gauged his task silently for a moment, then brought the gelding up close to the side of the house. As though he knew what was needed of him, Thunder braced himself as Colin kicked off his boots and pulled himself up onto the horse's back. His balance precarious, he crouched, then stood up, one foot on the gelding's withers to try to make his weight more bearable for the old horse, the other resting just in front of the animal's kidneys. Thunder groaned beneath his weight, but remained faithfully still.

"Good boy," Colin murmured, already feeling his bad leg beginning to protest, and without being told, the gelding took a step closer to the house. The movement was enough to upset Colin's already shaky balance, and wildly, he managed to grab the stony ledge of the windowsill, there to swing desperately by his fingertips while his feet dangled into space.

He cursed and gritted his teeth. Then, with all his strength, he pulled himself up onto the ledge, tossed the rope over a grinning gargoyle just above his head, and began to climb ... .

Never seeing Maxwell's servant watching him, nor the shadow he made as he darted from the beneath those trees and ran for the house.

Chapter Twenty-Two

Tristan had just worked up the courage to knock on Maxwell's door, a half-baked plan in his mind to rescue Ariadne, when he heard Shareb-er-rehh's high, piercing whinny coming from the stable.

Ari *was* here, then. *Oh, God...* .

Leading his mare, he crept around the back of the building and slipped inside. Horses moved in the darkness. He smelled their warm hides, and heard his own nervous breathing shattering the still quiet.

There, in a roomy box at the end, was the stallion.

He glanced apprehensively behind him, but his entry had gone unnoticed. By the meager starlight beaming down through the window, he could just see Shareb-er-rehh's proud, beautifully chiseled head, his small, pricked ears, the arched crest of his long neck. The stallion was staring fixedly out the window, the moonlight gleaming in his dark eye; then he turned his head and saw Tristan.

Both man and beast froze.

Shareb's huge, shell-shaped nostrils quivered, taking the air. Tristan saw and recognized the horse's distinctive white blaze.

The two stared at each other, neither one moving—and then the stallion's low, welcoming whinny came softly through the darkness.

Tristan had never heard a sweeter, more comforting sound in his life. He ran forward and put his arms around the horse's neck, his eyes stinging with emotion as he laid his cheek against the sparse black mane and hugged the horse nearly hard enough to strangle him. Relief and courage coursed through him. Shareb was just a horse, but he had been his father's horse, and there in the darkness, the young Lord Weybourne felt his father's presence and knew it was time to confront the devil.

For he hadn't posted the rewards, worried himself sick, and chased Ariadne all the way to Norfolk to lay claim on a horse that was already his.

He'd chased her to stop her before she could marry that fiend that Father had unwittingly pledged her to.

A fiend who belonged in the very pit of Hell itself.

Steeling himself, Tristan turned and made his way toward the big manor house.

ARIADNE, wearing a green gown trimmed in peach and ivory that had been hastily procured from the nearby Weybourne estate, paced the confines of the bedchamber to which she'd been brought.

Fresh from a bath and a maid's attention, her coppery locks entwined with artfully arranged strands of pearl and her hands wrapped in butter-soft gloves, she was once again the Lady Ariadne who had both captivated and scandalized London society. But the bath had failed to leave her feeling clean, the gown (even though it had come directly from her own armoire) was restrictive and uncomfortable after the clothing she'd spent the last week in, and this room that Maxwell had provided for her—*until you can safely return to your family's home, my dear*—seemed more like a prison than a haven.

Especially after she had tried the door and found it locked.

The discovery enraged her. Did Maxwell think her an impulsive child who didn't know her own mind? No doubt he knew she'd go racing off after Colin, and thought a few hours of confinement would restore her to sanity—and, a wish to rethink her decision and honor her betrothal. Well, she objected to such high-handed treatment, knew her own mind very well, thank you, and had no intention of marrying Maxwell, not today, not tomorrow, not *ever*.

And Colin—she clenched her fists in rising anger, the gloves stretching tightly across her knuckles. She had a word or two to say to him, as well! Oh, she didn't believe for one minute that he'd been bought off by Maxwell's fifteen-thousand-pound cheque, especially after he'd ripped up the first one with such contempt. She remembered how he'd refused to speak about his past, how he was so ashamed to tell her about his deep, dark, secret. Maxwell was lying. Colin had not deserted her because of a large sum of money, he'd left because of his shame about the court-martial.

Oh, when she caught up to him—

There was a noise outside. Something moving against the side of the house. The sill. Her window. Frowning, she tiptoed to the drapes, drew them aside—and nearly screamed.

There, his face reflecting the glow of candlelight behind her, was Colin, crouched precariously on the ledge and motioning desperately for her to open the window.

With a little cry, she threw it open.

"Colin!"

It took him but a second to haul himself over the sill and into her arms. She sobbed with relief as he crushed her to his chest and held her fiercely, protectively, against his body. Never had she been so glad to see anyone in her life.

"Oh, Colin, I thought you'd run off and left me here—"

"Shh, Ariadne," he whispered, against her hair. "We don't have much time. I want you to put your arms around my neck and hold on tight. We're going back down—then, we'll have to seize the horses and make a run for it."

She felt movement, and pulling back, Ariadne saw that his bad leg was visibly shaking with the effort of having made what had to have been a difficult and excruciatingly painful climb up the side of the house. But he had done it—and he had done it for her.

"Come, Ariadne, we must leave, now!"

"But your leg—"

She never finished. The door crashed open and a horde of men, pistols in hand, charged inside. Ariadne had no time to even utter a scream before Colin thrust her aside and out of the way. She stumbled and grabbed the edge of a chair, hearing the sickening thuds of fists against flesh. Shouts and curses echoed in her ears; a gun went off, someone screamed, and she gained her feet only to see Colin slam his fist into the jaw of a big, powerful brute with greasy black hair and a mouthful of broken teeth.

"Run, Ariadne! For God's sake, get out of here!"

He whirled, ducked a chair that came swinging around at his head, and managed to dispatch the assailant with a strong uppercut to the chin. The man went down, and Colin whirled to meet another attack—but his leg, shaking with fatigue, gave out from under him and he fell heavily to the floor. He rolled aside, but it was too late; hands hauled him roughly to his feet, someone landed a hard blow to his belly, and as he doubled over in agony, one of the attackers brought the butt end of his pistol cracking down hard against the back of his skull.

With a groan, he collapsed and fell sprawling to the floor. One finger twitched, and then he lay still.

For a horrified moment, Ariadne could not move. Then, with a cry of anguish, she fell to her knees on the rug beside him, her arms going protectively around him and pulling him up against her even as the door opened and Maxwell himself stepped inside.

Instantly, everyone fell silent.

Brows raised, the earl surveyed the room with a cool, appraising eye. Outside, a dog —*Bow*, Ariadne thought dazedly— was barking frantically. Maxwell jerked his chin, and one of his minions ran to the window and slammed it shut.

Then he turned and regarded his men, Ariadne, and, with a smile of contempt, the man who lay unconscious in her arms.

She pulled him protectively close.

"Well, well, is *this* what my meeting with the new Lord Weybourne was interrupted for?" Sighing, he put his hands behind his back and peered down at the veterinarian. "Ah, look. A thieving intruder." He gazed at one of his servants, just picking himself up from the floor and groaning in pain from Colin's well-placed blow, then the butler who stood faithfully behind him. "Critchley? Please arrange to have this refuse carted out and *shot*."

"You can't do that!" Ariadne cried, holding Colin's lolling head to her shoulder. "That's *murder*!"

"That's *justice*," Maxwell corrected her coolly. "The blackguard broke into my house. He shall get the punishment he deserves."

For a moment Ariadne could only stare at Maxwell in horror and disbelief, the blood draining from her face. She suddenly remembered the feeling of danger, fear even, as Maxwell had strode calmly back and forth in front of the fire, the poker clenched behind his back, his one sighted eye black and bottomless.

Oh, my God ... .

"Please stand up, my dear," Maxwell said softly.

"No!" she cried, locking a trembling arm behind Colin's shoulders and clasping his heavy weight against her. "You'll have to shoot me first, Maxwell, I swear it!"

The earl sighed. His cold gaze flickered over his rival's still body, and Ariadne's skirts pinned beneath it. "I wouldn't dream of harming a hair on your pretty head, my dear," he murmured. "Get up."

"I *said*, no!"

"My lady." Maxwell's smile widened, and he reached to take the cheroot offered by his butler. "If you do not get up, I will have you forcibly hauled away from your lover by your hair, and *still* have him shot as a thief before the sun is up."

Ariadne glared at him, splaying her fingers up through Colin's hair and pressing his head against her even more tightly.

"Or," Maxwell continued, gesturing with his cheroot, "You can obey your father's wishes and honor your betrothal to me." He flicked an imaginary bit of dust from his sleeve. "The choice, my dear, is yours. Honor your betrothal to me, or I shall have the good doctor shot."

"That's *blackmail*!"

"That's my offer. Make a decision, or I will make it for you."

Swallowing hard, Ariadne was acutely aware of Colin's weight in her arms, his lifeblood flowing through his veins, the slow beating of his heart, so close to hers. She felt his hair against her palm and between her fingers, the weight of his brow against the cup of her shoulder—

"What will it be, my dear?"

She directed a cold glare at the earl. "You leave me no choice, do you?"

"No more than you leave me."

An icy chill pervaded the very marrow of Ariadne's bones, and tears leaked from her eyes. *Oh, Father ... why did you ever pledge me to this man, didn't you know what a monster he is?*

She pressed a kiss to Colin's brow, whispered a plea for forgiveness that she knew he never heard, and then, one hand supporting the back of his head, carefully eased him down to the floor. Her hands were trembling as she pulled her skirts out from beneath his heavy weight, and it was all she could do to maintain her courage, and her dignity, as she coldly refused Maxwell's offered hand and got to her feet; harder still as his men shoved her roughly aside and picked up Colin's body as though it was nothing but rubbish for the compost pile. As they lifted him, she reached out to touch his hand a final time, and found it deathly cold. Then, at a nod from Maxwell, the men shouldered her aside and carried him out of the room.

Maxwell followed, closing the door behind him. And so it was that Ariadne didn't hear the earl's last, cold order to his faithful servant, Daley.

"Take him out to the far pasture and put a bullet in his head. And I don't want to see your face again until the deed is done. Is that understood?"

"Yes, my lord."

Ariadne, alone in her room and crying into her pillow, never heard the single shot that cracked the night. By the time the sun came up three hours later, Daley was back, his face sober, his trousers smeared with grass stains, his hands filthy with the dirt of the grave. He gave his hasty report to the earl, who nodded with satisfaction and then, calmly sipping his tea, called for his morning paper.

For Maxwell, life had never looked better. His rival was out of the way. The Fastest Horse in the World was in his stable.

And now, nothing—not the chit's father, her stupid, spineless brother, nor even her lover himself—could stand between him and the great St. Aubyn fortunes.

TRISTAN WAS QUITE proud of himself. Not only had he cleverly disguised his plan—and a desperate plan it was, too—as a gamble that Maxwell could not resist, but he had carried it through with a cool directness of purpose that would have done his father proud. Surely, it was only the thought of his endangered sister that had infused him with such courage, but nevertheless, Tristan was almost grateful for the abrupt appearance of Maxwell's butler, and the subsequent conclusion of the meeting. Now, as he stalked out of the house, a servant running to open the door before he reached it, his heart was pounding as much with relief as it was with fear, because there were a million and one things that could go wrong with his plan to rescue Ariadne.

A plan that depended entirely upon the very one who had gotten her into this mess:

Shareb-er-rehh.

The meeting was still fresh in Tristan's mind... .

"What do you mean, she's agreed to marry you?" Tristan had said, jumping to his feet and staring angrily at Maxwell. "I forbid it! You know what my father's wishes were, you know what my sister's wishes were! I demand to see her immediately!"

"Sit down, Tristan."

"I said, I want to see her, *now*!"

"Your sister is indisposed. She retired early, pleading a headache and expressing her wish to take tea in her room. Surely, this reunion between siblings can wait until morning."

He stared into Maxwell's eyes. They gave nothing away, and as usual, were as cold as the soul of the monster that looked out of them. Shaking with anger, Tristan sat heavily down in a chair and drained his port with one quick, fluid flick of the wrist. He slammed the glass down, and the elegant crystal shattered into a thousand pieces.

"My, my ... what has the aristocracy come to, if its fine young men can no longer show proper poise and manners in other people's homes," Maxwell drawled.

"Don't goad me," Tristan said heatedly. "I'm not afraid of you. Not this time. Not anymore. My father told me, not two hours before he died, that he'd sent you a letter terminating the engagement between you and my sister! He didn't want Ariadne married to you, not after I told him what you are *really* like!"

"Now Tristan—" the earl began, condescendingly.

"And isn't it strange, that somebody *mysteriously* set fire to his stables the very night he sent that letter?"

"Quite strange indeed," Maxwell said, fixedly staring at Tristan and smiling a thin, evil little smile.

"One would think it was almost in *revenge*," Tristan taunted, knowing he was walking at the edge of an active volcano.

Maxwell lit a cheroot, appeared to study it thoughtfully. "Pity, that some things can be surmised ... but never proven."

"You will not marry my sister."

Maxwell, still gazing at his cheroot, smiled without looking at Tristan. "Oh, but I will. The betrothal is still on."

"I say it's not. And I would like to see my sister, *now*."

"Of course, there *is* the matter of ... the veterinarian," the earl said, offhandedly. "Tell me, does your sister fall in love with every handsome man who happens to come her way? She arrived here looking like a grub worm that just crawled out of the garden. 'Twould be a pity indeed, if society were to find out that she traipsed across half the English countryside unchaperoned, save for the company of a man who managed to get himself thrown out of the Royal Navy for losing not one, but two of its finest warships... ."

Tristan was not prepared for this. He had always known that his sister was impulsive and flighty, but to think she could fall in love with someone she'd only known for what, a week?

"My time is valuable. What do you want, Tristan?"

His mind whirling, Tristan had no choice but to seize opportunity from despair. He sat back in his chair, plucked a book on foxhunting from the table beside him, and to still his shaking fingers, casually flipped through the pages, all the while feeling Maxwell's malevolent stare boring into him behind a cloud of blue smoke.

"You are a gambling man," he said, turning another page and pretending to be absorbed in a drawing of a hunting scene. He let a moment go by, just enough for drama and effect. "Therefore, I have a proposal for you, Maxwell. A proposal that, as a sporting man, should prove unbearably tempting to you."

Out of the corner of his eye, Tristan saw one sinister black brow rise, ever so slightly. Maxwell gestured with his cheroot. "This ought to be interesting. But go ahead. I'm listening."

"Black Patrick is the unbeaten king of the English turf," Tristan continued, casually reciting a well known fact but feeling his own hands beginning to sweat at what he was about to propose. "In thirty-five races, he has never been defeated."

Maxwell's unnerving stare was leveled on Tristan's face.

"Shareb-er-rehh is the last of my father's Norfolk Thorough-breds, excepting, of course, Gazella. He is the Fastest Horse in the World—"

"Purportedly, Tristan, but never proven." Maxwell took a long draw on his cheroot, blew out a perfect ring of smoke, and stamped the thing out. "After all, the beast has never been raced."

"Precisely. Which is why my proposal should interest you greatly."

"And just what is it you propose?" he asked, condescendingly.

"A match race between Black Patrick and Shareb-er-rehh."

Maxwell laughed softly, a soft, thready sound that froze the blood in Tristan's veins. He shook his head.

"With the horse himself as the stakes," Tristan finished, quietly.

Maxwell stopped laughing. He turned the full effect of his eyes on Tristan, and on a note of scared triumph, Tristan saw the sudden, keen interest that flickered in those chilling depths. "Really, Tristan ... haven't you learned your lesson? You are hope-lessly in debt to me already, with no means of paying me off until you reach the age to inherit." He smiled, threateningly. "That is, *if*, you reach the age to inherit. All you have left is that horse ... and you would risk even *that*?"

"I love that horse ... but I love my sister more," Tristan said, his voice beginning to tremble, for the thought of losing Shareb-er-rehh filled him with as much grief as the last memory of his father.

"Well ..."

"Despite what my sister thinks, Shareb-er-rehh belongs to me," Tristan said firmly. "Therefore, what becomes of the horse is my decision, and what I propose is this: If Shareb-er-rehh wins the race, you must free me from all debts owed to you — and, my sister from a betrothal that neither she, my father, nor I, wish. *Publicly*."

Maxwell leaned back in his chair and calmly folded his arms behind his head, his gaze boring into Tristan like nails. "And if Black Patrick wins the race?"

Sick dread pulsed through Tristan's stomach, making jelly out of his nerves, for such a thing did not even bear thinking about. He raised his chin and resolutely met the earl's black stare. "Then ownership of both Gazella and Shareb-er-rehh goes to you."

Maxwell looked at him for a long, thoughtful moment, his eyes glinting with greed. He kept that calculated stare on Tristan until the young lord felt his heart beginning to pound, the sweat popping out on his brow. *Please, God, let him accept the proposal, it is the only way I know to save both my sister and my horse—*

"Has it ever occurred to you, Tristan, that the stallion is already *mine*? As part of your assets—assets that will be sold off to pay me, I'll remind you, if you don't come up with the money—I can rightfully claim him anyhow as payment of your debt." He smiled, threateningly. "One way or another, the horse is mine."

Tristan met that black gaze, sudden rage bubbling up in his throat like acid. "He is *not* yours, Maxwell, and if you resort to such lowly means to try and gain him, I will sell him to one of my friends for the sum of a mere pound, if only to keep him out of your clutches."

Maxwell laughed softly then, and Tristan's very bones felt cold.

"If you love this horse so much, then why would you risk losing him in a match race?" he said, patronizingly.

"Because I know that you won't be able to resist the opportunity to make money—lots of money—that such a race would offer, for not only will it draw crowds from Norfolk, but from all over Britain as well. It will be the sensation of the century."

Maxwell's eyes glinted. "And... ?"

"Because I will do anything to save my sister from marrying you."

"And ... ?

Tristan leaned forward in his chair, gripping its arms and locking his gaze with Maxwell's. "Because I have every faith in the world that Shareb-er-rehh will win."

He sat back, his heart hammering painfully against his ribs. Maxwell looked at him for a long, assessing moment. Then, he gave a slight nod, and reached for his calendar.

"You are a fool, Tristan. But then, I have made a fortune off of fools, idiots—and people who don't know when their luck has run out. But what do I have to lose? We shall run the race." He pulled the calendar toward him. "Shall we make it, say ... one week from tomorrow?"

"One week from tomorrow."

"I shall send a courier to Newmarket, then, to alert my racing friends so they can spread the word," Maxwell said, and Tristan could see that the fire had caught hold of the earl, just as he'd known, hoped, gambled, that it would. "Some advertisements there, in the newspapers, in London—"

The door opened suddenly, and the butler, gaunt and skeletal, stood there, looking like a corpse that had just crawled out of the coffin—save for the eyes, which were bright with desperation.

"Excuse me, my lord. There is a small ... disturbance, that demands your immediate attention... ."

Maxwell had risen to his feet, bid Tristan good-evening, and that had been the end of a confrontation that Tristan had been dreading with every waking breath of the last week. Now, he wanted only to escape this Hades incarnate, find this veterinarian of Ariadne's—*bloody hell, why didn't she just run off with the damned groom?*—and demand some answers. And as for the race... . He'd see Maxwell in hell before he gave up either Shareb-er-rehh or his sister to the soulless fiend!

The night was dark, lit only by the silver wash of starlight and the eerie bars of gold slanting across the lawn from Maxwell's windows. Tristan was almost to the stable when he heard shouts and pistol shots coming from behind him.

Within the house.

He froze.

His first instinct was to rush back inside, his only thought the safety of his sister. But rationale took hold of him and he dove for cover behind a block of shrubbery, peeking out just in time to see a door open and several men, carrying a dead body between them, hurrying across the dark lawn. Dread iced Tristan's spine, numbing his limbs and settling in his stomach. In horror, he watched as they slung the corpse over the back of an old, sway-backed gelding, exchanged quick words between themselves, and leaving only one of their number behind, returned to the house.

He nearly blacked out for holding his breath. The man that remained, a wiry, skittish-looking bugger, was just pocketing a gun and carrying a shovel. As Tristan watched, he took the gelding's halter and tried to lead him away. A little dog came racing out of the darkness, barking frantically; the servant shouted at the animal to no avail, finally raising the shovel until it ran, yelping, into the shadows. The gelding's eyes rolled with fear and he began to stamp and snort, nearly spilling the corpse from his back. The servant jerked down on the animal's halter, hard, then, dragging the shovel behind him, led the frightened beast off into the darkness.

Tristan didn't need anyone to tell him where the servant was heading.

Toward the lonely Norfolk pastures.

He scrambled out from behind the shrubbery, half-expecting

gunfire to ring out behind him, but the night remained still and quiet save for the scraping, increasingly distant sound of the shovel moving over the ground. Tristan waited until he was sure the servant couldn't look back and see him, and then, driven by morbid curiosity and fear, sprinted across the lawn after him, keeping to the shadows and behind trees. For a minute, he thought he'd lost the odd trio; then he saw the old gelding just ahead, and thirty feet away, the little dog following at a safe distance. He heard the panicky drumming of his heart, and felt the bile of fear in his stomach at sight of the corpse, the fingers dangling just above the horse's knees and the lifeless head and arms swinging above the grass with every plodding step the old beast took.

Who was the dead man? Another debtor who had fallen afoul of Maxwell and couldn't pay up? Tristan shuddered, seeing a sudden vision of his own dark fate. Unless he came up with the money—or Shareb won the race—*he* would be the next one to be murdered and buried in a dark, Norfolk field.

He wiped icy sweat from his brow, and continued on.

The house was well behind them now, the night growing darker, deeper, blacker. Out over the lonely pastures he followed the servant and the broken-down old horse. Here the grasses were thick and damp, the brambles clawing, and he felt the moisture seeping through his shoes until his feet were wet and clammy. Somewhere off in the distance a night bird called; closer, an owl hooted. Finally, a mile away from the manor house, the servant stopped the horse, pulled the corpse from its back, and let the body drop bonelessly to the earth. It landed on its back with a heavy thud, arms outflung and face turned toward the night sky.

Tristan stole closer, unnoticed.

The servant began to dig. Cold starlight flashed against the shovel, and the sound of metal striking rock and flint, the servant's labored breathing as he worked, and loose dirt thumping against the steadily growing pile of earth, filled the night. On and on it went. The digging sound was horrible, and the sweat turned to ice the length of Tristan's spine as he wondered how many other unmarked graves were out here on this lonely, windswept hill.

He crept closer.

And saw the body move its hand.

He froze, the scream hanging in his throat. Then reason and reality swept in, and with it, horror. The bugger was burying the man alive!

The shovel flashed, the servant grunting and cursing as he struck rock. Holding his breath, Tristan crept forward. He was thirty feet away now ... twenty ... fifteen—

The old gelding stepped quietly toward the fallen man and nosed his shoulder, as though trying to rouse him. The hand moved again, then the arm, and Tristan heard the poor fellow moan, saw him drag open his eyes and reach up to gently touch the horse's lowered muzzle.

At that moment, the servant turned and saw the whole thing.

Swearing, he tore a pistol from his pocket and trained it on the defenseless man.

But he was too late. Tristan had already leapt forward, his elbow deflecting the servant's aim, and the shot went wild into the Norfolk night.

Chapter Twenty-Three

The crack of a pistol, the ground vibrating beneath him as bodies wrestled in the grass, grunts, curses, fists against flesh—and the dark mass of Thunder moving to stand protectively over him. Colin, dazedly aware of the struggle, tried to sit up, couldn't. He fell back in the grass and must have blacked out, for when he opened his eyes there was only a hand against his cheek and someone hovering over him, breathing hard.

"Ariadne—" he murmured, desperately trying to get to his feet. "Got to get her out...."

The stars wheeled above his head and began to fade out. From a great distance away he felt his rescuer shaking him, slapping his wrists and cheek, forcing him back toward consciousness. An arm slid behind his nape, pulling him up. Dragging open weighted eyelids, Colin saw a youthful but handsome face, intent gray eyes staring worriedly down at him, and a tense, determined mouth that broke suddenly in a relieved smile.

"Another one of Maxwell's debtors, are you?" the youth drawled, in a voice that was educated and high-bred.

"Colin Lord ... veterinarian, London."

The wry smile vanished and the youth leapt to his feet.

"You're the bloody bastard who helped Ariadne get to Norfolk! Damn you, I ought to just finish what that idiot started and kill you right here and now!"

Colin, too ill to stand, drew his legs to his chest, and rested his brow against his knees.

"Please, after I get my bearings. Make it a fair fight, at least."

"If it weren't for you I'd have caught up to her and stopped her before she ended up in the clutches of that—that *monster*, Maxwell!"

"And pray, who are you?"

"Tristan St. Aubyn, her brother," the lad declared, with high-born indignation.

"Ah, yes, of course." Colin bent his head and wincing, massaged the back of his skull. "Young Lord Weybourne. If you're after the stallion, I fear you're too late, lad."

"I'm not too late. Shareb-er-rehh belongs to *me*, not my sister. Besides, I didn't chase her all the way from London because I wanted to get my hands on that horse! That isn't what she thinks, is it?"

"I'm afraid so."

"Bloody hell." The young lord, no less high-strung than his sister, began to pace, cheeks bright with color, fists clenched at his sides. "I chased her all the way to Burnham because she *cannot marry Maxwell*, she doesn't know the danger she's in, doesn't know what Father tried to do, damn it, she doesn't know *anything*—"

"She thinks you want the horse to pay off your debts," Colin said, carefully.

"Debts! I'll tell you about debts!" Then, lowering his voice as though he feared anyone hearing him out here in this desolate pasture, the young lord spat, "I'm in debt to the tune of thousands, and it's all owed to Maxwell. Gambling debts, horse racing debts, cock-fighting, dog-fighting, and boxing debts. I made wagers, lost, borrowed from Maxwell because he was the only person I could find who'd lend me the blunt to support my obsession, gambled more, lost more ... before I knew it I was in over my bloody head."

He paused, raked both hands over his eyes, dropped them on a sigh of self-disgust before turning his face away.

"Maxwell threatened me with bodily harm if I could not come up with the money. So I went to my father, and when he realized what a fiend Maxwell is—I mean, what kind of a man would lend money to someone my age?—he tried to break off Ariadne's engagement to him. He sent a note to Maxwell but before anything could be made public, before he could even tell Ariadne, even, that he had broken it off, there was a f-fire—"

"Easy, lad," Colin said gently, in a voice he might've once used to steady a frightened midshipman.

"There was a ... f-fire, and my father ran into the barn to try and save Shareb-er-rehh. He was the last of the Norfolk Thoroughbreds, but Father, he—he had an attack, and I was the one who ... who ... f-found him. Damn it, damn it all to hell—" The youth bent his brow to his fingers, unable to mask his grief from Colin's sympathetic eyes. "And to think that my sister believes I came here to steal Shareb-er-rehh back... ."

Colin pulled himself to his feet. Swaying, he leaned heavily against Thunder's stout old shoulder until the fog cleared from his brain and the waves of nausea and dizziness passed. It was then that he saw the shovel lying in the grass, the partially dug grave, the unconscious servant nearby. He had no doubts as to what his fate was supposed to have been.

"By the way," he said, when the hitching sobs finally stopped, "thanks for saving my life."

"Yeah. Well, I couldn't just let the bastard bury you alive."

The youth walked a little distance away, misery emanating from his proud, narrow shoulders as he gazed off into the night.

"So how do you propose to settle your accounts, then?" Colin asked, gently. "If you are not yet of age to claim your inheritance, it would seem that you have to give up Shareb-er-rehh in order to pay your debts, and will still lose him after all that your sister went through to keep him."

"Mr. Lord—" Tristan faced him, his composure intact once more, his tone far older, wearier, than his face was. "Shareb is all I have. I had no choice."

"No choice?" Colin stepped forward, the fingers of dread already inching up his spine. "What did you *do*, lad?"

Tristan kicked at a tuft of grass and looked away, his mouth hard.

"You signed the stallion over to Maxwell," Colin said.

"No."

"You plan to sell him and give the money to Maxwell, then."

"No."

"Then what on earth have you done?"

Tristan looked up, his eyes defiant. "I proposed a match race between Shareb-er-rehh and Black Patrick, and made a bet with Maxwell on its outcome. If Shareb wins, then Maxwell must not only publicly declare that the wedding between himself and my sister is off, he must release me from my debts. All of them."

"And if Shareb loses?"

Tristan's throat moved, and he turned away. "He can't."

Colin stepped forward, and grasped the youth's shoulder. "I repeat, Tristan, if he loses?"

The wind suddenly whispered through the trees, making the leaves shake ominously above their heads.

"If he loses, ownership of both Shareb-er-rehh and Gazella goes to Maxwell, and I'm as good as dead."

IF ANYONE NOTICED that young Lord Weybourne's personal groom bore a resemblance to the intruder that had been shot and buried in one of the far pastures, no one commented on it. If anyone noticed that Daley was unreasonably skittish and unable to meet anyone's eyes, they never guessed the reason for it. And if anyone heard the Lady Ariadne's pitiful sobs far into the middle of the night, no one, not even the maid that Maxwell had assigned to her, made any move to comfort her.

For their master was not a man to be crossed, and those who were in his employ knew that more than just their positions were at stake if they were to rouse his ire in any way. And so the household went about its business, Lord Weybourne—who insisted on seeing his sister—was assigned a room in a guest wing, and the servant Daley kept his silence, desperately praying that Maxwell would never find out that the man he was supposed to have killed had escaped and disappeared.

It was Daley's most fervent wish that that man would not turn up in an unexpected—and close—place. Luckily, his tasks did not include anything remotely connected to the earl's stable of prized thoroughbreds, and so it was that he did not recognize Lord Weybourne's bespectacled, crippled groom for the man he actually was.

The idea of the disguise—and to get Tristan placed within the manor house in order to keep a watch over his sister—had been Colin's. It was no difficult task to exaggerate the limp that would always pain him, and spectacles, a change of clothes, and a feigned, stooping gait was enough to fool anyone who might have gotten too close a look at him during his failed attempt to rescue Ariadne. He waited just long enough to make himself comfortable in his new role—and then he sent the young Lord Weybourne to bring his sister to him.

WHEN A HAGGARD-LOOKING Ariadne was escorted to the parlor, she found a slim figure leaning against the mantle, hat and gloves in one hand, brow resting tiredly in the other.

With a shock, she realized it was her brother.

Her first impulse was to flee the room. Her second was to curse him for making her life hell these past few weeks, and forcing her to become a fugitive in order to save Shareb-er-rehh. He, like Father, had spent most of his life ignoring her, and yet here he was, wanting something from her. Shareb, most likely. She stared contemptuously at his drawn face, his elegant hands, and shot him her most withering look of disgust.

"I have nothing to say to you, Tristan. Good day."

She turned to leave.

"No, Ariadne!" Abandoning his place by the hearth, he rushed across the room, seized her elbow, and forced her into a chair. She fought him, struggling angrily, until his intent gray gaze was inches from her own.

"Unhand me this instant, Tristan, or so help me God I'll scr—"

"Colin Lord is hiding in the stable, waiting for you," he hissed, desperately, in her ear.

Instantly, she froze and fell silent. Her body all but sank into the depths of the chair, where she sat with bent head and hands folded demurely in her lap. She squeezed them to stop their sudden shaking. She could not speak.

"Maxwell tried to have him murdered," Tristan whispered, just above her ear. "Luckily for your animal doctor, I happened to come along at the right time."

"Oh my God, I must go to him—"

"He's *fine*," Tristan said tightly, restraining her. "A bit sore, but otherwise quite well. Ariadne, I ... I did something you must know about."

He told her about the match race.

"For God's sake, Tristan, how *could* you?" she cried angrily. And then she saw his stricken eyes and knew that despite everything, and all that had happened, he was still too young to know any different, still too young to weigh the risks, and still ...

Her brother.

Her brother, who had also, in many ways, been ignored by a

benevolent but largely absent father who cared more for horses than he did his own children, and whose neglect had caused Tristan to resort to plenty of "bad behavior" of his own.

"Oh, Tristan—"

The two siblings rushed into each other's arms, sobbing with relief, despair, and grief for all that they had so recently lost.

And all that they still had left to lose.

&.

TRISTAN DISCREETLY LEFT her at the entrance to the stable, and picking up her skirts, Ariadne ran past the box containing Black Patrick, past the demure and elegant Gazella, past the stall where Thunder—never looking more sad and deplorable than he did in contrast to a stable containing some of the finest horses in England—quietly munched his hay, and straight toward the big box where her stallion resided.

Shareb-er-rehh—staring lustfully at Gazella—saw her coming. He pricked his ears and then, walking forward, thrust his muzzle over the partition, his forelock falling over his eyes as he whickered in welcome.

But Ariadne brushed past him and the two dogs and threw herself into the animal doctor's arms.

"Oh, Colin ... I'm so frightened, Tristan told me what Maxwell tried to do to you, and now he's got this match race planned and I want nothing more than to leave here and to do so straightaway, because all I keep seeing is you lying hurt on the floor and reliving that awful moment all over again and oh, please, please tell me you're alright? I've been worried sick—"

But he was grasping her by the shoulders and setting her back and away from him, looking like someone had just dealt him a stunning blow. "My God, Ariadne... ."

Confused, she came up short. "What?"

And then she saw the direction of his gaze. He was staring at her, speechless and awestruck. His throat worked, and almost reverently, he reached out to touch her coiffed, upswept hair and the bodice of her gown, to trail his fingers down her sleeve.

Then his gaze lifted to regard hers.

"I have never seen such exquisite beauty in all of my life," he murmured, hoarsely.

Heat swept into her cheeks. "Surely, it's not as if you've never seen a lady in a gown before."

"No, dearest, I have never seen *this* lady in a gown before. I am totally undone. Overcome."

"Oh, Colin—" she gave a pained little smile. "Are you certain you're alright?"

"Yes, thanks to your brother. I owe him my life."

She went back into his arms, and rested her head against his chest, feeling his arms closing about her with fierce protective-ness and holding her tight. Tears rose in her eyes and she blinked them back, thinking of how close she'd come to losing this man who loved her so much that he'd scaled the side of a house for her—and did it with a bad leg. "I can't imagine what my father was thinking, pledging me to someone so evil," she murmured, sniffling. "Tristan said he had Father fooled, that Father didn't know how terrible Maxwell really is, and that all Maxwell ever wanted was to get his hands on the Norfolk Thoroughbreds and I was the only way he could get to them." She reached up and laid her hand against his cheek. "Are you sure you're alright, Colin?"

"I am. And as much as I relish the sight of you, you cannot stay here, Ariadne. It is too dangerous."

"No, I'm *not* leaving," she declared, pulling back. "Besides, Tristan is standing guard just outside, and will cough if anyone comes. Oh, please don't tell me you are actually sleeping out here—"

"I have to. I don't trust Maxwell, Ariadne. Not with the race coming up. God only knows what he'll do."

"Do you think he might sabotage the race? Even harm Shareb?"

"I wouldn't put it past him, my dear. You and your brother have too much riding on the outcome of this race, and I'd hate like hell to see that stallion end up in Maxwell's hands—or worse, see anything happen to either of you." He took her hand, enfolding it within his own. Then, poking his head out of the stall to be sure the way was clear, he hurried her out of the box, and toward the stairs that led up to the loft.

Ariadne followed eagerly, mindful of her skirts. A beam of sunlight, adrift with dust swirls, slanted through a window. Colin gained the loft first and kneeling in the hay, reached down to pull her up. Stifling a giggle, she went into his arms, clinging to his solid, comforting warmth before he picked her up and carried her through the whispery hay to a far corner. There he set her on her feet, and pulling her close, kissed her long and hard.

She melted against him, never so relieved and happy to see anyone in her life. Just being near him made all the fear and anguish of the past days go away, and she wearily gave herself up to him and his solid, comforting strength. His hands came up to cradle her cheeks, then one drifted down to graze her neck, her bodice, her stomach, as though to reassure himself that she was truly well and unharmed. She felt the fire starting within her, as it always did at his touch, and she broke the kiss to gaze at his beloved face.

To think that Maxwell had tried to have him killed ...

Dear, gentle Colin, who had dedicated his life to saving God's creatures from pain and illness—

Her eyes filled with hot tears, and his face suddenly went blurry behind them.

"Ah, sweetheart ..."

His arms went around her, holding her close and cupping her head against the inside of his shoulder. Choking sobs bubbled out of her throat, were muffled against his heartbeat. Her tears soaked his shirt, dampening the warm, hay-scented skin just beneath, and she fisted her hands in the fabric beneath her cheek. How close she had come to losing him, and how much peril they were all still in.

And then she remembered Maxwell's revelation.

Managing to get her tears under control, she pulled back, even as Colin pulled the tail of his shirt free and gently dried her eyes. She stared up at into his handsome face, the beautiful, soul-deep eyes that were filled with love and tenderness as he went about this humble task.

"Why didn't you tell me?" she asked.

He stared at her, uncomprehending. "Tell you what?"

"About your former career ... *Captain* Lord."

His flinched, and his hand, just beneath her eye with the shirt-tail bunched in it, froze. He stared at her as though she had struck him, then began to lower his hand.

She caught it, unwilling to let it go.

He looked away.

"So ... you know."

"Yes," she replied, steadily. "Maxwell told me."

"Everything?"

"Everything."

He gave a great sigh, and sat down in the hay, looking defeated and broken. "I told you you wouldn't want me if you only knew what I'd done."

She sat down beside him, arranging her skirts in such a manner that her bare ankles showed temptingly. "Colin Lord, you are one of the most intelligent men I have ever met, but some-times you really *are* a thick-headed dolt."

His gaze had been on her ankles. He looked at her, confused. "What do you mean?"

"How can you believe that I would think any less of you for what you did?"

"I disobeyed my admiral." He looked down, picked up a piece

of straw, began to tie it up in a series of little knots. "Because of me, we lost two ships that night, Ariadne. Not just one."

"You disobeyed him because you were trying to save his life, and that of every man aboard that frigate."

She sidled closer to him, put her hand beneath his chin, and forced him to look at her. His eyes were full of pain and anguish. "Maxwell told me about it," she said. "And fiend that he is, did so with all the triumphant malice in his black heart. But it did not have the intended effect on me, Colin, because I love you all the more for what you tried to do—"

"The wind was too strong," he murmured, looking down at the piece of straw he still held. "Sir Graham—he was my admiral, and I was his flag captain, the man whose ship he had chosen to carry his flag, the man who was, in his absence, second in command of the entire fleet—had gone aboard one of our frigates to dine with its captain. The hour was late, and there was no moon. We were in the Caribbean, and there was nothing, nothing at all, to signal that a squall was bearing down on us. Suddenly and without warning, we were hit with winds that came out of nowhere, and before we knew it, we were on a lee shore in the dark of night, with the frigate closest to the peril." He paused, his eyes haunted. "Sir Graham ordered me to save the flagship, to just get out of there while I still could, and leave the frigate to dash itself against the rocks. He *knew* the wind was too strong, that in trying to save him and the frigate, I'd imperil my own vessel, my own people, as well. But I couldn't do it, Ariadne." He looked up at her, his eyes anguished. "He was my admiral. My friend, my superior, the man who wouldn't let the surgeon take off my leg after I was hit during the height of battle. He was the finest commander I ever served under... ."

She put her arms around him, laid her cheek against his shoulder.

"The frigate was doomed, try as I did to save it. And God help me I tried, though Sir Graham was bellowing at the top of his lungs for me to leave off—but I deliberately disobeyed him, deliberately ignored him, and ordered my crew to anchor, and rig a tow rope between the two ships to try and help the frigate to claw off —" He put his hands over his eyes, trying to shut out the horrible memory. "The wind was too strong, Ariadne ... just too damned strong... ."

"Oh, Colin... ."

"The anchors began to drag, and the tow line broke. It *broke*. After that—after that it was too late to save either ship. It was a disaster of unimaginable proportions. A ship, no matter how large and strong, no matter how mighty, has no chance against rocks on a lee shore. Some of our crew were able to claw their way through the surf and make it to shore, but many men drowned that night. Had I obeyed Sir Graham's order perhaps not so many would have been lost." He raised his head and looked at her then, and although sorrow was etched in every line of his face, his eyes were almost fierce. "But I swear to you, Ariadne, that if I could go back and face that same decision all over again, I would not have done any different. *I would not have abandoned my admiral.*"

No, he would not have, this man who, despite a bad leg, had scaled the side of a house in order to save her when everyone else in her life had left her to her own devices. He had not abandoned her, and loyal as she knew him to be, he would not have abandoned his admiral.

"But he abandoned *you*, Colin" she said softly, feeling a sudden, unreasonable hatred for this unknown officer who had done nothing to save the career of the man who had tried to save *him*.

"No. He didn't, Ariadne. He was Nelson's own protégée, the brightest star in the Royal Navy, and angry as he was with me for what I'd done, he was right by my side throughout the entire court-martial. If anyone could have saved me from ruin, or my family from the shame and disgrace they suffered because of the whole affair, it was Sir Graham. And God help him, he tried." He tossed the piece of straw aside and looked bleakly at the beam of sunlight slanting over the hay. "But nothing he could say in my defense made a damned bit of difference. The fact of the matter was, I disobeyed my admiral and in so doing, was responsible for the loss of many fine men. In so doing, I cost the Navy one of its finest, most expensive, warships. An eighty-gun *flagship*."

She squeezed his hand.

"Afterwards, I had little money with which to support myself. I was too proud to ask my father for help, and though he didn't say as much, I knew his shame ... he was an admiral himself, from a proud family with a long naval tradition that I had been expected to uphold; I couldn't disgrace him further. And so I found myself in London, and one day, when I came across a horse being beaten by a cab driver, I intervened." He gave a sad smile. "It was rather like what happened with Thunder, I guess ... only this horse's name was Ned. Something happened, then—I have always shared a rather unusual bond with animals, but when that horse looked up at me, I knew, I just *knew* what my calling was, and what I had to do to atone for all the lives I had destroyed, not only in disobeying my admiral, but in the name of war." He looked at her, unashamed of the path his life had taken. "I couldn't ask you to marry me, Ariadne, until I'd told you about my past. And I was so afraid that if I did, you'd no longer want me. No longer respect me. That you'd pity me—"

"I love you, Colin," she said, touching his lips.

"I do not move in the same circles that you do, Ariadne, not anymore, and soon enough you will tire of me—"

"Colin."

"And what of your future, you do know that marrying a veterinarian will probably get you ostracized from polite society, that you will be an outcast just like me, and here I can't even earn enough money in my profession to keep you in gowns half as beautiful as this one—"

"*Colin*."

He shut his eyes and leaned his forehead into the heel of his hand.

"I don't *care* about gowns," she murmured. "I don't care about those stuffy people that will turn their backs on me, as those that are my true friends will not; the rest can all go to the devil. I don't care about money, though God knows I have enough of it to put the whole of *Norfolk* in beautiful gowns, and I would gladly trade every penny I own to find the one thing I always wanted—to be loved."

He just looked at her, uncomprehending.

Tears rose in her eyes. "For heaven's sake, can't you see what you mean to me? I was a pawn to be used so that Maxwell could get his hands on the legacy of the Norfolk Thoroughbred, nothing more. My mother died when I was young, my father had no time for me and even less interest in me. Nobody has ever cared. But you—*you* have shown me what it feels like to be trea-sured, valued, cherished, *loved*. Not used, not neglected, not aban-doned, but *loved*. *You* are all that matters in my world, don't you see? *You*. I love you, Colin. And I wouldn't care if you're a poor veterinarian or the richest lord in the land, I'm still going to love you." And then, looking into his eyes, she pulled off his cap, removed his spectacles, put them on the hay beside them, and began to kiss him.

He shut his eyes, the long lashes draping his cheeks, his hands clenched into fists as her kisses feathered against his face. She pressed her lips to his, tasting him, loving him. His breathing grew deeper, and finally, his hands came up to caress her back, at first tentatively, then with increasing confidence as he realized that he *hadn't* lost her, that she loved him, still, and perhaps more, now, than ever. She felt her heart beginning to pound, and her hand drifted down to slip beneath his shirt and touch the warm skin just beneath.

His belly was flat and hard and warm. She leaned against him, until he finally sighed and drawing her close, lay back in the hay. It rustled beneath them, its fragrance coming up to envelop them in its sweetness.

"Colin ... will you make love to me?"

His lips curved in a boyish grin. Somewhere beneath them, one of the horses stamped; from beyond the window a pheasant made a harsh, squawking noise before it departed with a whoosh of its wings.

And from just outside came Tristan's loud cough, and the sound of approaching footsteps.

"Someone's coming!" she whispered. "I have to go—"

He hushed her with kisses, and she felt only the strength of his arms, the heat of his mouth against hers, the feel of his hands ... caressing her back, moving down her leg, catching the hem of her gown in his fingers and dragging the fabric up her leg, until the pin-prickliness of the hay was sharp against her flesh.

She sank down atop him, even as the footsteps grew louder and voices came from outside.

"Fine day, m'lord, eh?"

They clung together, breath and bodies hot and close, as the conversation wafted up to them.

"Indeed," came Tristan's drawled reply.

"'is Lordship wanted me to take Black Patrick out f'r some exercise, seein's how the race is in just a few days. Not that the beast ain't in good condition, but ye can't be too sure, eh?"

"Of course."

Ariadne began to giggle. She felt Colin's fingers dragging the heavy skirts up over her bottom, and his warm touch upon her skin. She sighed and pressed closer, touching her mouth to his.

"I wish Tristan would *leave*," she whispered, against the curve of Colin's neck. "I have no wish for him to hear us!"

"He won't. Not if we're quiet."

"Can you be quiet?"

"Aye. *I* can." His fingers roved around the silken skin of her thighs and back over her bottom, until the searing ache was blossoming between her legs and her pulse was beginning to beat in her ears. "But, can *you?*"

She settled onto her side so that she could reach his trousers. From below, she could hear the servant entering Black Patrick's stall, the slap of his hand against the powerful neck, the steed's squeal and the challenging whistle of Shareb-er-rehh.

"You're hard, Colin."

"Mmmm ... Painfully so, I think."

"Do you need some *medicine*, my good doctor?"

He gave a short burst of laughter even as she thrust buttons through holes, slid her hand beneath the flap of fabric, and began to stroke his growing arousal. Softly. Agonizingly. He groaned, and she pressed her mouth against his, her hand against his rigid flesh, her thumb running up and down its side with torturous slowness.

"My God, Ariadne—"

"Shhhhh!"

He grimaced as the pad of her thumb circled and teased the engorged tip, and buried his face against her neck, his breathing coming hot and hard.

Downstairs, the sound of Black Patrick's shod hooves rang against stone as he was led outside.

"This is your punishment for not telling me about your past," she murmured, smiling.

"Then I swear I'll never tell you anything again." He sucked in his breath as she stroked and teased him, a sheen of moisture breaking out on his forehead.

She leaned over, kissed his eyebrows, his long, sweeping lashes, his mouth—and then his hand grazed her hip and swept over her inner thighs.

"*Co*lin!"

"Fair is fair," he gasped. "Dear heavens, you keep doing that and I'm not going to be able to last—"

She persisted, lightly dragging her fingers up, over and around his hard length, until a warm pearl of moisture came oozing out to dampen her thumb. She gasped as he wreaked havoc on her senses as well, his fingers slipping beneath the heavy folds of her skirts and into the silken, cinnamon-colored hair at the junction of her thighs; beneath her the hay stabbed, and a burr was sticking against her ankle, but none of that mattered, for—

"Oh!" she gasped, nearly crying out as his fingers parted her damp warmth and slid gently inside her.

"Tell me to stop, then," he murmured, suddenly clenching his teeth as she ringed his arousal with thumb and forefinger and slid her hand slowly up and down his length. "I'll bet you can't."

"You know very well that I—oh!—that I can't ..."

"So hush, dearest, and let me make love to you." He kissed her, his finger finding parts of her that she didn't know existed, until sobs of pleasure were clogging the back of her throat. His mouth was there, against hers, and she felt him straining against her hand, heard the hay rustling beneath their bodies, heard his hot, heavy breathing and the frantic slam of her heart in her ears—

"Make love to me, Colin. *Now*."

With the very likely chance of someone discovering them, time was not a luxury that they could afford. Colin gently rolled her onto her back, withdrawing his hand only to coax her thighs apart. Her skirts lay bunched between their bodies and he impatiently pulled them aside, even as he looked down at her fair, flushed face with the damp strands of fiery hair caught across her cheeks, even as her hand continued its slow and wicked massage, even as her eyes, jewel-like with passion, gazed up at him through the dark fringe of her lashes.

He could not wait any longer. The hay pricking his forearms, he eased himself down to her tiny body and drove himself deeply into her, feeling himself sliding in on a tide of wet heat all the way to the hilt. He groaned with the feel of it. She arched up to meet him, sighing, and then her hands were cupping the back of his head, sliding down his neck, his shoulders, her nails driving into his back as he began the slow, agonizing rhythm, trying to hold out, trying desperately, frantically, futilely, to make it last, even as he felt the first waves of climax beginning to seize him and knew that he was lost.

She convulsed beneath him, her soft cries quickly muffled by his mouth as he, too was carried away by the sweet agony of passion. And when it was over and they lay panting and gasping in the hay, Colin raised his head and put his lips against the damp hair at her ear.

"Ariadne?"

"Yes, Colin?"

"Thank you ... for loving me, just as I am."

Chapter Twenty-Four

Midnight.

Hours before the great match race would start, hours before the sun would claw its way out of the sea, hours before the crowds would line the racecourse, pressing and shoving and making last frenzied bets, Clive Maxwell was awake.

He was sitting in the library, calmly thumbing through a book by the light of a single candle, when the knock came.

"Enter."

The massive doors opened and the sleepy-eyed Cook stood there, a burlap bag clenched in one hand.

"Here ye go, m'lord. Early breakfast, just like ye wanted." She opened the bag, bending her grizzled old head over it and inhaling deeply. "Peach pie, apple pie, and some of those blackberry tarts yer lordship fancies ... fresh from the oven and enough t' feed a horse, if ye don't mind me sayin' so meself!"

Clive Maxwell took the bag with an icy smile that never reached his eyes. *If you only knew... .*

"Thank you, Cook. You may bring it here, please."

"Though Oi don't know why ye be wantin' me to pack it up

like ye did, less'n ye be plannin' t' take it with ye t' the racecourse to share with those friends o' yers—"

"Yes, Cook, that is exactly what I intend to do. The bag, please?"

She handed it to him, stifled a yawn, and left.

Maxwell waited until her footsteps faded and the great manor house was silent once more. The candle flickered in a draft, striking tiny diamonds of light off the sugar that still clung to the outside of the bag. He snuffed the single flame and headed out of the room, malice in his heart and a smile on his lips as he envisioned how this race on the morrow was going to go.

"Milord?"

Maxwell swore beneath his breath. It was a footman, young, eager to please, just passing in the hall outside and probably on his way to bed.

"Ah, Edward. Just the man I wanted to see."

"I beg your pardon, Milord?"

Maxwell thought fast. "Lady Ariadne has entrusted me with a favor, but I wonder if I might transfer its execution to you. It appears that her ladyship's horse runs best with his favorite treat in his belly, and she has implored me to give this to him in preparation for tomorrow's race." Maxwell offered the bag to the young footman. "I'm tired and on my way to bed, so take this down to the stable, and give it to her horse. You can't miss him; he's bay, with a wide blaze and a black mane and tail."

"Yes, Milord!" the youth said, puffing up with importance as he took the bag.

"Thank you, Edward. Good night." Maxwell turned and, smiling maliciously, headed for the stairs.

Young Edward, swinging the bag, left the great house and quietly made his way to the stable. He had not been down here before, his duties requiring him elsewhere, and glad he was of it, too, as horses were big, frightening beasts that made him nervous. He pushed open the door. The stable was dark, the air thick with the mingled scents of hay, grain, horse-sweat and leather. *Bay horse,* he thought, trying to get his bearings in the heavy gloom. *Bay horse... .*

He moved down the single row, looking in each stall. In the darkness it was all but impossible to tell color, save that they were all some shade of brown, but even so, none of these had a wide blaze. Edward continued slowly on, and there, an animal he'd seen from a distance, was the famous Black Patrick, inhabiting the biggest stall in the barn. Filled with a sense of awe, he paused for a moment to admire the huge beast. He could see a tiny star in the middle of the great racer's forehead, the bandages that protected its fine, long legs. He reached out to touch the animal's nose and jerked back in alarm as it struck savagely out at him. Another inch, and he would have lost his fingers.

His heart pounding, Edward moved quietly on. Past more stalls. Past the only white horse here, which must, he reasoned, be the fabled Gazella, her mane like a unicorn's and her coat so bright it almost glowed in the darkness. He paused, his eyes searching the pitchy gloom, trying to locate the Weybourne horse by the wide blaze that Maxwell had told him the stallion possessed. Somewhere, a horse gave a low whicker, and got to its feet. Swinging toward the sound, Edward turned and saw the animal he sought.

It was wide awake and staring at him.

He let out a sigh of relief; the master wasn't the only one who was eager to get to bed, and the sooner he could complete this task and turn in for the night, the better. Still nervous after Black Patrick's attempt to take off his fingers, he moved hesitantly toward that tell-tale blaze, the only thing he could see in the darkness, and slipped quietly into the stallion's stall, thinking that if he were silent and quick, it would be less likely to attack him.

But unlike Black Patrick, this horse was not vicious. The big head swung toward him, only the blaze visible in the stygian gloom and the animal's breath coming in short, inquisitive blasts against his hand. He stroked the warm muzzle, and pulled a piece of still-warm pie from the bag.

The horse sniffed it, warm breath blowing against his fingers; then, ever so gently, the animal lifted the treat from his hand with velvety lips, and began to chew, slowly at first, then, as the taste apparently agreed with it, faster.

No mere legend then, what they'd been talking about in the kitchens this afternoon: the Weybourne horse had a taste for pastry.

Warming to the animal's friendliness, Edward gave it another piece of pie.

The big head pushed against the bag, eager for more, and he quickly dumped the contents of the bag into the food trough.

Then, with a pat on the animal's neck and a whispered wish of good luck on the morrow, he left the box, the horse's happy munching fading behind him.

❧

GRAY LIGHT STREAMED through the windows of the sleeping stable, touching first upon partitions and walls, then hay racks, buckets, and troughs. Both Colin Lord and Shareb-er-rehh were in the deepest stages of sleep, the veterinarian's head pillowed against the stallion's glossy croup, the animal's wiry black tail laced with straw and lying haphazardly over Colin's legs and the speckled brown-and-white bird-dog that lay sprawled against them. One dreaming of a red-haired noblewoman, the other of a white-maned mare, neither Colin nor Shareb was aware of the agonized moans coming from the bay horse in a nearby stall.

But Ariadne, sneaking out to the stable for a pre-dawn tryst with her lover, did, and investigating, found Thunder down in his stall and rolling about in anguish.

She took one look at the old gelding and knew he had colic.

Bad.

Colin had been more pleasantly awakened by ship's servants in times of impending battle. One moment he was making love to Ariadne in a dream-hazed field; the next, hands were rudely shaking his shoulders, his teeth were snapping together, the equally startled Shareb-er-rehh was lunging mightily to his feet, and Colin's back and head thumped painfully to the hard-packed earth beneath the straw.

"For God's sake, Ariadne—"

"Oh, Colin, you must come, *quickly*!"

"Come where?" he muttered, thickly, as he pushed the rumpled hair out of his eyes.

"Thunder! He has colic!"

Together, they ran to the gelding's stall, Marc at their heels and little Bow crawling out of the hay to come flying after them. Sure enough, Colin found the old horse down, his flailing hooves cutting the air as he rolled about in an attempt to relieve the agony.

"You have to save him!" Ariadne cried, her eyes desperate. "Please, Colin, *do* something, he's suffering, please, please do something, now—"

He reached out, caught her arms, held her until she calmed down. "Stop it, Ariadne!" he ordered, holding her tightly. "I need your help, do you understand?"

Numbly, she nodded her head and stared at him. Then he turned, strode past the curious horses that were now watching him from their stalls, and hauled his sea chest out of the chaise, which had been drawn up in a nearby annex. Hoisting the heavy trunk, he hurried back into the stall.

He found Ariadne down on her knees beside the old horse, stroking the sweating hide. Thunder's eyes rolled in his head upon seeing Colin, and desperately, he tried to lunge to his feet, back straining, lips peeled back in pain. He managed to stand, and began pawing his bedding before his legs buckled and he went down once again.

Outside, the day grew a shade brighter.

"Stand back, Ariadne," Colin ordered, and quickly entering the stall, he seized Thunder's halter and with all his strength began hauling on his head, trying to get him onto his feet.

"Come on boy, get up—"

Thunder groaned, tried to get a leg beneath him, began to roll onto his side.

"Ariadne, help me!"

She dove forward, instinctively swatting at the gelding's heaving flanks, the sunken rump, while the veterinarian heaved and hauled on the halter. Thunder got a leg under himself once more; another; a good, sharp swat on the rump and he was standing, lurching, walking—

"Why, Colin?" Ariadne was asking, as she stared miserably at the suffering horse. "He seemed fine last night—"

Colin, however, had looked into Thunder's feed bin and seen the remains of what the gelding had been eating—several chunks of fruity, sugary pie and pastry, crawling with flies, lay in the trough. He pulled out his watch and putting his fingers against the ramus of the mandible, took the gelding's pulse.

Should be forty beats per minute, he thought, his mind racing, his eyes closed as he counted. *I'm counting sixty-five... .*

"Look in his feed bin," he said darkly.

Ariadne did—and cried out in alarm and horror.

Thunder groaned, tried to lie down. Roughly, Colin jerked the gelding' head back up, knowing if the animal went down again he might never get up.

Now, servants and stable hands were beginning to filter into the stable to start their morning work, their faces shocked as they saw Lord Weybourne's personal groom attending to the old horse.

One by one they came running, eager to offer their help.

Colin, putting his ear to Thunder's flank, looked at the small gathering. "Where's Maxwell?" he snapped.

"Gone. Went to the track," one of them offered, lamely.

Colin swore beneath his breath.

"What are you listening for?" Ariadne breathed, holding Thunder's head so the old horse couldn't collapse.

"Abdominal sounds. But I'm hearing nothing. No stomach noises, nothing."

"He's going to die, isn't he?"

"Not if I can help it."

But he noted that Thunder's mucus membranes were a dark red instead of the normal, healthy pink, and that the sweat was pouring off of him. His patient's prognosis didn't look good at all, but at least he knew the etiology of the colic—not constipation, nor a blockage, but an overload of pastry.

Ariadne was there beside him, brave, frightened, wanting to help. "What's happening inside of him, Colin?"

"Too much pastry," he muttered, flipping open the lid of his sea chest with one booted toe. "It's fermenting in the stomach, probably the large colon as well. Expect diarrhea. Then, laminitis."

"Laminitis?"

"Founder," he said, darkly.

Some of the stable hands had come forward, their faces angry as word was quickly passed about what had brought on the gelding's colic.

"Who would do such a bloody awful thing?"

"Don't know; ain't like this here hoss is anythin' valuable or anything—"

Ariadne, stroking Thunder's drooping face, jerked her head up. "He's valuable to *us*," she retorted, her eyes glassy with tears.

"Aye, but who would do such a thing?" one of the stable hands insisted, coming forward to help should the gelding's legs buckle once again. "Why would anyone put all that pastry in the feed bin?"

"Because they were trying to sabotage the race," Colin muttered, his voice hard and angry.

"But this here horse ain't racin'!"

"No. But he bears a marked resemblance, in color and markings, to the one that *is*. Somebody obviously poisoned the wrong horse."

Kneeling, he rummaged through his sea chest until he found what he was looking for. Shadows blocked out the light as the small group drew close, exchanging hushed comments and speculations about the strange instrument he was uncoiling. He looked up and saw curious faces, all staring down at the snake-like thing he held in his hands.

"What in God's name is that?"

"A stomach tube. I need help here, and quickly, if I'm to have a chance at saving this animal. Someone, please get me a bucket."

A pail was set before him, and while Ariadne walked Thunder up and down the aisle to keep him on his feet, while the day grew brighter and the birds began to sing, while he sent grooms running to and fro until he had most of the ingredients he needed, the veterinarian began to mix the laxative.

He knew the formula by heart.

Two ounces of venice turpentine, dissolved with two egg yolks ... an ounce of diascordium and a pint of red wine, to help tranquilize the poor fellow ... a quart of water to restore fluid and correct the dehydration...

Ariadne was there, watching him stir the evil-looking mixture. She reached out and put her hand on his shoulder, her gentle encouragement bolstering his own fading spirits. "A physick?" she asked, peering down at the mixture.

"Aye. We've got to get that pastry through and out of him as soon as possible. This will help speed it from the stomach and into the intestine so he doesn't absorb so much of it." He stood up, the bucket in his hand.

And saw the stable hands all staring at him—no longer with curiosity, but narrow-eyed speculation.

"You ain't no mere groom, are you?"

Without skipping a beat, Colin took the stomach tube from the hands of the nearest one. "No, I'm not."

"He's a veterinarian," Ariadne offered, proudly.

"A what?"

"An animal doct—"

Just then, Tristan entered the stable, his face flushed. He caught sight of the sick horse, the group of people gathered around it, and his "groom," armed with a bucket in one hand and a long, snake-like, leather-wrapped tube in the other.

Instantly, he ran forward to help, his face darkening with rage as he heard bits and pieces of the tale, all coming at him from every direction from stable hands, grooms, and his sister alike. "Maxwell," he spat, for Colin's ears alone. "That bastard's behind this, I'll bet my bloody balls—"

"We'll deal with *him* later. Right now all that matters is saving this horse."

The veterinarian stepped toward the gelding, laying his hand on the sweating, trembling old neck. Sick as he was, Thunder turned his face against his ribs in a quiet, trusting plea to make the pain go away, to make him better.

It was a tall order, but Colin was determined. Some patients— like old Ned, whose life he'd had to mercifully end with a bullet between the ears, the tears rolling down his face as he'd pulled the trigger—he could not save no matter what he did. But by God, Thunder wasn't going to die.

Not on *his* watch.

Face set, mouth determined, he retrieved the mouth gag from his sea chest. Resembling a metal halter, it was a cruel-looking assembly of bars, screws, and a strap of leather, with a metal plate to keep the jaws forced open. Stroking Thunder's face, he pulled the animal's head up, removed the halter, and put the mouth gag on.

One by one, the stable hands, the grooms, and even the horses in the stable all fell silent.

"I'll need an assistant," Colin said as he fastened the leather strap, and even before he straightened up, knew it would be Ariadne who would be the first to get to his side.

As indeed it was.

He eyed her dubiously, wondering if her fair sensibilities would withstand what he had to do. But she recognized his hesitation, and put her hand on his arm.

"I'm strong, Colin. Please—allow me."

"This will not be pretty."

"I don't expect it to be," she said, her concerned gaze going to Thunder once more and the tears welling up in her eyes.

"Very well then. Hold him steady."

The stable went hush-quiet in anticipation. Grasping the stomach tube and feeling like an actor on a stage with so many people watching him, Colin moved to Thunder's left side and gently inserted the tube into the braced-open mouth. The gelding was too sick to protest. Glancing up, Colin saw the color fading from Ariadne's face, but she remained steadfast and still, determined to do her part.

Slowly, he pushed the tube into the horse's mouth; he felt Thunder swallow it, and watched intently for the tell-tale gulp as it passed into the esophagus. There he met with the expected resistance.

"God almighty, how do ye know ye got it in the right place, and not the windpipe?" one of the grooms whispered, his voice filled with awe as he peered over the shoulder of one of his colleagues.

"He's not coughing." Colin pushed the tube slowly into the esophagus, watching the customary ripple slide down the left side of the neck; he put his hand there to ensure its progress, envisioning it going through the thorax and past the diaphragm, where he met with mild resistance at the cardia of the stomach. He jiggled the tube a bit to get it into the stomach, held his breath as a sudden wave of foul-smelling gas came welling up through it, and heard Ariadne's voice from beside Thunder's head.

"I think I'm going to be ill."

"Don't," he warned, and shot her a sharp glance. She was pure white, nearly green, one hand on the gelding's head, the other pinching her nose shut to block out the smell. Something in his look must've sustained her, for she gave a tremulous smile, swallowed hard, and glanced away.

Outside, a rooster began to crow.

"Alright, someone get me the bucket," Colin said, and three of the grooms scrambled to do his bidding. Still holding the tube in place, he affixed a funnel to its end, lifted the pail, and poured the physick down the stomach tube.

"You're going to be just fine, old boy," he murmured, gazing into Thunder's suffering eyes as the physick went down. "Just fine... ."

But the words suddenly felt like a horrible lie, for he'd made the same promise to poor old Ned before having to destroy him. A lump rose in his throat and unable to look into the gelding's trusting eye a moment longer, he finally removed the tube, his face grave and expressionless. Then he made his way through the small crowd, got the blanket that had been his bed for the past several nights, and returned to find the stable hands exclaiming over the stomach tube they passed amongst themselves while Ariadne quietly watched them.

She raised her head and her gaze—shining with pride, adoration, and hero-worship—fastened on his.

Her lips moved to form the silent words. *I love you.*

He gave a little smile that offered no promises, and unable to face her reverent eyes, turned away to put the blanket on Thunder's back. The old horse was not out of the woods yet.

"Will he founder?" Tristan asked, watching him remove the metal gag and replace it with the halter. Colin heard himself make some noncommittal reply; then, squatting down, he placed two fingers at the gelding's pastern and checked the pulse at the posterior digital artery. The hoof itself was too warm, but thankfully, there was no increase in pulse. Nevertheless, he called for several buckets of cold water, and shortly afterward, the blanketed horse was standing in them, head cradled to Ariadne's chest, little Bow standing on her hind legs to reach up and lick the ugly old nose.

At last, Colin stood back and surveyed his patient, his eyes worried behind his spectacles. In several hours he could give another laxative, but for now there was nothing more he could do. Sunlight was already streaming in through the windows, and soon servants would arrive to tack up Black Patrick; the race would go on, and the late earl of Weybourne's legacy, his children's future and happiness, hinged upon its outcome.

An outcome that was dependant upon one thing, and one thing only.

The stallion met his gaze from across the aisle, and something unspoken passed between them.

Shareb-er-rehh.

Chapter Twenty-Five

✣

In a special, roped off area beside the dunes, Lord Maxwell and his Jockey Club friends sat drinking wine and plucking morsels of food from trays carried by servants whose faces were trained to be expressionless. The long beach that lay between the sea and Burnham Overy Staithe's marshes and sandy dunes was not the best race course he might have imagined, nor was it one that he would've selected had circumstances given him more time to choose otherwise. Nevertheless, his racing friends had come up from Newmarket, Epsom and London to see the much-heralded contest between the undisputed "King of Newmarket" and Weybourne's purported "Fastest Horse in the World," and the race had drawn villagers, farmers, fishermen, and people of every class and description for miles around.

Maxwell was just far enough away from the crowd milling against his private, roped off area that he couldn't hear their broad Norfolk accents, couldn't smell their sweaty bodies, didn't have to listen to their gossip and news about births, deaths, and sicknesses. But he could see the money being passed at the betting booth, could feel the excitement in the air, could sense the eagerness the crowd had for its first glimpse of the late Lord Weybourne's mystery horse.

An eagerness that was equally shared by Maxwell's cohorts. After all, old Weybourne had never made a secret of the fact that his lifelong goal was to breed the fastest horse in the world.

And now, it was time to see if he had succeeded.

"I say, Maxwell, this is a most unusual site for a match race!" drawled Sir Randall Tapworth, quirking his thick gray brows. He gestured toward the sea with his wine glass. "A beach! Whoever heard of such a thing?"

"Most unusual, indeed," muttered Lord Chittick sourly, who had journeyed all the way from London for the event.

The Marquess of Sunningwell, looking polished and elegant despite the day's warmth, stared disdainfully at the long beach. "I daresay you take the Sport of Kings to new lengths, Maxwell." A friend of the late Lord Weybourne, he had bet an enormous sum of money on Shareb-er-rehh.

Too bad he would lose it all, Maxwell thought, as he watched several men pounding a marker into the sand a mile down the beach. *Most unusual indeed.* Well, a good, flat-out, run was what he wanted—a race that would leave Shareb-er-rehh in the dust and the fortunes—and legacy—of the late Lord Weybourne in his hands.

But what was taking so long?

He hoped he hadn't given *too* much pastry to the stallion. He'd merely wanted to throw the animal off, not make him deathly ill.

He was just opening his mouth to reply to Sunningwell's taunt, when a roar from the crowd heralded the arrival of the contestants.

He stood up, the platform that had been erected for his and his guests' benefit affording him a superior view. He smiled with satisfaction. Ah, there was Black Patrick, undisputed king of the English turf, being led through the parting crowds. Maxwell's eye was unusually sharp; he needed no assistance to see that the Irish import was in fine form indeed, lather flecking his glossy jet hide, nostrils flaring red, noble head snaking out to lash viciously at a child who tried to reach out and touch him. Maxwell saw his jockey slash at the brat with his whip before the mother grabbed it up and shielded it to her breast.

He smiled and reached out to pluck a bit of fruit from a tray that appeared beside his shoulder, never sparing the servant a second glance.

"There's Black Patrick," noted Sir Randall, stretching his neck until its withered old cords stood out in high relief. "A fine animal, a fine animal indeed. Who's that on his back, Maxwell?"

"Spit Jordan."

"Ah, *wonderful*!" Randall exclaimed, rubbing his bony old hands together and making it obvious which horse he had laid his money on.

Maxwell smiled down into his drink, the sea wind ruffling his hair. Spit Jordan was a cunning blackguard who'd stop at nothing to win a race, and had been well paid to make sure that his mount didn't lose. He chuckled darkly to himself.

Soon, my financial problems will be over... .

"Where the hell is Weybourne's nag?"

Forever.

"You sure there's supposed to be two of 'em racing, Maxwell old chap?"

"Maybe he chickened out," Randall said, laughing. "There isn't a horse in England that can beat Black Patrick!"

Maxwell pulled out his watch, arching one brow as he idly studied the time. "I suppose they'll be along shortly."

"Who's riding him?"

"Weybourne's groom," he drawled, thinking that it wouldn't really matter who was on Shareb-er-rehh, for no jockey in the world would be able to coax speed from a horse that was too ill to run—

Suddenly the crowd sent up another roar, one that grew so

loud and deafening that Black Patrick, just emerging from the throng and stepping onto the beach, shied into several people who were unlucky enough to be near him. The cheering went on, until one by one, Maxwell and his companions were forced to stand up to see what the commotion was all about.

"Bloody rabble," Maxwell muttered—

And went slack-jawed with shock.

It was Shareb-er-rehh. Head high, huge nostrils cupped and flaring, forelock sweeping back from his brow and his tail floating on the wind behind him, he made a magnificent sight. His coat glinted in the sun. His muscles rippled with power. He was fire and beauty and speed incarnate, and now, as he caught sight of Black Patrick, he gave a half-rear, his shrill stallion-call ringing on the wind.

"Is *that* Weybourne's horse?"

"Great God above! I think I've put my money on the wrong one."

"Have you ever seen such bloody long legs?"

"Damn his legs, look at that depth of chest!"

Maxwell, blinking, could only shut his eyes and clench his fists in disbelief. Then, the fury began to build and swell deep within him, rising from the very pit of his soul like smoke from glowing embers, with nowhere to go but up. His head ached, and the rage popped out on his forehead as burning droplets of sweat. *Something must've happened. The damned horse must have neglected to eat the pastry. Either that, or it's built up a resistance to it, because that bloody stallion has never looked healthier.*

He opened his eyes, plucked a glass of wine from a passing tray, and pretended to toast the stallion. "Don't forget, gentlemen, Weybourne's horse has never been raced."

"He's speed. Pure, unholy *speed.*"

"Going to be a real contest, I tell you!"

"Yes, and look how well that groom is handling him!"

Following their gazes, Maxwell promptly dropped his drink.

It was Ariadne. Her fiery hair was stuffed under a cap, trousers covered her legs, and a light jacket concealed her figure—but there was no mistaking that exquisite, pixie face.

Nor was there any mistaking the identity of the tall, fair-haired man who walked beside the stallion's shoulder, leading it through the crowds.

Colin Lord.

Who was supposed to be dead and buried and no longer a threat.

He clenched his fists in fury, the very arteries pulsing in his temples. He managed to raise his hand, and instantly his servant was at his elbow. Lowering his voice, Maxwell drew the man hastily aside.

"See that bay horse coming through the crowd?" he snarled, his black gaze boring into servant's. "I want you to make sure he doesn't win this race, do you understand?" He drew the servant close. "*Do you understand?*"

The man nodded jerkily, staring into Maxwell's face.

Then Maxwell shoved him roughly away, and the servant melted off into the crowd.

"So, gentlemen ..." Maxwell murmured, the picture of aplomb and poise once more. "You were saying?"

SHAREB-ER-REHH TOSSED HIS HEAD, sending his black forelock spilling rakishly over his eyes. Fretting and prancing, he danced his way lightly through the crowd, neck arched, head tucked, mouth worrying the bit and his tail riding the wind behind him. Ahead, his rival's haunches flashed in the sunlight as he was led past the crowd to the starting line, and Shareb-er-rehh raised his head and screamed out a challenge. Seconds later, the other horse answered him, his call piercing the wind.

Shareb reared, his ears sweeping back, and fought for more rein.

"Easy, boy," Ariadne murmured, laying a hand against the stallion's hot neck. She felt the taut, raw power coiled beneath her, and had no doubt that her father's horse would leave Black Patrick floundering in the dust. But her mind was awhirl ... with the memory of poor Thunder, rolling about in agony ... with horror that Maxwell had tried to have Colin murdered ... and with raw, sickened rage at what Tristan had told her about the evil man to whom she had been betrothed.

She looked up. Sunlight was just breaking through the high clouds in a magnificent, reverse-crown of glory, as though God had opened up the heavens and was shining His light down upon them.

Oh, God ... please let this all turn out alright.

She looked down at Colin. He was tight-lipped and silent, and his eyes—normally gentle and expressive—were hard with fury as he scanned the crowds for Maxwell. If she didn't hate him so, she could almost pity the earl.

Then she remembered Thunder, and his suffering.

Almost.

Now, hands reached out to touch Shareb's burnished, gleaming coat as the veterinarian led him through the packed masses; the stallion's one white-ringed eye turned to regard the crowds, and he stepped up his fine prancing, showing off for his many admirers.

They were almost to the racecourse now. The last of the crowd parted to let them through, and then there was only the sea before them, wide open and stretching into forever, sunlight glittering on thousands of waves, the tide swirling in great arcs of foam before eddying back into the azure expanse with a timeless, rhythmic roar.

She glanced down at Colin, wondering at the pain and longing the sight must surely bring him. *I will buy you a sailboat,* she thought, the idea coming out of nowhere and filling her with determined resolve. *You may no longer be in command of a great warship, but I know the sea is in your blood, and since we will live near the sea, I'll make sure you have a boat so that you can always enjoy it... .*

Black Patrick was just ahead, his long strides carrying him along the beach.

Colin, however, was not thinking of the sea, but of Maxwell, and of Thunder, and his fears for Ariadne's safety in the upcoming race. He looked up at the little noblewoman, perched so high atop the great stallion's back.

"Can this nag of yours run in sand?" he joked, trying to bolster her courage and confidence.

"Shareb-er-rehh's ancestors came from the desert. Of *course* he can run in sand."

Exchanging private smiles, they neared the starting line, where Black Patrick was rearing up on his hind legs and striking out at his groom. A vicious animal, that one, Colin thought. He turned and looked up at Ariadne. "I want you to be careful up there," he warned. "Don't get too close to that demon."

"Really, Colin!" she said airily, tickling his shoulder with her foot. "We don't intend to be anywhere near him, do we, Shareb?"

The stallion tossed his head, and slammed it so hard against Colin's shoulder that he nearly knocked him over.

"Shear off, you arrogant beast!"

Shareb made a soft whickering noise that sounded suspiciously like laughter, and then settled down to business. He resumed his prancing, all elegance and grace as he moved past the crowds. He ignored the children that scooted out from beneath the ropes, trying to touch him before being hastily grabbed by their mothers. He ignored the gulls that wheeled and screamed just overhead. He ignored the waves pulsing at his hooves, ignored the thrumming roar of the crowds, ignored all but that huge, black rival that awaited him at the starting line.

The two stallions exchanged challenges, their high, piercing screams piercing the wind, and it took all of Colin's and Ariadne's combined strength to keep Shareb-er-rehh from attacking the other horse. The starter was there, gesturing to the red marker placed far down the beach.

"Easy course," he said, taking off his hat to wipe his thinning hair back from his brow. "Down to the post and back, two miles, and the first one back wins. Got it?"

Spit Jordan cast a malicious glare at Ariadne and curled his lip in contempt as he gazed at Shareb, as though dismissing him already.

"When you're ready," the starter said.

But Ariadne's heart was hammering, and she suddenly felt a tickle in the arch of her foot. She tried to press it against the stirrup iron, to no avail. Tried to rub it with her hand, but couldn't reach the itch through the leather sole. Finally, with a quick apology to the starter, she leapt down from Shareb's back and yanked off her boot, hastily rubbing the offending area while Colin raised a brow and bent down to help her.

"Problem?"

"My foot itches," she said, sheepishly.

No one saw the shadowy figure that darted up on Shareb's opposite side and was gone in the blink of an eye. But the stallion did, and let out a sudden scream, one hind foot lashing viciously out.

"Easy, Shareb!" Ariadne soothed, the sudden motion startling her. Then, stepping into Colin's cupped hand, she vaulted back into the saddle.

"*Now* I'm ready," she called to the starter, who nodded and motioned them forward.

Colin reached up and squeezed her hand for good luck. The course stretched ahead of them, open, free, and flat, the ocean on one side, the crowds pressing fifty feet away on the other. It would be a good race. A fast race. He let go of her hand, and slapped Shareb's glossy rump as a final farewell.

But as the fiery, prancing stallion moved up to take his place at the starting line, sudden dread seized his heart.

"Ready—"

Desperately, he tried to run forward.

"Set—"

And saw it. *The girth.* Cut.

"*Ariadne!*"

The pistol shot cracked the air, and the horses were off.

SHAREB-ER-REHH'S mighty lunge broke the threads that held the girth and sent the saddle tilting crazily from his back. Colin heard his shout of panic over the crowd's sudden roar as the saddle fell away, felt the pain in his bad leg as he ran to the tiny figure crumpled on the sand; then there was only Ariadne, clinging dazedly to him as·he fell to his knees beside her and gathered her up into his arms.

Shareb-er-rehh came racing back, reins flying, head turned to regard his speeding rival.

The crowd was screaming.

And Black Patrick was already gone, running like fire through a trail of gunpowder.

Ariadne raised her head, her cap falling off to reveal her fiery hair. "Got to ride Shareb ... got to ride him, Colin."

"You aren't riding him, damn it, *you aren't riding him*!"

"No, Colin ... *you* have to ... "

And then her eyes closed, and her head fell back against his arm. The crowd was in an uproar. The stallion circled his fallen mistress, mane and tail streaming in the wind. He made one pass by Colin. Another.

Ariadne opened her eyes. "Do it, Colin ... for Tristan ... and for me."

He looked up, seeing the black horse a quarter mile away now.

And then, before he could deliberate any further, the crowd had surged in and it seemed that a hundred hands were there, hauling him to his feet and tossing him up bareback aboard the rearing, plunging Shareb-er-rehh as he plowed to a halt before them, sand spraying up from his front hooves.

"Bloody *hell*," was all Colin had time for—and then the stallion exploded out from under him.

He'd been in battles with shot and lead flying inches from his ear. He'd faced storms, stood up to his admiral's temper, survived a hideous fracture that should've cost him his leg if not his life. But never had Colin felt the desperate, exhilarating fear he felt now, as the mighty steed beneath him thundered down the beach like a man-of-war's unleashed broadside, carrying him to certain death if he were to fall off. He heard the crowd screaming off to his left, where nothing but colors passed in a speeding, dizzying blur.

God help me. The wind tore at his eyes, slashed at his shirt, whipped the flying black mane into his face until tears ran down his cheeks. He bent low over the stallion's surging neck, desperate only to stay aboard the animal as it took him on a ride straight into hell.

And Shareb, running like a thing possessed, showed no signs of slowing, stopping, or tiring. He poured on more speed, his angry scream echoing through Colin's head, great muscles pounding beneath him.

The crowd was roaring. Through Shareb's mane and past the backswept ears, Colin could just see Black Patrick circling the far marker in a wide arc, beginning his homestretch run back up the beach.

They'd never catch him now.

Not in a million years.

"Go, Shareb," Colin cried, into the small, savage, backswept ears. "For God's sake, *go!*

Black Patrick galloped toward and past them, now into his

second and final mile, and Shareb slowed, teeth bared as he tried to go after his rival without completing the far turn. With all his strength, Colin hauled on the outside rein, the leather cutting into his hand as he tried to turn the stallion and keep him on course. The mighty body rose beneath him in protest, plunged to the ground, and then Shareb was back on course and galloping toward the marker. He swept around it, body angled toward the ground like a ship coming about, and as he finished the turn and plunged down the beach at a speed that defied belief, the crowd rose to its feet, hundreds upon hundreds of people screaming, roaring, cheering—

A quarter mile ahead was the churning black rump, the streaming tail. Far beyond, at the finish line, Colin could just see Ariadne, leaning heavily against the starter, Bow at her feet and Marc pressed against her calves.

"Go, Shareb, damn your lazy, bloody, spoiled, hide!" Colin cried, and touched his heels to the pounding flanks. "Win this damned thing and you can have all the pastry and ale your heart desires! You hear me? *Pastry and ale*!"

It was enough. The great body beneath him seemed to flatten itself to the sand, the reins were ripped from Colin's hands, and he buried himself in the whipping mane, the wind screaming past his face leaving him faint for lack of air—

Please, Lord, don't let me fall off now, please, not now—

Knees buried in the stallion's sides, fists anchored in the stinging black mane, he hung on for dear life, knowing that if he fell off now he was a dead man. Through flying mane and watering eyes he saw the black horse's hindquarters coming closer, closer...

By God, they just might make it—

—Heard the thunder of its hooves, saw its jockey glance under his shoulder to look behind him, felt clods of sand from the animal's hooves pelting his face. He couldn't see. There was no stopping Shareb-er-rehh. Not now. The black hindquarters were a length away now ... half a length ... and then Shareb's head was darting out, snakelike, lunging for his rival's neck as the two pounded furiously down the beach toward the finish line—

The other jockey's whip came savagely down on Shareb's nose; still, Shareb went for the other horse, more intent on killing him than winning the race, even as the two hurtled toward the finish line at a blistering speed, the crowd screaming in a wild frenzy around them.

Shareb was falling back, teeth going for Black Patrick's jugular.

And then Colin looked up and saw Tristan, running out beyond the finish line with a lure.

The lovely white mare, Gazella.

Up went Shareb's ears—and in a blazing burst of speed, he shot past Black Patrick and won the race.

Epilogue

In a roomy box stall piled thick with straw, a tiny colt stood with his mother, his belly full with milk, his body warm and ready for bed. His legs were wobbly, his eyes droopy with fatigue. Beyond the windows darkness had fallen, and it was long past time for the little fellow to go to sleep—but he seemed restless, and Colin and Ariadne, gazing fondly down at the new arrival with the newest little Lord held safely in his father's strong and loving arms, were reluctant to leave.

"Looks like his papa, doesn't he, Colin?"

The colt's tiny face, one eye ringed with white just like his sire, turned toward them. The fuzzy forelock seemed to stand straight up, and the tiny body swayed on the absurdly long, stilt-like legs as he took a hesitant step forward.

"Oh, I think he rather looks like Thunder, myself," Colin joked, enduring a playful swat from his wife as the old gelding whickered from a nearby stall. He yawned, tiredly. "Plague take it, is this little fellow ever going to call it a night?"

"He's not going to go to sleep until you tell him a tale, Colin, and neither is little Caleb, here." Ariadne leaned over to take the infant, now beginning to fuss, from her husband, and planted a loving kiss against the downy blond head. "Don't you know that all babies need a bedtime story?"

"You tell it, love."

"Oh no, you're much better at telling stories."

"And which one would you have me tell?"

"The one about ..." She thought for a moment, then her face lit up, her eyes sparkling. "About us. And how I took you by storm!"

He laughed. "Dear God, that will take all night."

The little colt looked at them, eyes huge and imploring, tiny muzzle frosted with droplets of milk. He stumbled forward, tottering precariously, and put his miniature nose into the palm of the man who had brought him safely into the world.

"See, Colin? He's *asking* you."

Colin gave a heavy sigh, affecting great weariness, but he was grinning. Gazella had had a rough time of it, and for a while there, as he'd struggled to help her through the hard delivery, he'd wondered if the legacy of the Norfolk Thoroughbred was going to die right along with her.

But she hadn't died, and neither had the colt, and now they had a tall, healthy baby to show for all their shared pain and effort. Still smiling, Colin opened the door to the box. He sat cross-legged in the straw to get down to the little one's level, and gazed into the huge, dark eyes.

"So you want to hear a story, eh, young fellow?"

The colt stared at him, waiting, tiny ears twitching back and forth. His dam stepped forward and touched her muzzle to Colin's shoulder, and in the adjacent stall, Shareb-er-rehh put his head over the divider, his rapt gaze, like his son's, on the veterinarian.

Even the dogs sidled into the stall. Marc lay down against Colin's thigh, and Bow put her paw on his knee, her scraggly tail wagging with anticipation as he patted her fondly.

Audience in place, his own little son watching him from the

safety of his mother's arms and finally beginning to settle, Colin ran his hand over the colt's sloping shoulder, his fine, long legs. He had a feeling this wouldn't be the last time he'd have to relate the tale—not only to Shareb-er-rehh's heir, but in the years to come, more babies of his own.

He couldn't wait.

And so he settled himself in the straw, smiled up at his wife and young son, and began, starting with the beginning ... about how the Lady Ariadne had all but abducted him, how they had fallen in love on the journey to Norfolk, how Shareb-er-rehh had defeated Black Patrick in the match race of the decade. His kept his voice low and mild, gentle and soothing, and at the door he saw Ariadne, her cheek resting lovingly against Caleb's golden head, an adoring smile on her face as she gazed down at him.

The good doctor sighed, and gazed affectionately at each equine face. "And then," he said, cradling the jaw of Shareb-er-rehh's tiny heir in his hands and gazing intently into the wide, attentive eyes, "just as we accepted the prize money for winning the race, Lord Maxwell's servant came running out of the crowd, babbling hysterically about how his employer had ordered him to kill me. Later, at the trial, he and several others came forward and testified that Maxwell had set the fire that burned down Ariadne's papa's barn, all because he was angry that he was trying to break off their betrothal. The authorities came and took the earl off to jail, Lady Ariadne married me so that we could live happily ever after, we settled here in Burnham, and then ... well then, your mama and papa had *you*."

The little colt wobbled with fatigue, but his eyes were wide with wonder. He turned his head and stared up at his proud father, as though seeing him for the very first time. Colin smiled, and touched the fuzzy little neck. "And someday," he said, "you, too, will grow up and be a famous racehorse—just like your papa."

Colin got to his feet, running his hand over the fuzzy back, aware of Ariadne watching him with her heart in her eyes. He moved across the stall, plumped the straw piled thickly in the corner, and beckoned the colt with his hand.

"Time for bed, little fellow."

But the colt's eye was challenging, his stance defiant.

"I think he wants a bedtime snack," Ariadne said, her voice bright with laughter. "Pastry and ale."

"Well, he can want it all he likes, he's not getting any!"

As though in understanding, the colt threw a tantrum, squealing and kicking his tiny heels against the door. He turned a mutinous stare on Colin, the breath whooshing in short, angry bursts through his flared nostrils.

Colin and Ariadne looked at each other and burst out laughing. And in the end, it was Shareb-er-rehh who sighed heavily, leaned over the divider, and flattening his ears with fatherly authority, scowled fiercely at the young scallywag.

The colt returned his stare; then, his tiny head drooped and with a heavy sigh, he turned and flung himself down at his dam's feet.

Grinning, Colin crept out of the stall and joined his wife and son, now fast asleep in his mother's arms, just outside. For a long moment, they stood gazing down at the tiny foal.

"What do you think Shareb just said?" Ariadne whispered, as Colin put his arm around her shoulders and the two stood watching the little Norfolk Thoroughbred drift off into slumber.

He looked up at Shareb-er-rehh. The stallion's dark eye gleamed, and he seemed to smile as he looked steadily at Colin.

"I think," the veterinarian murmured, returning that equine smile, "that he just agreed with me."

And then he took his sleeping son back from his wife, and arm-in-arm, with Marc and little Bow following at their heels, led her from the stable.

A Heartfelt Thank You!

Thank you from the bottom of my heart for reading my book. If you enjoyed it, please consider posting a review. Reviews don't just help the author, they help other readers discover our books and, no matter how long or short, I sincerely appreciate every review.

Would you like to know when my next book is available? Sign up for my newsletter:

Also, please follow me on BookBub to be notified of deals and new releases.

Thank you again for reading and for your support.

PREVIEW MY SAVING GRACE

Get you copy of My Saving Grace today!

Prologue

The ancient Celtic cross that hung from their mother's neck was a source of awe and mystery for all of Deirdre O'Devir Lord's children.

Gathering in a circle for story time was a bedtime ritual, and it had been so for as long as any of them could remember. Tales of her homeland in faraway Connemara. Tales of green pastures and brooding gray skies, windswept mountains, rocky cliffs and barren wastelands of limestone. Tales of the sea, of life in a small cottage, of a land far, far away from the stately English manor house the children knew as home. And most fascinating, tales of Irish heroes, heroines and saints vividly brought to life with each retelling. Finn McCool. Cu Chulainn. St. Patrick. St. Brendan the Navigator. Brigid and Aoife and Queen Maeve of Connacht. All well and good, but she always saved the best for last.

Grace O'Malley.

Or rather, as their mother called her, *Gráinne Ní Mháille*.

They'd push their way closer, tightening the circle and staring up at her with wide eyes as she began to reach for the chain around her neck that held the cross. *Shhhushing* each other for quiet. Upturned faces rapt with attention. Squirming. Waiting.

And then, she would begin the story of Ireland's fierce and famous lady pirate who had lived during the time of Queen Elizabeth so long, long ago and to whom the ancient relic had belonged. The story never changed, though over the years, the children's ages did. Colin, fair-haired and handsome, the image of their English father. The four girls, born one after another and each, like Colin, a pale blonde.

And finally, Del. Sensitive and serious, he was the youngest of Admiral Christian and Deirdre Lord's brood and the only one to inherit the wild black curls of their mother.

He sat now, quietly waiting his turn to hold the heavy cross of beaten gold and raw emeralds as it began to make the round of their circle. Colin, the oldest, preparing to go off to sea under the watchful eye of their uncle Elliott, quickly passing it to the sister beside him with a shrug, as though such childish things were now quite beneath him. Niamh, Kathleen, Brigid and Tara, each fingering it with wonder and reverence before passing it to the child on her right. Del waited his turn. He knew what to expect. But today...

Today was different.

Beside him, Tara stared down at the relic while their mother told the familiar tale of their ancestress, the formidable *Gráinne*, sea-queen of Ireland's wild western coast.

"Her blood runs through your veins," she murmured, speaking in her native Irish—a language she had taught each of the children. "And every so often—" her voice softened, grew so low that the children had to lean forward to hear her— "*Gráinne* returns for the sake of one of her descendants. Someone that she herself chooses, someone she takes a fancy to, someone that needs her protection. Her wisdom. Her guidance."

Tara passed the heavy cross to Del. He had held the relic many times before, had felt its metal against his palm, the heavy chain falling over his fingers. What stories could it tell? What things had it seen? Did it still bear a trace of the salt spray it must have gleaned as it had hung from around the neck of *Gráinne* herself?

Wonder. That had been all he'd ever felt.

This time was different.

He closed his hands around the ancient metal, and something moved in his blood. At just five years old he couldn't identify it, but it was there all the same and he felt it in a way that was raw and physical. A quickening. Something ignited. Awakened. He couldn't put words to it but it made him uneasy, aware, and he was quick to pass the cross to the last person in the circle, his mother.

She took it from him, smiled, and fastened it around her own neck, tucking it back beneath the bodice of her gown so that it rested near her heart. Storytelling was over. It was time to go to sleep. She listened as each child recited their prayers, helped them into their beds, kissed foreheads and tucked blankets around little shoulders and finally blew out candles, taking her stories and her warmth and the cross, which was suddenly no longer mysterious but frightening to little Del, with her.

He lay there in the darkness of this room he shared with Colin, whose soft breathing he could hear from the curtained bed nearby. Colin, who seemed a million miles away. Colin, whose dreams would surely be of ships and the sea and girls, most particularly the Honourable Miss Jane Drury of the neighboring Rathmore House. Colin, who had fallen asleep quickly, not a care in the world.

But Del was afraid to go to sleep.

Afraid to close his eyes, and be all alone with himself.

He had felt shaken and somehow different since holding the cross tonight, but as the stars wheeled in the heavens above, passing in and out behind the clouds scudding across the Hampshire sky, and rain fell gently against the heavy, lead-paned windows from a very English night, his young eyelids grew heavy. It was probably raining in Ireland, he thought. The Ireland of Grace O'Malley, a place he had never seen but which, thanks to his mother's stories, lived vividly in his imagination. Rain and mists, seabirds and rock, church ruins and lonely wind and rest-less, wandering spirits...

The wind hit him, and pelting rain, and he realized he was on a boat. Not a massive, stately square rigger such as the one his father was off commanding, but a primitive, many-oared vessel like those he'd seen in ancient paintings. The boat was empty save for one person.

A woman.

She stood there near a long tiller, feet braced against the motion of the sea and arms folded across her bosom, her head thrown back and her very stance commanding and bold.

She was about his mother's age and her hair was wild and dark and long, dull with sea mist and spray, lashing her cheeks and mouth. Her eyes were fierce beneath slashing black brows, her nose strong and her lips full and smiling. She wore strange clothes, partly masculine, partly feminine, but he recognized the good serviceable sea-boots and the dagger in a heavy belt at her waist, the easy way her body absorbed the wild roll of the ship as though she were born to it.

"Delmore," she said, and greeted him warmly in Irish.

He spoke Irish, of course. Spoke it as well as he did English. He understood.

He reached up to clutch the shrouds, steadying himself against the vessel's pitch, sea-spray as cold as ice soaking his clothes as the galley's bow dipped, rose, and flung it aft in a hissing shower of foam that spattered the woman's long skirts and the mannish coat she wore over it, belted at her waist.

"Do you not speak, young man?" she asked, humor in her bold eyes. Her voice was strong. Father would call it a quarterdeck voice. Again, she spoke in Irish.

"I don't know what to say, nor whom I'm addressing."

"You know who I am, Delmore."

He was suddenly afraid to speak. His fist tightened on the tarry rope and he shook with cold.

"Gráinne Ni Mhaille," she said. "Your English father—" at this, her smile changed ever so subtly, and he caught the disdain there— "would call me Granuaile."

"Grace O'Malley?"

She inclined her head, her smile broadening, and he wondered why there was nobody on this strange boat except for the two of them, and how it could sail with just her to crew it.

"Then that makes you my grandmother."

"Aye, several times great," she replied.

"Am I dead?"

She laughed, no ladylike twitter but a full, gusty sound that cut through the roar of the thrashing sea. "Not dead, young man, but dreaming. It's the only way I could reach you. Now listen closely, because you will not see me again for a long, long while."

"I'm listening," Del replied, wide-eyed, holding on for dear life as the galley's pitch and yaw grew more noticeable, his small arms straining with the effort.

"You, like so many in our family before you, will grow up to be a great and famous mariner. This, despite the wretched English blood you carry from your sire's side!" The wind strengthened, snapping the pennant above, pushing the galley over on her lee rail until Del's arms began to ache. The wind tore at the woman's hair, flung wild, wet strands of it across her fierce eyes. "You will grow up and you will find your true love. There will be many who'll have your heart, and many who will break it, but don't despair, little lad. I'll send someone who will be your soulmate. Someone that God made just for you. A mariner, like yourself. A woman worthy of the man that you'll be."

Del just stood there. Girls, marriage, a wife... they were the farthest things from his mind.

The howl of the wind strengthened, and water was streaming through the scuppers now, washing down the decks, soaking his feet, pouring out into the sea. His body was tiring from the effort it took to cling to the shroud as the vessel leaped and dove beneath him. The apparition was fading, losing substance, losing form, and Del felt a great pulling and wondered if the sea was sucking him down into its depths or if the galley was driving herself into the rising waves, into the sea itself, with each building swell.

"Gráinne!" he yelled, desperate, unwilling to be left alone on what he now knew was a sinking ship. "Don't leave me!"

She was already moving away, the waves washing over her boots, her cloud of dark hair tangling in the wind, whipping across her face and shoulders in a wild, snarling cloud.

I will never leave you.

"Gráinne!"

She was fading into the sea mists, the ship going with her.

"How will I know her?" he cried desperately. "How?"

She turned back then, and through the screaming wind he heard her strong, resolute voice.

"She will bear my name."

The wild pitching gentled and ceased. His ancestress shimmered in the salty mist and flying foam and was gone. Del jerked awake, his heart pounding so hard that he felt the throbbing in his throat. The dream was vivid. Real enough that he felt he could reach out and touch it. He lay there in the bed, quite dry save for the sweat beneath his back, staring up into the darkness and his pulse hammering in his ears. *Bang, bang, bang.* He shuddered and blinked, finally hearing the sound of Colin's measured breathing in the other bed as his heartbeat began to quiet.

A dream.

He could not know then that it would fade, as dreams almost always do, and as he grew to adulthood it would be all but lost in the pick-and-choose array of memories that the adult mind remembers when looking back at its childhood years. He could not know then that he would suppress his imaginative and sensitive side to become the mariner the strange woman had said he would be, not because she'd foretold it but because it was in his blood, like it was for all the Lord men and, truth be told, all of the O'Devir men of his mother's side as well. He could not know that the dream would become less vivid, its colors and emotion fading as the years passed and that eventually he'd dismiss it entirely, when he even bothered to think about it as all, as silly childhood fantasy.

But for now, he lay there in the darkness, trembling in fear and awe.

It was a long time before he slept.

Also by Danelle Harmon

Introducing

The Bestselling, Award-Winning, Critically Acclaimed

DE MONTFORTE BROTHERS SERIES

"The bluest of blood; the boldest of hearts;
the de Montforte brothers will take your breath away."

1 **Kindle Store bestseller:** The Wild One

The Wild One

The Beloved One

The Defiant One

The Wicked One

The Wayward One

The Admiral's Heart

The Fox & the Angel

My First Noel

The Homecoming

OFFICERS AND GENTLEMEN

Captain of My Heart

My Lady Pirate

Wicked at Heart

Lord of the Sea

Heir to the Sea

Never Too Late for Love

THE NOBLE LORDS

Master of My Dreams

Taken by Storm

Scandal at Christmas

My Saving Grace

Pirate in My Arms

About the Author

New York Times and *USA Today* bestselling author Danelle Harmon has written many critically acclaimed and award-winning books. A Massachusetts native, she has lived in Great Britain, though these days she and her English husband make their home in New England with their daughter Emma and numerous animals including three dogs, an Egyptian Arabian horse, and a flock of pet chickens. Danelle welcomes email from her readers and can be reached at Danelle@danelleharmon.com or through any of the means listed below:

CONNECT WITH ME ONLINE!
Danelle Harmon's Website
Danelle Harmon's Blog

Want to know when the next new title from Danelle is released? Click here!

Even more ways to connect: